"You think I might [...]

Lydia asked.

Jesse kept his gaze on the road as he drove her home. "I hope not, but it's a possibility if the bomber thinks you can ID him."

"I can't. Yet. But what if I did see him and I can't remember?"

"You suffered a head trauma," he reminded her. "Not remembering, especially right away, isn't uncommon. Don't force yourself."

"Are you sure you work for the police? I would have thought you'd have wanted me to remember right now."

"I know you. Force won't work." He threw her half a grin.

"I've been trying, and I can remember a few bits, like how I felt when I heard the laugh track. After that, nothing much else. Lunch was starting," she said, shifting toward him. "I just thought of that."

He glanced at her smile, which lit her whole face. "See? It will come."

Jesse pulled into her driveway, the same house he had picked her up at as a teenager. A memory flashed into his mind—of eons ago when he was a different person.

USA TODAY Bestselling Author

Margaret Daley
and
Carol J. Post

Dangerous Memories

Previously published as *The Protector's Mission* and *Buried Memories*

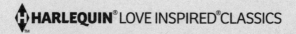

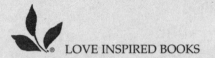

LOVE INSPIRED BOOKS

Recycling programs for this product may not exist in your area.

ISBN-13: 978-1-335-14305-1

Dangerous Memories

Copyright © 2019 by Harlequin Books S.A.

First published as The Protector's Mission by Harlequin Books in 2015 and Buried Memories by Harlequin Books in 2017.

The publisher acknowledges the copyright holders of the individual works as follows:

The Protector's Mission
Copyright © 2015 by Margaret Daley

Buried Memories
Copyright © 2017 by Carol J. Post

www.Harlequin.com

Printed in U.S.A.

CONTENTS

Margaret Daley, an award-winning author of ninety books (five million sold worldwide), has been married for over forty years and is a firm believer in romance and love. When she isn't traveling, she's writing love stories, often with a suspense thread, and corralling her three cats, who think they rule her household. To find out more about Margaret, visit her website at margaretdaley.com.

Visit the Author Profile page
at Harlequin.com for more titles.

THE PROTECTOR'S MISSION

Margaret Daley

God is our refuge and strength,
a very present help in trouble.
—*Psalms* 46:1

To Mike, Shaun, Abbey and Aubrey

ONE

Lydia McKenzie swung open the door to Melinda's Bistro and plowed right into a middle-aged man wearing a navy blue hoodie that shrouded his gray eyes and the scar slashing his cheek. "Sorry."

The guy, holding one of the restaurant take-out sacks, mumbled something and scurried away.

Lydia spied Bree Stone, a doctor and friend from childhood, and headed toward her table. "Sorry I'm late. Had an emergency at work. I hope you got my text." After several hours in surgery at the veterinary hospital, Lydia finally eased into a chair and relaxed.

"I certainly know what an emergency is. We're a doctor short at the hospital, so I'm taking an extra shift to fill in." Bree gathered her purse and put money on the table to pay her tab. "What kind of emergency?"

"It involved one of the rescue dogs from the bombing at the church. A police K-9." Right now she could use a neck and shoulder massage. Pain radiated down her back. "A few days ago, I tended to two rescue dogs that had been injured while searching for survivors at the church, but one of them took a turn for the worse this morning. I had to remove his left hind leg in order to save him. The decision broke my heart because it ends his career, but he'll live."

Bree started to rise but sat back down. "Jesse Hunt's Brutus?"

The mention of Jesse made Lydia's breath catch. She tried to avoid seeing him as much as possible, which was hard since she worked with Northern Frontier Search and Rescue and went to SAR sites to be there if a dog needed medical help. Jesse was often there with his Rottweiler. "No, Officer Nichols with the Anchorage K-9 Unit. He sometimes works with your husband at search and rescue sites."

"Yes, Nichols was brought into the ER last Friday. David was upset. He came to the hospital as soon as he could to see how he was."

"How's he doing?" Lydia shook the image of Jesse Hunt, once a friend, from her mind. When she returned to Anchorage last year, she renewed several friendships, but not with Jesse, whom she'd betrayed right after she'd graduated from high school.

"He's still on the critical list. His accident shows me how dangerous my husband's job is, but David wouldn't do anything else." Bree rose. "I wish I could stay. But I have to be in early because the other doctor is sick."

"We'll catch up later." Lydia rolled her shoulders and released a long breath.

Bree smiled. "When we both slow down. Tell Kate hi for me. She's been asking me about being a doctor."

"She has?" She should know that, but she and her seventeen-year-old sister had clashed a lot since she'd become her guardian last year.

"Yes, she doesn't think she can work with animals

like you and your dad, but she's interested in the medical field. See you."

Lydia watched Bree weave through the tables starting to fill up with people coming in for an early lunch. She scanned the bistro, trying to decide whether to stay and eat or order and take it back to the Aurora Animal Hospital down the street, the veterinary practice she inherited from her father when he died last year. They treated large and small animals as well as the Northern Frontier SAR dogs and the K-9s that worked with the police.

Her gaze settled on Melinda, the owner of the restaurant, talking to a man with dark brown hair sticking out of a black ball cap. The guy took Melinda's hand and moved closer. Was this Todd, the boyfriend she'd been telling Lydia about this past month?

Lydia started to look away to give them some privacy when she spied the man lean toward Melinda, a furious expression on his face. Melinda jerked her hand from his grasp, and the guy pivoted and stormed away, passing Lydia's table.

She averted her look toward a man and a young woman sitting at the table next to her. She knew the guy. He worked at the drugstore—

"Sorry you saw that, Lydia."

She looked up at Melinda. "I'm the one sorry for staring. Are you all right?"

The bistro owner waved her hand. "Boyfriend problems. He isn't too happy with me at the moment." Melinda slipped into the chair next to Lydia. "How have you been?"

"Tired. I had to operate on one of the K-9 dogs that

was hurt at the church bomb site. It's been all over the news."

"That's what everyone's been talking about. Two bombings close together."

Lydia shivered when she thought about the pictures she'd seen on the news. "I know some police officers, and they're working overtime."

"Yeah, I heard there's no connection between the hardware store and the church, but they were only ten days apart. Do you think it's the same person? Have you heard if it's the same MO?"

"It sounds like it. Both times there was a laugh track that sounded seconds before the bomb went off."

"What a sick person!" Melinda rose. "Are you going to eat lunch here or order takeout since Bree left?"

"Takeout. The veggie wrap."

"It shouldn't take too long." Melinda headed for the kitchen in the back.

Glad to be sitting for a few minutes, Lydia glanced at the different people coming into the bistro. Some she recognized because they were regulars, like herself, but a couple were new to her—a young, petite woman with an older gentleman, a young man with long brown hair and a bald man about thirty-five or forty. She loved to people watch. She'd once considered being a writer, but her love of animals clinched her decision to be a vet and follow in her father's footsteps. She'd hoped that decision would reconcile them. It hadn't.

Before Melinda brought her takeout, she made her way down a long hallway to the restroom. A man slipped out the exit door at the end of the corridor. Odd, it wasn't used much.

A few minutes later as she came out of the woman's bathroom and paused, she panned the dining area, pleased to see the restaurant doing so well. But one of the new customers had left. Maybe the bistro didn't serve what he wanted. She noticed Melinda carrying a takeout bag toward the table where she'd been sitting.

But before Lydia moved forward, a blast of maniacal-sounding laughter resonated through the restaurant. Melinda dropped the sack, a look of horror on her face. Lydia took only two steps back into the hallway before her world exploded.

Sergeant Jesse Hunt took Brutus out of the back of his SUV, secured his leash and walked toward the rubble of the church he attended. One person still remained missing and two were found dead in the bombing last Wednesday. He was on duty and had only stopped by to see David Stone, the head of Northern Frontier SAR, at the bombing site to assess it after the two people were hurt searching it Friday.

"Have they stabilized the structure?" Jesse asked as he approached David.

His friend turned toward him, a grim expression on his face. "Yes, this morning. At least this time I hope nothing else happens. I don't want any more people hurt, but we need to check thoroughly for the one missing."

"Yeah, I've seen people found days later and I heard of someone who lasted a week in the wreckage. That's why I'm here. I can help later after my shift."

"Good. It's nice that late August still gives us long days."

"Is Pastor Paul around?"

"No, he went to a parishioner's house. They're making plans for holding a church service here on Sunday."

"That sounds like him. Someone bombing his church isn't going to stop him from having worship services." Jesse surveyed the large mounds of debris, noting some were marked already searched. His church had been large and thriving. At first the authorities wondered if it had been a crime associated with religion, but as they investigated they discovered too many links to the hardware store destroyed a week and a half before the church. The establishments weren't connected, but the way the bombings were carried out indicated the same person or persons did both, down to the type of bomb, detonated with a timer and the sound of a laugh track.

"At the hardware store there weren't any deaths or injuries, but you and I know the two who died here."

"And the one missing." Jesse's cell phone rang. As he answered the call, he saw it was his commander. "Hunt here."

"There's been a third bombing at Melinda's Bistro, down the street from the Aurora Animal Hospital."

"I know the place. Brutus and I are on our way." Jesse hung up as David received a call, no doubt about the new bombing.

Jesse waved at David, then jogged with Brutus toward his SUV. Settled in his car, he switched on his engine and sirens. Fifteen minutes later he parked his car with other police cruisers and hurried toward the crime scene. The whole street was blocked off. So far, if this was the same MO, there had been only one bomb going off, but this bomber was escalating with each site, the amount of time between each bombing and from the look of the site the size of the bomb. Melinda's Bistro would have just started serving lunch, which meant probably more deaths than the previous one. Did the killer take it even further with the addition of another bomb?

When he arrived at the command post, he assessed the destruction up close. A shudder snaked through him. A cloud of dust hung in the still air where the restaurant had once been, a two-story building brought to the ground, except for one small area where the top floor remained, but heavily damaged. Cries floated to him, some from within the massive debris of concrete, wood and brick.

His gut knotted, and his determination to catch the perpetrator intensified. He'd ask Thomas Caldwell, the detective overseeing the first two bombings, if he could be on the task force the department was forming. He searched the police officers, found his longtime friend and headed straight for him.

"When can we start searching for survivors?" Jesse asked. The site had to be stabilized first to protect everyone, including the survivors.

Thomas shifted his attention to Jesse, his shoulders slumped as though he'd been up forty-eight hours, which was possible. A scowl carved deep lines into Thomas's face. "As soon as we get the okay that it's safe. Until then I could use you and Brutus to check for any other bombs in the area."

"Will do, and I want on the task force you're heading."

"I already put your name down. You were at the top of the list. I have two other K-9 officers searching this side of the street. One that way. The other opposite." Thomas pointed toward the buildings flanking Melinda's Bistro. "But if the bomber is getting more violent, it won't be long before we start seeing multiple bombs. All the shops have been evacuated, necessary personnel only, so be on the lookout for looters."

Jesse started at one end of the street and investigated anything that remotely looked suspicious. Most of the buildings' windows were blown out, and the structures suffered minor damage. He was acquainted with Melinda and most likely she had been in her bistro. Would there be any survivors? From what was left of the restaurant, he didn't have high hopes for anyone, even after hearing the faint cries.

At the other end of the street, he saw Bree Stone admitted into the blocked off area. She had some medical personnel with her. He detoured to meet her in the middle of the street. "Are you setting up a medical tent?"

"Yes. Have you heard of any survivors? I haven't been told anything."

"They're stabilizing the site and making sure there aren't any other bombs. As you can tell, it's pretty chaotic."

"David is coming."

"I know. I was with him when we both got the call."

Bree chewed on her bottom lip. "I was in that restaurant ten minutes before the bomb went off. I had to get back to work, but one of my friends was still there."

"Have you checked to see where she is?"

"Yes, and she hasn't returned to the animal hospital." Bree studied him. "You two dated in high school, if I remember correctly. Lydia McKenzie."

Lydia McKenzie. Jesse could feel the color drain from his face. His heartbeat slowed to a throb, and his breathing became labored. He thought if he kept his distance, even when they both were at the same SAR site, he'd be all right. He'd thought they would marry after high school. When she'd eloped with Aaron, one of his good friends, he had locked away the unbearable pain of rejection. Until she'd returned to Anchorage last year. Then the lid had lifted on that pain and leaked out.

"You need to report that. Thomas is over there." Jesse waved toward his friend, then before he said something he'd regret about Lydia, he rotated away and said, "I still have one more building to inspect."

With Brutus by his side, he hastened toward the last store. As his Rottweiler sniffed around, Jesse examined the clothing store, the large plate window gone in front. Through the opening, he caught a movement out of the corner of his eye in the appliance shop next door. He pulled on Brutus's leash and headed for the place. As he peered inside, he glimpsed a door closing at the rear.

He entered the appliance store with Brutus and unsnapped his leash. "Check it."

While his K-9 moved around the large open space, Jesse removed his gun and strode toward the back exit. When he opened the door, he spied a black Chevy driving out of the parking lot. He took down the part of the license number not covered by mud. All employees, shop owners and customers were evacuated an hour ago, so why did this guy stay behind?

Going back inside, he did his own search of the premise while Brutus finished. Nothing. That was a good sign, but a troublesome feeling about the man who left nagged at him. He headed back toward Thomas who was talking with David in low tones.

Thomas wore his deadpan expression that didn't give anything away if reporters were watching. "So far we think at least twelve people were inside. I imagine more names will come in as people wonder where someone is. We have four employees and eight customers we know of at this time. We have been given the go-ahead to search the left side of the building."

Jesse and Brutus started for that area, the one where the second floor had crashed down on the first one. There was little to shore up, and it was probably where the bomb originated as well as where most of the casualties would be.

The thought of finding Lydia dead soured his stomach. He might be angry with her, but he prayed to the Lord she was alive somewhere in the rubble.

Lydia tried to drag deep breaths into her lungs, but the effort sent pain through her. Cracked or broken rib? She eased her eyes open to find debris all around her. Pinpoint streams of light filtered through the rubble.

A beam lay across her torso. Dust in the air caused her to sneeze and intensified the sharp constriction in her chest. The lack of oxygen and the pressure bearing down on her made her light-headed. Her eyelids slid close. She focused, as much as she could, on any sounds that indicated people were searching for survivors. Creaks and groans, as though the building were protesting its destruction, surrounded her, but she couldn't hear any voices.

She tried to move her legs. She couldn't do more

than wiggle her toe, which meant she wasn't paralyzed. One arm was pinned against her side, the other free. She pushed on the beam, but it wouldn't budge. The effort drained what strength she had. She stopped and concentrated on filling her lungs with at least shallow breaths.

Then thoughts began to invade her mind. Who would take care of her seventeen-year-old sister? She came back to Anchorage for Kate. When their father died in a climbing accident, Lydia finally returned for the funeral, not intending to stay except to settle her dad's affairs and move her sister back to Oklahoma where Lydia lived. None of her plans had worked out. Kate refused to leave her friends, and Lydia discovered her father left her his practice and part of the animal hospital.

Then Bree showed up to help her deal with her father's death. They had been close friends in school, and suddenly she felt as though fifteen years had vanished, and their relationship took off where it had stopped when she'd left Anchorage to elope with Aaron.

Why did You bring me back, God, only to have this happen? I was beginning to settle in again and forget why I'd left all those years ago. She'd even started to contemplate staying after Kate graduated from high school. She'd tried to hold on to her faith, but so many things happened. And now this. She didn't know what to do anymore.

Then there was Jesse, her first love. They had dated for over a year but broke up their senior year at Christmas. She'd started dating Aaron, which in retrospect was a rebound. She'd been trying to forget Jesse and made a big mistake that affected her even today. She and Aaron broke up after a few months and she and Jesse reunited—more in love than ever. But when she discovered she was pregnant with Aaron's baby, everything changed. Jesse had been devastated when she left without telling him why. Aaron's dad and her father had insisted they get married and keep the child a secret. Aaron's dad was a prominent citizen and her father was an elder in his church. She was to accompany Aaron to Stillwater where he was going to attend Oklahoma State University. As long as they did as they said, Aaron would have money to support them and his education paid for. The memories of those years married to Aaron chilled her. She'd never been so alone in her life.

What good was it to look back? It was too late to change anything. She didn't even know if the rescuers would find her.

Her head pounded like a jackhammer. With her free hand, she touched her hair and came away with bloody fingers. A darkness tugged at her. It offered comfort and peace.

Through the haze that clouded her mind, a noise penetrated her thoughts. A bark. Then another. The rescuers had found someone. Hope flared until another sound drowned out all others. A crash—something collapsing?

Brutus barked and wagged his tail. He found someone. As part of the second floor fell to the ground in the section not stabilized yet, Jesse headed for his Rottweiler. He reached the spot and caught a glimpse of something blue under the debris.

"Over here," Jesse shouted, and several rescuers without dogs climbed through the remains of the structure.

Jesse knelt by Brutus and tried to see through the rubbish. He glimpsed some more blue and began removing bricks and wood, praying the person — maybe Lydia—was alive beneath them. Jesse knew that time was against the trapped people. If they were alive and injured, their wounds could eventually lead to their death if help didn't get to them.

"I'm here," he heard faintly from below. Or was he imagining a voice that sounded like Lydia's?

"Lydia?" Jesse kept removing bricks.

"Yes. A beam is on me." The familiar voice grew a little stronger.

"This is Jesse. We're going to get you out."

"I need air, and it's getting dark."

"Okay. Let me see what I can do."

"Thanks, Jesse. I knew I could count on you." The last part of the sentence ended with a racking cough.

"Lydia, are you all right?"

"O—kay. So cold."

"You'll be out in no time." He worked as fast as he could. "Are you still all right?"

Nothing. His gut clenched.

"Get that air and camera over here," he shouted while David and Thomas hurried with his request. "Lydia is alive." He refused to acknowledge the possibility that she had died—just moments from being rescued.

He searched the debris until he found what he hoped was a hole that led to where Lydia was. He snatched the air tank and shoved the hose through the opening. *Please, God, keep her alive. We've already lost too many.* He said that over and over as he pushed the camera with a light down into another small crack. It was in moments like this that all he could do was believe the Lord was taking over.

TWO

Lydia blinked her eyes open. In the dim light, she saw the hose to the left of her. The air seemed fresher, although she still couldn't breathe too deeply without a shooting pain knifing through her.

She went in and out of consciousness to the noise of people removing the building on top of her. The sound of voices fueled her hope. Memories of that time she'd gotten lost in a cave swamped her—the fear of the dark, of being alone. She shivered. Then she remembered when she'd first seen Jesse with a flashlight, coming to her rescue. She'd rushed into his arms and wouldn't let him go until he'd pulled back, stared at her for a long moment and then kissed her for the first time.

What happened to that puppy love? She'd only been seventeen—Kate's age—but she'd never felt so close to another as in that moment.

Her eyelids were so heavy, like the beam across her torso. She closed them again, trying to think of a warm place. Every part of her was cold, as though she'd been in a refrigerator for hours, dressed in her scrubs. She hadn't even changed out of them when she'd gone to meet Bree. At least she wasn't there with her.

But the others…what of them?

Again she began to drift off.

Hold on, Lydia.

Did someone say that? Jesse?

A rush of cool air brushed over her. She looked up and saw Jesse's smiling face.

"She's alive." His grin grew. "Don't move. We'll get you out of there."

"I know," she whispered, her throat so dry she doubted Jesse could hear her.

When the rescuers finally reached her, all she could do was peer at Jesse as though she were back in the cave and he alone had come to save her. His almost-black hair was covered with a helmet. Dust and dirt coated him. He was more muscular and taller than when they'd been teenagers. When he and Thomas hoisted the beam from her, it seemed so easy for him while she couldn't budge it an inch.

Jesse's golden-brown gaze fastened on hers. Lines at the sides of his eyes deepened. "We've almost got you out, then Bree will check you before we move you. Do you want some water?" His voice held a tender note, as though he cared.

But she knew better. Since she'd returned to Anchorage they had spoken few words, only when necessary because of a search and rescue or Brutus, who she treated as the department veterinarian. "Yes" squeaked out of her mouth.

He couldn't prop her up to drink until Bree said it was okay to move her, but he did squirt some cold water into her mouth.

Nothing tasted better. She swallowed. "Again."

When Bree appeared next to her, she tried to hide the worry in her eyes, but Lydia knew Bree.

"I'm okay," Lydia murmured, her voice stronger now. "Get me out of this hole, and I'll be good as new in no time."

"I'll be the judge of that." Bree ran her hands over Lydia, especially examining the wound on her head, then put a neck brace on her. "She's okay to be lifted but be careful. Slow and easy. No jarring."

"Honey, stop telling us our job. We've done this before," David said from above, ready to take Lydia when Thomas and Jesse hoisted her up.

Jesse positioned himself at her head while Thomas was at her feet. "On the count of three."

Bree stabilized her midsection as Lydia was brought up out of the hole.

Sunlight bathed Lydia. She was put on a stretcher and carried from the rubble. The last sight she saw was Jesse's handsome face—but he wasn't smiling. Worry knitted his forehead.

Lydia gave in to the black swirling abyss beckoning her.

Lydia heard an annoying beep. Pain quickly followed, radiating from her head and chest. She moaned and lifted her eyelids halfway. A hospital room greeted her, and she remembered why she was here and hurting. She'd been in and out of consciousness since an emergency surgery to have her spleen repaired.

She wondered where her sister and Bree went. Earlier they'd been in here. Probably to grab something to eat. At least she wouldn't have to worry about Kate while she was in the hospital. She'd stay with Bree and David until Lydia was released, which she hoped was soon.

Lydia closed her eyes and tried to relax. But the second she did, visions of the bombing assailed her mind. The sound of hideous laughter right before the bomb went off. The expression on Melinda's face when she knew what was going to happen. Was she alive? The feeling of helplessness she experienced trapped under the building debris. Her heartbeat began to race. A cold clamminess blanketed her, much like when she'd been trapped.

The swish of her hospital room door opening pulled her away from the memories. Kate returning? She needed to have a few moments with her sister. When Lydia fastened her gaze on the person who entered, her pulse rate sped faster. Jesse Hunt. She wasn't prepared to see him.

He looked like he'd come straight from the crime scene. As a search and rescue worker for Northern Frontier, he'd probably work as long as he could function. The only time he'd rest was when Brutus needed to.

So why is he here?

He stopped at the end of the bed. "Bree told me you'd been awake earlier and coherent after your surgery, so I took a chance and came to talk to you."

His stiff stance and white-knuckled hands on the railing betrayed his nervousness, but his tone told her he was here in his professional capacity. Saddened by that thought, Lydia said, "Thank you for finding me."

"I was doing my job yesterday."

"Knowing the people who would be searching kept my hope alive. Have you found everyone?"

"We don't know for sure. Names of missing people are still coming in. I was hoping you could tell me how many people were in the restaurant when the bomb exploded."

"I'm not sure. Let me think." As much as she didn't want to, she tried to visualize the moments before the explosion. "Melinda, and I remember seeing another waitress. I don't know how many cooks she had in the kitchen. They're always in the back."

"How about customers?"

She had to think. She didn't want this person to get away with what he'd done. She fought the weariness that kept edging forward. "People were coming in and out. Some ordered takeout for lunch and didn't stay long. I came out of the restroom, saw Melinda seconds before the laugh track played. I'd estimate maybe nine besides me. Most of them were regulars."

"Who?"

"I don't know their names. I just see them there a lot. I go get lunch there once or twice a week…" The thought that the bistro was totally gone inundated her. She dropped her gaze to her lap, her hands quivering. She balled them, but that didn't stop the trembling sweeping through her body.

"If I bring you photos, could you tell me if they were there?"

Emotions crammed her throat. She turned for her water on the bedside table, but it was too far away without leaning for it. She started to and winced from the movement.

Jesse was at her side, grabbing the plastic cup and offering it to her.

She took it, their fingers brushing, and she nearly splashed the water all over her with her shaking.

Jesse covered her hand and steadied her drink, then guided it to her mouth. The feel of his fingers against hers for more than a second jolted her. "I know this isn't something you want to talk about, but we want to recover all the bodies as quickly as possible."

"Bodies? Did anyone else survive?"

"A waitress and two cooks. We found them in the kitchen area, the waitress just inside the entrance while the cooks were across the room."

She didn't want to ask but she needed to know. "Did Melinda survive?"

"No, we ID'd her body. So far we've recovered eight bodies, including Melinda. Four people are missing, according to their families, but we haven't found them yet. The bomb squad thinks the bomb originated in the dining area where the customers were. They'll know more when the bomb fragments are all found."

"Eight dead." How did she survive when the others didn't? "I was in the hallway to the bathrooms when it went off, not in the main dining room. Do you think that protected me some?"

"Possibly. Do you know where the laughing sound came from?"

"Not sure." She closed her eyes and tried to think back to that time. Nothing. She massaged her temple, forcing herself to dig deeper beyond the pain throbbing against her skull. "I don't think from behind me. When I heard the laughter—" she shuddered "—I took two steps back. Then everything went blank."

Jesse put the cup on the bedside table. "I know this isn't easy, but anything you can remember could help us piece together what happened. We've got to stop this man."

"Nobody wants that more than me. I... I..." Tears blurred her vision. She couldn't voice what she felt, not even to herself. She remembered coming to in recovery, and all she'd wanted to do was surrender to the darkness. Stay there. But that wouldn't help. She'd learned long ago she couldn't escape from the truth.

"I'm sorry, Jesse. I'm tired. I'm sure I'll remember more later." She hoped she could. She needed to. If no one in the dining area survived the bombing except her, she might know something that could help find the culprit. But at the moment her head felt as if it would explode.

"I understand. I'll come back later."

Was that sympathy in his voice? She looked up. His expression was neutral. When she'd first returned home last year, she'd tried to talk to him about what happened all those years ago. He'd shut her down. He never acted angry or upset around her although she'd wronged him. Instead, he'd been more like a stranger. Even as a teenager, he'd kept his feelings to himself. That was part of the reason they broke up that first time at Christmas, and she began dating Aaron.

She watched him leave. But hadn't she done the same as him? When her mother left their family she'd shut off her emotions entirely. Even now she wouldn't think about the woman who had abandoned her family. She couldn't deal with that on top of everything else.

The emotions she'd kept checked while he was there

gushed to the surface. Tears ran down her cheeks for the people who'd died, for her foolishness as a teenager, for the rift between her and her father and for the times she'd missed her mother so much it had hurt deeply. And now, she couldn't even remember anything to help the police.

Later that day, Jesse loaded Brutus into his crate in the back of his SUV and left the bombing scene. His dog needed a lengthy break if he was going to work late into August's twilight hours for the third straight day, searching the rubble for victims or clues to identify the type of bomb used. There were still two people unaccounted for, and he was going to pay another visit to both Lydia and the waitress who survived. Maybe one or both of them could tell him if the two missing people were at the restaurant. Thomas talked with the cooks, but they didn't know anything because they always stayed in the kitchen.

He drove toward the hospital, the bright yellow sun splashed across the sky in all God's glory. Life went on in spite of the tragedy that occurred yesterday. The death count with the bombings was climbing and so was the fear sweeping through the city. The mayor was demanding answers, and he'd gladly give him some if he had any.

The closest surveillance camera had been disabled before the bombing. The others didn't have a good angle on the entrance to the restaurant. Even if they had there were two other ways for a person to leave Melinda's Bistro—the back door where the kitchen was and the emergency exit down the hallway to the bathrooms. There were no cameras on those two places. In fact, each building targeted didn't have a lot of security. The police were urging businesses to increase their security.

When he rode the elevator up to Lydia's floor, he tried to prepare himself for seeing her again. He didn't want to think about their past, but as he neared her hospital room, he experienced relief and…joy all over again, like when he heard her through the rubble. She'd been alive. After finding several dead bodies, he'd started to think no one would be alive.

He'd thanked God he found her. He'd never felt that kind of relief. And yet, he had to keep his distance. Too much happened between them when they were teenagers. He'd grown up in a good foster home, but early on when he bounced from one family to another, he learned to keep himself apart from others. He would have to rely on that ability now.

He couldn't afford to be hurt by her again.

Pausing at the door, he lifted his hand to knock and froze. He couldn't go inside. *I've got a job to do. Get in. Get out.*

He rapped his knuckles against the wood, heard Lydia respond and pushed the door open. He'd prefer to stay at the end of the bed, but he had to show her the photos. He'd have to stand next to her, only a couple of feet away.

When he entered, a neutral expression fell over her features. Her brown eyes held a guarded look. She'd been pretty as a teenager, a little gangly, but now fifteen years later, she was a tall beauty, nothing awkward as she moved. What he'd observed at search and rescues was a self-assured woman who was aware of herself at all times. That had changed over the years. What else?

"Is this a good time to talk?" Jesse asked, almost wishing she would say no.

"Yes. Bree and Kate went to lunch. They should be back soon." Her voice, husky laden, was the same, and its sound renewed memories best forgotten. "I haven't remembered anything new. I wish I could. Everything is fuzzy. Maybe it's the meds they have me on."

"That could be. But it also may be the trauma. The waitress doesn't remember anything, either, but I wanted to show both of you the photos of the two people still missing and see if you can place them at the restaurant when the bomb went off."

"I'll try to help any way I can. I want this madman caught before others die."

"On that, we agree." But on so many other things, they hadn't agreed on. Aaron had been a good friend, but Jesse had known Aaron wouldn't be good for Lydia. Obviously she hadn't felt that way. Even after they got back together in April, out of nowhere she left Anchorage with Aaron in June.

Jesse removed the two pictures from his shirt pocket. One was of a young woman and the other an older gentleman. He laid them on the tray table. "Does either one seem familiar to you?"

"Maybe the older gentleman. There was one that came into the bistro when I was there. The woman I didn't see at all. I'd remember that red hair."

A smile tugged at his mouth. He thought back to a time Lydia had dyed her long brown hair that color and it turned out more a neon orange than red, especially toward the ends. She'd fixed it the best she could by cutting her hair short, which was the way she wore it now.

She stared at him. "I know what you're thinking. It turned out to be a good thing although I hated the stares I received those few days before I cut my hair. It's easier to keep this way." She combed her fingers through her strands.

"I tried to warn you."

"That's because you didn't like redheads."

"I liked you the way you were." But she never understood that. She'd wanted to be constantly reassured how he felt, and feelings had never been easy for him to express.

She handed him the photos. "I wasn't much help. I hope the waitress knows for sure. I'd hate for families not to know what happened to a loved one."

"Like what happened to your father?"

"Yes, not knowing one way or another when he disappeared in the wilderness was nerve-racking. Kate and I felt in limbo. I understand you were one of the K-9 teams that went out searching."

"Alex Witherspoon found your father at the bottom of the ravine." Ten days after he went missing. "That's one of the things David does. If we don't find the person right away, we don't give up. We keep going out until every possibility is covered."

"Thankfully he died instantly and didn't linger, injured and without food and water. But he shouldn't have gone in the first place. It was stupid to go by himself, especially with Kate living at home." Anger laced each word. "But then he never changed, even after Mom left us. He always did daredevil stunts, testing his limits with no regard for the family left behind."

Jesse stuck the pictures in his uniform shirt pocket. Things were getting too personal. He didn't want to go there. "Thanks for your help. I've got to show these to the waitress. If you do remember anything else, call Thomas. He's lead detective on the case."

Jesse left as quickly as he could. He'd almost told her to call him. That wouldn't have been a wise decision on his part. He was on the Laughing Bomber Task Force, but he'd leave Thomas to deal with Lydia.

The waitress was hospitalized in another corridor on the same floor. When Jesse made his way there, a code blue was issued. Several staff members hurried past him. As he neared the room, a sinking feeling took hold of him. A nurse pushing a crash cart cut him off. The door swung wide to reveal a team of medical personnel fighting to keep the waitress alive.

Jesse leaned against the wall, waiting to see if the woman made it. Only Lydia and this woman had been out in the dining room area and seen who the customers were. If she died, that only left Lydia.

THREE

"What do you mean I have to escort Lydia home from the hospital? Why don't you?" Good thing Thomas was Jesse's friend, or he'd never get away with challenging a superior's order.

Thomas started for his vehicle at the church bombing site. "Lydia requested you when I told her I wanted an officer to escort her home."

"Are we going to guard her or something?" He didn't want to be on that detail.

"Not at this time. The situation doesn't warrant the drain on our manpower although I have authorized the police to drive by and periodically check on her and the two cooks who are still alive. I don't think the cooks know much, but Lydia might. She was in the area that took the worst of the bombing. With the waitress dying, Lydia is our best chance. We're focusing all we can on finding this maniac."

"Do you think she's in danger?"

"Not at the moment. Her name hasn't been given to the press. If it gets out, we'll reconsider what to do or if the autopsy findings on the waitress who died last night indicate murder. We reviewed the surveillance tapes of people going in and out of her room and only saw staff members. The doctor has no reason at the moment to think someone killed her. She was injured more severely than Lydia." Thomas opened his car door. "I have a lead to follow up."

"Trade you?"

Thomas shook his head. "You're complaining because I asked you to make sure a beautiful woman gets home okay? I'm beginning to think you were the one who suffered a head trauma."

"Cute. You know Lydia and I have a history."

"Which is even more reason to put you with her. You know her. You know what to expect. I'm not asking you to be her new best friend."

"You owe me."

"You wanted in on this case."

"Because this was my church that was bombed." Jesse waved his arm toward where the building used to be.

"While you're with her, help her to remember. Somewhere in her mind she might have seen the bomber and can ID him. Now, that would be a lead."

Jesse watched Thomas drive away, then stormed to his police cruiser with Brutus. Before opening the rear of his SUV, he knelt next to his Rottweiler and petted him. "At least you understand why I don't want to see her. I've ranted to you enough this past year. This city of nearly three hundred thousand doesn't seem to be big enough for the both of us."

Brutus barked, then licked Jesse on his cheek.

He laughed. "I like your reply. I know I've got to do my best. Nothing less." He rubbed his hand down Brutus's back. "Load." Jesse gave the command for his K-9 to hop into the rear and crawl into his crate. He fastened the door, although in an emergency Brutus could undo the latch.

Yesterday when the other survivor had died, he'd interviewed the staff and reported it to Thomas. He'd asked the staff not to talk about the death. The police didn't want rumors flying around. With Bree at the hospital, he'd keep tabs on anything being said.

Now he'd return to take Lydia home and have the task of informing her about the waitress's death and finding the older gentleman's remains in the last area to be searched at the bomb site. Since the young woman who had been the other missing person showed up at work, everyone was accounted for.

When he arrived at Lydia's room, after dropping Brutus off at home, she sat in a wheelchair looking out the window. She glanced back at him as he entered.

"Thomas called and told me you were driving me home. I appreciate it."

He approached her and clasped the wheelchair handles to roll her out of the room. "Why did you request me?" His voice sounded even, belying his frustration.

"Because I think we should talk, and you've been doing a good job of avoiding me. We were friends once—"

"Yes, once. We aren't now."

"I realize that, but I owe you an apology. I've been meaning to talk to you since before the bomb went off. If nothing else, I can take away from this situation how fragile life is. Don't put off what you should do. In one second, a lot of people died at the hands of this madman. The more I think about what happened, the more I get the feeling I know something."

"Shh." Jesse scanned the hallway leading out of the building. "We'll talk when we arrive at your house. I don't want anyone overhearing us. We haven't released your name to the press. The bomber doesn't know who the survivors are." If that truly was the case, then the waitress died naturally.

He waited until he brought the car around and assisted Lydia into the front passenger seat to tell her about the death of the waitress. He didn't want a public reaction to the news.

On the drive to her house, after a long silence, Jesse stopped at a red light and looked at Lydia. "I didn't want to say anything until we were alone, but the waitress died last night. An autopsy is being performed to determine the cause of death."

"You don't think her death is a result of the bomb explosion?"

"Probably. She was in more critical condition than you were, but she had been responding to treatment and improving so I can't say for sure."

"What does the press know?"

"How many died in the blast and that there were four survivors. No names at this time because we were still identifying victims and notifying family. That will change now since everyone is accounted for."

Lydia stared out the windshield. "You think I might be in danger?"

"I hope not, but it's a possibility if the bomber thinks you can ID him. That's why we won't release your name, but the press have their ways of finding out."

"I can't. Yet. But what if I did see him and I can't remember?"

"You suffered a head trauma. Not remembering, especially right away, isn't uncommon. Don't force yourself. If you have any information, it'll come to you in time."

"Are you sure you work for the police? I'd think you should be pushing me to remember right now."

When the light turned green, he threw her a half grin and pressed on the accelerator. "I know you. Force won't work."

"I've been trying, and I can remember a few bits like how Melinda looked when she heard the laugh track, how I felt when I did. After that nothing and not much else before other than remembering Bree thankfully left ten minutes before the bomb went off."

"Yes, I talked with Bree. She remembered some of the people we found in the rubble."

"Lunch was starting. The door opened and closed—four times after she was gone." She shifted toward him. "I just thought of that."

He glanced at her smile, which lit her whole face. He'd always loved seeing her grin from deep inside her. "See. It will come."

"I feel like I need to remember right now because someone else might die if he strikes again."

"We're interviewing a lot of people who were there earlier or on that street sometime that morning. You're not our only hope."

Jesse pulled into her driveway, the same house he would pick her up at as a teenager. A memory flashed into his mind—of kissing her on the front porch. Eons ago when he was a different person. His chest tightened. He wouldn't go down that path again.

"I'll see you to your door."

"Will you stay until Kate comes home from school?"

"I—I…" He didn't want to be with her any more than necessary, but one look into her pale face and he couldn't say no. "Fine. When does she get home? I'll need to let Thomas know what I'm doing."

Lydia checked the clock on the dashboard. "No more than an hour. She carpools with a few friends."

As they walked slowly toward the house, Jesse just thought of something. "How are you going to get in? Your purse was destroyed by the bomb."

She slipped her hand into her jean pocket and pulled out a key. "Bree had the locks changed and gave a key to me and Kate. Alex went grocery shopping for me, so I won't have to do that right away. My friends have been so helpful, especially with Kate. Reconnecting with Bree and Alex when I came back to Anchorage has made my return home easier." Lydia opened her front door and entered.

Jesse followed, scanning the house. He was glad he'd taken Brutus home so he could run and play in his large fenced backyard. These past days, his K-9 had worked long hours and needed the break.

Lydia dropped the small bag of clothes Bree had brought her in the hospital on a chair in the spacious living room and walked through the dining room toward the kitchen. "I'm fixing myself a good cup of tea. What they had at the hospital isn't what I call tea. Do you want some?"

"I'm a coffee drinker. No, thanks."

As he strolled through the house, snatches of his time spent here continued to bombard him. Lydia always had to come right home from school to babysit her little sister who stayed with a neighbor until

Lydia arrived. Her dad didn't get off work until six and sometimes didn't come home right away. Lydia hated being alone and usually their friends would gather at her place.

Jesse caught sight of a recent photo of Lydia with her younger sister. Picking up the framed picture, he realized he hadn't seen much of Kate since those early years. She looked a lot like Lydia at the same age. Quickly he returned the photograph to the end table.

Why had he agreed to stay until Kate got home? He didn't want to be pulled into Lydia's world again, and yet he had allowed himself to be persuaded to wait an hour.

"I have some…" Lydia opened the refrigerator "…I guess only water. Kate likes soft drinks, but there are none in here."

"Water is fine." He remained in the entrance of the dining room until the memory of sharing Thanksgiving dinner with Lydia and her family a few weeks before they broke up their senior year faded. He stood at the bay window that overlooked the unfenced backyard with woods a hundred yards from the house.

"Do you still get moose around here?"

"Yes, also caribou and occasionally a bear. That's why I keep the garbage cans in the garage except on pickup day."

"Have you had any trouble with them?" He could do a generic conversation with Lydia. Nothing too personal.

"Kate's an animal lover and takes photos of all our visitors. Once she was at the window in her bedroom, snapping a picture when the bear came over and tried to get inside. He tore the screen, and we had to replace it. The way she screamed, I thought the bear was inside. I ran and got my dad's gun, then went to rescue her." She appeared behind him.

Jesse pivoted from the window, and the familiar scent of apple floated to him. She held out the glass of water, and he took it.

But she remained where she was—too close. When she looked up at him, for a few seconds the years apart fell away, and he was a teenager again and in love for the first time.

Then she smiled, and no one else existed for that moment. It was as if fifteen years vanished along with all the hurts and words exchanged between them.

The shrill whistle of the kettle pierced the air. Lydia gasped as though she'd been transfixed as much as he had.

When she crossed to the stove to make her tea, he sat in a chair and took deep sips of his iced water, relishing the cold liquid. "What happened with the bear?"

"I closed the blackout curtains and hoped he would forget that we were inside. He hit the screen a couple more times, then left. We both collapsed on the bed, laughing."

"Laughing?"

"In relief that we were still alive. I'd been checking out the bedroom door and wondering if that would stop a bear if he did get into the house through the window. I'd decided no."

Chuckling, Jesse relaxed, surprised by both actions.

When Lydia returned to the kitchen table and sat across from him, she blew on her tea and took a sip, a habit she'd had since he'd first known her. What else did she still do? She used to chew on her thumbnail when she was nervous. He looked at her hand and saw each fingernail was cut short.

"I'm glad you're having a good laugh over my bear encounter. There is a downside to living a little ways out from the main part of the city. More wildlife."

"To me that's what's appealing about this place. I live in town with a fenced yard. Brutus needs to have a place to exercise when he isn't working. I can't risk him encountering a bear."

Lydia shifted in her chair and cringed. "I'm trying to ignore my bruised ribs, but they love reminding me they've been mistreated."

"Being in that hallway protected you some from the main blast."

She stared at her tea, tracing her finger around the rim. "I know. I…" She shook her head. "Can we not talk about the bombing?"

"You need to remember, and talking sometimes helps."

Her mouth tightened. "Not right now. When I start trying to think about that day, my mind shuts down."

"That's not an unusual reaction for a traumatic experience. So what do you want to talk about, if not the case?"

"The way things ended for us. I never wanted to hurt you. If I could have done that over—"

He held up his hand. "Don't. We can't change what happened and discussing it to death won't help. What was done is done."

"I understand, but ignoring something doesn't make it disappear."

"Maybe I want to be reminded to be cautious."

"With me?" Her eyes darkened. "I made a couple of

big mistakes as a teenager and have learned a lot from them. I hope we can be friends at least."

Friends. That was how things started originally. "Listen, I'm sorry it didn't work out with you and Aaron, but when you eloped it changed everything."

A noise from the foyer charged the air between them.

"Lydia, I'm home. Where are you?"

"I'm in the kitchen."

He stood, the sound of his chair scraping across the floor echoing through the kitchen. "I need to check in with Thomas before I call it a day. I'd better leave. I'll lock the door on my way out." He passed Kate in the dining room, nodding at her but not slowing his step.

Always in the back of his mind, he wondered why she'd married Aaron so fast after going out with him again. He'd thought they really had a chance to make it work that second time. He was a foster kid while Aaron came from a good family with some influence in Anchorage. Had money in the end meant something to Lydia? Or was it something else that changed her mind? They had started to make up after their breakup at Christmas, but in a snap of his finger, everything had fallen apart. And Jesse had only himself to rely on, again.

Lydia forced a smile when Kate came into the kitchen. The sound of the front door slamming came just as Lydia realized she'd have to tell Jesse the whole sordid incident of her becoming pregnant and having to marry Aaron. One foolish night and her whole life had changed. She lost so much then. Although she'd communicated with Kate on a regular basis over the years, they weren't close. And her father had made it clear she wasn't welcome in Anchorage.

"How was school?"

Kate shrugged. "Nothing earth-shattering. Everyone is still talking about the bombing. They're scared."

"So am I."

"They've locked down the school tight. No one gets inside without a valid reason and everyone gets searched at the main entrance."

"Good. I'm glad they're taking precautions. I imagine other places will, too."

Kate went to the refrigerator and looked inside. "We shouldn't have to live in fear like this. Have you remembered anything?"

She already felt pressured. She hated that it was also coming from Kate. "I'm trying." Lydia took her cup to the sink. "I'm going to lie down. Just doing this little has worn me out."

"Can we order pizza tonight?"

"Sure. That way I don't have to come up with something." Lydia left the kitchen while Kate sliced cheese to put on crackers.

Emotionally and physically drained, Lydia moved slowly toward her bedroom at the end of the hallway. Luckily there were no steps to climb.

Crossing to the dresser, she decided to get comfortable and put on her pajamas, although it was only four thirty in the afternoon. In fact, she might sleep most of the evening and only get up to eat pizza, which she loved.

After she took a pair of pj's out, she swung around, her gaze skimming over the items on her desk as she made her way to the bathroom connected to her bedroom. She stopped and stared at the wooden surface. Something was wrong. Her cup of pens seemed askew. Her desk didn't look ransacked, but it didn't look right. A shiver wracked her weakened body. Someone had gone through her desk.

FOUR

Lydia racked her brain trying to figure out what felt so wrong. She hugged herself and rubbed her hands up and down her arms. Didn't she close the top drawer all the way? She always did. Keeping everything neat and in order helped her get through her busy schedule.

"What's wrong?" Kate lounged against the doorjamb, popping the last bite of her cheese and cracker into her mouth.

Lydia pointed a shaky forefinger at the drawer slightly ajar. "Did you get something from my desk?"

Kate frowned and straightened, squaring her shoulders. "I didn't go through your desk. Bree and I came in here and got some clothing for you, but that was all. Why do you think I would?" Anger edged Kate's words.

Lydia stepped closer and pulled the drawer open. She spied the notebook with a snow scene on the cover inside and sighed. It was still there. Every night she would write in it and then put it up, shutting the drawer. Not that there were any big secrets in her journal, but the idea someone else read her innermost thoughts made her blood go cold. It was one place where she would let everything out.

Lydia shut the drawer completely and looked toward Kate. "Sorry. I must have left it open. I'm such a creature of habit I thought someone had been in here going through the desk. Do you remember when you were getting the clothes if it was ajar?"

"I don't even remember looking at the desk. I know you have a place for everything, but maybe you were upset and for once didn't close it all the way."

The last time she wrote in her journal, Lydia had poured her heart out about the fight she and her little sister had over a boy Kate was dating. Lydia shook her head. She'd said some things that she regretted. To say there was tension between them after their argument concerning Connor was an understatement.

Kate surveyed the room. "Is anything missing?"

Lydia didn't get thrown off her game easily, but when she did she had trouble regaining focus. Her attention fixed on her laptop, sitting exactly as she would have left it sitting on the top of her desk. "Not that I can see. I guess with all that has happened lately, I'm jumpy. But still…" She stared at the drawer, not able to shake the thought she was right. No, it was only her overactive mind. Obviously she'd gone through a traumatic experience she hadn't dealt with yet and was imaging problems when there weren't any.

"Maybe you should call Sergeant Hunt. Let him know. He's been working on your case."

"And say what?" Lydia walked around the room, opening and closing other drawers. "Nothing seems to be gone. My most valuable possession in here is my laptop, and it's on the desk." When she looked into her walk-in closet, she stiffened. Clothes and hangers were tossed on the floor.

"Maybe I should call him. My closet is a mess," Lydia murmured before she could stop herself.

Kate came up behind her and glanced over Lydia's shoulder. She flinched at her little sister's quiet approach and stepped back.

Kate pushed past her into the closet and began picking up the shirts and pants.

"Leave it. It could be evidence."

Clenching a blouse in her hand still on its hanger, Kate glared at her. "I did this. I was upset and hurrying to get back to the hospital. I was looking for the green shirt you like to wear because it's so comfortable. I thought you could wear it home."

Her tension deflated, Lydia sagged against the door, holding herself upright. "I'll take care of it later. Right now I just want to lie down." She made her way to her bed and sank back against the pillows. "I'm sorry I accused you of going through my desk."

"Yeah, right." Kate huffed and stomped into the hallway.

I should get up and go after her. But exhaustion swamped Lydia. She closed her eyes and decided she would in a little while after Kate calmed down. After Lydia rested…

As Jesse drove toward the bistro bomb site after being at Lydia's, he couldn't shake from his mind the brief conversation about that last year before she eloped with Aaron and didn't return to Anchorage. All he wanted to do was forget it. Why did women always want to discuss things to death? The past was just that.

And as far as he and Lydia being friends, he didn't see that as an option. He didn't want her to hurt him again. It was like when he was a young boy and touched the hot stove. He never did it again. Once was enough to teach him to stay away.

Thomas wanted Jesse to follow up with the appliance store's owner today. The black Chevy with the partial license plate number Jesse had written down hadn't been found yet.

Not long after the bombing, Thomas had sent two police officers to interview each store owner on the street. Yesterday Officer Williams hadn't been able to get much from Mr. Pickens, the man who owned the appliance store. He'd been so shaken up that he could barely remember anything about that morning. This was the first day the police had allowed people back on the street after another thorough search for a follow-up bomb or any evidence. Besides Mr. Pickens, Jesse would also interview the manager at the clothing store and drugstore next door.

Jesse parked in front of Pickens Appliance, and after retrieving Brutus from the back, entered the shop. He immediately homed in on the tall, overweight man watching two men measure the area where the plate glass window used to be.

Jesse approached Mr. Pickens, recognizing him from his driver's license photo. "Mr. Pickens, I'm Sergeant Hunt, and I need to have a few words with you about the day of the bombing."

"I was in the back when the bomb went off. Shook the whole building. By the time I came out of the office, everyone was fleeing, screaming, scared."

"When did you leave that day?" Jesse gave Brutus a short leash and signaled for him to sit next to him.

"When you guys asked us to evacuate the area. I wasn't gonna wait for another bomb to go off."

"I checked your store not long after noon and found someone in here. He fled out the back. Do you have any idea who it could have been? An employee? A customer who didn't leave?"

"Everyone was gone when I locked up. Don't know why I bothered because all any person had to do was climb through the window." Mr. Pickens waved his hand toward the large gap at the front of the building. "We spent all morning picking up the glass. It shattered everywhere."

"Do you have a surveillance camera in here?"

The man pointed to two mounted cameras. "They don't work. It's not like someone is going to shoplift a stove. What did the person look like that you saw?"

"I got a brief glimpse of a dark hoodie before the door shut. When I looked out back, all I saw was a black Chevy driving away. Couldn't tell you the year. Do you remember seeing anyone park there that morning?"

"No, but it was here when I came to work at ten. I thought it belonged to an employee of the stores next to me. Like I said, I was in my office most of the time on the phone to the bank."

"Who were the employees working the floor that day?"

"Bill Campbell and myself."

"So Bill is here?"

Mr. Pickens nodded. "He's the one with the broom."

Jesse approached Bill Campbell, a medium-sized

lanky guy, with a sour expression on his face. After introducing himself, Jesse asked, "I understand you were on the floor the morning the bomb went off across the street. Did you see anything strange? Someone hanging around watching the building?"

He stopped sweeping and leaned on the broom. "It wasn't busy that morning. We usually get more customers in the afternoon or evening. There was a woman in here looking, but she wasn't here when the bomb went off. Don't know her name. Then there was a young man, maybe twenty-five in here. He wandered around looking at all kinds of appliances." Campbell stared at the hole where the window used to be. "You know he kept looking out front as if he was waiting for someone."

"Do you know his name?"

"Nope but he was here when the bomb went off."

"Did he leave right away?"

"I don't know. I was hiding behind the counter. When I finally stood up, all I focused on was the bistro."

"Would you be able to describe the man to a police artist?"

Campbell's eyes grew round. "You think he had something to do with the bombing?"

"I'm looking into everything."

"I'll do what I can. We've got to catch this guy before another bomb goes off. Business was slow before this last bomb. I don't expect much now."

"Will you be here tomorrow?"

"Yes."

"I'll send the police artist then." Jesse shook Campbell's hand, then left with Brutus.

Jesse visited the clothing shop then the drugstore, flanking Pickens Appliance. Neither place had any promising leads. The few employees in those establishments were scared and jumpy. Phillip Keats, the pharmacist and manager, even told him one longtime woman employee called in sick and hadn't returned since the bombing.

As he strolled to his SUV his phone rang. It was Lydia's house number. He quickly answered, praying nothing was wrong. "Lydia?"

"No, this is Kate."

"Has something happened?"

"Lydia thought someone had been in her bedroom. I'm scared."

Jesse turned on his engine. "Is anyone there now?"

"No, but—"

"I'll be there as soon as possible." After disconnecting, Jesse pulled out of his parking space. Why didn't Lydia call him? *Because you told her to contact Thomas.* He realized the foolhardiness of that. They might not be friends now, but they were close once. He couldn't walk away because she hurt him in the past—not if her life was in jeopardy.

A sea of black surrounded her, but Lydia couldn't move. Something held her down. Her heartbeat began to race. She couldn't breathe.

Lydia's eyes flew open. Darkness blanketed her. A band felt as though it constricted her chest. Panic drove her off the bed. But when she stood, she began to see shapes and glimpsed the clock. It was 9:30—obviously at night. She wasn't trapped any longer. She was safe and at home.

Just a dream—no, a nightmare.

She flipped on the overhead light and drank in the sight of her bedroom. She eased onto the bed and dragged deep breaths into her lungs until her heartbeat slowed to a normal rate.

Quiet melted the tension that had gripped her, and she thought of going back to sleep. But immediately dismissed that notion. She'd already slept over four hours, and her stomach rumbled. She decided to check on Kate and see if she'd ordered that pizza.

Thoughts of her sister brought back what happened earlier and the fact that Kate was no doubt angry with her, her usual attitude toward Lydia. She hadn't handled her sister right. She needed to apologize. She didn't want what happened to disrupt her life any more than it already had.

Out in the hallway, she found Cheri waiting at her door. Scooping her cat up into her arms, she started for the living room. The sound of Kate's voice as well as a deep, masculine one floated to her. Who was here? She hoped it wasn't the boy Kate was dating. Connor was a senior and from what she'd discovered, wild. Lydia didn't want her sister making the mistake she'd made.

She followed the voices to the kitchen. Stopping in the entrance, she stared first at Brutus, then Jesse sitting at the table with Kate across from him.

"Are you sure you don't want any more pizza? Lydia might not wake up until morning." Kate was finishing off a piece, then slurped a long sip of her soft drink.

Jesse's gaze snagged Lydia's.

Kate twisted around in her chair and looked at Lydia. "How long have you been there?"

She moved into the kitchen, Cheri wiggling in her

arms. "A few seconds. Why?" She placed her cat on the floor, and Cheri stared at Brutus, then walked to him and settled down beside the Rottweiler as though that was where she belonged. Brutus gave her cat one look and closed his eyes.

Kate shrugged. "Just wondering."

What had they been talking about? Lydia switched her attention to Jesse, his expression his usual neutral one whenever they were around each other. "Why are you here? Has something happened on the case?"

Jesse and Kate exchanged a glance. "Kate called me."

"How? Why?" Her sister had met Jesse at the hospital and had seen him again when she'd come home from school earlier, but that had all been casual.

Kate scraped the chair back and shot to her feet, rounding on Lydia. "I called Bree and she gave me Jesse's number. I started thinking about how someone might have been in the house, and I got scared."

"Why didn't you wake me up?"

"And you'd do what? You're hurting. Bree was working, and David is tied up. I thought of asking Connor to come over, but then you'd freak out if you found him here."

If she'd seen Connor, she probably would have. Connor reminded her of Aaron, and she didn't want her sister to have anything to do with him, especially when she was sound asleep in another room. "I was wrong. I'm sure no one has been in the house while we were gone. The evening before the bombing, I was late going to bed, and I just didn't shut the drawer all the way. I can't even remember what happened at the bistro, let alone the night before." *I'm panicking at the small things.*

Kate curled her hands and then uncurled them. "Yeah, I guess. Anyway, I've got homework." She looked over her shoulder at Jesse. "Thanks for sitting here with me."

"No problem." He gave her a smile that died the second Kate left the kitchen.

Leaving them alone.

The past few minutes left Lydia drained. She sank onto the chair Kate had vacated. Brutus came over and put his head in her lap. She began stroking him, and the feel of his fur soothed her. Finally she looked up at Jesse, studying him.

"You should have called Thomas if you thought there was a chance someone was in your house."

"But not you," came out, and she wished she could take those words back. Even she could hear the regret in them. Cheri jumped up on the table and purred, then plopped down in front of Lydia while Brutus lay on the floor by her chair.

Jesse glanced out the window over the sink.

When she could no longer take the silence, Lydia made a decision. Right now she felt her life had shattered into hundreds of fragments. "I can't change what happened, but I'm asking you to put what happened right after graduation in the past. I could use a friend right now."

He swung his attention to her, but she couldn't read anything in his expression. "What about Bree or Alex?"

"You knew me better than anyone did at one time."

One eyebrow rose. "Did I? I used to think I did, but

then you took off. One day you were here. The next gone and married."

"I called you and left a message on your voice mail."

"Yeah, at the airport right before you got on the plane to leave. With no real explanation."

Stress knotted her shoulders and neck, the pain surpassing the ache from her bruised ribs. She remembered the tears she'd cried when she'd agreed to marry Aaron and leave. The disappointment on her father's face was engraved in her mind—a vision she couldn't shake even after all these years. She'd let everyone down, but mostly Jesse. He deserved better than her.

She swallowed several times, but still her throat was as dry as the ground in the midst of a severe drought. She walked to the sink and drank some water, then returned to the table, combing her fingers through Cheri's thick white fur. "I couldn't because we'd promised our parents we wouldn't tell anyone."

"What? That you were eloping?"

"That I was pregnant with—Aaron's child."

For a few seconds his mouth pressed together in a thin, hard line, and his eyes darkened. Then as though he realized he was showing his anger a shutter descended over his features. But she saw a tic in his jawline.

Finally after a long moment, he asked, "Where's your child? With Aaron?"

That he would even think she'd let Aaron have full custody of her child devastated her. She rose, gripping the edge of the table and leaning into it. "I lost my little girl when I was seven months pregnant. I had to deliver her stillborn." She spun on her heel and stalked toward the hallway.

She heard the sound of the chair being scooted across the tiles, and all she could think about was getting away from him before she fell apart and poured out the pain she'd locked deep inside.

He caught up with her and clasped her arm, stopping her escape. "I'm sorry, Lydia. I know how much you wanted children."

A houseful, she'd once told him when they'd talked about the future. "Dreams have a way of changing," she whispered, remembering the few times she'd dated after her divorce from Aaron. No one had been Jesse. Instead, she'd thrown her life into her career and her love of animals.

"Yes, I know." His hand fell away from her.

And she missed his touch. For a second, she'd felt connected to him again like when they were teenagers. "Why didn't you come back to Alaska?"

"I was married to Aaron and I took that seriously. I wanted to make our marriage work even after our daughter died."

"What happened?"

"He had an affair with one of his professors while I worked to support us and allowed him to go to college full-time."

"He came back here a couple of years ago with an older woman as a traveling companion. He talked with Thomas but didn't get in touch with me." One corner of his mouth hitched up. "Good thing, too, even though I didn't know all the details of your elopement." He swept his arm toward the table. "I'll warm up some pizza while we talk about what happened earlier. Kate had herself worked up by the time I arrived."

His softer expression coupled with his coaxing

voice urged her to accept, especially because she was hungry. "That sounds nice. Food was what drew me out here in the first place."

After Jesse heated up the remaining slices and fixed a cup of tea for Lydia, he sat across from her. As she took several bites, he finally asked, "Explain again why you initially felt someone had been in your house. I've taken a look around and haven't seen a forced point of entry. I was surprised you didn't have a dog or two until your assistant brought the cats."

She placed Cheri on the floor, then took several sips of her warm tea. "I had Bree take both of my cats to the veterinary hospital for boarding. I didn't want her to have to deal with them and Kate. JoAnn, my assistant who brought them home, told me they were being thoroughly spoiled. Charlie and Cheri are siblings left at the back door of the hospital. One look into Cheri's green eyes and I knew I had to keep them."

"No guard dog?"

She shook her head. "But Charlie growls like a dog, and anytime someone comes to the house, he's at the door growling."

"That's better than nothing."

"Yeah, but as soon as the person comes in, he runs and hides, whereas Cheri is all over the visitor. She's never met a stranger."

"So that's why I've only seen her." Flipping his hand at Cheri, Jesse relaxed. "I'm surprised you have cats. You always had a dog growing up."

"The cats needed me." *And I needed them.* It had been within a month of her arrival in Anchorage. She'd been dealing with a hostile sister, who was grieving but not expressing those emotions. Many nights she'd been up late cuddling Cheri and talking to her about her day. In those first months she and Kate had argued every day. At least now it wasn't as often.

"Tell me about going into your bedroom."

"I didn't notice anything at first, but when I looked at my desk, I saw the top drawer was open about an inch or two. I always make sure I close drawers and cabinets. Remember when I fractured my wrist?"

"Oh, yeah. You told me you fell, not how."

"I'd opened the drawer a few minutes before, then the phone rang and I was in a hurry to answer it, but I rammed right into the drawer and fell. It's become second nature to me to shut them now, which is why it stood out, but I couldn't find anything missing or out of order. I was upset, so I supposed I could have forgotten to shut the drawer. The night before Kate and I had a big fight over Connor. That boy isn't good for her, but she won't listen to me."

"And you find that strange?" A grin twitched the corners of his mouth.

"Okay, you don't have to remind me about my dad and me. He changed so much after Mom left, and I could be stubborn."

"You think?"

She narrowed her eyes and pinched her lips together but couldn't maintain the tough act. She started chuckling. "I seem to remember you could be quite determined, too."

"Still am, and I'm especially determined to catch this person setting off the bombs. If you don't mind, I didn't check out your room earlier. May I look at it?"

"Sure." She frantically reviewed how it looked and breathed a little easier when she remembered everything was neat and put away—except for the clothes on the closet floor.

"Do you want me to check it out now?"

"I have something I need to do first, then you can."

"I don't care if it's messy."

"I do."

"A mess you made?"

"No, Kate did when she was getting something for me to wear home from the hospital. The clothes I came to the ER in were given to the police and then I hope thrown away."

"Nothing is going to be tossed until this case is over. The police are scouring each bomb site for any clue to who is behind this. Because this bomber is so erratic we can't predict where he will go next."

For a few seconds the sound of the laugh track blared through her mind. She shook. "So you think he will strike again?"

"Yes."

The one word froze her as though a blizzard swept through her kitchen. And somewhere in her memory she might have a picture of the killer. If only she could remember...

"Are you okay?"

Jesse's question pulled her from her thoughts. "I want to remember what happened at the bistro, but the more I try, the harder it is."

"Then don't try. It will come to you."

"But in time to stop another bombing?"

He reached across the table and took her hand. "We're working on the case. A lot of manpower and resources are going into this. You might not have seen anything. Don't do that to yourself."

He was right. She had enough guilt to handle without adding to it. She and her dad never really reconciled their differences before he died. That was why her relationship with Kate was so important. She didn't want to have that regret again. She could even apply that to Jesse. She didn't see their relationship returning to the way it was, but she wanted to mend it enough to remain friends.

"I'm trying, but then I think of the people I was acquainted with who died in the bombing and it's hard not to put pressure on myself."

"You suffered a severe concussion. It takes time for your brain to heal."

She inhaled a deep breath and was reminded it would take time for her ribs to heal, too. "Give me a couple of minutes to pick up the clothes. My bedroom is the last one on the right."

A minute later, she bent over in her closet to scoop up the clothes, but as she straightened, she winced. She was constantly rethinking how to move to keep from sending pain through her chest. Not an easy task when she was used to being on the go. After hanging the shirts and pants up, she surveyed the floor for any signs that meant someone besides her sister could have been in here. Everything appeared as she'd left it. At least from what she could remember.

She emerged from the closet to find Jesse in the entrance while Cheri sauntered into the room and jumped up on her bed. His gaze captured hers, and for a moment she couldn't think of anything to say. Transfixed by his presence, the seconds ticked off until he finally dragged his attention away and took in the room. He crossed to each of the windows and checked to make sure they were locked. She should have thought of that. When he walked to the desk and opened the top drawer, she tensed, but he didn't touch or say anything.

"Nothing seems unusual. The windows are locked, and I can't find any evidence of tampering. Who has a key to your house besides Bree?"

"No one except Kate and Bree."

"Nothing outside under a rock or something?" Lines at the corners of his eyes deepened, drawing her full attention to their color, a heart-melting caramel, her favorite candy.

"No. Kate lost her key once, and she had to call me at the animal hospital to come home and open the door."

"When?"

"Months ago, but I changed the locks since she never found it." She started for the hallway, needing to put some space between her and Jesse. There had been a reason she'd kept her distance between them this past year. Seeing him made her regret even more what she did, and now they were different people. After Aaron, she didn't trust easily. While she'd dedicated herself to their relationship, he'd been having an affair that destroyed their three-year marriage.

Kate opened her door across the hall from Lydia's room. Her sister glanced from her to Jesse. "I can get you some bedding for the couch in the living room. It's very comfortable."

Lydia stood in front of Jesse, who was still in her doorway. "What do you mean, Kate?"

"Jesse said he would stay if he thought someone had been in our house."

"But we've decided I overreacted and no one was.

He doesn't have to stay." Although the idea had merit, and she would have asked if she really thought someone had been in the house, it was still clear he was uncomfortable around her. She'd offered a partial explanation of what happened years ago, but they really hadn't discussed it.

"You might feel all right, but I don't. What if you had died?" Tears filled Kate's eyes, and she whirled around and disappeared into her bedroom, slamming the door.

FIVE

Lydia stared at the closed door, understanding the emotions her sister was going through. She was still experiencing a gauntlet of feelings, ranging from anger to dismay to sadness, each striking her over and over.

Jesse cleared his throat. "Lydia, go talk to her. I'll wait in the living room with Brutus."

"Thanks. She was pretty quiet at the hospital. At least now she's talking about how she's feeling." She approached the bedroom, hoping she could find the right words to say to her sister. She didn't want this to make a bigger mess out of their relationship.

After rapping on the door, she fortified herself with thoughts that could bring them closer together. Something good could come out of this tragedy.

"Go away," Kate shouted.

Lydia knocked again.

Suddenly the door was wrenched open, and Kate's usual glare pierced through Lydia. Right now her sister's anger was front and center. It was hard to reason with her when she was like this. Had Lydia been this difficult for her dad? Was this why they had always butted heads? "I'd like to come in and talk."

"Why? You never listen to me. You aren't my parent."

"No, I'm your guardian, but that has nothing to do with what we need to talk about."

Kate stepped to the side and let her enter the room. At least she didn't slam the door this time. Lydia sat on her bed, exhaustion creeping in.

"Why did you really call Jesse? Other than my initial reaction, there wasn't any indication someone had been in our house."

She fisted her hands. "Only a few survived the bombing. What if the bomber comes after you? What if…" Kate's voice thickened, and she swung around and stared at the laptop and papers on her desk.

"I don't remember anything. I'm not a threat to him."

"But you could be." Kate's back was still to Lydia. She pushed off the bed and closed the space between them. She started to touch her sister's shoulder, but her stiff stance told her to keep away. "If it'll make you feel better, I'll have Jesse stay the night, but we need to move on and put this behind us because that solution is only temporary." She almost laughed at that statement. She didn't know if she'd be able to do that, but she didn't want Kate to be afraid. "He has a job to do. He's on the task force looking for the bomber. I want him to be a hundred percent rested."

Kate slowly turned. "So do I, but he has to sleep somewhere. Why not here?"

Because I can't deal with that. I wronged him and every time I see him that's reinforced. "Let's take it one day at a time," was all Lydia could come up with, which really wasn't a solution. But she didn't have the energy to hash this out with Kate tonight. "I'll ask him to stay…" an idea popped into her head "…or better yet, I'll have him leave Brutus here if he's willing to. I've treated Brutus, and he knows me. The dog could sleep in your room."

"I'm not the one the bomber would be after. You are."

"How about Brutus sleeps in the hallway between our rooms?"

Her sister's frown melted. "Okay."

Lydia left Kate to talk with Jesse. She wasn't sure he would agree, but all she could do was ask. When she entered the living room, Jesse knelt next to his Rottweiler and was rubbing his stomach and play wrestling.

"You've got a good dog. Well trained."

Jesse peered toward her and smiled. "Yeah. We work well together."

"Kate is still scared even though I told her we didn't think anything happened here. I believe it's all leftover emotions from the day of the bombing. With our dad dying last year, she had her legs knocked out from under her. My death would have been a second big blow in a short time."

At the mention of her possible death, Jesse's eyes widened slightly and his grin dissolved. "I can certainly understand that. I was a foster kid. You not only have to deal with your parents' death but living with strangers."

As a teenager, Jesse rarely mentioned living with a foster family. In fact, he wouldn't talk about his past, something that had frustrated her because she wanted to know everything about him. "Would it be possible to leave Brutus overnight with us? It might put Kate's mind at peace."

"What about tomorrow night and the one after that?"

She pushed her fingers through her hair. "I'm hoping when nothing happens she'll begin to calm down. Right now I'm taking it one day at a time." Because that was about all she could handle. "That way you can go home and get a good night's sleep. The couch is okay but not as good as a bed. I know you've been working long hours…" Her voice faded as Jesse rose and cut the distance between them.

"I'll do what is needed. If you want me to stay, I'll make do with the couch. I love to go camping, and the hard ground is way worse."

His very nearness robbed her of any reply. She moistened her lips and stepped back. "She was happy when I suggested Brutus sleep here. It'll be easier to transition back to being just the two of us." And easier on her. She hadn't spent this much time with Jesse since they were dating.

"Then we'll do that. He doesn't eat until the morning. I'll bring his food over before I go to work. If there's a problem, call." He slipped his card into her hand, his fingers lingering a couple of seconds longer than necessary.

His touch set off a myriad of buried emotions flowing through her. "I'll take good care of Brutus."

"I know. I've seen you with the SAR dogs." His gaze snagged hers and bound her to him as though with invisible ropes.

Her heartbeat accelerated. She turned away and headed for the front door.

Jesse called Brutus and put on his leash. "I'll take him for a walk since you don't have a fenced-in backyard. It won't take long."

While Jesse and his K-9 descended the porch steps, Lydia made her way outside to stand and wait for them to return. In the darkness, she could study Jesse without him seeing. She always loved the fluid way he moved, usually as though he didn't have a care in the world. But then she'd seen him in action, quick to do whatever was needed.

When he ascended the steps with Brutus five minutes later, Lydia walked toward him and schooled her features into a neutral expression—at least she hoped, because light streamed from the open door.

"I'll need to come by early. We'll finish up at the bistro hopefully tomorrow and what remains will be for the crime scene techs to handle."

"Everyone was accounted for?"

"Yes, finally. But Brutus is a bomb detector, and we're making sure we have all the pieces left. Any evidence we can gather will help us find this guy."

"I'll be up early. I'll take Kate to school, then I'm going to the animal hospital."

"I thought the doctor told you to take it easy."

She chuckled. "You know me. When have I ever done that? I'm not staying long, but I want to check on the dog I operated on the day of the bombing. I know a lot of the staff want to see me, too. I promised Bree I would wait to go back full-time until next week."

"Okay. I'll be here by seven thirty. I'll wait to leave until you and Brutus are inside."

She strolled toward the door and glanced back.

"Thank you." Maybe they could be friends again. She hoped so.

Then Jesse said, "I became a police officer to protect others. Stay, Brutus."

In other words, he was only doing his job. Jesse had a way of reminding her their time together as a couple was over. She knew that in her mind, but her heart was struggling with it.

In the living room, she watched him drive away, then switched off the lights and went into the kitchen to make sure there was water in a bowl for Brutus. In the garage she had an old cushion that she would use as a bed for Brutus. After he was settled in the hallway, she finally sank onto her bed. Jesse's parting words ran over and over through her mind. She couldn't blame him. She deserved them. She was a victim in one of his cases, and that was all.

After Jesse picked up Brutus, Lydia dropped off Kate at school, and then she drove to the animal hospital and parked in the lot on the side of the building. As she walked toward the front entrance, she stared at the bomb site where the bistro had been. She noticed Jesse's SUV near it. When he came to get Brutus, she'd invited him to have breakfast, but he'd declined. She wished he hadn't because she and Kate had argued about having the Rottweiler back that night.

Lydia hadn't slept much the night before, not because she was scared but because of Jesse. She hoped she could forget about him long enough to take a long nap.

As she entered the reception area, she came to a stop. Streamers and balloons hung from the ceiling

with a large banner over the check-in counter. She'd
mentioned to Dr. Matt Muller she was coming but
wouldn't be staying. He and her dad had been good
friends, but she never imagined Matt would do something like this.

When she looked behind the counter, the receptionist stood and started clapping. Others came from the
back and joined in. Heat flamed Lydia's cheeks. She
waved her arms. "Thanks. I'd planned on sneaking in,
but this beats that idea."

Matt opened the door to the hallway that led to the
exam rooms and entered the reception area. "That's
what I figured. We couldn't let you do that without letting you know how happy we are that you survived."

Her assistant, JoAnn, followed him. "We all pitched
in and brought goodies. The Lord was watching out
for you. That's something to celebrate."

"Hear! Hear!" someone shouted.

There was a time when Lydia hadn't thought God
cared what happened to her, especially in those dark
days when she'd lost her baby and realized Aaron
wasn't really there for her, either. She went through
the motions of worshipping the Lord, but she'd decided
years ago He was too busy to listen to her prayers.

"Thank you. I'm not going to say you shouldn't
have done this because I'm hoping JoAnn baked her
cinnamon rolls."

Her assistant grinned and nodded. "We have everything set up in the break room. I even made you
some to take home."

"Thank you! I'm going to check on Mitch, then
we'll party."

"He's a trouper. He's going home today." Matt gave

Lydia a hug. "And his partner, Officer Nichols, is getting better. We have a lot to celebrate."

Like Matt she'd become attached to the SAR dogs and the K-9s that were partnered with a police officer. She'd enjoyed having Brutus last night. He was so well trained that he even got along with Cheri, while Charlie remained hidden under her bed, one of his favorite places.

"Who's taking Mitch until Jake Nichols gets out of the hospital?" Lydia headed for the back where Mitch would be.

"Jesse Hunt is coming to pick him up this morning on his break. Brutus and Mitch have always gotten along." Matt stepped to the side to allow Lydia into the large room with cages for the animals.

"This is the time I wish I had a fenced yard. I'd have taken Mitch."

"You could walk him. He'll need the exercise. And you can make sure he continues to progress."

Lydia opened the cage door as Mitch struggled to stand. Before he hobbled two steps, she was next to him, kneeling down and petting the tan-and-black German shepherd. As she checked him out, he nuzzled her. "You're looking good, Mitch. Would you like to come home with me?"

The dog barked.

"That's your answer," her partner said. "You should talk with Jesse about taking Mitch."

"I think I will. I saw his SUV at the bistro. If he hasn't come by here, I'll go see him when I leave." Having Mitch at her house would make Kate feel better—and if she was honest with herself, she would, too.

Matt glanced at his watch. "Let's go eat. My first appointment will be here in fifteen minutes."

"How's Dr. Stutsman fitting in?"

"He's not you. A bit set in his ways, but at least he could help us while you're recuperating. He should be here soon."

"He's seventy and prefers camping and fishing now."

"Yeah, I know. That's all I hear about."

Closing the cage door, Lydia chuckled. "He reminds me of my father."

"Your dad was kind of set in his ways, too."

Lydia's chuckle evolved into laughter. "You think? *Change* was not in Dad's vocabulary."

"True. I guess you've spoiled me. I like going with the flow."

Lydia clasped Matt's shoulder. "You've made this transition easier."

At the break room, he paused. "Still want to leave after Kate graduates?"

She remembered telling him that when she'd met with him the first day. "I'm reconsidering."

"Good. I'm too old to go through breaking in another partner."

She studied the medium-sized man with salt-and-pepper hair and sharp eyes. "You're not old. You can't be a day over fifty."

"Fifty-four, and thank you for saying that." He indicated she go into the room first.

Lydia ate a bite from every dish brought and spent some time with the staff she'd come to care about. Maybe she could return earlier than she'd planned.

"I see the wheels turning in that mind of yours."

JoAnn presented her with the leftover cinnamon rolls wrapped in aluminum foil to take home with her.

"I've only known you a year, and you think you can read my mind."

"I see the yearning on your face."

Lydia's gaze fixed on Dr. Stutsman, who had come in a few minutes ago. She leaned close to JoAnn and whispered, "Are you two getting along okay?"

Her assistant turned her back to the room full of staff. "Sure. I can get along with a grizzly."

"It's that bad?"

"Today's Friday. Aren't you coming back Monday?"

Lydia nodded.

"We're fine, but I've learned to appreciate you." JoAnn winked and pointed toward the door. "You look exhausted. Go home."

Lydia saluted. "Aye, aye." Then to everyone, she said, "Thank you so much for this party. I needed it after the week I've had. I'll be back on Monday." As the last word slipped from her mouth, she pictured a few days ago when the bomb exploded, and shuddered. So much had changed in that time. She would be glad when she returned to her normal routine.

She made her way toward the front entrance with her goodies. When she reached for the handle, the door opened, and she quickly stepped back. Jesse with Brutus beside him filled the entry.

"I saw your car. I thought I'd catch you to make sure Mitch will be okay to go home today." Dust covered Jesse's black uniform.

"Did you go Dumpster diving?"

One corner of his mouth hiked up. "Searching for clues can be a dirty job."

"I was coming to see you to give you and who-ever else is working the site this." She thrust the foil-wrapped sweets into his hand. "JoAnn makes the best cinnamon rolls."

"Thanks." He stared at the gift for a few seconds, then looked her in the eye. "Is Mitch cleared to leave?"

"Yes, but I want to take him home."

"You think he might need a vet?"

"No, but Kate wasn't happy when I told her Brutus wasn't coming back tonight. Mitch is familiar with me. I've treated him several times this year, and best of all, I think Kate won't give me a hard time."

"But you don't have a fenced backyard."

"I think Kate will jump at the chance of walking him around out back. My little sis has taken after me as far as loving animals." *Not much else, though.*

"Are you sure you don't need Brutus?"

"Yes." She wanted to see more of Jesse, but she needed to remember it was only a case to him.

"Then that's fine with me. I'm so used to Brutus being around that it was lonely without him."

"Great. I'm going to load Mitch and some food into my car and take him home now. I need a long nap."

Instead of leaving, Jesse moved inside and shut the door. "Did you get any sleep last night? I was hoping Brutus would help you feel safe."

"He did. It was probably my four-hour nap yester-day that threw me off schedule." Although that could be part of the reason, the main one was the man stand-ing in front of her. Even in a dusty police uniform, he commanded a person's full attention.

"And you're taking another one today?"

"Yep. You can carry the canned food."

After she showed him where it was kept, she took a leash and retrieved an excited Mitch from his cage. She adjusted her gait as the German shepherd adapted the way he walked with a missing back leg.

Out in the parking lot, Jesse set the food on the seat in back while Lydia helped the dog climb into the front seat of her gray Jeep. She shut the passenger door and came around the hood of the car.

"I thank you, and so does Kate, for letting us have Mitch."

Jesse peered at the bomb site and back to Lydia.

"Does Jake know about Mitch's leg?"

"No, I wanted him off the critical list and stabilized first. He was really attached to his dog."

She'd known that, but she had no choice if Mitch was to live. "I'd like to go with you when you tell him."

"You don't have to. I can break the news to him."

"It'll devastate him, but I feel I need to be the one. I made the decision and can explain the reason why Mitch lost his leg."

Jesse's barrier he kept between them fell in place. "I'll let Jake know now that he can receive visitors, then if you want you can talk to him."

Lydia slipped in behind the steering wheel, started the car and lowered her window. "Have you found anything helpful this morning?"

"Not yet, but every area has to be combed through."

While Lydia drove away from the animal hospital, she glanced at Jesse in the rearview mirror, his legs planted a foot apart, his gaze tracking her as she pulled out into traffic. She sighed as he disappeared from her sight. Probably a good thing. She didn't need to have a wreck, staring at him when she should be driving.

* * *

Jesse squatted next to Brutus and rubbed his hand down his back. "Break time is over. We have to get back to work. Sorry about your buddy not coming home with us."

As he rose and stretched, he thought about yesterday and spending more time with Lydia than he'd wanted. And yet, in the end, he didn't mind it because leaving Brutus with her and Kate felt like the right call. Even so, he'd stayed outside her house for an hour before leaving.

He couldn't shake what she'd told him about marrying Aaron. If he ever saw his high school friend, he'd throttle him. He'd known Aaron was a player and tried to warn her, but she'd refused to listen. If only she had… Would they have been together today? He'd asked himself that question quite a bit with conflicting answers each time. Now it was too late.

When he reached the bomb site, he picked up where he and Brutus had left off. Fifteen minutes into searching his section, his cell phone rang, his ring tone the call of a bull moose. He saw it was Thomas and asked, "I thought you were going to be at the bomb site. Has something happened?"

"Yes, but not another bomb. I got the autopsy information back on the waitress. She died from a large air embolism. After some investigation and looking at video feed, it has been ruled a murder. A medium-sized man was caught going into her room, dressed as an orderly, but no one on the staff fits his description. It turns out an orderly's badge was stolen in the locker room the day the waitress died."

"Then we have a photo of the guy."

"Sort of."

Jesse surveyed the area. "What do you mean?"

"It looks like a disguise, although we'll use the photo. Even if our bomber is using disguises, maybe this will help us. I'm just not sure how accurate it will be and the orderly had an uncanny way of avoiding the cameras. I can't find anyone he interacted with on the floor. I'm almost at the bomb site."

Jesse clicked off. If the waitress was murdered, then she must have seen something in the dining area or the bomber thought she did. What about Lydia? She couldn't remember, but the man wouldn't know that, and even if he did, he killed the waitress to get rid of a witness. Jesse tried calling Lydia on her cell phone, but she didn't answer. Spying Thomas's car pulling up, he hurried toward the detective.

Thomas met him partway. "I'm worried about Lydia. Did you just see her? Is she still at the animal hospital? I want to show her this picture."

"Yes and no. She's taking Mitch home with her. I'd feel a lot better about that if the dog wasn't injured. I tried calling her cell phone, but she isn't picking up. She wouldn't be home yet."

"Maybe she stopped somewhere. Doesn't have her cell. It died. We could be overreacting."

Jesse frowned. "I'd rather be overreacting than have something happen. I'm going to her house. I'll take the picture to show her."

"I'll have a patrol car near there go by Lydia's until you arrive. With this development, she needs police protection. Stay with her until I get everything set up. If this guy thought he needed to kill the waitress, then he must have thought she saw something. Lydia probably saw it, too."

"Yeah, let's hope she did. There's no guarantee." Jesse strode to his SUV and settled Brutus in the back. On the way he called her again, praying he was over-reacting.

Lydia pulled into the driveway and punched a re-mote button to raise the garage door. "We're at my house, Mitch."

The German shepherd perked up on the seat be-side her.

"I'm going to take the food in first. I'll be right back, then I'll show you my house. I have a couple of cats I need to put in the bathroom until you all are properly introduced."

Mitch cocked his head as though he understood every word she'd said. Dogs were attuned to a per-son's body language and tone of voice, so maybe he got the gist of it.

She rubbed the top of his head. "Then I'll take you for a walk out back."

Lydia slid from the backseat and grabbed the box of cans. When she lifted it, a pang of pain stabbed her chest. Her bruised ribs were healing but not fast enough for her. With the dog food in her arms, she fumbled to open the door into the house. When it swung wide, she almost fell through the entrance. She recovered her balance but not before the box crashed to the tile floor. Her actions only reinforced her ear-lier pain. She hurried to close the door to the garage before one of her cats got out and decided to investi-gate the strange dog in her car.

As she picked up the dog food that had rolled from the box, she began to have reservations about Mitch.

She hadn't really thought about her two cats. Mitch could appease Kate but cause an animal war in the house.

One of the cans landed under her kitchen table. She scooted a chair away and eased herself down to crawl after it. She grabbed it and backed out.

A sound caught her attention. Footsteps? The cats? Where were they? They were always in here greeting her when she returned home.

She rose slowly, her body already protesting the physical exertion. Her gaze swung from one end of the room to the other. Her cats weren't in the kitchen. She needed to find them to lock them up. It would take time to acclimate Charlie to Mitch. Cheri wouldn't have any trouble, so she would start with her.

Lydia headed for the dining room that flowed into the living room, calling their names. They usually came when she called, but occasionally they would ignore her. When she stopped in the foyer, she heard a cry coming from the hallway to the bedroom. She didn't want to leave Mitch alone in a new place for long, so she hurried toward the sound Cheri was making, like the cry of a baby.

The noise continued, emanating from her room at the end. As she approached, she tried to remember if she'd closed the door. Sometimes she did. She'd been rushing this morning and—

Her home phone rang.

The ringing of the phone cut through the silence. She gasped at the sudden sound and glanced over her shoulder. She froze. A man in a ski mask emerged from her bathroom. All she saw was the long knife in his hand.

SIX

Jesse disconnected his phone and stepped on the accelerator. She didn't even answer her house phone. Was she outside walking Mitch?

He was still ten minutes out, and he couldn't shake that something was wrong. What if the bomber followed her from the animal hospital and ran her off the road or...

He shook the what-ifs from his mind. It would only distract him from getting to Lydia. He took a sharp curve ten miles over the speed limit. At least Thomas had called for a patrol car to go to Lydia's. But what if there wasn't an officer available in the area?

He clenched his jaw, hoping to make her house in half the time.

Not taking her eyes off the knife in the man's hand, Lydia lunged for her bedroom door, shoved it open, whirled around and banged it shut. She threw the lock in place, then backed away.

Off to the side Cheri perched on her bed, wailing as though she was being assaulted. Something slammed against the door. The lock held. But not for long. The wood wasn't thick. She went to her bedside table to retrieve her father's revolver. As her assailant attacked the flimsy barrier, his pounding fist vied with her heartbeat—ever increasing. Although the weapon was always loaded, she checked to see if the gun had bullets in every chamber. Empty! The spare ammunition was kept in a hall closet.

Her cell was in the car. Why wasn't there an extension of the home phone in here? She frantically looked around for any kind of weapon to use. Nothing useful against a knife. Her gaze fell on the window at the end of her bed. Maybe if she could climb out of it and escape…

A crashing sound, as if the intruder was throwing his body against the door, rattled the pictures on the wall nearby. She rushed to the window and fought to unlock it. It wouldn't budge. After wiping her sweaty hands on her jeans, she poured all her strength into trying one last time before she searched for something to break the glass. The bolt gave way, and she shoved the window up.

The sound of sirens—not far away—echoed in the air. Suddenly an eerie silence came from the hallway. What was the intruder doing? Looking for something else to smash the door open? Either way she had to get out of her bedroom. The sirens probably weren't for her.

She poked her head out to see how far down she would have to jump to the ground. A motion out of the corner of her eye caught her attention. A man dressed in black jeans and T-shirt ran across her yard from her back door, heading for the woods nearby. It had to be her attacker, although earlier she hadn't even noticed what he was wearing. Or could there be two people and the other one was waiting out in the hallway for her?

Jesse turned the corner onto the road that ran in front of Lydia's home. He spied a patrol car parked in front with the lights flashing. As he shut down his emotions, preparing himself to handle anything coming his way, he pulled up behind the cruiser and glanced toward her house.

Lydia came out onto the porch with Officer Williams, her arms crisscrossed over her chest. The look on her face twisted his heart. Something happened there, but at least she was alive.

He climbed from his white SUV and rounded the rear to release Brutus. He strode toward Lydia, and her head swiveled toward him. She bit her lip, then returned her attention to Officer Williams.

"What happened?" Jesse asked as he approached them.

"Dr. McKenzie found a man in her house. I was going to have her sit in my car while I take a look inside."

"He's gone. He ran out the back door toward the woods." Lydia's voice quavered, and she clamped her lips together.

Jesse headed for the left side of her house. "How long ago?"

"Four or five minutes ago," the police officer answered.

"Stay here and guard her. Brutus and I will follow the intruder's trail. Don't leave her alone."

Officer Williams nodded his head.

Jesse disappeared from their view, hurrying his steps. He wanted to catch this man—put an end to the past weeks' terror. Brutus picked up a scent at the back door, and Jesse gave him a long leash as they charged across the yard into the woods. His partner weaved through the trees as though the intruder wasn't sure which way to go. Good. Maybe he had a chance to catch the guy even with his lead.

In the thick brush to the left, a flash of black caught Jesse's attention. He turned Brutus loose, and his dog made a beeline toward the heavy foliage a couple of football fields to the west. The sound of a motorcycle's engine revving spurred Jesse on faster. When he broke out of the line of trees onto a path, his K-9 raced down the trail after a person in black hunkered over a motorcycle speeding around a curve.

Jesse ran twenty yards behind his Rottweiler and rounded the turn onto a paved road. Brutus and the motorcycle had disappeared from view.

So cold. Lydia sank onto a chair on her front porch, her whole body shaking, and massaged her hands up and down her arms.

Leaning against the house, Officer Williams stood next to her, panning the yard. "Can you remember anything about the guy in your house?"

"I wish I could give you a description of the man in the hallway. I just don't remember anything other than the knife he had."

"But you think it was a man?"

Yeah, she did—even before she glimpsed the person running away from her house. She tried to recall anything to help catch the intruder. Did he have on jeans, a black T-shirt? Although she only stared at the knife, it was against a dark background. "Yes."

"Okay, you said the guy running from the house was medium height and build. How about his hair color?"

She'd given the officer a brief description right when he showed up, thinking he might go after the intruder, but he'd told her Detective Caldwell had insisted he stay with her. She visualized in her mind the man escaping toward the woods. "He had on a black ball cap, and dark brown hair was sticking out of the back."

"Then dark brown hair, medium height. At least it's a start."

One that fit a lot of men in Anchorage. Why didn't she think to study the guy? Because she was too busy trying to get away from him. "Is Detective Caldwell coming here?" she asked, glad that at least Kate had been at school.

"I don't know."

Lydia looked toward the left, wondering where Jesse was. He knew how to protect himself, but this man — if he was the bomber—had nothing to lose by killing him. Or her.

She clasped her hands together in her lap, squeezing so tightly her knuckles whitened. She checked her watch. Jesse had been gone fifteen *long* minutes. What if the intruder hid and then attacked him? No, he'd be all right. Brutus, too. They worked well together.

Lord, I haven't asked for much, but please keep Jesse and Brutus safe.

The prayer came to her mind unexpectedly. She

hadn't prayed much in the past years. She'd given up when hers went unanswered after her daughter died.

Finally, five minutes later, Jesse came around the side of the house with Brutus but no intruder. She sank against the back of the chair and unclasped her hands. He was unhurt. But the man was still out there.

Jesse mounted the steps. His look zeroed in on her. "Are you okay?"

She started to nod, but she couldn't. She wasn't all right. A huge knot twisted her stomach. Her ribs were sore, and finally she was beginning to realize how close she had come to being hurt or killed. Again. The trembling sped through her body, and there was nothing she could do to stop it.

"Officer Williams, why don't you walk through the house? See how the man got inside."

Her head lowered, she heard the screen door bang closed. She sensed Jesse moving toward her, but for the life of her, she couldn't look at him. If she did, she might totally fall apart, and she couldn't. It wouldn't change anything.

Jesse squatted in front of her and laid his hands over hers.

She finally looked into his eyes. The kindness in them battered at the dam she desperately tried to shore up. They weren't even friends anymore. All she was to Jesse was a possible witness to a crime…one who couldn't even remember anything to help the police— to help herself.

He cradled her hands between his as though he cared. His gaze softened, and for a few seconds, she was swept back to when they had been dating and she'd fallen while skiing. He'd been there by her side almost instantly, holding her like this and asking her if she was okay.

She slid her eyes closed before the emotions cramming her throat turned to tears and demanded release.

"Lydia, I'm not going to let anything happen to you. Thomas is going to move you to a safe house, and you'll have a guard with you at all times. That's what he's working on right now."

She coated her dry throat and asked, "How did you know what was going on? If the officer hadn't turned on his siren and arrived when he did…" The sounds of the intruder attacking her door echoed through her mind as though it were still happening. She flinched with each strike.

Jesse released her hands and drew her to her feet, then wrapped his arms around her. "We now believe the waitress was murdered. When I was told about the autopsy report, I headed here while Thomas dispatched a patrol car in the area."

"If the officer had been five minutes later, the intruder would have gotten into my bedroom. My gun wasn't loaded. It should have been." She pulled back from Jesse. "I never unloaded it. Dad had it there, and I kept it in the same place."

"Would Kate have?"

"I'll ask her, but I don't think so. She doesn't like guns, and when Dad tried to teach her to shoot, she refused. But she never had a problem with me having it for protection. She just didn't want to be the one holding it."

Jesse glanced around. "Let's go inside. I see a few of your neighbors are getting curious." With his arm around her shoulder, he walked with her into the foyer.

"When you feel ready, I want you to tell me and show me what you did when you came home."

Lydia cupped her hand over her mouth. "Oh, no. Mitch is still out in my car in the garage." She hurried toward the kitchen and almost ran into Officer Williams coming out of the room. She could vaguely hear Jesse talking to the police officer as she entered the garage.

When she opened the door, Mitch perked up and slowly climbed down. "I'm sorry it took so long." She petted him, glad he hadn't been with her. He might have gotten hurt further trying to apprehend the intruder.

The German shepherd was learning how to compensate for his lost leg. The K-9s she treated were always very smart dogs and able to adapt to different kinds of situations they found themselves in. He followed her into the house. His tail began to wag when he spied Brutus near Jesse.

"Where's Officer Williams?"

"Checking the perimeter. We haven't figured out how the man got into the house."

"You think he had a key?"

"I don't know. If so, how did he get it?"

Which also brought up the question why did he kill the waitress at the hospital but not her? He didn't try until now. "If he's trying to kill me, why now and not at the hospital?"

"Several reasons possibly. You had people in your room coming and going all the time. Kate. Bree. Me. Your assistant from work. The waitress didn't have any family nearby. She'd recently moved to Alaska. Usually it was just staff moving in and out of her room. If he impersonated an orderly, he could find enough time when no one else was around."

"Do you have a photo of the man you think did it?"

"Yes, a couple, but not any good ones." Jesse opened his cell phone and showed her the ones Thomas sent him from the surveillance cameras at the hospital. "I know that part of his face is hidden, but does this trigger anything? Was it the man you saw today?"

She stared at the pictures—one with the left side of his face while the other was a full-body shot, but in the distance and not clear. "This guy has blond hair so that's different from the intruder."

"Hair color can be changed."

"It's hard to tell for sure. His build seems familiar if I use the door as a reference point for height, but he's chubby around the waist. I don't think the guy in my house was." But uncertainty nagged her. Was she trying to fill in details because she wanted to remember? Was she missing something? She thought back to the visitors and staff who were in her hospital room and…

Jesse started to take his cell phone back.

"Wait." She clasped his wrist to still his movements. "I remember seeing a guy like this in my room. Bree had me walking in the corridor, and when we came back into the room, he was there. He said he had just finished changing my sheets and he rushed out. So many staff came and went, I really didn't think about it, even though he struck me as a little weird. You know how it is in a hospital. The parade of people through your room makes it difficult to get much rest."

"That's why I avoid hospitals as much as possible."

"Have you ever had to stay in one?"

"Only twice in the ER. They almost admitted me the time I was shot, but I managed to avoid it."

"You were shot? On the job?"

"Yes. It wasn't that big of a deal. Hardly more than a flesh wound."

There was so much she didn't know about Jesse now. And there was much he didn't know about her. They were strangers in many ways, and that thought saddened her.

After Lydia put some water down for Mitch and Brutus, Jesse said, "Tell me what happened once you came inside the house."

She went through the steps she'd taken earlier. "Cheri was carrying on, and I was following her cries and looking for where Charlie was. Neither one came to greet me." She paused. "Wait. Where is Charlie? Cheri had been shut up in my bedroom." She surveyed the hallway and began checking the rooms—the third bedroom that her dad had turned into an office, the bathroom, Kate's room and then she came to hers, the master bedroom, with the door nearly destroyed. It drove home how close she'd come to being killed. "Cheri was on my pillow. When the pounding started, she went under the bed."

Lydia knelt on the floor and peeked under it. Two sets of eyes stared at her from the dimness. "Charlie is with Cheri. I didn't put them in the bedroom. The intruder must have." She pulled Cheri out and Charlie followed until he spied Jesse with Brutus and then he dashed out of the room.

Lydia rose with Cheri in her arms and sank onto

her bed. "Thank God he didn't kill them. I don't know what…" Her voice quavered, making the rest of the sentence difficult to finish. She hugged Cheri against her, her eyes watering. What could have happened hit her like an avalanche, and this time she couldn't contain the emotions overwhelming her.

Jesse sat next to her, his side pressed against hers as though to let her know he was there for her. She wasn't alone. She buried her face in Cheri's long fur as she struggled to stop the tears slipping down her cheeks. She appreciated Jesse's silence because he knew how she felt about crying in front of others. She'd always fought not to, even when she attended her father's funeral and Kate had bawled in her arms. As the older sibling with a grieving father, Lydia had learned to shut her sorrow down quickly after her mother left.

Cheri's purrs calmed her, and she drew in deep breaths to compose herself. "I start thinking about what could have happened to my animals or Mitch if circumstances had been different."

"And you. I want you to pack your clothes. After Officer Williams checks the perimeter, he's going to pick up Kate from school a little early. I'll need you to call the school and let them know. Then she'll need to pack, and we'll get out of here. I'm not sure they'll find anything, but I'm going to have the crime scene techs here to check. Do you remember if he had on gloves?"

The vision of the knife in the intruder's hand materialized in her mind. "Yes, black ones. Not thick winter ones."

"I'll still have them go through and take latent prints where they can." His gaze latched on to the revolver on the bedside table. "Also go over the gun. See if there are other prints beside yours on it. And if he was here before you came home from the hospital maybe he left something or took something that would give us a clue."

"So you think he took the bullets?"

"Unless Kate did. Probably."

"I'll ask Kate about that, but I don't think she'd have done it."

"Which means you might have had an intruder before today who went through your possessions."

So she hadn't overreacted. "Why?"

"I can only speculate." Jesse twisted toward her and framed her face with his large hands. "Why would he be going around bombing different places in Anchorage? Or, why would he go through your belongings? Maybe to get a sense of you. We may never know. Not all people think in a normal, logical way. Their reasoning won't make sense to us."

"Is there any way the person in my house was a robber and had nothing to do with the bombings?"

"Have there been any break-ins around here?"

"Not that I've heard of."

"It's possible, but usually when they break in, we can tell. This person didn't. We need to proceed as if the guy behind the bombings either came himself or sent someone."

"To kill me," she finally said aloud.

Frowning, Jesse nodded.

A shudder rippled down her body. "Then I'd better remember what he thinks I know. Somehow I must have seen him, but there were a lot of people there that day in the bistro, coming and going."

"You will."

"How can you say that? You don't know for sure."

"Yes, I do. I've been praying you will."

She twisted around, leaning back as she looked at Jesse. "When you were in high school, you never went to church. What happened?"

"I blame Thomas. After you left, he dragged me to his church. At first I didn't pay much attention to what Pastor Paul was saying, but slowly the words began to sink in. My faith has helped me make sense of all the evil I see in this world. If I didn't have the Lord to fall back on, I'm not sure I could be a police officer."

"And I did the opposite. I went to church all the time here, but when I left Anchorage, I grew further away from my faith. After losing my baby and Aaron's betrayal, I was struggling just to get through each day. Working a full-time job and going to college took all my time. I'd come home and collapse on the bed."

"I'm sorry you went through that."

She tilted her head to the side and tried to read the true meaning behind those words. "Do you really feel that way? You have every right to say, you made your bed and now you have to sleep in it."

Jesse looked away from her. "I'm not going to tell you I wasn't angry. I was. I felt betrayed. It took a long time to get beyond those feelings."

"I'm sorry." She touched his arm, needing the tactile contact with him.

"You should come to church. Pastor Paul is such an inspiration."

"I might, but wasn't your church the one that was bombed?"

"Yes, but that won't stop Pastor Paul. We'll have

service in the part that still remains. If you want I'll take you this Sunday."

The invitation took her by surprise—a reversal of roles from when they were teenagers. "I'd like that."

"Good."

His smile warmed her and gave her a seed of hope that they would at least become friends again. "You never said what happened when you and Brutus went after the intruder. Did Brutus find his scent?"

"Yes, but we were a minute or so too late. I saw a man dressed in a black T-shirt and jeans riding away on a motorcycle. I only got a glimpse before he went around a curve on the trail in the woods. Brutus went after him, but the intruder had a good head start. I ran after Brutus and had to call him back. I think he would have raced after the bike until he dropped."

"Sounds like you had a good workout."

"You could say that." Jesse pushed off the bed and faced her. "I'm walking through the house with Brutus while you pack. Don't forget to call the school. Williams should be through and on his way to pick up Kate."

Lydia watched the pair walk from her room with Cheri hot on their trail. She was a busybody, always wanting to know what everyone was doing in the house while Charlie hid.

After calling the school, she retrieved a piece of luggage and began filling it with clothes. She wanted to take her dad's gun, and she needed some ammunition, which was in the hall closet. The door was ajar—no doubt Charlie's handiwork. He was a master at opening them if they weren't totally latched. As she swung it wide, Charlie darted out of another one of his favorite hiding places and charged toward the living room.

As she reached for the box of ammo on the top shelf, a loud crash filled the air.

SEVEN

Charlie raced from the living room and down the hallway. Lydia grabbed the box of ammunition, then strode to the entrance of the room, almost afraid to see what happened. A ceramic lamp lay on the wooden floor, shattered into several pieces. Mitch sat by the mess with Cheri next to him. Jesse came from the dining area with Brutus.

Jesse kneaded his nape. "Maybe I should have left Mitch in the kitchen, but Cheri kept whining and scratching on the door. I gave in when Mitch began whining, too."

"Who did this? Did you see?" Lydia moved toward the busted lamp.

"Charlie. I think Mitch was trying to be friendly and Charlie jumped up on the table to get away." Jesse joined her and stooped to pick up the pieces.

"He tries to go to high ground."

When Jesse reached for a second shard, his hand paused for a few seconds. "Here take this one." He passed her the first chunk, then took the second one and examined it. "This is a bug. And not the kind that crawl around."

Lydia stared at the small device on the underside of the lamp, too shocked to say anything.

"I'll get a bug detector out here and see if there are more. Do you have a paper sack?"

She nodded and hurried into the kitchen to grab one.

When she returned, Jesse had on latex gloves. He carefully put the sections of the lamp into the bag. "There might be latent prints on this that aren't mine or yours."

The events of the day caught up with her. She collapsed on the couch nearby, trying to assimilate what was going on. It had been bad enough an intruder was in her house, but to have someone listening to what she had said unnerved her even more. "If Charlie hadn't knocked it over, we would never have known."

Jesse set the sack on the coffee table and sat next to Lydia. "The crime scene techs would probably have found it."

"When will they be here?"

"Half an hour. Kate should be here soon, then we'll leave when they show up."

"Will Kate be allowed to go to school?"

Jesse rose and pulled her to her feet and headed for the porch. "We don't know how many bugs he planted or where."

"I didn't think about that."

"To answer your question, Kate isn't the target. I'll discuss it with Thomas, and if he thinks it's okay, I don't see why not. Over the years schools have become more secure because of school shootings." He cocked a grin. "And I have a feeling Kate wouldn't want to be locked in a house indefinitely. She'll have to have an escort, though, to and from."

"Where will we be?"

"My house. I told Thomas if I'm going to be the lead on your detail I want a place I know has a top-notch alarm system and neighbors who are vigilant. Several other police officers live on my street."

"You're the lead on my detail? You didn't even want me to call you a few days ago if I remember correctly."

"Can't a guy change his mind?"

"Well, yes, but—"

Officer Williams pulled into the driveway. Kate stalked toward them, zeroed in on Lydia and headed for her with Officer Williams right behind her. The poor man must have gotten an earful because Lydia knew that thunderous look on Kate's face.

Kate tossed her backpack onto a porch chair. "We're leaving here? Why?"

Stay calm. Losing my temper won't make the situation any better. "Because someone was in our house today when I returned home from the animal hospital. He had a knife, but I managed to get into my bedroom and lock the door." Lydia slanted a look at Jesse. "The autopsy of the waitress indicates she was murdered. Jesse was already on his way here, and Thomas dispatched a patrol car until Jesse could arrive. If they hadn't, I don't know what would have happened." Her voice remained even, but her stomach roiled and the muscles in her back and neck tensed as she thought of her near miss.

Color drained from her sister's face, and her mouth hung open. "In our house? How?"

"We think he had a key. Where is yours?" Jesse rose from the couch.

Kate moved to her backpack and dug into a side

pocket, then held the key up. "It's a new lock. We haven't had these long."

Lydia shoved to her feet and closed the space between her and Kate. "There's a chance he had access to the one that Bree brought me at the hospital."

"But you had yours when you came home."

"He could have had it copied." Jesse indicated for Officer Williams to follow him.

When they were gone, Lydia faced Kate. "I don't like this any more than you do. You'll be escorted to and from school until this guy is found."

Kate stomped toward the front door and went inside. "You're kidding! When can I see Connor?"

"Never" almost slipped from Lydia's mouth, but she knew that would make the teen even more attractive to Kate. She followed her sister into the house. "We'll see. I'll have to talk to Jesse about that, but in the meantime, don't let anyone know where we're staying. If someone asks you, just say a safe house."

Kate huffed. "I didn't even witness anything. I'm not the one the bomber is after. Why am I being restricted?"

"Because I would worry. We don't know what this maniac is thinking. By what he's done so far, he certainly isn't rational and sane." She didn't care if he'd bugged her house and heard what she thought about him.

"Go on TV and make a statement that you have no memory of the bombing. Then he'll leave you alone."

"Again, we don't know that." Lydia wanted to hug her sister. In all her bluster, she could tell Kate was worried, because she was twirling her long, sandy-colored hair. She did that when she was nervous or upset.

"We can talk more after we move. You need to pack a bag. I'll feel better when we're at…our safe place." She surveyed the living room, her gaze pausing on where the lamp had been. She wasn't sure she ever wanted to come back even after the man was caught. He was in her house, possibly twice, and obviously got in easily.

"Okay." Kate started to turn toward the foyer, stopped and swung back around. She threw her arms around Lydia, then hurried toward her room.

The hug brought tears to Lydia's eyes and gave her hope that somehow their sisterly bond could be renewed. Their relationship had been strained, especially ever since Connor came into Kate's life three months ago.

Later that evening, Thomas sat with Lydia and Jesse at Jesse's kitchen table while Lydia's sister was in the bedroom they shared, probably video-chatting with Connor. The other police officer who would be guarding them through the night would be arriving in the next hour.

"So how is this going to work?" Lydia shifted her attention from Jesse to Thomas. "I'm going to have to tell Kate something. Thankfully other than that initial outburst, she has been quiet. I told her she would be escorted to and from school, but otherwise she needed to be here. She wasn't happy about that. She wanted to know how she was going to see Connor."

"Young love. They tend to have tunnel vision when it comes to each other. All they want is to be together, no matter what." Thomas put his notepad on the table.

"You've described Kate and Connor's relationship accurately. But she'll get to see him at least at school." Lydia could remember how she'd felt about Jesse when she was her sister's age. She'd always wanted to be with him. Those feelings could be intense, whether they lasted or not.

Thomas's lips set in a tight line. "I do have one stipulation. Since tomorrow is Saturday, I'll be meeting with the principal and going through their security precautions. I know they have more in place since the second bomb went off. But Kate will have to agree to have the officer escort her to and from the building."

"She won't like that. Is it possible to have a young female officer and not have her dressed in a uniform?" Lydia could already imagine what Kate would say.

"That can be arranged, but I like the idea of a uniformed cop with you at all times. I want to make this as painless as possible, but I want that guy to know you are being protected. If you go to work, there'll be two with you. The person taking Kate to school will join you at the animal hospital and be in the reception area. All outside doors except the main one will be locked, and you'll also have a police officer by your side at all times."

"Even when I operate on an animal?"

Thomas nodded.

"Who?" Lydia looked toward Jesse. "You?"

"No, I'm going to be investigating the case while you're at work, then take over after that. We're doing two twelve-hour shifts."

"When are you going to sleep?"

Jesse's golden-brown gaze gleamed, totally directed at her as if Thomas weren't even in the room. "Don't worry. I'll get my sleep. The department can only spare four officers right now. Although the cooks haven't been threatened like you, we have to give them pro-

tection, too. The bombings have really taxed our resources. We're asking for some help from the state
police because I'd like to have two-person teams on
eight-hour shifts. I'm hoping one of them is Chance
O'Malley. You're familiar with him since he's involved
in search and rescue. Hopefully that can be arranged
by the time you go to work on Monday."

She was *not* going to melt at that look that made
her feel so special. In high school he'd do that in the
one class they'd shared. She didn't even know how she
made an A in the subject. "Good. The more people I
know around me the better."

"You're taking this awfully calm," Thomas interjected.

"You should have seen me when Officer Williams and Jesse first showed up. There was nothing
calm about me. Will Officer Williams be one of my
guards?"

"Yes. He requested it." Thomas leaned forward and
looked at his pad. "Here's what we know. The fragments of the bomb found at the bistro are similar to
the other two that went off at the church and hardware
store. C-4 plastic explosives were used, but the one
difference between the first two and the bistro is the
amount. The bomb was more powerful at the bistro."

"We finally have an array of photos of all the victims," Jesse said. "We thought if you take a look at
them, you might remember something—someone you
saw who isn't among the pictures. Then you can describe the person to our artist. We have some other
leads that we're developing into sketches. Bree is doing
what she can. We're trying to track down people who
left before the bomb went off."

Lydia closed her eyes and tried to visualize the bistro before she went to the restroom. Who was there? Anyone who left at that time? But all she saw was Melinda's look when the laughing track sounded. She couldn't seem to get past that. "I'll do what I can, but I don't know if I'm ever going to be a help to you."

Jesse began lining up the photos of the victims on the table. "Relax. If you can't, then you can't. Look at each one. Do you remember seeing them?"

Relax? The first picture she homed in on was of Melinda, smiling as she so often did while greeting customers. Everything else vanished. Her vision blurred, and she looked away. Flashes of the explosion like a strobe light raced through her mind.

Jesse put his hand over hers. "It's okay. You take all the time you need. If you want, we can do this tomorrow morning before we go see Jake at the hospital."

"You two are going to see him?" Thomas asked.

Until he had said that, Lydia again felt just she and Jesse were the only two in the room. His comforting touch centered her in the here and now. "Yes, now that he's stable, I want to take Mitch so he can see he'll be all right."

"Good. He needs something to cheer him up. I know what a special bond an officer and his K-9 develop." Thomas closed his notepad. "We have a few leads we're running down, Lydia. You aren't the only one. The C-4 is homemade so we're looking at the ingredients and places that sell them. We're going through all the videos at the hospital, trying to find a better photo of the orderly. We're looking for a vehicle that might have been the getaway car from the last bomb site."

"When is Melinda's funeral?" Lydia needed to say goodbye to her friend.

"The family is planning a memorial service at the end of next week. We're going to be there filming it to see if people who go are on some of the surveillance tapes we have." Thomas rose. "But we're hoping we catch the guy before that."

Lydia latched on to Melinda's photo again. "I need to go to the service."

"I think it'll be all right. They're holding it at a park, and we're covering each service for the victims, even staking the place out beforehand and having a bomb dog go through before it starts. Now, I'd better go. I know it's been a long day for you."

Lydia started to stand, but Jesse clasped her shoulder. "I'll see Thomas out and be right back."

While she waited for Jesse to return, she picked up the nearest picture and studied it. She knew the woman. She was one of the regulars. By the time he came into the kitchen and refreshed his coffee, she'd singled out a few more familiar faces, all regulars like the woman.

"Would you like another cup of tea?" Jesse placed his mug on the table.

She shook her head.

He sat next to her. "Who are these people?"

"The ones I don't know or remember seeing." She waved toward the group segregated off to the side. "These people I know, but honestly I don't necessarily remember them there that day except for Melinda." She stared into his warm, kind eyes. "What's wrong with me? I should be able to identify more than Melinda."

"When you go through a trauma, you often shut the incident out. You don't want to relive it."

"No, but I've been trying. I need to. The more I

think about it, I believe I saw something." Lydia massaged her temples. "But my mind isn't cooperating."

"I know a therapist you might talk to. She works with trauma victims."

"Please. I have to do something. I don't want to live my life in fear that this guy is going to come after me."

"He isn't if I can do anything to stop him." Jesse took a sip of his coffee. "Thomas wants me to tell you what the crime scene techs found at your house. He got the report right before coming over."

"Why didn't he say anything?"

Jesse gathered up the photos. "He didn't want to overwhelm you all at once, but I know you're tough and would rather know everything we know."

"This doesn't sound good."

"There were several listening devices in your house—in the kitchen, your bedroom and of course, the living room, but there was also two cameras found. One in the living room and the other in your bedroom."

Stunned, Lydia stared at Jesse, but no thoughts came into her head for a long moment. She opened her mouth to reply but snapped it close. She sagged back in her chair.

"We're doing everything we can to track where the surveillance equipment came from." Worry knitted his forehead.

Slowly, Lydia began to process his words. She released a long breath. "Listening devices are one thing, but cameras give me a chill." Goose bumps covered her whole body, and she rubbed her hands up and down her arms. "Why the cameras?"

Jesse shrugged. "Covering all his bases. I think I

know why he came after you. Remember when we talked last night in the kitchen?"

She nodded. "He didn't want to take the chance I'd remember something because I certainly was determined enough. So that's why he came to my house before I was let out of the hospital. It was hard to get to me there so he wanted to keep track of what I was remembering."

"If we'd only known, we could have set a trap for him."

"I'm willing to be bait if it will put an end to this."

"No! That wasn't what I meant. I won't risk your life like that." Jesse's mouth firmed to a hard, straight line.

"Then how do we end this?"

"By investigating, looking for any kind of connection between the hardware store, the church and the bistro. I've been digging into that aspect. We think it's random and it might be, but what if it isn't? I've been working with Pastor Paul about the parishioners, newcomers and visitors. We have to look at all possibilities."

"Because the bomber is escalating and he'll probably hit another target soon?"

"Yes, and we have no idea whether it's random or connected. We're cross-checking people associated with the hardware store and my church. It will be harder with the bistro because the owner was killed and her records were destroyed."

Massaging her temples, she needed to change the subject. "Are Mitch and Brutus still outside?"

"Yes. I'm leaving Brutus in the backyard during the night. He has a doghouse. I'll bring Mitch inside. He may have only three legs, but he is a well-trained

K-9. Between them we should be alerted if anyone comes here."

"And your alarm system will help, too. I'm going to have to invest in one, although I don't know if I can go back to that house."

"Give it time."

She and Kate grew up in that home, but the bomber had spoiled it for her, and she wouldn't be surprised if her sister didn't want to return, either. She had good memories there until her mother abandoned them when Kate was three months. Everything changed after that, but at least at that time Jesse was a big part of her life.

"Maybe you should get a dog, too. I can help you find a good guard dog."

"I'm not sure after what happened earlier with Charlie and Mitch. He isn't a social animal. At least he gets along with Cheri."

"It's still something you might want to consider. Animals do adapt over time, especially when things settle down."

"What's that?" Lydia chuckled. "Charlie needs stability. Both of them are going to start thinking I abandoned them. But with them back at the animal hospital, at least I can see them during the day. I'm hoping that will help him because I'd hate to split Cheri and Charlie up. He does respond to her, but then they've been together since they were born."

Jesse rose. "I'll get Mitch. I've set up a place for him in the bedroom you're sharing with Kate."

"You don't want him able to roam your house? Or, are you putting him with us to make us feel safe?"

"That's part of the reason. But the night detail will

take care of making sure the house isn't breached."
Jesse stepped outside for a minute and called the dogs.

Lydia took Jesse's and her mug to the sink and
rinsed them out. She liked his house. The comfortable furniture invited a person to relax. The walls were
painted beige with photographs of different places in
Alaska hanging up. Did Jesse take the breathtaking
pictures? He used to love photography when they were
teenagers.

She moved into the great room with a large stone
fireplace and her gaze immediately fell on a photo in
a wooden frame over the black leather couch. It was
of a mountain at sunset, and the play of colors on the
snow-covered terrain dazzled her with its brilliance.
Whoever took it had to have been on a taller mountain
looking down on the scene.

"I took that last winter when Chance, David and I
went mountain climbing."

She gasped and swung toward him standing in the
entrance to the room with Mitch beside him. "I didn't
hear you. I was too engrossed in the picture. Did you
take all the ones hanging in your house?"

"Yes. I'd rather be shooting with my camera than
my gun, although I always take one with me in the
wilderness for protection."

"Then why did you decide to be a police officer?"

"Because I wanted to help protect people. When I
was twenty and attending a community college, there
was a male student who came on campus with a gun,
shooting people at random. There were four of us hiding in a room as he went through the building. I knew I
was in God's hands, but the other three were freaking
out. I was there that day to keep them calm and quiet.

The shooter didn't find us. After that day, I wanted to help others feel safe, not helpless."

What else had Jesse gone through since they parted? That incident shaped his future like her failed marriage to Aaron had changed her and made her more determined to do what she'd always dreamed of—becoming a veterinarian. Her father and she had become estranged because of her relationship with Aaron, but she'd still wanted to follow in her father's steps, even if he never knew or cared.

"Well, this person—" she pointed to herself "—feels that way right now. Thank you." She held her breath, hoping he wouldn't say it was his job.

"I'm glad you feel that way."

Enjoying this subtle change in their relationship, Lydia started to ask him about the photograph of a mother polar bear with her cub, but the doorbell rang.

"That must be Officer Collins, the other half of the nightshift." As he strolled into the foyer, he put his hand on his gun in its holster at his waist.

That action underscored the danger she was in.

When the tall female officer came into the living room, Lydia shook her hand and said, "Thank you for being here, Officer Collins."

She grinned. "Please call me Mary. I want to do my part to bring this bomber to justice."

"I'll give you the grand tour and we'll discuss duties," Jesse said.

"I'm Lydia, and that's my cue to go to bed. It's been a *long* day."

"Yeah, I heard what happened at your house. I won't let it happen on my watch." Mary petted Mitch before following Jesse into the kitchen.

Lydia made her way to the master bedroom with Mitch by her side. This was Jesse's room, but he had insisted that she and Kate stay in it because of its large size and the private bathroom. When she entered, Kate sat on the king-size bed working on a school project on her laptop.

Her sister looked up. "Who was at the door?"

"Officer Mary Collins, the other one staying tonight." Lydia shut the door after Mitch hobbled into the room, spied a bed on the floor next to the bedside table and settled down on the large pillow. "Mitch is sleeping in here."

"Good. What's gonna happen to him? He can't be a K-9 dog anymore." Kate closed her laptop.

"He'll be retired. It's possible his partner will keep him."

"Even if a new K-9 is assigned to him?"

"Sure. You see how well Brutus and Mitch get along."

"If he doesn't want him, can we have him?"

Kate's question reminded Lydia of Jesse's suggestion about a guard dog. "That's definitely something to consider, but Jake is attached to Mitch so maybe we'll need to think of getting a different dog."

"Good. We agree on something." Kate glanced at her cell phone, then back at Lydia. "Can Connor come over tomorrow?"

Her first instinct was to say no, but her disapproval of the teen wasn't changing Kate's mind. She would leave the decision up to Jesse. "You need to run it by Jesse. This is his house, and he's in charge of the officers protecting us. Did you tell Connor where we are?"

Kate stared at her lap. "No, you told me not to tell anyone."

"Kate?"

Her sister looked right at Lydia. "Really, I didn't."

"Okay." Lydia took her pajamas out of the drawer Jesse emptied so they had a place for their clothing. "I'm going to bed. I'm exhausted." She started for the bathroom.

"I told him. It just came out. I didn't mean to."

Kate's words rushed out of her mouth so fast it took Lydia a moment to digest what she'd said. Lydia turned toward her sister. "Then you'll need to tell Jesse that, too, but thank you for telling me the truth."

"Connor won't tell anyone. He loves me." Kate's upper teeth dug into her lower lip.

"You've only known him three months. It takes—"

"I'm seventeen. I know what I want and what I need. Do you? You certainly made a mess of your life at my age, so I'm not so sure you're the one to give me any advice."

"Because I made mistakes at your age, I know some pitfalls I hope you don't fall into."

"You're not me." Kate's glare drilled into Lydia.

Without another word, Lydia pivoted and marched into the bathroom, closing the door. She sank onto the tub's edge and stared at herself in the mirror, her hands gripping the cold ledge. How was she going to bridge the rift with Kate?

Lord, it's me again. What am I doing wrong? Why is my life falling apart around me? I feel paralyzed. Abandoned. First Mom left, then Dad and even Aaron. I can't go through that again. Please don't abandon me, too.

EIGHT

"I think that's what he looked like." Lydia studied the sketch the police artist drew from her description of the orderly in her hospital room. "I really didn't pay much attention, and he didn't stay long at all. I only saw him that one time."

The artist pulled out another drawing. "This is what Dr. Stone described."

Lydia swung her attention between the two pictures of a man with medium-length blond hair, a mustache and closely set dark eyes. "They're similar, so hopefully that'll help your case." Lydia glanced over her shoulder at Jesse. "Does that fit anyone who works at the hospital?"

"No. After I got Bree's sketch, I checked. The man in your room wasn't an orderly."

The sketch artist closed his pad and stood. "If you need me again, call. I want this guy. My wife is having our groceries delivered because she's afraid to leave the house. Of course, the store is charging an extra price for time and gas. I'll make copies at headquarters and start distributing them to everyone."

Jesse shook his hand. "Thanks for coming. I'll walk you to the door."

While Jesse left the kitchen, Lydia made herself some tea and stood at the window overlooking the backyard. Mitch and Brutus were basking in the sun. With Mitch in her bedroom last night, she'd actually slept nine hours, which surprised her because in strange places she didn't normally sleep well. But the mental and physical exhaustion took over the minute she laid her head on the pillow.

Jesse entered the kitchen and poured another cup of coffee. "With the dogs out back, I think we're secure since Officer Williams is sitting in the living room with a good view of the front yard."

Lydia turned from the window. "When are we going to the hospital?"

"Bree was going to figure out a good time and text me."

"She got it cleared for us to bring Mitch." Lydia returned to the table, sat and drank some of her tea.

"I have another sketch I'd like to show you." He unfolded a photocopied sheet and passed it to Lydia. "Have you seen this man?"

Lydia examined a man with short sandy hair and gray eyes, plain features with nothing that stood out, and yet there was something that nagged her. She couldn't pinpoint what.

"Have you seen him?" Jesse stood behind her, looking over her shoulder.

The hairs on her nape tingled. "Maybe. I'm usually good with faces, but not necessarily where I might have seen that person."

"So you can't say if he was in the bistro or not."

"No, just that he seems familiar. Why do you have this sketch? Who gave this description?"

"A man who worked in the appliance store across the street from the bistro. This guy was in the store when the bomb went off and seemed interested in what was going on. He hung around for a while until everyone was told to evacuate the street. Most people fled when the bomb went off."

"But there are always some who hang around to see what's going on." Lydia studied the sketch again. "You know the gawkers who stand around watching a fire, a wreck or something like that."

"When I was checking that side of the street before we got the go-ahead to search for survivors, all the buildings were supposed to be empty. I saw someone going out the back door at the appliance store. The owner said he and his employees left and thought that the store was vacant."

"You think it could have been this guy?"

"When I checked out back, a black Chevy peeled away from the parking lot. We haven't been able to find it yet. "

"If that is the case, this guy doesn't look like the orderly. He's older than the orderly. Could there be more than one person?" The thought of two or more maniacs out there knotted her stomach, her body tensing.

Jesse clasped her shoulders. "I won't rest until we get this guy or guys." His strong hands kneaded her tight muscles as he spoke. "The man might have hired someone to go to the hospital, so it still might be just one person. This last bomb site has garnered more leads than the other two put together. Those bombs went off when not many people were there, not like the bistro."

"Trial runs?" Slowly the tension melted under his expert manipulations.

"Could be that, or he's getting bolder or refining his MO." He squeezed her shoulders, then took the chair kitty-corner from her. "How's Kate taking this? She stayed in your room most of the evening."

"My sister is scared, but she's also mad that she has to be guarded. She wants to be safe but free."

"Kate probably has nothing to worry about, but I prefer being extra cautious rather than regretting a decision after the fact."

"I know one thing. Come Monday morning, she'll be eager to go to school. Most Mondays I have to drag her out of bed to get her up."

He chuckled. "I seem to remember you used to have trouble getting up, too. There were several Mondays you were late for school."

His teasing look flushed her cheeks with warmth. "I'm still that way. I've been known to be late Monday for work, and I can't always blame it on Kate."

"Blame what on me?" her sister asked from the doorway.

Lydia glanced at her. "Being late for work on Monday."

Kate harrumphed and shuffled toward the coffeepot. "Where are your mugs?"

"In the cabinet right above."

"Thanks," her sister mumbled, then retrieved one and poured coffee into it. "That was the last of it. I can make more."

"Unless you want more. I'm fine." Jesse took a long drink of his.

Kate made her way to the table and plopped down. Her long brown hair was a tangled mess, and she finger combed it. "I can't believe I slept so late."

"So you slept all right?" Lydia finished her tea.

"Better than I thought I would." Kate smiled at Jesse. "Thanks for having us and letting Mitch stay in our bedroom."

Lydia pressed her lips together before she laughed out loud. When Kate wanted something, she could turn on the charm, and in this case she wanted to see Connor. Lydia relaxed back and waited to see what her sister would say.

"Since we can't go anywhere, I was wondering…" she lowered her gaze for a few seconds then reestablished visual contact with a contrite expression on her face "…if I could have a friend over here. Two days staying inside with such beautiful weather is a long time without at least seeing someone. Please." Kate batted her eyelids.

Lydia dug her teeth into her lower lip and fought to keep a straight face. Jesse slid a glance toward her. "You're in charge of the protection detail, not me."

The look he sent her made it clear she would hear about it later. Then he switched his attention to Kate. "It's important that people don't know where Lydia is. It makes protecting her easier."

"Oh, that's all right. I let it slip when I was talking to Connor, so he already knows."

"You did?" His jaw twitched. "Didn't I say not to tell anyone?"

"Yes, but he's my boyfriend. We see each other every weekend."

"Video-chatting is the next best thing. Feel free to do that with him, but no visitors here."

"But I told him we'd get to see each other this weekend. That's not fair." Kate swiveled her attention between Jesse and Lydia and started to say something else when Jesse's cell phone blared the moose call.

He rose and went into the other room to answer.

"You need to convince him Connor would be all right to come visit. He isn't gonna say anything. He loves me."

"No. I told you his word was final."

Kate bolted to her feet, glared at Lydia and rushed from the room, nearly colliding with Jesse returning to the kitchen.

"I figure she isn't too happy with my answer." Jesse pocketed his cell.

"Join the list. I'm right at the top. At least once a week, I get 'you're not my mom,' which means I have no right to set boundaries."

"I noticed you deferred to me to tell her she couldn't."

"I tried, but it didn't sit well with her, so I told her this was your house and you had final say."

"Chicken."

Laughing, Lydia held up her hands, palms outward. "Yep. I'm tired of fighting with her."

"That was Bree. Jake can see us. He'll be in his room the rest of the morning."

"Good. Until he sees Mitch, he won't know how well his dog is adapting to three legs. I'll go get ready and meet you in the foyer in ten minutes." Lydia rose.

Jesse took several steps toward her, shrinking the space between them. "She'll come around. You used to get mad at your dad when you were stuck at home babysitting Kate."

"But at least you got to come over and help."

"This will pass. She'll appreciate you one day. It took me a while to realize how much my last foster parents did for me."

"Do you see them much?"

"After church on Sunday, I usually eat with them, but I won't this weekend."

"Surely someone else can guard us while you get some downtime."

"It wouldn't help. I'd worry the whole time."

"You'd worry about me?"

He framed her face. "Yes. My job is to protect you, and I wouldn't relax much wondering if you were all right or not."

Did that mean he had forgiven her about Aaron? That they could be friends at least? She didn't ask because she didn't want him to tell her he would feel that way about anyone he was assigned to protect. For a while she wanted to think she was special to him. It made this whole situation bearable.

"Wait until I get Mitch out of the back." Jesse climbed from his SUV at the hospital, and once he had the K-9 harnessed, he came around to Lydia's passenger door and opened it.

He held out his hand to help her down, and she fit hers in his. He wished he could say her touch meant nothing to him, but he couldn't. Having Lydia in his home had affected him more than he thought it would. For years, he'd fooled himself into thinking he was over Lydia. But this morning, seeing her in his kitchen, he realized he wasn't. He cared, and he didn't want to. Every close tie he'd allowed himself to have had ended badly. He wasn't going through that again.

"I hope this helps Jake recover faster." Lydia's soft voice pulled him from his dilemma.

Its sound flowed through him, sparking a need he'd kept buried for years and making a mockery of his earlier declaration to keep his distance. When she was safe, he would stay away from her, but right now he was responsible for protecting her and hoped she could remember enough to catch this bomber before he struck again. Then he could get back to the way things were before.

"I know if I were in his shoes, I'd want to see Brutus. Jake and Mitch have been partners for years."

"How long have you and Brutus worked together?"

"Six." Jesse opened the hospital door and waited for Lydia to go inside first.

"No wonder you two are such a good team. Like an old married couple."

"Yeah, I'm married to my job."

Lydia pushed the elevator button. "Is that why you don't have a wife?"

The doors swished open, and Jesse entered the elevator after Lydia, relieved another couple got on, too. It gave him time to try and figure out what to reply. When they exited on Jake's floor, he started down the corridor, hoping Lydia would forget the question.

But as she walked beside him, she slanted a look at him. "You have so much to offer a woman."

"It's not like I'm a hermit, but between being a K-9 officer and taking part in search and rescues, my time has been limited." He stopped outside Jake's room and faced her. "Why haven't you remarried? You and Aaron have been divorced for years."

"Two reasons, my schooling and then work took so much of my time, and I'm gun-shy."

"Sounds like we have that in common."

"All-consuming work or being gun-shy?"

"Both." Jesse knocked on the door, then pushed it open.

Jake's grandfather shook hands with Jesse who introduced Lydia to him.

"I'm going to the cafeteria to get something to eat." Mr. Nichols bent to pet Mitch, and then he left.

His head wrapped in a white bandage, Jake sat partway up in his bed, his leg in a cast and suspended in the air. "This has been difficult for him. He's hardly left this room since the accident. I've told him I'm getting better and to go to my home and get a good night's rest, but my grandfather can be stubborn." Jake's gaze fell on Mitch. "Come, boy."

The German shepherd hobbled toward Jake and managed to lean his front legs on the bed while supporting himself with his hind one. Jake leaned forward and rubbed his K-9, tears shining in his eyes. He buried his face against Mitch. "Thanks for bringing him here." Jake's thickened voice underscored the emotional tie he had with his partner.

Jesse could identify with that. What would he do if something happened to Brutus? Until this moment he'd refused to think about that.

Lydia approached the other side of the bed. "I did what I could. I'd hoped I could save his leg, but it wasn't possible."

Jake swung his attention to her. "I knew he was in good hands with you. You remind me of your dad. He'd do anything to save an animal and give it the best life possible. Mitch can't be a police K-9 dog, but he can do other things with his training."

Lydia glanced at Mitch "He's amazed me how fast he's adapted to having three legs."

"Yeah, he's always been a quick learner and has a streak of determination a mile wide." Jake turned to Jesse. "He reminds me of your Brutus. Everything okay with them together?"

"Brutus has a playmate. You should see them in my backyard."

"And Mitch is guarding me and Kate at night in our bedroom."

"He's a good guard dog and tracker. But he's also cross-trained to detect drugs. His career isn't over. It'll just be different." Jake sank back against his pillows but kept his hand on Mitch's paw. "Tell me what's going on with the investigation. My grandfather won't tell me anything."

Jesse went through what they knew, but toward the end, Jake's eyelids slid closed. "Jake?" He looked at all the machines his friend was hooked up to, and everything seemed all right.

"We wore him out." Lydia rounded the end of the bed. "I know how exhausted you can get from even carrying on a conversation when you've been injured."

"We accomplished what we wanted to do. I think he'll rest better after seeing Mitch. Let's go."

Seeing Jake with Mitch touched a deep chord in Jesse. He loaded the German shepherd into the back of his SUV and slipped behind the steering wheel, but he didn't start the car. Remembering the tears in Jake's eyes when he greeted Mitch made Jesse confront a concern that he'd refused to acknowledge until he'd seen Jake.

Finally Jesse started the SUV and grasped the steering wheel. What was he going to do if he lost Brutus? His Rottweiler was eight, and his years as a K-9 partner were limited. He would have to break in a new dog, but worse he would have to deal with the loss of Brutus eventually.

"What's wrong?" Lydia's question penetrated the fear he'd been holding at bay for years—having to handle yet another loss. He should be used to it by now—after his family and Lydia, but…

"Jesse?"

He blinked and glanced toward her.

"What happened? You're pale."

"Seeing Jake and Mitch was hard. That could be me and Brutus at any time. In fact, we've had a few narrow escapes in the years we've worked together. I should be used to death, to goodbyes."

"I don't think anyone totally is immune to them. I think instead we ignore the emotions generated as if they don't exist, but one day they'll come to the surface. When my baby died, I refused to talk about her death, after all I never got to hold her. I tried to convince myself she didn't really exist. Then one day I was holding a friend's two-month-old girl and everything crashed down on me. That's when I really began to mourn her."

He squeezed his hands around the steering wheel and gritted his teeth. "I don't think I ever mourned my parents' deaths."

"You went to a service for them, didn't you?"

"Yes. My foster mother at that time took me, and people from my dad's work paid tribute to him. The caskets were closed. For the longest time I didn't understand why, but then I became involved in search and rescue and found my first body in the wilderness left to the elements and animals. Then I realized why no one would let me see them."

"You never told me how they died."

"They were park rangers who got caught in a sudden blizzard early in the season. Everything changed after that. Fear became part of my life until I just shut it all down."

Lydia laid her hand on his arm. "I'm so sorry."

Her touch pulled him away from the past, and he shook his head. "Everyone suffers losses. Life goes on." He never talked about his parents, and he realized the reason why. It opened up too many memories. He pried his hand from the steering wheel and flexed his fingers, then put his SUV in Reverse. "We need to get home. Chance is coming to take my place while I track down some leads. The sooner we find this man, the quicker we can get back to our normal lives." And then he could put Lydia in proper perspective.

When they arrived at his house Chance's state trooper car was out front. "I'm glad we've gotten some assistance from the state police. The sketches from this morning are being circulated and will be on the news. Maybe someone will recognize the person in either of the drawings."

Lydia slid from his SUV in his garage. Before she opened the door to the house, she turned toward him. "I'm a good listener if you ever want to talk about your parents. I joined a support group after my baby died, and it really helped."

"They died twenty-five years ago. I'm fine."

"Are you? You were left alone at a vulnerable age."

Jesse reached around her and shoved his door open. "I have work to do."

As he retrieved Brutus from the backyard, the hurt that flashed into Lydia's eyes niggled his conscience and made him regret his abrupt end to their conversation. She was getting to him again, and he needed to keep his focus on finding the bomber and keeping her alive. Then he could move on with no regrets.

"I thought Officer Williams would be guarding me at work today," Lydia said as she climbed into Jesse's SUV on Monday.

Jesse pulled out of the garage and headed toward the animal hospital. "He will be there. He's meeting us. I'll take you to and from work. Officer Williams will be out in the reception area while Officer Collins will drop Kate at school, then come and relieve me as your guard. Then I'll relieve her later, so she can pick up Kate from school. She'll take her to my house and stay with her until you leave work with me."

"You've changed things around."

"With work and school the schedule needed to be adjusted. Chance has agreed to be one of the guards at night. During the day I'll be helping Thomas run down leads, but if for any reason you need to talk to me, call me."

She tried to relax, but tension knotted her neck and shoulder muscles. She wanted—needed—to get back to work. Sitting around resting was driving her crazy because she couldn't remember anything to help the police. Maybe getting back to work would help her. "I think I'm trying too hard to remember and nothing is coming."

"Probably. Have you ever forgotten a name or some tidbit of info, and as long as you try to concentrate on the answer, nothing comes to mind, but hours or even days later you remember?"

"Sure, but we don't have days."

"I want you to know we're making some progress. There are several names connected to both the hardware store and church."

Lydia angled toward Jesse, taking in his strong profile, remembering the times she'd freely touched his face, kissed him. No, she had to forget those times. Too much had happened since then. Staring out the windshield, she brought her thoughts back to their conversation. "How about the bistro?"

"That's a bit harder, but there is a waitress who's been on vacation and we're trying to get in touch with her. She may be able to help us with some of the names on the list at the other two bomb sites. Did someone frequent all three or even two of the places?"

"How about me? I go—went to the bistro at least once a week. I know some names, but I mostly remember faces. If you have a picture with a name, I could take a look."

"I'll have that for you tonight." Jesse pulled into the parking lot next to the animal hospital.

As he and Brutus escorted her into the building,

Jesse scanned his surroundings, his gaze lingering on where the bistro used to be. His mouth firmed into a fierce look. Lydia followed the direction he stared and shivered. Every time she came to work, she would remember what happened that day the bomb went off. She would never forget it.

"I wish this place wasn't on the same street," she said as Jesse reached around her and opened the door.

Inside, some of the stress of seeing the bomb site faded as she saw familiar faces and surroundings. She greeted the staff as she made her way to her office with Jesse and Brutus. She put her purse in the drawer of her desk while Brutus and Jesse walked around the room.

"Everything all right?" she asked, slipping into the white coat she wore over her clothes.

After he completed his inspection, Jesse looked at her. "It seems to be. I wish I could leave Brutus with you, but the people I'm interviewing are people who have ties to the hardware store and the church. If one of them worked with the bombing materials, the scent could be on him, and Brutus will be able to alert me."

The idea that he would offer to do that touched her. "It wouldn't work anyway. Brutus is well trained, but I can't take him into an exam room when I have a patient. Some animals aren't well trained like he is, and there could be a problem." She could imagine the chaos it would cause with certain pets, especially cats and high-strung dogs.

"We'll at least walk through the whole building each morning and when I come back in the afternoon. I know Williams will be out in reception so that should be enough, but you can't be too cautious."

"We're going to be fine with two officers and an alert staff. I want you out there tracking down this man."

Jesse stopped in front of her. "I wish we had enough dogs trained to search for bombs. I've heard some businesses are shutting down or only letting people in they know. The thing about a bomb is it doesn't have to be left in a building to do damage. It can be placed anywhere nearby."

"All we can do then is pray the person is found quickly, and put our safety in the Lord's hands. And be as vigilant as we can." Even more lately she'd come to realize she couldn't control the actions of others and what happened around her. But she couldn't stay in her house and never leave it. The bomber found her at her home. God was the only one who could protect her ultimately.

"If anyone finds something left unattended, we're asking them to report it. That has kept our officers even busier because we're getting a ton of calls and each one has to be checked out."

"While the bomber is sitting back enjoying the fear he's caused in the city." Lydia balled her hands, her fingernails digging into her palms. "I've got to remember."

Jesse clasped her upper arms. "Listen to me. This isn't all on your shoulders. We are going to find this guy."

She nodded, trying not to put pressure on herself. It wasn't easy, though. The urge to press herself against Jesse and wrap her arms around him flooded her. He made her feel safe as though the Lord had sent him to guard over her.

"Good. Now give me a tour of the hospital."

Jesse followed her into the hallway, Lydia very aware of him behind her. She walked him through the examination rooms and Matt's office. They ended up in the break room where she fixed him a coffee to go.

JoAnn appeared in the doorway. "We have an emergency. Are you ready to see an American Eskimo dog?"

"What kind of emergency?"

"He's alive but hardly responding. His master just carried him inside. And Officer Collins is here."

"Put the owner and dog in exam room one, and show Officer Collins back here."

"I already did." JoAnn smiled.

"I'm leaving. See you this afternoon." Jesse smiled at her and headed for the hallway as the female police officer came into the break room.

Lydia snatched an extra white coat from a hanger and gave it to Mary. "Put this on over your uniform. I'm going to introduce you as an intern, here observing. I don't want to frighten people any more than they already are with what's been happening."

Mary slipped into the white coat that came to her knees and hid her gun belt, then removed her hat.

"I have an emergency patient." Lydia left the break room at a brisk pace with the police officer right behind her.

Once she stepped into the exam room one, she went into professional mode, her gaze falling on a white furry dog on the table, lying listlessly. Then his legs twitched, and he tried to get up.

JoAnn moved in to calm the animal while Lydia

turned to the owner, an older gentleman, with gray hair and beard, his shoulders slumped forward. "What happened?"

"I had a box of candy on the counter, and he somehow knocked it onto the floor and ate some chocolate." The man's eyes misted. "I thought it was out of reach."

"How much chocolate?"

"A lot. Most of the box." The man closed his eyes and rubbed his hand across his forehead. "Fifteen, twenty pieces maybe. He started vomiting and having seizures. He could barely walk. I grabbed him and put him in the car, then came here. You were the nearest vet. Can you help him?"

This wasn't the first time she'd seen a dog poisoned by chocolate, which could be lethal to them. "Was it white, milk or dark chocolate?" She positioned herself on the other side of the table from JoAnn and listened to the animal's rapid heartbeat.

"I'm not sure. No white. A mix of milk and dark. I'm never gonna have any chocolate in my house again. Please help Calvin."

"We will. You'll need to leave him here at least overnight. Okay?"

"Anything."

"I'll try to counteract the theobromine which is making him sick, and give him some medication to control his heart rate and seizures. My assistant will show you to the front to fill out the paperwork. Is this the first time you've come here?"

"Yes."

"We'll need your contact information, and I'll keep you updated." She walked the older gentleman, who limped, to the door. "JoAnn, we're moving Calvin to the treatment room."

The second the owner left, Lydia released a long breath. As she picked up the dog to move him, he began another seizure as Mary hurried around to open the door.

"Calvin, I'm going to make you better," Lydia said in her soothing voice, praying she could save him.

Jesse had worked his way through two-thirds of the people—many of whom had stopped at the hardware store and attended his church. There had been a few visitors that Pastor Paul couldn't recognize. Nothing jumped out in the interviews and Brutus hadn't alerted him to the scent of C-4 or any kind of bombing material. But there had been a few on the list of twenty who weren't home. He had to ask their whereabouts the days of the explosions, but he'd run out of time. He had six more to question tomorrow. There were times he felt like he was chasing his tail.

Tired and disappointed, he pulled into the parking lot to the animal hospital. The thought of seeing Lydia picked up his spirits as he and Brutus made their way inside. He paused in the doorway and surveyed the area. Two women were waiting, one with a poodle and another with a cat in a carrier. He headed toward Williams, a bored expression on his face. When he saw Jesse, he straightened.

"I gather nothing exciting happened here today." Jesse could remember his own assignments that consisted of standing around, watching and waiting for something to happen.

"It's been slow. Dr. McKenzie told me there have

been a few cancellations for routine yearly checkups. I can't blame people for that."

"Then it's been a successful day if nothing happened. Are these two ladies the last for the day?"

"I think another one is coming and that should be it unless there's an emergency like this morning."

"I heard about that. What was it?"

"At lunch I found out it was an overdose of chocolate."

"That'll do it to some dogs. Did he make it?"

Williams nodded. "Dr. McKenzie has two more patients and after that she wants to check Calvin, the dog who ate too much chocolate. Then she'll be ready to leave. I think the day has been long for her."

Jesse approached the receptionist. "Where is Dr. McKenzie?"

"Exam room two."

He walked down the hall, rapped on the door and opened it. Officer Collins saw him and said goodbye to Lydia and then left to pick up Kate at school. He stood in the corridor, watching Lydia finish up with a beagle and then escort the young lady with her dog on a leash out into the hallway.

"The medicine should take care of her allergies. If you can, and I know it can be hard with Lady, keep her inside for a while to give the pills a chance to work."

The woman smiled. "Thank you. She was scratching so much she was bleeding. I'm glad you're all right, Dr. McKenzie." The lady glanced at Jesse.

"Officer Hunt is a friend from high school," she said as she strolled a few feet down the hall.

When Lydia came back toward Jesse, Brutus took a whiff of the air and moved closer to her. The K-9 sniffed her white coat, then sat in front of her and gave one bark.

Jesse stiffened. "He smells a component of a bomb on you."

NINE

Lydia heard the words Jesse said, but for a moment their meaning didn't register. A bomb ingredient? What? How?

"Take off your coat and let me see if it's on your slacks or shirt. Something on you has triggered Brutus." While Lydia took it off, Jesse said to Brutus, "Good boy," then gave him a treat.

As Jesse went into the storage room at the end of the hall, he said, "I'm hiding the coat, then I'm going to see if he does the same thing."

When he returned, Lydia followed him and Brutus. Her heartbeat galloped as though she'd run a mile at full speed. How did she get the scent on her? She held her breath while Brutus checked the area and sat, then barked at a cardboard box.

Jesse retrieved the coat from behind the carton. "Do you have a paper bag? I'm going to take this to the lab and see if they can tell what Brutus is smelling."

"Yes, there are some in the break room." Lydia's legs shook as she made her way there.

Jesse and Brutus were right behind her. "I'm going to assume it's connected to this case until the lab tells me otherwise." He dropped the coat into the sack. "So the question now is how did this happen?"

She shook her head. "It could be anything. I handled animals all day."

"I want to evacuate the building while I walk through with Brutus and see if he can detect it anywhere else. I'll have Officer Williams guard you outside in my SUV." Jesse started for the front of the hospital. "Who's all here?"

"I'll let Matt and his assistant know. They're in exam room three. JoAnn is getting my last patient."

As Jesse disappeared through the door into the reception area, Lydia swiped her hand across her sweaty forehead and hurried to let her partner know what was going on. In the doorway, she called him out into the hall.

Matt frowned. "What's wrong?"

"Brutus detected a bomb ingredient on my coat. Jesse is evacuating everyone. I think more as a precaution."

Matt settled his hand on her shoulder. "I'll let Chris and Mrs. Marlowe know. We'll be right out."

"I'm so sorry, Matt. I shouldn't have come back to work. I put everyone in danger."

"Let's not jump to conclusions. We don't know what's going on." He squeezed her shoulder and turned to go back into the exam room.

Lydia rushed down the corridor, her heart beating as fast as her steps. In the reception area, Officer Williams waited for her. "Where's Jesse?"

"Outside with the staff and people in the building. He wanted to make sure no one else triggered a response from Brutus. Then he's going to go through the building. He's called Detective Caldwell." He escorted her to the parking lot at the side of the building.

Brutus sat in front of JoAnn, and Jesse instructed her to remove her coat.

Lydia watched the scene as though she were viewing a movie, not really part of what was happening, just an observer. If only that were the case.

Five minutes later after sending everyone but JoAnn and Lydia home, Jesse reentered the building. The bomb squad as well as Thomas were on the way. But he'd questioned Williams, and he reassured Jesse that he didn't see anything unusual. And yet Brutus found a suspicious scent on both Lydia's and JoAnn's coats that wasn't there when he left in the morning.

He started in the reception area with Brutus, who stopped, sat and barked in front of one of the chairs. But there was nothing around it that could be a bomb. Jesse put a marker on the chair and continued the walk through. Exam room one was another place that Brutus indicated the scent. Jesse searched the whole place, but nothing appeared to be a bomb.

When he checked a room next door, again Brutus smelled the steel table and area around it and sat immediately. An animal had left its scent on it?

When he reached the area where the sick or recovering dogs were kept, once again Brutus gave the sign he'd sniffed an ingredient in a bomb. An American Eskimo was still hooked up to an IV.

His phone rang, and he answered, "Thomas, I've almost completed my search of the building. Brutus has found several places, but there isn't a bomb. Is the bomb squad here?"

"Yes, they're moving the people and animals away from the veterinary hospital and evacuating the surrounding stores. I'll send in the commander. You two will need to decide what to do. I'm having Officer Williams take Lydia home."

"No. I need her to walk me through the people who were in these rooms. This could be the break we've been looking for. When it's safe in here, I need her to come back in."

Jesse wanted her as far away from the building as possible, but she and her assistant had more than likely interacted with the Laughing Bomber.

"So you think the bomber was at the animal hospital today?"

"Yes. I'll be outside after I finish my search." Jesse disconnected, wishing there were more dogs like Brutus in the city. Had this become some kind of game to the man behind the bombings?

Lydia chewed on her fingernail as she paced in a circle near Officer Williams, five hundred yards away from the animal hospital. What if a bomb went off while Jesse and Brutus were inside searching for it? *Lord, please keep them safe.*

She stopped when another man went into the building. "Who's that, Officer Williams?"

"The commander of the bomb squad."

"What's that mean?"

"Probably the sergeant found more evidence or a bomb."

Her chest constricted as if someone were trying to squeeze the breath from her lungs. She gasped for air. "Then they should be getting out of there." She began her pacing again, needing to move, to do something other than stare at the building. She felt so helpless.

No, I'm not. I have the Lord. He can give me peace. It had taken her a while after her daughter's death and Aaron's adultery to understand that. She began to pray. All she wanted was to see Jesse emerge from the animal hospital unharmed.

Ten *long* minutes later, Jesse and the commander came outside and made their way to Thomas. She started for them.

Officer Williams blocked her. "My orders are for you to remain here." He cocked a smile. "You don't want to get me in trouble, do you, Dr. McKenzie?"

"Please call me Lydia since we're going to be hanging out together for a while. What's your first name?"

"Don."

"No, Don, I don't. At least they are outside the building if it goes up." She intended to have a few words with Jesse when she spoke to him. This waiting was tying her up into knots.

Finally Jesse headed across the street toward her while the whole bomb squad went into the building. Did that mean they found a bomb and they were going to try to dismantle it?

She went around Don and took several steps toward Jesse, the grim expression on his face solidifying her stomach into a huge lump. "What's wrong? Is there a bomb inside?"

He shook his head. "But there were more traces of one of the ingredients that triggered Brutus with you and JoAnn. The bomb squad is going through the building, then I need you to go back in with me. I think the bomber was at your hospital today."

"But he didn't leave anything?"

"An American Eskimo dog."

JoAnn, who stood not far away, approached. "That would be Mr. Jacobs."

"The dog, Calvin, ingested chocolate. I remember his owner. You didn't pass him in the reception room?" Lydia tried to grasp the fact she'd possibly stood in the same room with the Laughing Bomber, not once but twice.

"I went out the back door to check the rear of the building." Jesse waved Officer Williams to join them. "The first patient this morning was an American Eskimo, a white dog. Do you remember the man who came with Calvin?"

"He was carrying the dog," Lydia said.

"So if Mr. Jacobs had the smell on him, he transferred it to the dog and that's how you and JoAnn got it on you. Did you move the animal to the room next door?"

"Yes, that's where I washed out his stomach and gave him activated charcoal. We started an IV, too. When he was stabilized, Calvin was transferred to the area where we keep an eye on the recovering animals. I'd planned to call Mr. Jacobs to let him know his dog was getting better, but we wanted to keep him at least overnight."

"But you haven't yet?" Jesse asked.

Lydia shook her head. "I was going to check on Calvin one more time before I made the call."

"We need his owner's address, phone number and a description. Also, I want you to make that call and tell Mr. Jacobs he can come pick up his dog."

"He was about seventy years old and walked with a

limp and had slumped shoulders. He had gray hair and a pasty white complexion. I thought he was sickly. I don't remember the color of his eyes. JoAnn, do you?"

Her assistant thought for a moment. "Blue or gray—not dark eyes. But he'll be on our security tape."

Like the color of eyes I keep seeing in my thoughts. "Yes, we had that installed last week as one of the security measures. It's monitored by an outside source, so even if something happened to the building, there would be a record."

Jesse smiled for the first time since he arrived. "Good thinking. This is all promising."

"So you think this old man is the Laughing Bomber?" Lydia couldn't picture the frail man as a maniacal murderer.

"It's possible or he's working with materials that make up a bomb. That's what Brutus is trained to sniff out. We don't know yet if it's the ingredients in C-4. Brutus found four places in the building. A chair in the reception area, the exam room and the one next door as well as the place where you monitor the animals. Did he seem familiar to you, Lydia?"

Again she tried to run through the faces she remembered at the bistro while she was there. Again nothing but Melinda's image popped into her mind…a vision of the waitress, Eve, serving a young couple materialized. "I remember a few others, but they aren't Mr. Jacobs." She'd been looking at the photos over the weekend that Jesse had left of the victims, so was that a true memory or wishful thinking? "The waitress put two plates down at the table next to me. A young couple sat there."

"You can show me their photos when we get home.

The more you remember the people who are in the photo array, the more I think you'll remember the rest of what you saw."

When we get home. If she hadn't made a bad mistake with Aaron all those years ago, she could have married Jesse.

"No one wants it more than me. This man is holding the city hostage."

Jesse glanced toward the animal hospital. "Tyler is waving at us. We can go inside. JoAnn, I want you to go, too."

"You betcha. The very idea he was in our building standing only a foot away from me gives me the willies." Without waiting, JoAnn marched across the street.

"The Laughing Bomber better watch out. JoAnn is fierce when she's on a mission." Lydia walked beside Jesse. "But she's right. The 'willies' are a good description of how I feel."

"I'm not going to let anything happen to you." A steel resolve laced each of Jesse's words. "You can't go to work until we find this guy. He hasn't given up trying to get to you."

"I agree. While I was waiting for you to come outside, I told Matt I wouldn't be back tomorrow. He's thinking of closing down the animal hospital and sending everyone on vacation for the next week at least."

"He wouldn't be the first. I've heard of a couple of other places closing, too."

"He thinks he can make house calls if one of our clients has an emergency."

Jesse introduced the bomb squad commander to

her, and she shook his hand. "I'm glad you didn't find a bomb. That it was a false alarm."

"We've been kept busy this past week with false alarms, but I'd rather people be cautious and call than the alternative. I've collected the evidence to see if we can narrow down the ingredient Brutus smelled. I'll put a rush on it. We should hear back soon."

Lydia and JoAnn entered the building with Jesse with Brutus while Thomas kept the others out until they retraced their steps. JoAnn stopped at the reception desk and found the contact information for Mr. Jacobs and gave it to Jesse.

Then Lydia proceeded through what she and JoAnn did with the American Eskimo. The only places Calvin went were where Brutus indicated.

"JoAnn, you've been a big help. You can let the others come in." Jesse waited until she disappeared down the hallway. "Lydia, let's go into your office and give Mr. Jacobs a call about Calvin."

She sat at her desk and picked up the phone, her hand trembling as she punched in the numbers the old man had left. She let it ring ten times before she hung up. "No answer."

"I'm taking you home and then Thomas and I are going to the address he gave JoAnn. I'll have Officer Williams stay until I get back."

"Just the two of you are going? He could be the bomber."

"Reinforcements will be hiding, waiting for a signal from us if we think it's him or he makes a run for it."

"I can't imagine Mr. Jacobs running. And he looks nothing like the drawing of the man in the appliance store or the fake orderly who was in my room."

"I know. This case has more questions than answers."

"Do you want me to continue trying to call him?"

"No. Let me see what we discover first. Are you ready to leave?"

"In a minute. I have a couple of animals to check on."

"I'll come with you."

Lydia began listing in her mind all the instructions she would have to give to Matt about the animals left until their owners were able to pick them up. "There are a couple of dogs and one cat that needs to stay, but Matt should be okay if the place is locked down."

"Yes. The security system is good, or I would never have let you come to work at all."

The intensity in his look and voice made her feel protected but also something more. If she didn't know better she would think that Jesse cared about her. Of course, he cared if she were safe. That was the kind of person he was. Expecting more was setting herself up to be hurt—like she'd hurt him.

Jesse pulled up in front of a small white house, well kept, with a fenced backyard. The blackout shades were down on every window they could see. The hairs on his nape tingled. It didn't feel right. He called Thomas, who was behind him in his car. "It doesn't look like anyone is home."

"Let's park up the street. Maybe we should check with a couple of neighbors to find out about Mr. Jacobs. He isn't the man who owns this house, and there isn't a driver's license for the guy."

"He won't be the first person to drive without a license. And the house is listed as a rental."

"But I haven't gotten in touch with the owner to see who is occupying it right now. I'll take the neighbor on the right. You visit the one on the left."

Jesse parked and unloaded Brutus from the rear, then approached the house on the left. He rang the doorbell and waited. Turning, he noticed a car in the driveway so this time he knocked. Still no answer. He decided to go across the street and see if that person was home.

An older woman, probably in her late sixties, opened her door but left the half glass/half screen shut. "Is something wrong, Officer?"

"Do you know your neighbor directly across the street?"

"No one has been there for a while or at least no one I've seen. I keep an eye on the street since I'm home all the time. I thought Mr. Sims would have rented it by now, but he hasn't put up a sign."

"Who lived there last? We haven't been able to get in touch with Mr. Sims yet."

"A young man, not very friendly. I'd say hi to him, and he would ignore me."

"Did this man have a dog?"

"If he did, I never saw it." The petite woman frowned. "What's going on? Is something wrong?"

Jesse glanced at Thomas talking to a man on a porch. "Do you know a gentleman around seventy years old? Mr. Jacobs?"

She shook her head and unlocked her screen door, then stepped out on her stoop and pointed toward the man Thomas was talking to. "That's his name. But as you can see, he isn't seventy."

Jesse removed a business card. "If you see anyone at the house across the street, please give me a call."

The lady's brown eyes widened. "What's this about?"

"It has to do with a case I'm investigating."

Her mouth twisted in a thoughtful expression. "I can call. I figure you have your hands full with the Laughing Bomber. I don't leave much so I might see something." She looked at the card and slipped it in her dress pocket. "I'm Anna Dodson."

"Could you describe the man who used to live there?"

"I could hardly see his face with all the hair and beard. He was normal height, certainly not as tall as you. Thin. Probably no more than thirty but again not sure."

"Thanks." Jesse turned to leave.

"What's your dog's name?"

He looked back and grinned. "Brutus."

"He's well behaved. I used to have a dog that would never sit that long. Always getting into things."

"Good day, Ms. Dodson."

Jesse met Thomas in the yard of the house in question. "Did Mr. Jacobs tell you no one has been here for a while?"

"Yes, at least a few weeks. And while I was talking to him, the owner, Mr. Sims, called me. He didn't realize it wasn't occupied. The man living here, a Sam Alexander, paid the rent this month. I asked him if we had permission to go inside. He gave it and is actually on his way here with the key."

"While we're waiting for him, I'm going to take Brutus around the house and check out what's in the backyard. See if he picks up anything." Jesse nodded his head toward the neighbor to the right. "I know Mr. Jacobs doesn't fit the description Lydia and JoAnn gave us, but do you think he could be involved somehow?"

"I'll be checking him out. And I'll send someone out to talk to the neighbor to the left. When I saw you walking across the street, I asked Mr. Jacobs if they worked. It's a middle-aged couple, and they both work at the hospital."

Jesse started across the yard, letting Brutus sniff around while he checked if he could see inside, but all the shades were pulled. When he tried the back door, the knob turned. He wanted to go inside, but he didn't want any legal issues. This case was too important. Jesse completed circling the house as a white Ford Escort pulled into the driveway.

Mr. Sims greeted Thomas, then Jesse, but as the owner started for the house, Thomas said, "I'd prefer you stay outside. We don't know what we'll find inside."

"But it's my place."

"As soon as we think it's safe, you're welcome to come inside, but there's a possibility this place is tied to a crime and therefore there may be evidence we don't want compromised."

Mr. Sims opened his mouth but snapped it closed before saying anything. He nodded.

Jesse took the key the owner held out for them and walked toward the porch. "Let me and Brutus go first. For some reason the fake Mr. Jacobs went to a lot of trouble to send us here."

His K-9 sniffed around the porch and especially

the entrance. Jesse waited until he was through before unlocking the door. He eased it open, looking for
any trip wires. Then Jesse and Brutus entered going
to the right. His K-9 checked the living room for any
scent of a bomb.

Thomas came to the doorway. "Okay for me to come
in?"

"So far nothing. But you should stay there until I
check everything." Jesse strolled into the dining room
and stepped onto an area rug where a table and four
chairs were.

Brutus went to the right, smelling a cabinet. He sat
and barked.

"Get out," Jesse yelled.

Following his friend, Jesse ran for the door with Brutus.
Two feet from the exit, a laughing track sounded.

TEN

When the doorbell rang at Jesse's house, Lydia came from the kitchen to see Officer Williams checking the peephole, then opening the door with his hand on his gun handle.

"Yes?" Don asked the teenage boy on the porch.

"Kate invited me over."

"Wait here." As Lydia walked toward the hallway to the bedroom they shared at Jesse's house, she wanted to throttle her sister. After the day she'd had at work, this was not what she wanted to deal with.

When she turned the corner, Lydia spied Kate coming out of the room. Lydia hurried her steps and blocked her sister's path. "Where do you think you're going?"

"I saw Connor's car parked out front."

"Did you invite him over here?"

Kate lifted her chin and narrowed her eyes. "So what if I did? I need help with my Algebra II homework. Who do you think has been tutoring me?"

"This is the first I've heard that you needed a tutor. Why didn't you tell me this earlier?"

"You haven't been home but ten minutes. Connor is early." Kate started around Lydia.

But she stepped to the side, preventing her sister from going anywhere. "Is that the truth or another lie?"

"What lie?" Kate's voice rose several decibels.

"You did great last year in geometry. Math has never given you a problem before."

"How would you know? Until this year you were never around."

"You made a B in Algebra I."

Kate got in Lydia's face. "Because I had a tutor. If you hadn't stayed away, you'd have known that."

Lydia took a step back, her pulse racing at the anger pouring off her sister.

"You left me here with Dad. He didn't care what I did. So why do you? Mom left, you left and then Dad…"

The issues that had been standing between them spewed out. A lot of what Kate was feeling, Lydia had gone through herself—a bit differently but the end result was the same, the feeling of abandonment.

Kate opened and closed her hands at her sides, her glare cutting through Lydia.

"You two can work at the dining room table if Officer Williams says it is okay."

Her sister charged past Lydia while she gathered her composure. She'd never felt that she'd abandoned her little sister, but in her eyes she had. They would have to talk about this. This anger couldn't continue, especially when a mad bomber might have been at her place of work today.

She made her way toward the foyer, Kate's pleading voice drifting to her.

Don glanced at Lydia when she came into view.

"It's your call, Don. If you aren't sure, you should call Jesse and ask him."

At that moment Officer Collins entered the living room with Mitch beside her. She looked at everyone, then asked, "I think the neighbors heard the shouting." She directed her look right at Kate. "With all that's been going on, nothing can be that bad."

Kate pinched her lips together.

"Thanks for bringing Mitch in." Lydia stooped to hug the German shepherd.

Kate gave Don a huge smile and turned her back on Lydia. "Please let Connor stay. I need help with our homework. Promise."

Don withdrew his cell phone. "I'm calling the sergeant."

Kate's shoulder sagged forward.

When Don clicked off, he looked up. "He isn't answering." His forehead crinkled. "I guess since you're here you can stay at least until he comes home."

Kate grabbed Connor's hand and pulled him toward the dining room so quickly Lydia almost laughed

She straightened and moved toward Don, lowering her voice, "I think she's afraid you'll change your mind. I'm surprised Jesse didn't answer."

"So am I. Maybe they've got a good lead with Mr. Jacobs."

Lydia hoped that was the case. Before the Laughing Bomber totally turned this town—her life—upside down.

* * *

Against the backdrop of hideous laughter, Jesse ran behind Thomas and Brutus off the porch. A blast exploded behind him. Its force flung Jesse through the air and crashing against the hard ground. Air rushed from his lungs. His ears rang. Stunned, he tried to lift his head, but the world spun around. He collapsed back onto the grass.

Brutus. Thomas.

They were ahead of him. Maybe they were all right. Jesse drew on a reserve buried deep inside him and pushed himself up, supporting his weight as he scanned the yard. Brutus lay still a few feet from him. As Jesse crawled toward his dog, he scanned the area for Thomas. He couldn't lose either one.

To the left Thomas rolled over, shock reflected in his expression. His mouth moved, but Jesse couldn't hear what he was saying. The sound of Jesse's heartbeat thundering in his ears overpowered every other noise. He pointed to his ears. Thomas nodded his head once and removed his phone from his pocket.

Jesse continued toward Brutus and stopped next to him. His hand shook as he reached out and touched him. A movement under his palm sent a wave of relief flowing through him.

"Take it easy, Brutus," Jesse said the words, but he could barely hear himself.

His Rottweiler shook his head and tried to stand but wobbled and fell down.

Seeing his dog struggling, Jesse gathered Brutus to him and held him. "We're alive because of you. We'll be okay." Jesse didn't know if his K-9 heard him or not, but Brutus could feel Jesse's support as he stroked him.

He thought of Mitch and what happened. He didn't know what he would do if he lost Brutus.

Not another loss. Please, Lord.

Five minutes after Officer Williams called Jesse, Lydia tried his number, surprised again that he didn't answer her call or Don's. Did something happen?

When the doorbell rang, she was nearest the door and hurried to see who it was. She looked out the peephole and saw Chance. She started to open the door when Don's hand clasped her arm.

"Let me answer the door. You know the drill."

"It's Chance, your replacement."

"He's early." The police officer gently pushed her back and put his body between her and the opening of the door. "Is something wrong?" Don looked around the state trooper.

"I was told to come here. There's been another bombing. A house this time."

Lydia stepped around Don. "Where?"

Chance told her the address she'd given for Mr. Jacobs.

The strength flowed from her legs, and she sank back against the police officer, who clasped her arms to hold her up. "Who's injured?" *Not Jesse. Please, Lord. I can't lose him.*

"I don't know much. Thomas and Jesse got out before it exploded but were thrown from the blast."

"How about Brutus?" Lydia asked.

"Jesse called but said he couldn't hear me. He said he and Thomas were rallying, but Brutus was bleeding. He told me to come here and make sure you and Kate were okay."

Lydia pivoted and headed for her bedroom. "I'll be right back." When she brought her belongings from her house, she included her medical bag she kept for emergencies. She grabbed it and headed back to the foyer.

"Where do you think you're going?" Chance asked.

"You're going to take me to the bomb site while these two officers stay here with Kate."

"No, I'm not."

She stared at Chance. "If you don't take me, I'm going by any means. Brutus needs medical help." And she needed to see with her own eyes that Jesse and Thomas were all right.

His eyes cut through her.

She tilted up her chin. "My car is in Jesse's garage. I'll drive myself. You can't force me to stay here."

Chance started to say something.

"Please," Lydia added.

"Okay. It won't be the first time Jesse and me have argued about something. The bomb site is probably the safest place in town by now."

Kate came into the foyer. "You can't go. He's after you."

"We don't know what this man's agenda is. Why did he rig the house? I never take animals to their owners."

"I think this madman did this to taunt the police." Officer Collins leaned against the entrance into the living room next to Kate. "He knew if anyone would go into the house it would be police."

Kate gasped.

Lydia ground her teeth, thinking about how close she'd been to Mr. Jacobs or whatever his name really was. "None of this adds up, but I can't stand around talking about it. I need to get to Brutus. I'm his vet." She thought about how Jesse would feel if he lost his dog.

"Let's go." Chance turned toward the door. "Stay here with Kate."

As he escorted Lydia to his cruiser, he kept sweeping the area as though he expected the bomber to appear suddenly.

She wouldn't put anything past this maniac. Once she knew that everyone was all right, she had to remember what happened at the bistro. If she could recall a few details, then she could somehow recreate the whole time she was in the restaurant. Lives depended on her.

On the drive to the new bomb site, Chance said, "I know this is tough on you."

"Which part, not remembering what I saw or my past with Jesse?"

"Both. I've seen you two together. And I can imagine how hard it is on you to not be able to recall the bombing. But not surprising. Our minds have a way of protecting us against trauma."

"And remembering would be traumatic, not a relief?"

"Again, both." Chance turned onto a street with fire trucks and police cars, their red lights flashing.

The sight that riveted Lydia was the ambulance and two paramedics rolling a gurney with a body on it, covered by a white sheet. "Who died?" she asked in a breathless voice that quavered.

Chance parked and glanced at her. "I don't know, but Jesse called me. He's okay, Lydia."

Inhaling and exhaling deep breaths, she grasped her bag and opened the door. "Then what about Thomas?"

Chance scowled and strode next to her as they weaved their way through the crowd forming. When they neared the half-bombed house, Lydia saw Jesse by Brutus on the ground with Thomas talking with the fire captain. They were both okay. She spied the Rottweiler trying to get up and Jesse calming him with his hand. Relief trembled through her as she hurried to them.

Jesse looked up, his eyebrows slashing downward. "How did you get here?"

Pointing to Chance, Lydia knelt next to Brutus, seeing the blood matting his fur with a shard of glass stuck in him. "And don't be mad at him. I would have come one way or another. Brutus needs my help. And I had to see that you were okay."

"You need to speak up. My ears are still ringing. I was calming him down so I could pull the piece out."

She knew about the hearing problems and still had a little tinnitus since the blast last week. Lydia dug into her bag, prepared a tranquilizer and gave Brutus the shot. "This will calm him and then I can remove the glass and tend to the wound. Did you see any other wounds?" She glanced up at Jesse.

His brow knitted, Jesse locked gazes with her. "You shouldn't be here, but I'm glad you are. He tried to get up and collapsed."

Lydia touched one of Jesse's ears. "Like you, he could be experiencing hearing loss, dizziness."

"Yeah, that's what I thought."

Jesse kept stroking Brutus while Lydia pulled the shard out and tended to the wound. "I'll need to stitch this up. We'll have to take him to the animal hospital. Everyone's picked up their pets except Calvin. I'd like to bring him home with us and keep monitoring him. It's obvious Mr. Jacobs won't."

Jesse withdrew his pad. "I didn't catch all of that."

Lydia applied a thick bandage to Brutus's injury, then wrote on Jesse's pad and signaled Chance.

The state trooper approached. "I found out who was on the gurney. The young man who rented the house. Mr. Sims identified him."

"I need to take Brutus to the hospital and check him out more thoroughly as well as stitch up his wound." She looked at Jesse's SUV with its windows blown out. "Will you take us in your car?"

"Yes." Chance stooped and slid his arms under the Rottweiler.

While he lifted him, she decided to write on Jesse's pad what she was going to do. He nodded and began to stand. He wobbled. She wrapped her arm around him and guided him toward the cruiser. Whether Jesse liked it or not, she was going to have Chance take him to the ER after he saw that Brutus would be all right and was settled back at his house.

Later that night, Lydia finally sank onto the couch and sighed. She was so tired she didn't know if she could get up to go to bed. She wouldn't until Chance returned with Jesse from the ER. He hadn't wanted to go, but they'd finally persuaded him. Lydia suspected the adrenaline that sometimes kept pain at bay had finally subsided. While she'd taken care of Brutus at the animal hospital, Chance had picked bits and pieces of debris from Jesse's back. Not anything large like his dog's, but the back of Jesse's shirt was bloodied.

Both Brutus and Calvin were curled up on the floor

in the living room, much better and sound asleep. Connor left right after they returned home per Jesse's order. Now Lydia waited for Chance to either call or bring Jesse home. She'd managed to chew one thumbnail down to the quick and was working on the other when the front door opened.

She shoved to her feet while Don came in the foyer from the back of the house. Mary Collins, at the other end of the couch, stood. Both were alert, but Don immediately relaxed, which meant Jesse was home. Lydia hurried toward the entry, needing to see he was okay.

Moving stiffly, Jesse stepped through the entrance with Chance right behind him. Even Kate appeared from the hallway leading to the bedrooms.

No one said anything for half a minute. Jesse's left side of his face was starting to bruise, probably where his face hit the ground. His left arm had a bandage around it and no doubt his back was a patchwork of tended wounds. He had on his short-sleeve black uniform shirt, untucked and bedraggled.

With a shadow in his eyes, he swung toward Lydia. "How's Brutus doing?"

"I think better than you. He's sound asleep and probably will be through the night. Which is what you need to do."

"I can stay through the night with Chance," Don said. "Then we can figure out tomorrow."

"I appreciate that, but, Don, this isn't going to change anything." Jesse waved his hand toward his bandaged arm. "I had minor cuts. No big deal."

Chance shook his head but remained quiet.

"There'll be a lot to do sifting through the house tomorrow. This may be the break we needed." Jesse looked from Don to Mary. "Thanks for staying late. You don't need to be here until nine. I'll make sure Kate gets to school." He turned his attention to her sister. "We have a few things to discuss on the way."

Kate waited until Jesse trod into the living room before she spun on her heel and stormed down the hallway toward their bedroom. Her sister didn't think rules applied to her. Lydia was glad she could count on Jesse to stand strong.

Chance saw the two police officers out locking the front door. When he came into the living room, deep frown lines bracketed his mouth. "I believe I heard the ER doc telling you to rest for the next day or so."

Jesse sat on the floor near his K-9, stroking him. "I'll rest when we catch this guy. He set a trap for any police that came to search that house. If it hadn't been for Brutus being there, we wouldn't have had enough time to get out." He zeroed in on Lydia. "And I don't think the bomber is a seventy-year-old man with a limp. I think our bomber has been wearing disguises. With that in mind, Thomas wants you down at police headquarters tomorrow to give a description of the guy. Then we'll use the sketches we have to see if we can guess what he might look like. There's a computer program that looks for similarities."

"What if one of the sketches is really the bomber?" Lydia asked, still feeling as if she saw something she shouldn't have at the bistro.

"That's possible, and of course, each one is being taken seriously. Chance, I'm too wound up to go to sleep right now. I'll take the first watch."

His friend clamped his lips together, started for the spare bedroom but stopped. "Okay, but I'm relieving you in three hours. No arguments. You won't be worth anything if you don't get some rest."

Jesse nodded, then pushed to his feet, wincing once.

"Sure, you're fine." Lydia placed her hands on her waist. "If that's the case, why did you wince?"

He averted his gaze and headed toward the kitchen. Lydia followed. She wasn't going to bed until she knew he had. This happened because of her. If she hadn't gone to the animal hospital, the older gentleman wouldn't have come with Calvin. If only she could remember what the bomber thought she knew and help the police put him in jail.

Jesse stood at the counter, fixing a pot of coffee.

"It's obvious you aren't as wired as you think or you wouldn't need caffeine to stay up."

He threw her a scowl and plugged in the pot. "Chance is volunteering to help. He still has his day job to go to."

"And you shouldn't be doing anything tomorrow, but you are. Your stubbornness hasn't changed."

"I call it 'resolve.' Earlier today my foster mother phoned me to ask if I thought it was safe for her to go to the grocery store. I told her about one that's delivering."

"I've heard of other businesses doing that, but not everyone can."

Jesse leaned against the counter as the coffee perked behind. "Did you notice the traffic today? It's probably half of what it would be normally. The Laughing Bomber Task Force has doubled in size. We have help from the FBI on profiling this guy. ATF is also involved."

The tense set of his shoulder and the lines of exhaustion on his face prompted Lydia to bridge the distance between them and grasp his right forearm. "I'll bring you your coffee in the living room. At least sit on the couch where you'll be more comfortable and near Brutus."

He didn't move for a moment. Then he covered her hand for a few seconds before pushing away from the counter and trudging out of the kitchen.

When he left, Lydia tucked her hands under her armpits, closed her eyes and tried to picture the bistro when she arrived that day. She opened the door and collided with…who? A man. What did he look like? Was he a regular? Did she know him? A vague image of a middle-aged man wearing a hoodie. Odd? Usually she saw young people doing that. As much as she concentrated on bringing his features into focus, she couldn't.

Okay, she entered the bistro and made a beeline toward Bree. Then what? Who did she pass? Was the pharmacist from the drugstore sitting with…? The picture in her head faded and a black screen filled her thoughts. Her eyes popped open, and disappointment slumped her shoulders.

Lord, please. This needs to stop. Help me to remember.

But nothing came to mind.

The coffee was ready, so she poured a mug for Jesse and walked into the living room to find his head resting on the back couch cushion, his eyes closed. Quietly she put the coffee on the table and took the chair across from him. She still wanted to watch Brutus for another hour as the anesthetic wore off to make sure that he didn't try to scratch his stitches.

The urge to caress Jesse's bruised face overwhelmed her. A mistake she'd made all those years ago still haunted her with so many regrets. If she hadn't fallen for Aaron's charms, would she have ended up married to Jesse? Now she was in the middle of a horrific situation, in danger—but so was Jesse. Yes, it was his job, but if anything happened to him she'd feel it was her fault.

In that moment she realized she'd never stopped loving Jesse. He would always have a piece of her heart. But she didn't think he would ever forgive her. Like her father? He certainly hadn't forgiven her, and she had no way to repair that relationship.

She'd begun to think returning to Anchorage was a good thing in the end, especially for Kate, but also for her renewed friendships. She'd missed their support. She'd missed Jesse but hadn't realized it until they spent so much time together. They were different people, but the person she fell in love with all those years ago was still there.

Which meant he didn't share himself. He always had a part of himself he guarded closely, and she knew it stemmed from his parents' death and never really having a home. She'd pieced that much together but never from him.

Brutus stirred. Lydia rose and went to the Rottweiler to make sure everything was still all right. She placed her hand on his neck, and he settled down. She checked his wound, then stood. Her gaze collided with Jesse's.

"Is he okay?" A huskiness entered his voice.

"Yes. He's a trouper."

Jesse leaned forward and picked up the mug. "Thanks. I need this."

Lydia sat on the coffee table and stilled his hand from moving the cup to his mouth. "Don't. Take Chance up on his offer. You fell asleep just now."

"I was resting my eyes. I heard you come in."

"Really, Jesse. Don't play that macho act with me. I need you back to one hundred percent because we have to figure out who this guy is."

One of his dark eyebrows hiked up. "We?"

"Yes, tomorrow I want to talk about the bistro bombing until my memory is triggered."

"It doesn't work that way." He sat forward and put his mug on the coaster next to her.

His arm brushed hers and sent a jolt through her. What if he'd been inside the house when the bomb went off? He could have died. She covered his hands with hers. "Why not? I was waiting for the coffee to perk and I had another memory of what I witnessed in the bistro before the bomb went off."

He sat up straighter. "What?"

She told him about the people she remembered so far. "I want to look at those photos of the people killed in the bombing."

"I'll get them." He started to stand.

She halted his progress. "Sit. I'll go. Where are they?"

"On the desk in the kitchen."

She retrieved the pictures, and this time sat next to him on the couch. As she flipped through them, she was acutely aware of the man beside her, their shoulders touching. "I remember the pharmacist from the drugstore across the street, but he isn't here. He was with someone, but I can't remember her. Her! I didn't know that before, but I'm sure it was a woman, but I didn't get a good look at her—at least that I remember."

"Then we'll interview the pharmacist. I wonder why he didn't come forward. Some people did who had been there although they couldn't help us."

"Did a middle-aged man come forward? I can't remember much about the guy in the hoodie. I just thought it odd."

"I'll check with Thomas. If you can remember him, we'll have an artist draw a sketch of him." He shifted to face her. "See, you're recalling facts. Both of these might lead somewhere."

"How are you feeling, really?"

One corner of his mouth quirked. "I've had better days, but looking at you has definitely improved it." His voice and expression softened, his golden-brown eyes fixed on her face as though he were memorizing every line.

"Good. Because waiting for you to return from the ER made me a nervous wreck."

"Now you know what I went through when you were taken from the bomb site. I wanted to go in the ambulance, but I had a job that had to be done."

She ran her hand down his arm, then threaded her fingers through his. "I don't know how you did that job. I've been at search and rescue sites, but not that kind with those results, knowing most of the people you found would be dead."

"But there was always the hope we'd uncover a live person. That makes it all worth it to me, especially when Brutus found you."

Warmth suffused her face. His dreamy look held her riveted. Maybe when this was over with, they had a chance. She didn't realize how much she wanted that until that second.

He lifted his hand and cradled it against her cheek. "How are you doing through all this?"

"I'm getting better each day, but I want this to end now."

"We all do." His eyes smoldering, he combed his fingers through her hair and cupped her nape, then dragged her toward him. "I don't know what I would have done if you hadn't been alive," he whispered, his mouth an inch from hers.

Every part of her wanted him to kiss her. She inhaled sharply and let her breath out slowly as the moment hung between them. What was he waiting for?

ELEVEN

Jesse wanted to kiss her but hesitated. He felt the brush of her breath against his lips. He smelled the fruity scent that he'd come to associate with her. It comforted him—as if he'd come home.

He held her face and settled his mouth on hers. As she clasped his sides, he deepened the kiss, wanting to pour so much into it, but a part of him held back. The part that remembered the hurt. The part that had wanted to marry her and have a family with her. The part that had felt discarded every time he moved from one foster home to another.

He pulled back, his hands slipping from her face. When he did, she withdrew her touch and scooted away a few feet. She lowered her gaze and sat forward on the couch. A barrier fell between them, much like right before they broke up in December when they were seniors.

"We shouldn't have—" he said in a husky voice.

"Kissed? Why?"

"Because…because…" He didn't want to tell her he was beginning to fall in love with her.

"Never mind. It's not important. People say actions speak louder than words, and with you, that's the only way I know what's going on with you. That's not changed."

Anger shoved his doubts away. "Don't make me the bad guy in what happened between us. If actions speak louder than words, you made it clear how you really felt about me all those years ago." He pushed off the couch, grabbed his mug and left the living room.

If he hadn't, he might have said more than he wanted to. He didn't want her to know how close he'd come to telling her he wanted another chance to see if they could work out. Who was he kidding? Too much in their past stood in their way.

In the kitchen, he put the photos back on the top of the desk, then placed a call to Thomas. He'd been out of the loop and wanted to know if they discovered anything at the newest crime scene. He needed to keep his focus on the case to end this nightmare and get back to the way his life was before—what? Before Lydia came back to Anchorage? Before he was a teenage boy who fell in love with her?

"I'm glad you called," Thomas said the second he answered his phone. "I was debating whether to wait until the morning or chance waking you up. I knew you left the ER so I figure you're okay. Right?"

"I'm fine." Jesse sat back against the hard chair and flinched, making a mockery of his words. "They had to stitch a couple of my cuts up otherwise they cleaned them and sent me home." After checking his hearing and doing a CT scan on his head. "Did you go get checked out?"

"The paramedics did on-site. I was ahead of you."

"And they didn't tell you to go to your doctor."

A long pause, and then Thomas chuckled. "Okay, they did mention that, and I will when we have this guy behind bars."

"Lydia remembered a couple of things today that happened before the bomb went off." Jesse relayed what she'd told him. "I want to interview the pharmacist tomorrow. Okay?"

"Fine, but I want you to encourage Lydia to keep remembering. There's a reason the bomber has come after her and the waitress. And after today, he might be going for law enforcement. There was a message written on the only wall that withstood the blast today, 'Back off or you'll regret it.'"

"So you think it was directed at us?"

"Yes. We're checking around at other vets about an American Eskimo named Calvin since the dog seems to respond to that name. Nothing so far."

"Have you tried the pound?"

"That's next as well as putting out a picture of Calvin and asking anyone if they have seen this dog. The bomber will make a mistake. He's getting bolder and reckless. But we've got to stop him before someone else dies."

"I'll interview the pharmacist and then take Calvin by the pound. Maybe seeing him will help someone recognize him. I'll be in touch after I do that tomorrow." When Jesse hung up, he turned toward the entrance from the dining room and glanced at the clock.

He had an hour and a half until he would wake up Chance. Better get another cup of coffee.

Then he peeked into the living room, wanting to see if Lydia went to bed. She hadn't—well, not exactly. She'd gone back to sitting in the lounge chair, which gave her a good view of Brutus and Calvin, but her eyes were closed and her feet propped up in the recliner.

Taking his mug of fresh coffee, he walked through his house, checking the doors and the alarm system. He hoped Lydia was still asleep. He didn't have any more emotional energy left to deal with what was going on between them.

Lydia stood in the entrance to the bistro, the dark shadows slowly evaporating as though the haze was finally lifting from her brain. Part of the restaurant she saw clearly. Melinda standing near the counter with a man she'd seen in the place before. The look on Melinda's face shouted distress, but she kept her voice low. Was the man complaining about an order? Or something else? Her boyfriend?

When Lydia spied tears in Melinda's eyes, she wanted to comfort her friend. The man shoved away from the counter and pivoted toward Lydia. His featureless face made her remain in her chair. He came toward her. She tried to see anything—eyes, mouth, nose. Nothing. But he brushed against her, and a chill flash froze her.

Lydia shot straight up in the recliner, her heartbeat pounding in her ears. Her gaze crashed into Jesse's. He sat across from her on the couch.

He rose and came toward her. "What's wrong?"

For a long moment, she couldn't form her words to explain the dream—no, nightmare. "Some guy was arguing with Melinda when I came into the bistro."

"What did he look like?"

"I couldn't see his face. He came right toward me,

but it was blank. That's all I saw, but there was something wrong with that guy."

"What?"

"I don't know." She ground her teeth together. "I've seen him before?"

"Okay. It'll come to you." Jesse sat on the coffee table. "How tall was he?"

Lydia tried to picture the man leaning against the counter, almost in Melinda's face. "Maybe about five-ten."

"What color hair did he have?"

"Brown."

"Long, medium, short?"

"A little long. I saw it sticking out of a ball cap."

"Anything on the ball cap?"

"I don't remember." Frustration churned her stomach. That was all she'd been saying lately.

"Body build?"

Lydia closed her eyes and recalled the faceless man coming toward her. "Lean but not skinny."

"Anything else?"

She shook her head. When she looked at Jesse, there was no reproach in his gaze, only kindness.

"If you just recalled that, you'll remember more. It'll come."

"But in time?"

"This case doesn't hinge on you. You're only one part of it. Thomas is digging into the man who was renting that house. He might have a tie to the bomber. Tomorrow I'll be following up on the pharmacist and visiting the animal shelters about Calvin."

"Can I come? I can't sit home doing nothing."

"Not to the drugstore, but I think it might help if I

take Calvin with me to the shelters. Seeing him might trigger someone's memory, and I know the dog responds to you."

"You're letting me go?"

He cocked a grin. "Besides, it'll take a day for the windows to be replaced in my SUV. I was hoping you would let me borrow your car to use."

She chuckled. "You're sneaky but thanks for letting me help with Calvin. Now that I know that the guy who brought him in is the bomber, I could see him getting a dog from the pound and then poisoning him. But I have an argument about coming to see you with the pharmacist. Seeing him might jar my memory."

"I've got a way for you to watch him from a safe distance. I'll have him come into the station for questioning. He won't see you, but you can see him."

"Thanks." She put the footrest down and stood. "I was going to stay up with you, but obviously I need my sleep. And you should get some, too."

Jesse glanced at his watch. "I have an hour. It'll give me time to think about what we do know so far in this case."

Lydia knelt by the two dogs and reassured herself they were doing well. When she rose, she noticed Jesse had moved back to the couch. After Jesse's response concerning the kiss, she didn't think he was capable of sharing himself with anyone. She had to accept that and quit dreaming they might have a chance after all.

At least she finally had hope that she might recall what she saw in the bistro that would cause the bomber to target her. It had to be that she could identify him. Unlike her relationship with Jesse, which seemed hopeless, it was starting to seem likely that she'd remember…but would it be soon enough?

Lydia sat next to an FBI agent working on the Laughing Bomber Task Force while Thomas and Jesse interviewed Phillip Keats, the pharmacist. Thomas sat across from Phillip, but Jesse was right next to him with Brutus on the man's other side, as if the man were boxed in. When the pharmacist had come into the interrogation room, the dog had sniffed him but didn't indicate anything. Jesse crowded Phillip who leaned as far from Jesse as he could get without getting up and moving his chair.

"I understand you were in the bistro not long before it was bombed. Why didn't you come forward to help us with identifying the people who could be victims?" Thomas asked.

Phillip slid a look toward Jesse, then Brutus. "Am I safe with him not on a leash?"

"He would only attack if I gave the command. You didn't answer the detective's question. Why didn't you come forward?" The fierce expression on Jesse's face even gave Lydia pause.

Phillip swallowed hard. "I don't go in there much and didn't know anyone."

"Ah, that's interesting when you were seen talking to a woman. And from what I understand that woman didn't survive the blast. Didn't you think the police needed to know she was in there?" Thomas's calm voice held only curiosity, not blame.

Sweat coated Phillip's forehead and began rolling down his face. He lowered his head.

Jesse hit his palm against the table. "It's a simple yes or no question."

The pharmacist jumped and leaned even farther away from Jesse. "I couldn't come forward," the man mumbled.

"Why not? You left before her. Why?" Again Thomas's soft tone was meant to calm the man down.

While Phillip wiped his hand across his brow, the FBI agent asked, "Do you remember anything else? Anything that would help with the questions to ask Mr. Keats?"

She shook her head. Something nagged at her, but she couldn't pinpoint it.

Finally Phillip looked right at Thomas. "Okay. I was there with Miss Prince. You knew she was in there. Her name was listed as one of the victims, so what was I going to tell you that you didn't already know?"

"Oh, I don't know. Maybe who else you remember being there? Don't you want us to find the bomber? What if you saw him?" Jesse's taunts made the man wince.

"I don't remember anyone. I was there to see—my friend. That was all. I had limited time before I had to be back at work. I'm not a criminal because I didn't say anything."

"So why didn't you?" Jesse asked.

The pharmacist's eyes grew narrow. "Because I'm a married man."

Thomas wrote something on a pad. "Ah, are you saying you were having an affair with Miss Prince?"

"She was a friend, but someone might mistake us eating lunch together as something more."

"While you were there, did you see anything suspicious?" Jesse snapped his fingers, and Brutus came to his side.

"I saw a man storm out of the bistro after talking to the owner."

Then her dream last night was true. Lydia felt it was but couldn't be sure until now.

Thomas cleared his throat. "I thought you didn't go to the bistro much. How do you know who the owner is?"

"I saw her picture on the news. That bombing was plastered all over the place. Kind of hard to avoid."

"What did the man look like? Is he one of these?" Thomas laid an array of pictures on the table.

"Nope, I don't think so. I never saw his face. I just heard him say something to the owner. I wasn't sitting too far from them."

Lydia leaned forward as Thomas asked, "What?"

"You're going to pay for this."

She'd known the man was angry, but this was a whole new level.

"When did you leave the restaurant?" Jesse asked, pulling the man's attention to him.

The pharmacist shrugged. "I don't remember. I do know I was back at the drugstore when the bomb went off."

"How long?" Jesse fired back.

Phillip sighed. "I… I guess maybe a minute."

"Did you see him leaving?" the FBI agent asked Lydia.

"No. Maybe he left while I was in the bathroom."

"How long were you in the restroom?"

"A few minutes."

When she turned back to the screen, Phillip Keats

was on his feet, looking at his watch. "I have to get to work."

Both Jesse and Thomas rose at the same time and Thomas passed a card to the pharmacist. "If you remember anything later, please call me no matter how unimportant you think it is."

Phillip pocketed it. "Sure. I want this guy caught like everyone else in Anchorage."

Lydia stared at the screen, watching the three leave the interview room. It hadn't triggered her memory, but it had given her an uneasy feeling as though something he said should have sparked a memory of that day. What did the man with Melinda look like?

The FBI agent stood. "Did you remember anything else?"

"No." The answer was just out of her reach. She knew something but couldn't access it. Every time she tried to, her mind shut down. Jesse was right. Forcing her to remember wasn't helping. Other than a nagging feeling, she hadn't gotten anything from the interview.

The FBI agent opened the door for her to go into the hall first. As she emerged, she found Thomas and Jesse with Brutus waiting for her.

"Anything?" Thomas asked.

She shook her head. "I didn't know he was having an affair, and I'm glad he confirmed that Melinda and a man were arguing, but other than that I didn't get anything new."

"Technically, according to Keats, he and Miss Prince were just friends." Jesse smiled at her. "Ready to take Calvin for a ride?"

The warmth in his gaze shored up her flagging spirits. He used to do that when they were dating. Make her feel better. That was one of the many reasons why she fell in love with him. "I'd like to find the man who left Calvin, not only because he's probably the bomber but he poisoned the dog. I hope Calvin is the one who leads us to him. That would be apropos."

Jesse placed his hand at the small of her back and made his way toward the rear exit. As Lydia emerged from the police station, a cool breeze blew, adding a chill to the air. Jesse continued toward her car, surveying the parking lot.

As she unlocked the driver's door, she paused while Jesse had Brutus circle her vehicle and sniff for a bomb and put him in the backseat. She panned the area, goose bumps streaking up her spine as if someone was watching her. Or was it just the fact Brutus had searched for a bomb in her car? She quickly slipped behind the steering wheel. The feeling made her want to lock herself in Jesse's house and never leave until this man was apprehended.

While she started the car, Jesse climbed into the passenger seat. "Is something wrong? You're pale. Did you remember something?"

"Do you always have Brutus do that when you get into a car?"

"Lately, since we began working on the bombing case."

"He's valuable to have around." She pulled out of the parking lot and chalked up the feeling to watching Brutus checking for a bomb.

"Yes. He saved my life yesterday. When I was waiting with Brutus for the ambulance, I thought of Jake Nichols and Mitch. They were both injured critically, but worse, their partnership has come to an end. I've been thinking about that a lot. That could have happened to me and Brutus."

"What would you have done? Have you prepared yourself for that? You've been a partner for six years. Brutus is eight years old."

Jesse blew a long breath out. "I don't think I want to talk about that. The very idea unsettles me, and I need to be sharp to catch this bomber. The idea of losing…" His voice faded into silence.

Lydia slanted a look toward Jesse. "The idea of losing anyone in your life is hard. I've had my share of losses. My mother and dad. My baby daughter." She coated her dry throat. "And I'm afraid I'm losing my sister."

"How have you gotten through it, especially with your child?"

How? And with no support from Aaron. "I used to think the Lord had abandoned me after what happened between Aaron and me. My father certainly let me think that. But now, looking back, I've seen God's hand in my healing. It didn't happen overnight. It's been a long journey, but nothing is forever except for His love. I hope one day to have another child. Actually I hope two."

"Two?"

She decided to be bold. "Do you want to have children?" As teenagers they had never talked about it.

Silence lengthened into minutes.

She should have realized that would shut down their conversation. She turned onto his street.

"Yes. Before I lost my parents, I had a good home life. I want to give that to my child."

She wished he'd said *our* child, but of course he

didn't. As a teenager it had taken him a long time to admit he loved her. Once he did, that was all he would share—the words, not the feelings behind them.

"What happened? Why didn't you ever marry?" She pulled into his garage.

Jesse sat in Lydia's car, staring out the windshield at his wall of tools. He grasped for the words to tell her how he felt as a child and especially after she left Anchorage with Aaron. It went beyond anger and betrayal. He didn't know if he could describe the emptiness he'd experienced.

He angled toward her. "I never found anyone to replace you."

"I've regretted my impulsive actions so much. I've paid for that mistake tenfold. I still love you, Jesse. I don't think I ever stopped loving you."

"And yet, you became pregnant with Aaron's child. It should have been mine." The words tumbled out of his mouth before he could censor them. In that moment, he realized he hadn't forgiven her as he thought.

Her gaze wide, she sucked in a breath.

"I loved you so much. I thought you would be my family. The one I always wanted. Instead you left with Aaron. I… I…" The loneliness he'd fought all his life swamped him.

Tears shone in her eyes. "I'm sorry."

"I know that, and I'm trying to let go of the hurt I felt. So much has been happening lately, I feel like our lives are caught up in a whirlwind and we can't get out of it."

She nodded. "Exactly."

He needed her to understand. She had always accused him of keeping his emotions bottled up and she was right. "When my father went missing in the wilderness, my mother left me with our nearest neighbor who lived a few miles away and went out looking for him. It had been snowing some but nothing bad. The neighbor notified the closest town, and they were going to form a search party, but the weather turned and a blizzard came through. Later they found my mother dead. I still had hope my dad was alive. They both knew how to survive in the wilderness. A week later, his body was discovered, mauled by animals. I was eight and lost everything—home, family and friends. My grandmother wasn't well at all and couldn't take me in. I went into foster care in Anchorage."

She touched his hand. "When my mother walked out on the family, at least my father was there."

He clasped her fingers, needing the connection. "I was supposed to be adopted until the couple found a younger child. After that, I stopped dreaming about a new family. I began to rely on myself only. Then you came into my life, and I started to have hope again."

A tear slipped down her cheek.

His cell phone sounded, and he quickly answered it when he saw it was Thomas.

"The tail I had following Phillip Keats lost him. He didn't show up back at work."

TWELVE

"Thanks for letting me know," Jesse replied and looked at Lydia. He lifted his hand and ran his thumb across her cheek to wipe the tear away.

The gesture sent her pulse racing. "Who was that?"

"Thomas. The detail following Keats lost him."

Again she ran through the scene of seeing him at the table with a woman. She tried to remember when he got up. Did she see him leave? *Please, Lord, I need Your help. What am I forgetting?* "What are we going to do?"

"What we planned. If it's Keats, we need evidence to bring him in. Thomas has a BOLO out on his car as well as staking out the drugstore and his house. Meanwhile Thomas is digging into the man's life." He caressed her cheek one more time. "When this is over with, we'll figure things out."

"I want that." She started to get out of her car.

"Wait. I'll get Calvin. Last night we bonded." He threw her a grin and slid from the front seat.

While he was inside retrieving the American Eskimo, she turned to Brutus and petted him. "How are you doing?"

He barked.

Lydia had assumed he would put Brutus in the house when they came to pick up Calvin, but she realized with Phillip's location unknown he wanted him to check her car each time they returned to it. After Calvin was settled in the backseat with Brutus, she backed out of the garage and drove toward their first destination.

By the fourth one, Lydia tried to keep from being disappointed that no one at the shelters recognized Calvin nor had there been an adoption of an American Eskimo in the past six months. With a sigh, she parked near the entrance.

"I hope this produces a lead, but not all trails we follow lead anywhere. We have to rule this possibility out. For all we know the man had Calvin a long time."

"That makes it even worse that he would give his dog chocolate in order to send the police on a wild-goose chase."

"Let's go. We still have a few more to check. I told Williams to be at the house by one."

"Where are you going after you drop me off?"

"Wherever Thomas sends me. He might have something on Keats by then or the lead on the Chevy behind the appliance store might give us some information."

"What lead?"

"They found the car and Thomas is going to pay the man who owns it a visit. He looks like the sketch of the guy who was in the appliance store. At least his license picture does."

"Who is it?"

"Shane Taylor. Do you know him?"

"No, but I'm glad the police have found him. One of these leads will pan out."

They entered the shelter with both dogs on leashes. Jesse showed his badge and asked to talk to the staff members.

The silver-haired woman came forward. "What's this about?"

"It has to do with an investigation."

Lydia walked a few steps toward the woman. "Have you seen this dog? We believe he was at a shelter, and we need to find his owner."

"He looks a lot like Calvin. He was adopted a few weeks ago." The American Eskimo started wagging his tail and moving toward the older woman. She bent over and stroked him. "Where did you find him? The man who adopted him seemed glad to get him. He wanted a medium-sized dog, and Calvin fit what he was looking for. Calvin's original owner died, and I was hoping he'd find a home, especially because of the owner's sudden death in the church's bombing."

"Was that owner Ed Brown?" Jesse asked.

Surprise lit the manager's eyes. "How did you know?"

"I attend that church, and I knew the people who were killed. Do you have any security tapes of the person who adopted Calvin?"

She shook her head. "This is a small operation. Myself, DJ and a few volunteers are the only ones here usually."

"Can you describe the man?"

The woman tilted her head to the left and tapped the side of her jaw. "Let me see. About six feet. He wore a hoodie, but I believe his hair was blond, not too long."

Lydia recalled the man leaving the bistro had a hoodie on. "What color hoodie?"

"Dark. I think navy blue or black. I'm not sure. I did notice he had beautiful gray eyes though."

"How old do you think he was?" Lydia asked.

The woman lifted her shoulders in a shrug. "I guess thirty or forty."

Jesse pulled up on his cell phone the sketch of the person Lydia ran into going into the bistro. "Does this look like the man who adopted Calvin?"

Her forehead crinkled. "Maybe. I don't know for sure."

Jesse went through the rest of the sketches or photos he had. "Does anyone look familiar to you?"

"No, not really, but I'm not good with faces."

"Did this DJ see the man?" Jesse stuck his phone in his pocket.

"No, he was at lunch. It was only me. The man came just minutes after DJ left."

"Do you have his paperwork? Did he use a credit card or write a check for the adoption fees?"

The older woman shook her head. "Cash. Wait right here. I'll get the paperwork and make a copy of it for you."

"Wait. I need to handle the paper. It's evidence now."

The manager's eyes grew round as she headed into her office. "What did this man do?"

"He's a person of interest in a case."

She pulled out a file cabinet and found what she was looking for.

"I'll need to take your fingerprints to rule out yours on the paper."

"Sure." She passed him the document.

"Did DJ ever handle this?"

"No. He has nothing to do with the paperwork."

While Jesse went to the car to get his fingerprinting kit, Lydia looked around. "How many animals can you take in?"

"Not nearly enough. I have room for thirty and often need to turn away animals."

"Do you work with a vet?"

"Yes, but he's only here from May to September. I need to find another one."

"I'd like to volunteer." Lydia dug her business card from her purse and handed it to the woman. "I can fill in from October to April."

"Bless you. You are an answer to a prayer. Our vet just informed me he was going to start going to Arizona for winters." She stuck out her hand. "By the way, I'm Nadine."

"I'm Lydia."

Nadine glanced at the business card. "Are you related to Robert McKenzie? He was a vet who died last year."

"Yes. He was my father."

"He used to help us out. It's like it's come full circle."

Jesse reentered the office, bagged the adoption paper and fingerprinted Nadine. When they left the shelter, Jesse again had Brutus sniff for a bomb as though it were an everyday routine. But to Lydia, it drove home what was happening.

Lydia put the car in Reverse as he lifted the paper out of the evidence bag by pinching one corner with his gloved fingers. "Guess who adopted Calvin? Sam Alexander."

"The guy you found already dead in the house that exploded."

"Yes. Let's drop the evidence off before going home. We'll have to dig into Alexander's life. He can't be the bomber because he was dead from a drug overdose about two weeks before the bomb went off in his house."

"He could have bombed the hardware store."

"But that would mean someone killed him and continued bombing. Maybe he had a partner and they had a falling-out."

"But why?" Lydia massaged her temples, trying to make sense of what was going on. The Sam Alexander who adopted Calvin had to be wearing a disguise, so he could have been working with the bomber.

"I wish I had an answer to that. Then I would know who was behind all this."

By the time they arrived at the police station, Lydia's head throbbed. Before Kate came home from school she needed to lie down and catch up on the sleep she'd been missing. She wished she could stay in the car while Jesse went inside, but the memory of that feeling of being watched earlier reinforced her fear of being alone.

Lydia lay on the bed at Jesse's house, but no matter how much she wanted and tried to take a nap, she couldn't. It was good to get out for a while today, but she couldn't shake the feeling she was a target with a big, red bull's-eye on her. After listening to Phillip talking with Thomas and Jesse, she'd felt she was missing something. It was inside her mind, locked away, and she couldn't find the key to open it.

Maybe it was the fact she told Jesse she loved him and still everything was unsettled. What had she thought he would do—declare his love back?

She stared at the white ceiling, silence surrounding her. Jesse and Don were in the kitchen the last time she saw them going through the evidence, hoping something would jump out at them. Thomas had come back with the results of the fingerprints on the adoption paper.

No match in the database but Sam Alexander didn't have a record. Thomas had discovered Sam would have had access to the C-4 at his construction job. So it was possible he was tied to the bomber in some way, but sorting through the rubble of his house after the bomb would take a while.

She heard footsteps coming down the hall, and suddenly the door burst open. Kate charged into the room and flounced onto the bed, letting her backpack slip to the floor.

"Did something go wrong at school?" Lydia prepared herself for an onslaught of anger.

"Connor. When I left today, I saw him talking to Mandy and they disappeared down the hallway." Kate twisted toward her. "He gets tired of me telling him I can't do anything. He can't even come over here. You've made it plain he isn't welcome."

Here, it comes. It's all my fault.

Kate chewed on her bottom lip. "I don't think he cares about me as much as he says he does. We had a big fight about me not being able to see him after school. Why would he go with Mandy? I tried calling him. He didn't answer." Tears began streaming down her sister's face.

Lydia sat up and scooted toward Kate. "I'm sorry. If he can't understand why you can't be there right now after school, then maybe he isn't the boy for you."

"He should know. He was here the other day and knows what's happening to you."

"It can be hard to put yourself in another's shoes. Maybe he knows on some level, but doesn't really get it."

Kate pulled out her phone. "All I can say is he better text me. Soon." She knuckled the tears away and rose, heading for the hallway.

There was a part of Lydia that would love to relive her senior year, so she could undo what had gone wrong. But there was a part that was so glad she wasn't a teenager anymore, especially as she saw what Kate was going through.

She reclined back on the bed. Thoughts of Connor and Kate arguing morphed into visions of the dream she'd had about Melinda arguing with her boyfriend. *It was her boyfriend, I remember that now. But why can't I see what he looks like? What did Melinda tell me after they talked?*

Then a faded image materialized in her mind. Shadowy. Down at the end of the hall at the bistro, hand on doorknob. He glanced back at her and she met his— cold, gray eyes. That was all she could see. What did he look like? Why was he leaving the restaurant that way?

She lay there for a while longer, but nothing else appeared—a vague person with gray eyes. Was it the man she ran into as she came into the bistro? If so, why was he in the hallway?

Exasperated, she pushed to a sitting position. She

felt as though she were going crazy. Bits and pieces of information floating around in her mind, but nothing came together into a whole picture. People's lives depended on her remembering.

A dark screen fell over her thoughts and shut everything out.

Frustrated, she stood and decided to find Jesse. She needed a distraction.

As she walked through the living room, Kate sat on the couch talking to Connor. She lowered her voice as Lydia made her way into the kitchen.

Jesse looked up at her and grinned. "Thomas discovered that Sam Alexander had an older man visit him several times in the past month and that Alexander did get a dog but it hasn't been seen in a while."

"Who? How did he find out?" Lydia sat across from Jesse with Don next to her.

"From the neighbor who wasn't home. This morning Thomas was able to talk to the couple before they left for work."

"What did the older man look like?" Lydia hoped this would lead to the bomber.

Jesse's smile grew. "That's the best part. The husband identified him from the sketch of the man with Calvin at the animal hospital, except according to the neighbor, this 'Mr. Jacobs' didn't have a limp and could get around with no problem."

Moving like a younger man. Lydia could see why Jesse was excited. They were getting closer to the bomber and his true identity. "So he called him Mr. Jacobs?"

"No. He didn't know the man's name. Thomas checked with some of the other neighbors and another said they had seen an older man come and go from Alexander's house. This past month or so."

"So do you two think the bomber got his C-4 from Sam?" Lydia looked from Don to Jesse.

"Maybe. Thomas is coming over to fill us in on a couple of other developments." Jesse studied her for a few seconds. "Leads are starting to produce some results."

The doorbell rang, and Don hurried to answer it.

"You okay?" Jesse held her hand. "Mary told Williams when she escorted Kate to the house that she was extremely upset when Mary picked her up at school."

"Boyfriend problems. Connor wants her to spend more time with him."

"Since he's been here already, he could come over after school, on the weekends, if you think that will make things easier."

The more she saw of Connor the more Lydia likened him to Aaron. She prayed her sister didn't do something stupid like she had. When she'd tried to have a conversation with her sister about sex, Kate shut her down. Dad had already given her the talk, and she didn't intend to go through that embarrassing subject again.

Lydia rolled her shoulders to ease the tension setting in. "Frankly, I'm glad he's showing his true colors to Kate. He has a one-track mind, and I know he's been pushing Kate to do things that—"

"That you did when you were a teenager," Kate said from the doorway.

Lydia closed her eyes for a few seconds, then twisted in the chair to look at Kate. "Yes. I know firsthand the mistake it was."

"He called and explained that Mandy's locker was stuck, and he helped her get it open. That was all."

Don and Thomas came up behind Kate, and she stepped out of the entrance, disappearing around the corner into the living room. Probably to call or text Connor again. Lydia heaved a heavy sigh.

Thomas took the chair Don had used while the officer left to check outside. The detective slid the sketch to Lydia. "This is the sketch Nadine gave us of Sam Alexander. It fits the driver's license for that man. He worked in construction. The AFT agent is interviewing his employer about the C-4, but I've got a feeling some is missing."

Lydia's gaze fixed on the young man who was found in a freezer in the bombed rental house. "So you think he supplied the C-4 to the bomber and that guy killed him so he couldn't identify him?"

"They could have been partners for the first bomb and had a falling-out," Thomas said.

Jesse took a look at the sketch. "Or, maybe Alexander blackmailed the bomber after the first bomb went off."

Thomas frowned. "The descriptions of the person we think might be the bomber are different each time. Remember that couple out walking on the street where the church was, not five minutes before the bomb went off? They saw a guy wearing a hoodie, slender build. And on the traffic cam near the hardware store, a person we think was the bomber leaving the scene before the explosion early that morning had a hoodie but a potbelly. Physical body type keeps changing as well as facial features and coloring."

Lydia sat forward. "Hoodie? Like the guy I ran into

as I went into the bistro. We collided as he left and he was wearing a hoodie."

Jesse captured her gaze. "Did he have a potbelly?"

"I'm not sure. I think he was what I would call husky. Did the couple see the color of his eyes? The guy at the bistro had gray ones."

"No, he had on sunglasses even though it was starting to get dark." Thomas huffed. "We have thin, fat, old, young. Gray hair, dark hair."

"If the couple saw the bomber, then why didn't he come after them like he is with me?"

Jesse snapped his fingers. "That's it. You saw the real bomber. The others were disguises—someone who knew how to apply makeup and play a role convincingly."

"Okay, why the bistro?" Flashes of the fractured memories from that day paraded through her mind.

"Not sure. We may not have the bomber on that traffic cam and the couple might not have seen the guy doing this. But the person who brought Calvin in has to be the bomber." Thomas stood. "But in disguise."

"What about Shane Taylor and the black Chevy? What did you find out there? What does he look like?" Jesse rose and went to the coffeepot to refill his mug.

"He was like what the salesman in the appliance store described, and he has an alibi for the first two bombings. He said he was there looking for a washing machine." As Thomas paced in a circle he looked at Lydia. "We're getting close. Hang in there. Well, I've taken a long enough break."

Lydia chuckled. "You call this a break. You're going to need a month's vacation when this is over with."

"Let us know what you find out about the C-4." Jesse walked with Thomas toward the foyer.

Was the gray-eyed stranger she'd bumped into the bomber? And who was the man using the hallway exit?

So many questions and so few answers.

When Jesse returned and sat in the chair next to Lydia, she told him about the faceless person with gray eyes who haunted her. "I can't shake him. But I know the pharmacist has brown eyes. I can't picture who was fighting with Melinda yet, and the guy who left the bistro as I came in had gray eyes. And I'm sure the old man with Calvin had blue eyes. They misted with tears when he wasn't sure Calvin would make it. How reliable are my memories? They seem so disjointed."

"Contact lenses can change a person's eye color." Jesse stroked his hand down her arm, the gesture meant to reassure her.

What would happen when this was over? Lydia didn't want to think about that question. "I forgot to ask if Thomas ever found Phillip Keats. Did he find him?"

"Yes, he showed up at the drugstore around one with some story that he went for a drive to clear his head. At least that's what he told a coworker."

"I guess it's a good thing he's part owner. A lot of bosses would fire someone over that."

"I kind of know what Keats feels like. I would like to clear my head."

"So would I. I keep getting brief images, and I can't tell what's real anymore. If only the bomber knew I have no idea who he is, he would leave me alone."

Jesse pulled her toward him. "You're trying too hard."

"I know you keep telling me that. Then I get a dirty look from Kate because of what's going on and—"

He laid two fingers over her lips. "Shh. Don't tell Thomas, but this evening let's not think about the bomber or the bombings. A deal?"

"Sounds wonderful. Although I'm not sure I'll be able to do it."

"Tell you what. My SUV is ready. After dinner you can drive me to get it, then I'll follow you back here and we can go for a ride. Just you and me."

"I don't think—"

"You're thinking too hard. I'm thinking too hard. I believe it'll help us. Let's go to Point Woronzof and see the sun set. Okay?"

"I haven't been there since we were teenagers."

"Then it's a date."

A date? Casually said, but it sparked memories. And here she was, still in love with Jesse. How was she going to deal with real life when the bomber was caught?

Leaving the parking lot at Point Woronzof, Jesse held Brutus's leash in one hand and Lydia's in the other as they made their way carefully down the hillside to the small-pebbled beach. Glacial silt tinted the waves gray as they washed up onto shore.

Lydia stopped and turned in a full circle. "I'd forgotten how beautiful this view of Cook Inlet and Mount Susitna are."

"I've seen some glorious sunsets from here."

"Yeah, I remember."

As the sun started disappearing behind the mountain line across the inlet, Jesse recalled the first time he'd known he was in love with Lydia. It was the summer before their senior year in high school. They had a picnic dinner at this point and waited for the sun to go down. He'd wanted to tell her how he felt. He could never get the words out and didn't until they reconnected after she'd dated Aaron. At the time, he didn't realize it wouldn't make any difference. She eloped with Aaron not long after. Why did he suggest bringing her here?

Because while they were here, the world hadn't intruded and a feeling of peace pervaded, at least for a short time. They needed that right now, especially in the midst of all that was happening in Anchorage.

"Look. Do you see the whale?" Excitement flowed from Lydia as she moved closer to the water. "Seeing one never ceases to make me smile. They're so beautiful. The Lord has created a whole bunch of unique and fascinating animals."

He pointed to a bald eagle flying above. "Like that one. Majestic."

The joy in her expression spread through him as though it were contagious and for a moment it erased the tragedy and pain in their past and replaced it with the hope only the Lord could give them.

Jesse unhooked Brutus's leash and gave him the signal to play. His dog sniffed his surroundings, exploring a piece of driftwood on the beach.

Then as if to confirm Jesse's thoughts, the sky deepened to a rich orange golden color as the sun dropped behind the mountains. The peace he sought descended while the ravens performed their aerial tricks.

Jesse slipped his arms around Lydia and pulled her back against him. He rested his chin on the top of her head, smelling the apple scent in her shampoo. A memory from his childhood wound its way through his thoughts, bringing a smile to his lips. His mother had pulled an apple pie out of the oven and put it on a cold burner to cool. The aroma from the pie had filled the whole house. He'd started to pinch off a piece of the hot pie. His mom had quickly pulled him back and warned him of the hot plate, but she'd wrapped her arms around him, much as he now held Lydia, and hugged him.

Lydia twisted toward him and locked gazes with him. "Why are you sad?"

He hadn't realized that his expression revealed his sadness. The older he became, the dimmer his thoughts of his childhood with his parents became. He wanted to keep them close always. "The scent of your hair reminded me of my mother when she used to bake us an apple pie. I loved them. Now I can't eat a piece."

"Because the smell brings back the thoughts of losing her?"

He nodded. Since Lydia had come back into his life, he'd done way too much thinking about his past.

Lydia brushed back a wayward strand of hair caught in the brisk breeze. "My mother didn't die. She left us, but I kept wondering for years what did I do to make her go away."

"And?"

"Finally my dad sat me down and explained I didn't do anything wrong. She hated Alaska. Didn't want to be a wife and mother. For a while after that I was so angry with her for leaving. Then again Dad asked me why I was so angry. I told him, and he said to me as long as I hold on to the anger I'll never be totally free to enjoy life. I needed to forgive my mother."

"Did you?"

"Yes. I have no idea where she is, but our family never moved. If she wanted to get hold of Kate and me, she knows where we are. Are you angry at your parents for dying?"

His arms slid away from her, and he stepped back. He wanted to say, no. But he couldn't. "My mother went looking for my dad. Why didn't she wait until the search was organized? She went out alone. She knew better." He glanced to the colors in the sky morphing into a darker orange-red. "So, yes, I guess I have been. She left me with a neighbor and never looked back. That was the last time I saw her."

"You know we both dealt with loss at a young age. Yours was more life changing than mine, but I still feel like I can relate to what you went through."

She was right. Instead of pulling away from her, he should be drawing closer. She knew what he'd gone through. What was stopping him? He took a step toward her.

The loud sound of a large jet flying over them disrupted the moment.

He glanced around at the dusk beginning to settle over the area. "I guess life intrudes. We better head back. It's getting dark."

She remained still, clasping his hand. "I know what you went through as a child. Remember that." Then she gave him a peck on his cheek before starting for the parking lot.

He called Brutus and hooked his leash, then trailed after Lydia, unable to forget her words just now and her dad's advice about letting the anger go. He'd never told anyone he'd been mad at his mother for going out and looking for his dad alone. Lydia was entangling her life into his again, and the thought scared him.

Later that night another dream awakened Lydia, her face drenched in sweat. She knew what happened between Melinda and her boyfriend, Todd, at the bistro. She glanced at Kate sleeping and knew she wasn't going back to sleep for a while. She pulled on some comfortable clothes and crept from the bedroom to seek whoever was on guard. She didn't think she would forget the dream, but she didn't want to take a chance.

In the living room Jesse held a mug, probably with coffee in it, and peeked out the side of the blackout blinds. He looked toward her while Brutus remained asleep on the couch.

She chuckled. "He must not be too concerned about me being up."

"He's been working hard lately. Why are you up? Something wrong?"

"No, but I remembered something from the bistro."

Jesse turned from the window and closed the space between them. "What?"

"I remember the man Melinda was arguing with. It was for sure her boyfriend. They'd been dating for a month. She was at the end of the counter with him. When he stormed away from her, Melinda had an angry expression on her face." Relief washed over Lydia now that she'd told another person.

"Where did he go?"

"I don't know. He walked past my table, but I was trying not to stare."

"What did he look like? Can you give our sketch artist a description? Do you know his last name?"

"He had a black ball cap on with jeans and a blue T-shirt. Brown hair and gray eyes. He went right by me. I'd seen him one other time in the bistro a week before."

"Do you remember anything on the cap? A logo? Something that might help us ID him?"

She shook her head. "No, I was focused on his furious look. I can give a description of him for a sketch. Melinda only referred to him as Todd. A few days earlier when I picked up some food for everyone at work, Melinda had just gotten off the phone with him. I tried to comfort her. They must have been having some problems." Lydia thought back to that day. "The only thing she said was that maybe having a boyfriend wasn't all that it was cracked up to be. She didn't say anything else. The part I'm excited about is he had gray eyes. I keep seeing gray eyes. That's got to mean something." At least she prayed it did.

"Yes. We'll dig into Melinda's personal life and see if we can discover who this boyfriend is."

"I remember two guys with gray eyes. Maybe it was one of them."

"We don't know a lot about the man you ran into when you came in. We know he got into a truck but mud covered the license plate. We have a couple of people searching the traffic cams around town to see if they can catch it." His thumb caressed her face under her eye. "You need to go back to sleep."

"Do I look that bad?"

"On the contrary. You look great, but our lives aren't ours right now. Not until this bomber is found."

She smiled, the reassurance in his touch comforting her. This situation would come to an end, and she would get her life back. "The worst part is, I'm bored. I'm not even at my own house where I could at least clean and organize things."

"Go right ahead. Feel free to do that here."

She laughed. "That's okay. Although I am thinking of cooking a special dinner tomorrow. How about my made-from-scratch meatballs and spaghetti? It was my grandmother's recipe. No sauce out of a bottle. I won't go as far as she did and make my own spaghetti."

"You're making me hungry at two o'clock in the morning. If you need me to pick up any ingredients, just make me a list and I can get them before I start working on the case."

"Is there a chance I can come with you? You know that boredom thing."

Their easy bantering ended as he firmed his mouth and stiffened. "No. Remember what happened at Sam Alexander's house."

"But—"

"End of discussion."

"I got to go to the shelters with you."

"That's because Calvin knows you and responds to you better than me. I'm not taking you to a grocery store where you could be an easy target."

"I could argue the point—" he opened his mouth to say something, and she hurried to finish "—but I'm not going to. I don't want to distract you from your job." She spun on her heel and headed for her bedroom to the sounds of his chuckles.

* * *

While Don and Mary played a game of checkers at the kitchen table, Lydia finished up her homemade spaghetti sauce before she turned to making the meatballs. She would brown them and add them to the sauce. She'd already beat both officers and declared herself the checkers champion. Now they were deciding the runner-up.

Her cell phone rang. She glanced at the screen. Jesse. She quickly wiped her hands off and answered it. "Tell me you've solved the case," she said as she walked into the living room for some privacy.

"I wish I could. I did find out Todd's last name, and I'm heading to his apartment right now."

Her grasp on the phone tightened. "Be careful. He has a temper and could be the bomber."

"I'll have backup. Thomas is working on a lead on the guy you ran into as you entered the bistro. One of the traffic cams found him turning into a housing development. So this is all good news. If they have to, they will go door-to-door to find the truck. They already checked on black trucks of that make and no license plates had addresses in the subdivision, but that doesn't mean he isn't there or working there."

"I love your optimism. Come home hungry. I've made a ton of spaghetti sauce and asked Don and Mary to dinner. They both said yes. I hope we have something to celebrate tonight."

"So do I, but unless one of them confesses, it will take a lot of police work to get the evidence to convict the bomber."

When she hung up, she stood to the side of the picture window and peeked outside between the blind slats. She didn't want to scan the street blatantly and make herself a target, but she probably did this several times an hour. Would she ever stop looking over her shoulder?

She started for the kitchen when her phone rang again. This time it was the school. She hurried and answered it. Kate had been so upset when she went to class this morning.

"Dr. McKenzie, this is Kate's principal."

She hoped her sister didn't get into a fight. "Yes?"

"Kate didn't go to her class after lunch. We've looked everywhere in the building but can't find her."

"Someone kidnapped her?" Hysteria wormed its way through her.

"All outside doors are locked. You have to use the main entrance, and it's monitored so I don't see how that could have happened."

"I'm coming up there, and I'm calling the police." Lydia hit the end button.

Her hands trembled as she punched in Jesse's number and waited for what seemed like an eternity for him to answer. Before he could say hello, Lydia said, "Kate is missing at school. I'm going up there."

"No. Stay with Williams and Collins. I'll take care of finding her and figure out what happened. You said she was upset this morning. Could she be hiding?"

"I don't know what my sister is thinking anymore. The school is locked down and the principal is sure someone didn't come in and take her but..."

"Lydia, I'll handle this. Let the officers know and have them be extra vigilant."

"Okay." But when she finished talking with Jesse, she sank down on a chair nearby, the trembling spreading through her whole body. She didn't know if she could even walk into the kitchen.

This whole mess had been hard enough for *her*, let alone a teenage girl. Maybe she should take Kate to Oklahoma until they found the bomber. She could probably leave without the man finding—

The phone ringing again disrupted her thoughts. She quickly answered, thinking it was Jesse. "Did you hear something?"

"I heard your sister was kidnapped and the bomber has her," a chilling voice said, followed by hideous laughter.

THIRTEEN

Numb, Lydia nearly dropped her phone. "Who is this?"

The same laughter she heard right before the bomb went off assaulted her ears. "You know who this is, and I have your sister. Have you told the police who I am?"

"No, because I don't know."

"Maybe not now. You'll figure it out eventually. I can't have that. I'll let your sister go if you take her place. She hasn't seen my face, but you have. If I see any police around when we make the trade, I'll blow her up. You hold her life in your hands."

"Where do I go?" Lydia asked, a knot jamming her throat.

He gave her a location of a warehouse. "It's abandoned, and I'll know if you tell the police."

Had he bugged Jesse's house like hers? She scanned the living room, feeling as though she was being watched this very second. "I need to talk to Kate."

"Such a demanding person. Remember it's easy for me to set off a bomb. I've done four so far."

Another blast of repulsive laughter petrified her.

She couldn't string two words together. She swallowed hard, trying to push the fear down so she could do this.

"Don't make me do a fifth one. When you get to the warehouse, I'll give you a call for further instruction. Here's your sister."

"Lydia, I'm so sorry."

She didn't have to see her sister to know that tears were streaking down her face. "You're going to be all right."

"Please—"

"That's all. You don't have much time. Be here in an hour. Don't let your bodyguards know anything. I know you have two sitting with you right now."

He *had* bugged the house! No, probably just watching it. "I'll be there."

"Don't even think about telling your boyfriend. I can be vindictive if you cross me." The bomber hung up.

The cell phone slipped from her hand and fell onto her lap.

She looked around frantically. She couldn't let her sister die because of her. The man was after her, not Kate. *Lord, what do I do? How do I get out without Don and Mary knowing?*

"Lydia, do you want to play another checkers game? I beat Don," Mary said from the kitchen, her voice sounding as if she was walking toward the living room.

Lydia moved quickly, snatching up her phone and sticking it into her jeans pocket as she stood. She schooled her face into a mask of calm while inside she shook from head to toe.

"Your spaghetti sauce smells wonderful," Mary said as she came into the living room.

Turned away from the officer, she inhaled a deep breath, then swung around. "Thanks. I was telling Jesse you two are staying for dinner tonight. I'm going to let the sauce simmer for an hour while I lie down. Getting up in the middle of the night is wreaking havoc on my sleeping schedule."

"I know what you mean. Do you want me to wake you up in an hour?"

"Yes. Please." Because by then she planned to be at the warehouse.

Once her sister was let go, she intended to fight for her life.

"Thanks." Lydia walked out of the room at a normal pace. When she was out of sight, she disabled the house's alarm system and rushed down the hallway to her bedroom.

After calling for a cab to meet her at the corner, she stuck her car keys into her pocket with some money, then went to her medical bag and prepared a syringe with a heavy-duty tranquilizer that she hoped to use on the bomber. She should be able to conceal it in her long-sleeve T-shirt. She would save her sister and not go down easily.

Please, Lord, let this work.

She hurriedly scribbled a note to Jesse about what was happening and left it for Mary to find. She couldn't risk saying anything before her sister was freed, but by the time Mary found the note, Kate should be safe.

She moved to the window on the side of the house, unlocked it and raised it up. The screen popped out with a little encouragement from her, and she lowered herself to the ground. Without looking back, she ran for the end of the street and prayed the cab would be there soon. When she reached the corner, it wasn't. She paced, checking her watch every moment. Finally after five minutes passed, she pulled her phone from her pocket to call the cab company. She punched in the first three numbers when she spied a taxi coming toward her.

She chewed on her thumbnail while she watched it approach. Once the driver took her to her house, she would take her dad's car, which was stored in the garage.

The cab stopped a few feet from her. "Did you call for a taxi?"

"Yes." She climbed into the back and gave him her address. "I'll double the fare if you'll get there as fast as possible."

When she arrived at her place, she paid the driver, raced into the house and found the keys to the Buick. In the garage, she turned her key. A grinding noise filled the air. It hadn't been driven in weeks, she suddenly realized. The car wouldn't start. What now?

Several K-9 teams were scouring the high school after the dogs sniffed a sweater in Kate's locker as well as her backpack. Jesse covered the area from the girl's last class before lunch. Brutus trailed her scent to a side door. He went outside and followed his dog to the parking lot. He stopped at an empty space.

She left and got into a car? Forcibly? Or on her own?

He hurried back into the building and strode to the principal's office. He'd met the man when he first came fifteen minutes ago. "Mr. Carver, are students allowed to go off campus to eat lunch?"

"No. That would be a security nightmare."

"I traced Kate to the parking lot from her last class. She went out a side door. I need to know whose car she got into."

"We have monitors on the parking lot. I can pull up the video feed and see if it caught anything."

Five minutes later, Jesse discovered that Kate had gone with Connor off campus and neither one had returned. "I need to talk to some of Kate's and Connor's closest friends. Maybe they know what the pair were doing."

When Jesse interviewed a couple of Kate's friends, no one knew where she'd gone today, although the day before they'd snuck off campus and eaten at Bud's Hamburger Joint. Jesse sent an officer to check in case they went back to the same place.

The next student Jesse talked to was one of Connor's buddies. Quinn came into the principal's office with a closed look on his face.

"Quinn, we discovered that both Kate and Connor are missing from their classes after lunch. I know they left campus. I need to know where they went."

Quinn dropped his gaze to the table. "Don't know."

"You may not be aware, but Kate is being protected by the police because her sister is a witness in the third bombing. I'm concerned something has happened to both of them, so if you know anything you might be saving their lives if you tell me."

The teenager looked at Jesse. "Connor doesn't live far from here. He took her to his house. They probably lost track of time. I was at the door to let them back in, but they didn't show up. I figure they decided to cut this afternoon."

Jesse stood. "Thank you. We'll check it out. What is Connor's address?"

Quinn wrote it on a piece of paper. "They'll be okay, right?"

"I hope so." But he didn't have a good feeling about this.

After getting Connor's address, Jesse left the others to continue searching the high school. He thought about calling Lydia to let her know where Kate went but decided he would wait until he had Kate under his protection. He tried not to think of why the two went to Connor's house. Lydia already had enough problems. This would add to them.

When he pulled into the driveway behind Connor's car, he and Brutus approached the house. He'd get Kate and take her to Lydia. He figured she would want to see her with her own eyes. He would have a few words to say to the boy later.

He rang the doorbell, and when no one came to the door, he peered into the front window. He tried the door. Locked. The car was still there so they had to be inside. He strode around the house, looking into every window he could. From a back window he saw Connor on the floor, not moving. There was no sign of Kate.

In her haste, Lydia had flooded the engine. After sitting for a while, the car started and she backed out of her garage, praying she still had time to save Kate.

As Lydia drove toward the warehouse, the bomber called again. He told her to toss her cell phone out the window. At the warehouse there would be a phone that couldn't be traced. She had no intention of doing that. She could be tracked with the signal.

Her phone rang again. She didn't answer it. After a second call, she received a text from the bomber and pulled over to the curb. I know you haven't done what I said. Throw it out now or your sister dies.

He must be following her. She scanned her surrounding but couldn't tell where he might be. A few cars passed her. Was he in one of them? She had no choice. She flung the cell out the window and continued her journey to the warehouse.

Lydia approached her destination and drove around back. After parking where he had told her to, she looked for the cell and found it, then sat in her car to wait.

Five minutes passed before the cell phone rang. She snatched it from her lap and said, "Where do I go now?"

"Drive down to the warehouse at the end of the row. Then I'll let you know."

She followed his directions and again waited. This time it was ten minutes before she received another call.

"Go to the back door of the warehouse on the left. It'll be unlocked. Go inside and wait."

As she headed for the building, she wondered if it was another stall tactic. Would she be sent somewhere else? If only she could remember who the bomber was and why he wanted her dead. The two cooks who survived in the bistro kitchen hadn't been targeted. She had seen him in the dining room. But who?

Then a vision of the gray eyes filled her mind, but this time the face became clearer. It wasn't gray eyes she saw but reflective sunglasses he put on right before he went out the bistro's exit door at the end of the hallway to the restrooms.

Her hand shook as she opened the door to the abandoned building. Inside, she paced in a circle, afraid to go too far into the cavernous area. She looked into the dim shadows surrounding her. Was he here now—watching her? Her heartbeat raced so fast she felt light-headed. She inhaled deeply, then exhaled to calm herself as much as possible.

The man leaving the bistro wearing the sunglasses had glanced back when she went into the bathroom and she'd looked right at him for three seconds. Then he'd hurriedly left.

A movement to the right in the warehouse caught Lydia's attention. A man stepped out of the darkness. She gasped. "It's you."

After calling Thomas, Jesse picked the lock on the front door, then entered with gun drawn and Brutus off his leash, sniffing as he went. Jesse checked each room while he worked his way back to where the teenager was. He wouldn't put it past the bomber to have a repeat of what happened at Sam Alexander's place. When Sam's body was found in a freezer, it was determined he'd been dead for weeks. Jesse prayed that Connor wasn't dead and there wasn't a bomb ready to explode. He had to find Kate for Lydia.

When Jesse went into the teenager's bedroom, he hurried toward the boy while Brutus searched the area. He checked for a pulse and found one. As he called for an ambulance, he surveyed Connor, whose legs and hands were tied behind his back, to see the extent of his injuries. All he found was a head wound with matted blood around it. More had pooled on the floor. He untied Connor.

While waiting for the ambulance and Thomas, he scanned the room as Brutus went from one object to the next, sniffing. If the bomber was the one who did this, at least he left the teenager alive, but he must have taken Kate. They would have to assume that was the case and start canvassing the street for any information. They could look at traffic cams, but they needed an idea of what kind of vehicle the bomber drove. And they needed to know fast.

Connor stirred on the floor, his eyes blinking open. Obviously disoriented, he stared at Jesse for a moment, tried to move and groaned.

"An ambulance is on its way. I wouldn't move. You were hit on the head. Do you remember what happened?"

Connor tried to sit up and collapsed back against the floor. Jesse caught him before he hit his head. "Where's Kate?"

"He must…" Connor's hoarse voice gave out.

"She's not here. Who is he?" Jesse kept his voice calm as panic descended over Connor's features, his eyes rounding as he tried to get up again and could barely lift his head. Jesse held him still.

"Did he…" Connor opened his mouth, but no words came out for a few seconds then he continued, "… take her?"

"Kate is missing. Who is *he*?"

"He burst in here as we…" Connor averted his gaze.

"If Kate has been kidnapped, we need to know everything now. Time is of the essence."

"He moved so fast." Connor paused for a few seconds, closing his eyes.

Jesse thought he might have lost consciousness again.

But Connor continued. "He had a bat…he knocked me out."

"So you don't know who tied you up?"

"No." Connor opened his eyes.

"What did he look like?" Jesse asked as the sound of sirens grew louder.

"Wore a ski mask."

"Do you remember anything about him?"

"About my size." Connor sucked in a breath. "I heard Kate scream… He took her?"

"I'm assuming he did. She isn't here."

"Is he the bomber?"

"I think so. Anything you can tell me would be great."

Connor's eyes slid closed again. The teen might not be much help at this time, but maybe the house could tell him something.

As the paramedics came down the hall, Connor's eyes popped open. "He wore black. Even black gloves."

Thomas followed the paramedics into the bedroom. Jesse stood and made his way to him. "All he could tell me was the man was about his size and wore black. He had on a ski mask and used gloves so I doubt there are prints."

"Do you know how he got in?"

"I think he picked one of the locks on an outside door. That's how I got into the house when I saw the kid on his floor."

"Brutus checked for a bomb?"

"First thing. None of us, including my dog, wants a repeat of the other day. My body is still healing."

"I think the best use of our manpower right now is to go house to house and see if anyone saw something. Have you called Lydia?"

"I was going to after you all came."

"Not a call you want to make?" Thomas's mouth twisted in a frown.

"No. She's going to blame herself. This wouldn't have happened if Kate hadn't left school. But in Lydia's mind it will become her fault *her* sister is in danger. I'll also call Connor's parents. I'll get the contact information from school."

"Tell her it's the bomber's fault." Thomas left to organize a door-to-door canvas of the neighbors at home.

The first task Jesse did was to inform Connor's parents about what happened at their house and where their son was being taken. Finally he had no choice but to call Lydia. If he wasn't needed here to help find Kate, he'd rather tell her in person, but that wasn't an option. He let her phone ring until it went to voice mail. She hadn't slept well last night. She must be taking a nap.

He gave Williams a call, and the officer answered on the second ring. "Is Lydia asleep?"

"Yeah."

"How long?"

"An hour. Mary was about to wake her up."

"We haven't found Kate, but we know some of what happened. I need to tell her."

"Kate is missing?"

Jesse gripped his cell phone tighter. "She called me

about Kate being gone when the school called her. She was supposed to tell you."

"She didn't say anything to me or Mary."

Why didn't Lydia tell the officers guarding her? His gut knotted. Something was wrong. "Kate went to her boyfriend's house at lunch. It seems yesterday and today they sneaked off campus. The doors are locked to prevent people from coming into the building but not going out. I found Connor knocked out and Kate gone. A man in black came in and took her. As much as I hate it, you need to wake Lydia up."

"I'm making my way to her bedroom now."

Jesse heard Williams knock on the door. There was a long pause, then another knock, louder this time.

"She's not answering. I'm going inside," Williams said as Jesse heard a slight creaking sound as he opened the door. "The window is open. She's gone."

Jesse went cold. "I'm on my way. Check the whole house and let me know what you find."

"Where's Kate?" Lydia stared at the bomber dressed in black, not ten feet from her.

"Somewhere safe and alive."

"And why should I believe you?"

"Because you don't have a choice, if you want your sister to live. I have no issue with Kate, but I do with you. I know you were remembering. I could tell by the direction of the police investigation, but mostly from the bug I placed in Calvin's dog collar. I didn't think you were going to take him home with you. That was a bonus. I just hoped to get some info when the police realized the bomber brought the animal in."

"Calvin could have died."

He shrugged. "You could ID me. I took care of the waitress who served me. If you'd died like you were supposed to, I'd have stopped. Now I'll have to set off another bomb just to throw the police off. They need to think it's a lunatic who is doing this."

He was a lunatic. Anyone who did what he had done wasn't in his right mind. "Why are you setting off bombs?"

"Because I had to kill my girlfriend. She purposely got pregnant with my child. She actually thought I would leave my wife. She's coming into a lot of money soon when her father's estate is finally settled. I've stayed married to her for years. I'm not walking away from all that wealth now."

What a sicko! Lydia pressed the arm with the syringe against her side. Somehow if her plan was to work, she had to get close to him. Once she tranquilized him, she could tie him up with the rope she brought from her house and call the police. Then he wouldn't be able to set off any more bombs, and she and Kate would be safe.

"So you killed all those people to cover up one death." She couldn't keep the contempt from her voice.

He ignored her statement and said, "Toss the phone to me."

She did as instructed but hit him in the chest hard, then whirled around and ran for the door. She wanted him to come after her, but she had to make it look like she was genuinely fleeing. As she raced toward the exit, she lowered the syringe so one end was cupped in her palm. Then she stumbled on purpose and went down, using the commotion to free the shot completely.

He grabbed her and jerked her to her feet. "Stupid woman. If you escape, I'll just have to kill your sister."

Before he had a chance to push her forward, she lunged at him and stabbed the needle into his upper arm. He backhanded her, sending her flying into the door. When she struck it, all the air whooshed from her lungs.

He took a step toward her. She'd given him enough tranquilizer to put a horse down. He kept coming toward her, but he weaved from side to side.

It had to work.

He stopped in front of her, his eyelids sliding closed. As she fumbled for the door handle, he put his hands around her neck and squeezed.

As Jesse drove toward his house with Brutus, he put a call in to headquarters to track her cell phone.

He was turning into his driveway when he received a call about the location of the phone. He ran to his house to get the two officers and grab something with Lydia's scent on it. Then he headed toward the location he'd been given. The signal was stationary. He tried to think what was in that location. Not a house—it wasn't residential. A building?

He reached the short street and pulled over to the curb. A vacant lot stood where the cell signal was emanating. Not a good sign. "We need to find the phone. Maybe there's something on it that can help us."

Jesse let Brutus out of the rear of the SUV and let him smell the sweater. "Find."

When his K-9 sat and looked at him, Jesse hurried over. The cell phone was hidden in the tall weeds. He put on a pair of gloves and looked at the calls she'd received recently. When he read the text message, he figured the phone would be a dead end, but he called headquarters to see if the number of the person who called her last could be traced. While he waited, he surveyed the street. Not the best part of town.

After he received the call informing him the cell couldn't be traced, he turned to the two patrol officers. "We need to check around here to see if anyone saw her."

But as each minute ticked by, Jesse couldn't forget the words, "Throw it out now or your sister dies."

In that moment he realized he might lose the woman he loved.

Before Lydia had a chance to knee the pharmacist, his hands slipped from around her neck as he swayed on his feet, then crumbled to the concrete floor. She shoved him to the side, opened the door and ran to her car for the rope. When she came back to the warehouse, she retrieved his cell phone and called Jesse.

"Jesse, this is Lydia."

"Are you okay? Where are you?"

She gave him the address and told him which warehouse she was in. "I'm tying up Phillip Keats. Hurry. He has Kate somewhere. We have to make him tell us where."

"I'm not far away. I'm heading there now. Stay on the phone."

"First I'm putting it down to tie him up."

After she secured the bomber, she picked up the phone and stood. "This guy isn't going anywhere. He'll be out for a while. I'm searching for Kate."

"Wait. I'm pulling up behind the row of warehouses.

Brutus is with me, and I have something from school with Kate's scent."

Lydia moved toward the opened door, went outside and waved at Jesse. "I'm so glad to see you."

Jesse parked, said something to Williams, then rushed toward her. He scooped her up in his arms and hugged her. "I love you. I can't lose you again."

"I love you, Jesse." She gave him a quick kiss. "That hasn't changed in all these years. But right now I have to find Kate. She's here because of me." She stepped away and saw Don bringing Brutus with Kate's backpack. Mary was behind them.

"We will find her and then we'll need to talk about why in the world you came to meet him alone and without letting us know."

"I left a message on my nightstand."

Jesse looked at Williams.

He shrugged. "I didn't see it, but the window was open and the wind was blowing into the room. It's probably on the floor by the bed or under it."

"I only told you the general location because that's all I knew, but I think he was following me so I had to come alone. Oh, and he had put a bug in Calvin's collar so he knew what was going on."

"How did you knock him out?" Mary asked as she examined the pharmacist while Don handed Jesse a flashlight.

"I gave him a tranquilizer. That's one of the perks of being a vet. I had some lying around my house."

Jesse held the backpack up for Brutus to smell. "Find." He gave his Rottweiler a long leash and he and Lydia followed. He yelled back to the officers, "Call this in and guard him."

Brutus headed for a rickety staircase and started up. Her heartbeat thundering in her head, Lydia held the light on the area in front of the dog. He entered a room, and she prayed Kate was alive and unharmed.

Jesse went in first and came to a stop. He called Brutus to his side. Lydia peered around Jesse to see her sister tied up with duct tape, some of it over her mouth. Her wide eyes, full of fear, were all Lydia could focus on.

Until Jesse said, "She has a bomb strapped to her."

FOURTEEN

Jesse handed Lydia the leash. "Leave with Brutus. I'll stay but everyone else needs to get out." He glanced at her. "No argument, Lydia. I have experience disarming bombs, but I can't be distracted with you being here. Go. Now."

"I can't leave you."

"Now. If there's a timer on it, I'm wasting valuable seconds."

Kate nodded as though indicating there was a timer. Lydia pulled Brutus toward her, took one last look at Jesse and Kate, then hurried down the stairs.

Jesse realized how much he had to live for. *Lord, we're in Your hands. Please keep us alive.*

Remembering how he triggered the bomb in the house, Jesse approached Kate sitting in a chair with duct tape securing her along with the bomb. He saw the timer. In red numbers, it indicated he had four minutes, twenty-three seconds to get her out of the chair and out of the building. Or to disarm it.

With his pulse racing, he squatted next to Kate and studied the bomb, similar to one he'd handled before.

"We're going to be all right. I'm not letting anything happen to you. Lydia would never forgive me."

He dug into his pocket and removed his Swiss Army Knife. Then holding his breath, he cut the wire he thought would stop the timer. It did at two minutes, forty-one seconds.

After swiping the sweat from his brow, he removed the tape over Kate's mouth first.

Sirens blasted the air as Lydia stood at the end of the row of warehouses. She kept repeating her prayer to bring Jesse and Kate out alive.

Then she spied Jesse and Kate emerging from the building, and she raced toward them as the first responders arrived. Williams had called the bomb squad, and they were in the lead.

She threw her arms around Kate and held her tight. She pulled back, tears running down her face, the biggest smile on her face. "You are grounded for the rest of your life."

Her sister's eyes watered, and she hugged Lydia and sobbed. She stroked Kate's back, telling her she would be all right. Lydia's gaze connected with Jesse's, and she wanted to kiss him senseless.

On the drive home from visiting Connor at the hospital, Lydia looked at her sister while stopped at a red light. "We need to talk about what has been happening. You could have died."

"I'm so sorry, Lydia. I honestly didn't think anyone would be after me or watching me like that."

"How many times have you sneaked out of school?"

Kate lowered her head and twisted her hands together in her lap. "Four times." Her gaze reconnected with Lydia's. "But that was the first time we went to his house. I wasn't going to let anything happen. I was..." Tears glistened in her eyes. "He wanted to show me his room. We were gonna be back at school by our next class. That's only half an hour."

"As you can see a lot can happen in half an hour."

"He'd been so mad we hadn't spent any time alone together in a while. I was trying to please..." Kate sucked in a deep breath, tears streaking down her face. "I was an idiot."

The light turned green, and Lydia crossed the intersection, not far from Jesse's house. "I hope you never make the mistake I did. I paid dearly for it. I know sex doesn't seem like a big deal to some, but there can be big consequences."

Kate remained quiet for a few minutes, but when Lydia pulled into Jesse's garage, her sister asked, "Can I ask you a question?"

"Sure."

"Do you think you lost your daughter because of what you did?"

"I can't answer that. She contracted a virus and died in my womb. That can happen to anyone. I do know that I lost Jesse because of what I did. I loved him—still do—but I did the 'right' thing and married Aaron. That was such a mistake, and for a long time I was mad at God. But I've come to realize in this last year I'm a stronger person, and my faith is deeper now because of what I went through."

"Did Mom leave because of me?"

Lydia twisted toward her and took her hands. "No. She left because of her. She didn't want her life. It really had nothing to do with us. It's taken me a long time to realize that, too. We were abandoned, but our father did the best he could."

Kate's eyes grew round. "You can say that even after what he did to you?"

"Yes. I know he forgave me when he left me his practice and guardianship of you. Our dad was never a man of many words. He kept things inside." *So much like Jesse.* "But that action spoke volumes to me."

"Even though I've been a pain."

Lydia pulled her sister to her and hugged her. "You are my sister. I love you."

After a long afternoon and evening wrapping up the case, Jesse was glad to be home and to see Lydia. She'd wondered why Keats had gone to such lengths to cover up his mistress's death, and right before he left the station, Thomas had discovered Keats had a major gambling debt. He was using his wife's inheritance as a way to buy him some time with the collectors.

Jesse came into the kitchen from the garage and saw the two pieces of luggage sitting near the door. He could have lost Lydia today forever. He had no intentions of letting her go again.

He strolled into his living room. Lydia and Kate sat side by side on the couch, talking, smiling. Lydia glanced at him and whispered something to her sister.

Kate chuckled. "I'll be out back with Calvin, Mitch and Brutus. I want to say goodbye to them."

After she left, Jesse took her place on the couch. "Okay, what did you say to her?"

"We had a long talk together. I think we finally understand each other."

"No, I mean just now."

"I told her I was going to make sure you understand how important you are in my life."

One of his eyebrows lifted. "Oh, you are. Just how important am I?"

"This much." She held her arms out as far as she could. "I love you—always have, and I'm going to prove it to you."

His fingers delved into her hair, and he held her head still. "You don't have to prove a thing. I know you love me. I love you—always have."

His lips touched hers softly at first, then settled over her mouth as the kiss lengthened. He wrapped his arms around her and pressed her against him.

When he leaned back slightly, he gazed at her for a long moment. "I've always been so afraid to lose someone else important to me that I shut myself off from others. I promise not to, and if I do, let me know. I won't change overnight, but I want you to be with me for all the changes. Will you marry me?"

She cupped his face. "I've been waiting for those words for years. Yes. And soon."

He kissed her long and hard. "As soon as we can. I'm not waiting any longer." He'd finally found the family he'd been searching for.

* * * * *

Carol J. Post writes fun and fast-paced inspirational romantic suspense stories and lives in sunshiny central Florida. She sings and plays the piano for her church and also enjoys sailing, hiking and camping—almost anything outdoors. Her daughters and grandkids live too far away for her liking, so she now pours all that nurturing into taking care of two fat and sassy cats and one highly spoiled dachshund.

Books by Carol J. Post

Love Inspired Suspense

Midnight Shadows
Motive for Murder
Out for Justice
Shattered Haven
Hidden Identity
Mistletoe Justice
Buried Memories
Reunited by Danger
Fatal Recall
Lethal Legacy
Bodyguard for Christmas

BURIED MEMORIES

Carol J. Post

He heals the brokenhearted
and binds up their wounds.
—*Psalms* 147:3

Acknowledgments

A huge thank-you to my friend Chaplain (Major) Andrew Ropp, US Army (retired). I appreciate your willingness to share your experiences. Your help on this project has been invaluable.

Thank you to my critique partners, Karen Fleming and Sabrina Jarema. Your sharp eyes and creative minds always make my writing better.

Thank you to my editor, Giselle Regus, and my agent, Nalini Akolekar. I'm thrilled to be working with both of you.

And thank you to my husband, Chris. I might be able to do this without your love and support… but I wouldn't want to.

ONE

Nicki Jackson wheeled her bulging carry-on through the carport, the rumble of the plastic wheels against the concrete breaking the silence of the dark night. The golden retriever prancing behind her had enough energy for both of them. Of course, the dog hadn't spent the past eight hours trapped in the car, battling traffic.

Nicki sighed. The last of her single friends was now married. But at less than a year from thirty, what did she expect? In fact, she'd almost made it to the altar herself. Instead, she was free and single, and her former intended was facing a hefty jail term.

She hesitated in the glow of the Ram's headlights to finger through her keys, then dragged her bag the final few feet to the kitchen door. Bed was only a few minutes away. Unpacking could wait till morning. So could a shower.

She raised the key and stopped short. The door wasn't shut tightly, and the jamb was chipped and scratched.

The headlights clicked off automatically, casting her in darkness, and the hair rose on the back of her neck. Someone had broken in to her house. Heart pounding in her chest, she pulled her phone from her purse and dialed 911.

"Come, Callie." With a small tug on the leash, she moved to the truck and opened the door. The dog stared at her, a question in her big brown eyes. After a moment's hesitation, she jumped onto the seat, and Nicki slid in after her. Uneasiness crawled along her skin, the sense someone was nearby, watching. Why hadn't that call gone through yet?

She lowered the phone and stared at the screen. Half a bar. More like a dot. In several places on Cedar Key, her cell service was sketchy. Under her metal carport, it was nonexistent. Sitting inside the truck wasn't helping, either.

Leaving the driver's side door open, she moved out into the moonlight, pulling Callie with her. Two bars. It was better than nothing.

The dispatcher answered, and Nicki's hand tightened on the phone. Perspiration coated her palms, and all the strength seemed to have left her limbs. "Someone broke in to my house." She quickly provided the address.

"Is anyone there now?"

"I don't know. I haven't been inside." Her gaze darted across the front of the house, and she backed toward the road, putting as much distance between herself and the house as she could. But nowhere felt safe.

A shadow fell over her, and she lifted her gaze. Clouds rolled across the sky, obscuring the three-quarter moon. Thunder rumbled in the distance, a far-off storm that might or might not reach Cedar Key.

After finishing with the dispatcher, she slid her phone back into its pouch. The police would be there soon. Meanwhile, Callie was with her. Of course, Callie was a big pussycat.

She turned to head back toward the truck, the sense of vulnerability too strong to ignore. She was used to living out of sight of the neighbors. She'd grown up in the country, at least from age nine onward. That was when she'd moved to Crystal River and found out what a real family was. The dozen or so foster homes before that didn't count. Neither did the time she'd spent with her birth mother.

But now, looking at the trees shielding her house on three sides, the privacy she'd cherished when she bought the place felt more like isolation. And not in a good way.

A rustle sounded nearby and grew rapidly closer. Her heart leaped into her throat. Callie stiffened, a low growl rumbling in her chest. Something was barreling toward them through the strip of woods separating her yard from the one next door. Something large. She jerked Callie's leash, ready to run for the truck, but Callie wasn't budging.

A male voice cut through the noise. "Sasha, heel."

Sasha? The breath she'd been holding spilled out in a rush. Sasha was the German shepherd next door, her neighbor Andy's dog.

A fraction of a second later, sixty pounds of quivering excitement broke from the trees and charged across the yard toward them. Both dogs' tails waved back and forth at a frantic pace. By the time Sasha's human counterpart appeared, the two dogs were busy exchanging sniffs.

She watched him retrieve the leash and loop it

around his hand. The other end was attached to Andy's dog, but the man standing in her driveway wasn't Andy. In fact, he looked sort of like... No way. She squinted in the bit of moonlight leaking through the clouds.

"Tyler?"

He hesitated for two beats. Then recognition flashed across his face. "Nicki." He wrapped her in a hug, then held her away from him, his hands on her shoulders. "Wow, you look good." The recognition turned to confusion. "What are you doing here?"

"I live here." The hesitation in her tone proclaimed her own bewilderment.

Long ago, they'd been friends—close friends—until his mom got sick and moved him to Atlanta, where his aunt could care for them both. He'd been a scrawny fifteen-year-old at the time. She'd been a year younger and pretty skinny herself.

Now he was anything but. Her three-inch heels, added to her own five feet nine inches, put her almost eye to eye with him. But he outweighed her by a good seventy pounds, all of it muscle.

She shook her head, trying to clear it. "What are you doing here with Andy's dog?"

"Andy's my brother. I'm going to help him renovate that run-down inn he bought."

The confusion cleared. Andy's kid brother. The soldier. Andy and his wife Joan had told her he was coming and had given her a bit of his history, how two years ago, he'd been finishing his third tour in Afghanistan and had come under attack during a recon mission and how he almost didn't make it out alive.

Andy had just failed to mention his kid brother was Tyler Brant.

"He told me you were coming, but I didn't make the connection." With different fathers, they didn't have the same last name. And during the two years she and Tyler had hung out, Andy was already out of the house and married.

"I just arrived this afternoon, and we had a lot of catching up to do. Since I'd kept them up way past their bedtime, I told Andy I'd take Sasha out. I didn't realize she was going to bolt as soon as I stepped out the door, or I'd have kept a death grip on the leash."

The teasing grin he flashed her carried her back fifteen years. When she was a cranky adolescent, he'd had a knack for sending the dark clouds scurrying with his quirky sense of humor. Of course, she'd done her share of warding off his storms, too.

She returned his smile. "Sasha probably picked up Callie's scent. They're best buds."

He nodded down at the golden retriever. "She must like late night walks, too."

"Actually, I'm just getting home."

He had the *late* part right. It was three hours later than she'd planned. After the Saturday wedding in Miami, she'd stayed a second night and enjoyed a long lunch with friends. The northerly drive from Miami to the Gulf town of Cedar Key wasn't a lot of fun anytime. Independence Day weekend, it was the pits. The truck that had overturned and strewn produce all over the turnpike hadn't helped, either.

Sirens sounded in the distance and moved closer. When the glow of red-and-blue lights shone from the end of the road, Tyler raised his brows. "I've only been here a few hours, but when I used to come here as a kid, it was a pretty quiet place. I wonder what's going on."

"That would be me. Someone broke in to my house while I was gone."

He frowned, the concern on his face obvious in the light of the moon, which had once again made an appearance. "Is anything missing?"

"I haven't been inside yet." But considering the creep had had all weekend to clean her out, the possibilities weren't looking good.

"That's probably smart. I hope it isn't too bad."

"Yeah, me, too."

A cruiser pulled into the driveway, and the siren stopped midsqueal. The door swung open, and Amber Kingston stepped out. Amber was the newest member of the Cedar Key Police Department and among the group of people who'd taken Nicki under their wings from the moment she'd arrived in town.

"You had a break-in?"

Nicki nodded. "I left midafternoon on Friday and just got home, so no one's been here all weekend." Andy had agreed to collect Saturday's mail, and her friends Allison and Blake had kept Callie. She hadn't seen a need to have anyone keep an eye on the house.

Amber's attention shifted to Tyler. "And you are?"

"Tyler Brant." He jammed a thumb toward the house next door. "Andy's brother."

Amber gave a sharp nod before moving up the drive. "Let's see what we have inside."

Nicki started to follow, but Tyler's hand on her shoulder stopped her.

"Are you okay? I can go in with you if you'd like."

She hesitated, then shook her head. She didn't need anyone to prop her up. She was just overtired. She'd made the harrowing drive home on too little sleep.

But all the excuses in the world couldn't stave off the sense of vulnerability that had swept over her the instant she realized someone had come into her house. There were things inside those four walls that couldn't be replaced at any price, because they'd belonged to the two people she'd cared for more than anyone in the world. Two people who'd taken a foster kid with a chip on her shoulder the size of Texas and shown her a love that wouldn't quit.

She squared her shoulders and forced a smile. If there was one thing life had taught her to do well, it was to stand on her own two feet. "Thanks, but I'm sure I'll be fine."

He opened his mouth as if ready to argue, then reached up to jam his fingers through his hair. No longer in the military buzz cut she would have expected, it rested in soft layers, light brown or dark blond—it was hard to tell in the moonlight. "Let me know if you need anything."

She watched him lead the dog toward the road, a sudden sense of nostalgia sweeping over her. She had friends, close ones, but Tyler knew things about her no one else did. There'd been no pretense for either of them. Could they pick up where they left off and renew the friendship they'd had so many years ago? She wasn't the same person she'd been then, and after the horrors he'd lived through, he probably wasn't, either.

She turned and, with Callie trotting beside her, led

Amber toward the carport. She might as well get it over with.

"This is where he got in." She pointed at the door. "Looks like I'm going to need some work done on the doorjamb."

Amber removed her pistol from its holster. "I'm going to go in and clear the place, make sure no one's hiding inside. You might want to wait in the truck."

Nicki coaxed Callie up into the seat for the third time that evening. A few minutes later, Amber stepped back into the carport, her expression somber.

"You've got a little bit of a mess." She held up a hand. "Nothing major."

Nicki followed her into the house, her insides settling into a cold, hard lump. She reached to unhook the leash from Callie's collar, then changed her mind.

"I'd better close her up." Her house had become a crime scene. She didn't need the dog traipsing through and destroying evidence.

She opened the door leading into the laundry room, then filled a bowl with dry food. Callie dove in right away. That would keep her occupied for a few minutes. After a couple of pats on the dog's back, Nicki pulled the door shut and stepped into the kitchen.

It was the same as she'd left it two days earlier. The living room, too, appeared untouched. Two curios held thousands of dollars of figurines—Swarovski, Lenox and Armani—all undisturbed. A sliver of the tension eased. The intruder apparently wasn't interested in electronics, either, because the big-screen TV and pieces of accompanying equipment still occupied their cubbyholes in the entertainment center.

Which meant the mess Amber had referred to was in her bedrooms. The guest room she'd chosen for herself, leaving the large master bedroom to function as a combination hobby room and office.

As soon as she stepped into the hall, she gasped. The open door at the end revealed her wooden work table covered with papers and files. She closed the distance at a half run.

All of her tools and materials for making stained glass were where she'd left them, but both file drawers were all the way open, the majority of the contents removed and strewn across her work area. Her bulletin board hung above the table, her to-do list pinned in the center. The first three items were crossed through. The remaining four, she'd assigned time frames for completion. Organization in the midst of chaos. But the sense of control it usually gave her had evaporated the moment she stepped into the room.

She reached for one of the files on the table. Amber's voice stopped her.

"Don't touch anything. I'm going to try to lift prints."

Nicki let her hand fall to her side but scanned the items. Lots of papers lay on top, pulled from their folders. One stack was the paperwork from the sale of the Crystal River house, an hour from Cedar Key. It had belonged to her parents. Seven months ago, they'd taken early retirement to see the country and reward themselves for all the years of hard work.

Some reward. They'd been headed toward a picturesque small town in North Carolina when a tired trucker had crossed the center line. And she'd been left with a three-bedroom house on five acres and a great big hole in her heart.

Next to the Crystal River sale documents was the paperwork from the purchase of the Cedar Key house. And beside that was the file from opening her account at Drummond Community Bank upon first moving to Cedar Key. Her income tax forms were also there, along with some credit card statements.

All of her personal information was right out in the open—her name, address, Social Security number, date of birth—everything needed to steal her identity.

"You'd better file fraud alerts with the credit reporting agencies." Amber's voice was soft but filled with worry.

She nodded and followed Amber from the room, an emptiness weaving through her. She'd come to Cedar Key to regain her footing after life had kicked out one too many of her foundation blocks. The quaint town's peace and tranquility had gone a long way toward mending the tattered pieces of her soul. And she wasn't going to let this break-in take that away.

She squared her shoulders and started down the hall. Before she'd gotten very far, Amber stopped her with a raised hand.

"The intruder did some damage in this room, too. I'm hoping you can shed some light on what's going on."

During her mad rush to her work room, she'd hurried right past her bedroom without even looking inside. Now something in Amber's tone sent dread showering down on her. Could anything be worse than what she'd already witnessed?

Amber stepped aside and Nicki closed the remaining distance to her room.

Then froze in the open doorway. Her old plush rabbit was hanging from the ceiling fan with a noose around its neck. Stuffing protruded from a slash that ran from throat to tail and littered the carpet beneath.

Her knees started to buckle, and she gripped the doorjamb for support. Lavender wasn't just an old, scruffy stuffed animal. She was her childhood friend who'd gotten her through nights of terror while her mother was being beaten by her men in the next room. She'd been Nicki's constant companion through one foster home after another when the parents couldn't cope anymore with a disturbed, destructive child, and through weeks of uncertainty as she waited for her adoptive family to give up and throw in the towel. Lavender had been hugged and kissed and cried on. And had been there for a lonely, terrified little girl when no one else had.

Why Lavender? Houses got burglarized all the time. Maybe not in Cedar Key, but plenty of other places. Even going through her paperwork made sense. But why destroy a stuffed toy?

Nicki dragged her gaze from the rabbit to take in the rest of the room. Several dresser drawers were open, the contents hanging over the sides. The closet doors were open, too. Other than that, and the empty spot on the shelf Lavender had occupied, it looked undisturbed.

A soft hand on her shoulder reminded her she wasn't alone. Nicki dropped her hand from the jamb and faced Amber. "I'm guessing the intruder was ticked about

not finding any money and figured he'd do a little vandalism before he left."

Amber shook her head, eyes now back on the
stuffed rabbit. "That doesn't look like vandalism to
me. It looks like a threat."

Tyler stepped out the door behind Sasha and drew
in an earth-scented breath. Early morning sunlight
slanted over the landscape, and the final remnants of
pink still stained the eastern sky. The rain that had
passed through during the night had left behind glis-
tening droplets that clung to the shrubbery lining Andy's front walk.

Cedar Key was a nice change from the city. Maybe
he'd even stay awhile. He was committed to two
months, anyway. Andy had bought an old inn and
needed help with renovations. So he'd offered his services. He might as well put to good use those long-
ago afternoons and weekends he'd spent working in
his best friend's dad's construction business. Besides,
after all the care packages that had traveled from Andy
and Joan's doorstep to Afghanistan, it was the least he
could do. How long he stayed after the work was completed would depend on how quickly the nightmares
caught up with him.

In the months following the attack, they'd been re-
lentless. He'd been stationed at Fort Sam Houston,
Texas, undergoing treatment, both physical and mental.
After a year, the Army cut him loose with a monthly
disability check.

Now another year had passed, and the nightmares
were still pursuing him. Strenuous activity helped. So
did starting fresh. That was how he'd lived ever since

his discharge—move, find a temporary job, get semi-settled, repeat. So far it was working. Sort of.

Halfway down the drive, Sasha stopped walking, head angled toward the strip of woods and undergrowth separating Andy's yard from Nicki's. A few seconds later, a soft rustle sounded about twenty feet away.

The German shepherd lunged, and Tyler tightened his grip on the leash. "Oh, no, you don't." Callie would be inside, and he didn't need to be led on a chase after some poor opossum or armadillo. He gave the leash a tug and continued down the drive.

Nicki's in Cedar Key. The realization was still sinking in. He'd thought he'd never see her again. They'd promised to stay in touch. For a while they had. Then life got in the way and they'd each moved on. He'd had a terrible crush on her, something he kept secret throughout their entire two-year friendship.

When he reached the end of the driveway, he turned left and cast a glance toward Nicki's house. It was dark except for the single light burning by the front door, apparently turned on after he'd gone home.

Since she'd had such a late night, she was probably still asleep. The same place he should be. But he'd woken up in the darkness after his usual four or five hours. And once he was awake, he was done. Sleep invited nightmares.

He continued down Hodges Avenue at an easy jog, Sasha as far in front of him as the leash allowed. The dog would have preferred a full-out run. But he wasn't giving her the choice. Running long distances was one of several things he couldn't do anymore.

Just past Gulf Boulevard, he turned Sasha around and headed toward Andy's. Maybe by the time he got back, Nicki would be out and about. Last night, when he'd offered her his help, she'd stood straight and tall, projecting confidence. But her eyes had given her away. They'd held a fear and vulnerability even the nighttime shadows couldn't hide. And his protective instincts had kicked into overdrive. He should have insisted on going in the house with her. But if there was one thing he remembered about Nicki, it was that once her mind was made up, there was no changing it.

He slowed to a brisk walk and struggled to catch his breath. It was barely six-thirty, and already the humidity was getting to him. It had never bothered him before. But neither had running. That last mission had changed a lot of things. Even more for his men.

He pushed the thought from his mind. He wasn't going there. He had no say over where his thoughts traveled while sleeping, but he could control them when he was awake.

Today would be the first day on his new job, temporary though it was. He was looking forward to it. Over the next few weeks, he'd work hard. And when he and Andy finished, they'd have something beautiful. It was an appealing thought. He'd seen enough destruction to last a lifetime.

He'd almost reached Nicki's driveway when she stepped off her porch, holding Callie's leash. She looked up and raised a hand in greeting.

"Good morning."

As soon as Sasha saw Callie, she shot off in that direction, pulling him with her. He didn't resist. It gave him the perfect excuse to approach Nicki.

"How did everything go last night?"

She nodded, but there was something stiff about the action. "Okay. It doesn't look like he took anything. I'm guessing he was hoping for some quick cash."

"Good." He studied her. There was more to it than that. "And no damage was done?"

"The doorjamb where he pried the lock is pretty messed up. The lock itself is kind of iffy, too. I'm having it replaced, but I'm getting one with a dead bolt this time."

Callie led her down the driveway toward the road, and he fell in beside her.

"Can I install the lock for you? I brought power tools, and I'm sure Andy has a mortising kit I can borrow."

She waved aside his offer. "That's okay. There's a handyman in town who has done some work for a friend of mine."

"I want to help you out. Andy can tell you I know what I'm doing." He paused. "I like to stay busy." He *had* to stay busy. It was how he stayed sane.

She hesitated but finally nodded. "All right. But I'm going to pay you."

He grinned. Stubborn as always. Of course, he hadn't expected any different.

When they reached the road, Callie turned to go in the same direction he and Sasha had gone, but Sasha didn't seem to mind repeating their route. She pranced along next to Callie, ears erect, head held high, which left him to walk beside Nicki, something he didn't mind, either.

He'd thought she was pretty years before, but she was gorgeous now. Her features had matured, erasing the last traces of childish softness, and her green eyes held a determined sparkle, confidence replacing the scrappiness that had been there earlier. Her hair fell in soft waves around her face and brushed her shoulders. Previously a light brown color, it was now a shade of auburn too bright to be natural, but somehow perfect.

"I've got to be at work in an hour, so I won't be able to get the lock to you until this evening. We don't have a Lowe's or Home Depot here. I guess I need to find a hardware store." She glanced up at him. "I've lived here only a month."

"No problem. Andy and I will be hitting Home Depot in Crystal River to pick up some materials for the inn. I'll get your locks while we're there."

She released a relieved sigh. "I appreciate it. I was trying to figure out how to fit everything in today. I took off an hour early Friday to get a jump on my trip to Miami, so I hated to have to beg off again today, being the new kid on the block."

"You won't have to. I'll make sure we have everything you need, and by bedtime tonight, I'll have you secure."

She frowned. "As secure as I can be with my personal data out there."

He raised his brows.

"The intruder went through my files. Seemed to be especially interested in my financial information."

"Not good." No wonder she was ill at ease. "Have you filed fraud alerts?"

"I will in a few minutes. That's going to be my entertainment over breakfast." She gave him a wry smile, then tugged Callie's leash to turn her around. Sasha eagerly followed.

"Anything else disturbed?"

She hesitated, her lower lip pulled between her teeth. It was something she used to do whenever she was perturbed or confused or any number of other emotions. Apparently she still did. "Lavender."

"Lavender?" The purple rabbit? He'd once asked her why she was hanging on to an ugly, ragged-out stuffed animal, and she'd gotten rather...defensive. The bruises on his arm had lasted several days. "You still have Lavender?"

"Until this weekend, I did." She frowned again. "Someone was apparently not happy about finding no money in the house and decided to string her up to the ceiling fan and slice her belly open."

His gut clenched, and a cold wave of unease washed through him. "That doesn't sound like your regular, run-of-the-mill burglar."

She pursed her lips. "Amber took it as a threat."

"I'd tend to agree."

"But I don't have any enemies."

Maybe she didn't have any she knew of. "How about saving my contact info in your phone?"

She pulled it from her pocket and her thumbs slid over the screen. When she was ready, he gave her his number.

"If anything happens or you feel at all unsafe, call me. I'm right next door. I can be here a lot faster than the police can."

She slid the phone back into her pocket. "Thanks, but I think you're worrying over nothing. I'm sure it was a simple act of vandalism." She stopped at the end of her driveway. "I'll see you tonight. Meanwhile, Callie will stand guard."

"Let me walk you to your door." He would make sure she was locked safely inside, then cut through the woods.

Halfway up the drive, his gaze stopped on her porch. Something was attached to her front door. She saw it at the same time he did and picked up her pace.

It was a single sheet of paper, folded in half, secured with a piece of tape. As she removed it, he cast an uneasy glance toward the woods. When he'd first stepped out of the house, he'd heard a rustle. He'd assumed it was an animal. Was it possible...

When he looked at Nicki again, she was staring at the unfolded paper, brow creased. Before he could ask, she angled the page toward him. It was blank except for three words written in all caps—THE PARTY'S OVER.

She gave him a sudden dry laugh. It held no humor, just a lot of desperation. "Trust me, these past few months, my life has been anything but a party."

"Someone apparently disagrees and is planning to make sure things get unpleasant fast." He put a hand on her shoulder. "You need to call the police."

"I will. But it'll have to wait till tonight. I've got to get to work. I can't be late."

She pushed the key into the lock and turned it, then opened the door. Her hands shook, something she was trying hard to hide.

"Where do you work?"

"City hall."

"How about if I take you?"

"Thanks, but I'll be fine. No one is going to bother me here with Callie around, and I don't think anyone would dare approach me at work." She stepped over the threshold and raised a hand in farewell. "Later."

He watched her close the door, then moved toward the woods with Sasha. Nicki wasn't the only one who needed to get to work. Andy would be ready to start soon, too.

He'd just reached the driveway on the other side of the trees when the front door swung open. Andy stepped onto the porch holding up a cell phone. Tyler patted his pocket. He'd left the phone on the table after finishing his coffee.

"It's Bridgett."

Their older sister. He cringed. He'd forgotten to call her when he'd arrived yesterday. Of course, Andy could have assured her he was alive and well. But he knew Bridgett, and she wouldn't be satisfied until she'd heard it from him. She'd worried about him as much in the past two years that he'd lived stateside as she had during his tours in Afghanistan. Maybe more. His mom would have been right there with Bridgett. But the day before his eighteenth birthday, the cancer she'd fought since the summer he turned fifteen had finally won. His dad wasn't doing any worrying, either. He'd walked out years earlier.

He stepped onto the porch and took his phone from Andy. Once he'd convinced his sister that he was all in one piece, he headed to the back to dress for work. Tonight he'd get Nicki's lock replaced. While he was at it, he'd check the ones on her other doors and windows. Any he wasn't happy with, he'd replace the following day.

The fact was, he'd cared for her all those years ago, and he felt no less for her now. As young teenagers, they'd been drawn together by a mutual toughness. He'd had a chip on his shoulder from his dad walking out, and she'd still had an attitude from her years in foster care.

But things had been simple then compared to now. In the fifteen years since he'd left Crystal River, he'd faced too many battles. He bore the scars, both physical and emotional. Nicki probably had enough of her own issues to fight without having to deal with his. Besides, he couldn't stay in one place long enough to pursue anything more serious than friendship with anyone. He had to keep moving to hold the memories at bay.

But that wasn't going to stop him from doing everything he could to protect her while he was here. Someone was threatening his longtime friend, and he was going to get to the bottom of it. He wouldn't leave until he made sure she was safe.

Maybe, if he was successful, it would help make up for the other times he'd tried to protect someone but failed.

TWO

Nicki picked up the porcelain bowl in the corner and crossed the kitchen. The painted paw prints lining the bottom shone clean and clear, licked to a glossy shine. As she placed the empty dish in the sink, Callie watched her every move, tail wagging, eyes filled with doggy eagerness. She never gave up hope that maybe, just this once, there would be seconds.

Nicki strolled toward the side door and cast a glance back at the golden retriever staying right on her heels. "You behave yourself."

She would be out all evening for the midweek church service. But she hoped the admonition wouldn't be necessary. A year ago, yeah. When she'd first brought Callie home from the Humane Society, she'd been well past the energetic puppy stage, but past abuse had made her terrified of everything that moved and a whirlwind of destruction when left alone.

Now she didn't even need crating. Finding a forever home where she was showered with love had made a world of difference. Nicki bent to scratch the dog's neck. She could relate.

After stepping into the carport and closing the door,

she fished for the key. Two nights ago Tyler had installed a new lock, complete with a deadbolt, and made repairs to the jamb. And he'd done a great job. So much so she might see if she could hire him to do some other projects. She would love to have the pedestal sink in the hall bath replaced with a vanity, and some shelves added to the two closets in her hobby room.

She hadn't seen him since he'd made the repairs. Their times for taking the dogs out hadn't coincided, and they'd both been busy. She was almost disappointed. It had been fun having someone to talk to on her morning walk.

She inserted the key into the deadbolt and turned it. The lock slid home with a satisfying click. She'd regained a little of her sense of control, thanks to Tyler. He'd even checked the locks on all her windows to make sure they were secure.

Fifteen years ago, they'd been the best of friends, spending hours hanging out at the park or high on a branch of the huge oak overshadowing most of her backyard. As he'd opened up about his anger with his father, she'd let down some of her own walls. Back then, he'd just been Tyler, her friend and confidante, the one person in the world she'd been able to connect with, because he was as lost as she was.

He was still Tyler. But now he was Tyler all grown up. It was hard not to notice how well he filled out those T-shirts he wore, or how his golden-brown eyes filled with warmth every time he smiled. But with her track record, she didn't have any business contemplating anything that smacked of romance. She was still trying to ward off the repercussions of the last disaster.

She pressed a button on her key fob, and the Ram's

locks popped up. Tonight she would be occupied, with or without Tyler. She was going to church, something her friend Darci had talked her into. She'd been surprised to find she enjoyed attending. It was almost like belonging to a family again—a loving heavenly Father and lots of brothers and sisters.

That wasn't all she'd been talked into. After the crash that killed Nicki's parents, Darci was the one who'd suggested she sell out and come to Cedar Key. When her ex had dropped the second bombshell on her, she'd finally agreed. One month had passed since the move. She still missed her parents terribly, but she hoped the call from Peter a week ago was the final one. He claimed that everything he'd done was for her. So what? It was over.

She swung open the driver's door of her truck, but before she could get in, a dark sedan pulled into her driveway. As she watched a man and woman exit, tension crept across her shoulders. Both visitors were strangers.

"Can I help you?"

The man showed her his badge. "I'm Detective Granger, and this is Detective Mulling. We're with the Jacksonville Sheriff's Office."

As he spoke, her mind whirled. Maybe they'd learned something about her break-in. But Jacksonville? That was where she'd spent her early years. In a run-down shack with peeling plaster, grime-encrusted windows and puke-green shag carpet.

"Can we have a few minutes of your time? We need to talk to you about your mother's murder."

She nodded, a weight pressing in on her chest. She'd worked hard to leave those memories behind.

The steady stream of creepy men who'd paraded in and out of the house. The way some of them had leered at her, making her hair stand on end. The nights she'd spent curled into a ball with her pillow over her head, trying to shut out the thud of angry fists and her mother's muffled pleas.

She swallowed hard and led them toward the house. "It's been twenty-two years. Why now?" If they hadn't solved it then, with fresh evidence, how would they uncover anything leading them to the killer over two decades later?

"We're investigating an incident that happened two weeks ago, also in Jacksonville. There are some similarities, and we think they might be connected."

"I don't know how much help I'll be. I wasn't there." She unlocked the door and ushered them inside. After a few quick sniffs, Callie apparently decided the visitors were okay and plopped down in front of the entertainment center, dark eyes alert.

Nicki motioned toward the sectional sofa. "Have a seat."

Once they'd settled onto the couch, Mulling turned back the cover on a notebook.

Granger clasped his hands loosely in his lap. "Thank you for talking to us." Although the female detective was sitting closer to Nicki, it looked as if Granger would be the one asking the questions. "I'm sure it's going to be difficult, but I need you to tell me everything you can remember about that night."

She drew in a deep breath. Yeah, it would be difficult. Not because she still grieved for her mother. She'd come to terms with her death years ago. In fact, if events hadn't gone the way they had, Nicki's life would have turned out quite differently. Ending up in the Jackson home was the best thing that had ever happened to her. No, this was going to be difficult because she didn't want to remember.

She leaned back against the padded leather. "I was spending the night with a friend, Lizzie. She lived next door."

"Do you remember Lizzie's last name?"

"McDonald. Elizabeth McDonald."

"What about her parents' names?"

She shook her head. "I never met her dad, and I just called her mom Mrs. McDonald."

Granger continued while his partner filled up the first small page. "Was anyone there when you left to go to your friend's house?"

"My mom and my sister. I don't remember anyone else."

"When was the first time you learned about your mother's murder?"

"The next morning. Mrs. McDonald said something awful had happened. She was crying. And she wouldn't let me go home." In fact, Nicki never set foot inside her house again. By lunchtime, the authorities had gathered up her belongings and whisked her away to the first of many foster families.

"Did you know of anyone who'd have wanted to hurt your mother?"

Hurt or *kill*? "A lot of them hurt her."

"How?"

"Slapping her, punching her, throwing her against the wall, pushing her to the floor." Fights were a regular occurrence, especially after a night of heavy drinking and shooting up.

Granger leaned forward, sympathy filling his eyes. Or was it pity?

She drew in a deep breath and lifted her chin. She didn't need sympathy. She'd put her past behind her a long time ago. And she didn't want pity.

"These men who used to hit your mother, did you ever see any of them with a knife?"

She shook her head.

With a signal from Granger, Mulling removed a picture from the back of the notebook and handed it to her.

"Does this man look familiar?"

She looked down at what she held. Cords of steel wrapped around her chest and throat, squeezing the air from her lungs. It was a booking photo. Wicked tattoos reached out from beneath the wife beater shirt, and eyes as black as sin glared back at the camera with a lethal hatred. To a seven-year-old child, the man had seemed huge. Judging by the thick neck and monster pecs, her perception hadn't been far off.

All the men had scared her. But this one had frightened her the most.

She shook off the fear. He had no reason to hurt her. And her mother was beyond his reach.

"Uncle Louie." She handed the photo back to Mulling.

"No blood relation, I take it."

"No, same as all the others. I had more uncles than any girl alive."

Granger gave her a soft smile. It held the same hint of sympathy she'd noticed earlier. "What can you tell us about Louie?"

"He was there a lot the last few weeks before my

mom was killed. I think he was mostly living there."
A shudder passed through her. "I didn't like him."

"Why not?"

"I was afraid of him. He had an awful temper.
Whenever I was home, I'd stay in my room and sneak
to the kitchen to get something to eat once he and my
mom were passed out."

She closed her eyes, events she'd tried hard to forget
bombarding her. "Once I made the mistake of taking
the peanut butter to my room. He grabbed me by the
hair and slammed me into the wall. When my mom
tried to stick up for me, he turned on her and beat her
to a bloody pulp."

She suppressed another shudder. At the time, she'd
thought it was her fault. Now she knew better.

"You haven't heard from him since that night,
right?"

"No."

"He was picked up near Ocala the morning after
your mother was found and jailed on drug charges.
Ended up doing fifteen years. But he was never
charged with the murder. He had an alibi, albeit a
shaky one, and although he was a suspect, we were
never able to find enough evidence to convict him.
Two weeks ago, another woman was stabbed to death.
She'd recently ended a rocky relationship…with Louis
Harmel."

Nicki nodded, a cold numbness spreading inside
her. Maybe her mother's killer would finally pay for his
crime. But how long would it take? And what would
she go through in the meantime? How many memories
would have to be dredged up before it was all over?

"Do you have any contact with your sister?" Granger's words cut across her thoughts.

"No. We were separated after our mother was killed." And even before that, they hadn't been close. They'd shared a room—a dinky space hardly big enough for the two twin beds and single chest of drawers. But Nicki hadn't taken much comfort in her sister's presence. No matter how terrifying the sounds coming from the next room, Jenny had never let her share her bed.

"Six months ago, I hired a private investigator to find her," Nicki said. Although the dysfunctional home and five-year age difference had kept them from being close, she'd thought of Jenny often over the years. Now Jenny was the only family Nicki had left.

"Are they making any progress locating her?"

"Yes and no. Three different times, the investigator has gotten leads, but every time he gets close, she disappears. It's as if she doesn't want to be found."

There was probably a good reason. A criminal background check had turned up a hefty list of arrests. Nothing too serious. Just a bunch of petty stuff—forged checks, shoplifting, possession of marijuana, disorderly conduct. And likely plenty of other stuff waiting to catch up with her. No wonder she kept running.

"We've had the same experience. We haven't been able to get close enough to explain what we want with her."

"My guy is going to keep trying." As long as she had the money. Her inheritance had allowed her to start the search and would enable her to keep it going for some time. "He's making it clear to everyone he talks to that it's her half sister looking for her, not law enforcement."

Nicki hoped the message would eventually reach her. At least she was pretty sure that was what she wanted. Twice the investigator had asked her if she wished to continue, his tone heavy with doubt both times. Jenny's life was a mess. She'd stayed in the foster care system until she aged out and had never known the love of a real family. Nicki didn't even try to deny what she might be getting herself into seeking a relationship with her long-lost sister.

But she couldn't turn her back on her. Yes, Jenny was messed up. But Nicki had been pretty messed up herself when Chuck and Doris Jackson chose to look past her faults and love her anyway. She could do no less for Jenny.

Granger stood, and his partner closed the notebook and followed suit. He extended a hand to shake Nicki's, then handed her his business card. "We'll be back in touch. Meanwhile, if there's anything you remember that you haven't told us, please give us a call. It doesn't matter how insignificant it seems."

She walked them to the door. "I will. And if you happen to find her, you'll let me know?"

"We will."

She watched them walk toward the sedan, then closed and locked the door. It was too late to go to church. Wednesday night services started at seven, and it was already seven-twenty. She crossed the room to sit on the couch, the same spot she'd vacated earlier. Callie approached and rested her head in Nicki's lap.

Was Louie the one who'd killed her mother? Any

number of men could have done it. But from everything she remembered, he seemed the most likely. He had the worst temper. And it wasn't just that. He seemed to radiate evil.

She shuddered again and reached for the remote. An evening of brainless television held a lot of appeal, the opportunity to lose herself in someone else's life for a short time. She let her head fall against the padded back of the couch and closed her eyes.

She'd spent the last two decades trying to forget.

Now they needed her to remember.

Tyler emerged from the bathroom, hair still damp but free of drywall dust. He'd hoped the days would be a little longer. It was Friday, and all week, Andy had been ready to call it quits by seven o'clock. Tonight it had been even earlier. Nine years Tyler's senior, maybe Andy was slowing down. Or maybe he'd been thinking about Joan's cooking and couldn't hold out any longer.

Tyler drew in a slow, fragrant breath. The scent of baking roast beef that had plagued him since he stepped onto the front porch wrapped around him again, and his stomach growled. When he entered the kitchen, Andy was already there, helping Joan cut up salad ingredients.

She smiled over one shoulder. "Dinner will be ready in twenty minutes. You guys messed me up coming home early."

The doorbell rang, cutting off his response. Leaving them to their meal preparation, he made his way to the front door. When he swung it open, Nicki stood on the porch, Callie next to her. A smile spread across her face and lit her eyes, sending an odd warmth straight to his core.

"I was walking Callie and saw you guys were home." She shifted her weight and cocked her head to the side. "You said you like to stay busy. How would you like to do a few projects for me?"

"Sure. What do you have in mind?"

"Several things. When you get a chance, stop by and I'll show you what I'm looking for."

He stepped onto the porch and closed the door behind him. "I've got almost twenty minutes till dinner. And if I'm a few minutes late, I'm sure Joan and Andy will save me some."

Nicki walked several feet down the driveway, then cut across the yard and into the woods. She glanced back at him, grinning. "Shortcut."

"Yeah, I found this one myself." It was the same route he'd taken Monday morning after seeing her to her door.

When they reached her yard, she pulled a set of keys from her pocket. "I used to not worry about locking up if I was just stepping outside for a few minutes. Now if the house is out of sight at all, you can be sure it's locked."

"That's a good idea."

He followed her into the house. Before Monday night, he'd made an assumption based on the simple block exterior. But on the inside, the place looked like something out of one of Joan's home decor magazines. A leather sectional sofa wrapped around an oak-and-glass table set on a wrought iron base. A marble-type floor tile in varying shades of brown and beige met three walls the color of Dijon mustard, the fourth a deep burnt orange. Two curio cabinets held a variety of figurines, and a floor lamp with amber globes bathed everything in a warm glow.

"This looks great." Whatever projects she had in mind, they probably didn't include this room.

"Thanks. The prior owners made some updates but never finished. I like the floor tile, but they'd painted all the walls a boring off-white." She grinned over at him. "I had to jazz it up a bit."

"That picture is perfect." He tilted his head toward the seascape hanging over the sofa. It was a sunset scene, depicted in colors that complemented her decor.

"Thanks. I had Meagan Kingston, a local artist, do it for me. It was my birthday present to myself."

"Happy belated birthday. And what about the stained glass wall hangings?"

"Those are mine."

"I thought so. I saw your supplies when I was checking the window locks."

"That's my hobby. Or maybe it's more than that, since I sell them. I've got them downtown at the Cedar Keyhole Artist Co-op and Darci's Collectibles and Gifts."

She led him into the kitchen. "The prior owners stripped and refinished the cabinets and replaced the appliances. I had the granite countertops put in. But I've got to get rid of that light fixture."

"Yeah, it looks sort of industrial. Do you have something picked out?"

"Not yet." She walked from the room and headed down the hall. "I plan to make one trip and do it all at once." She stopped at the open door to the bathroom. "Pedestal sinks look great, but they're not very practical. I'd like to replace it with a vanity and a cultured marble top. Are you up to it?"

"Sure." He was more than up to it. The broken arm had mended, and the burns were as good as they were going to get. All that was left of the smoke inhalation was some shortness of breath if he overexerted. Most of the damage to his body had healed. The effects on his mind, not so much. Splints and bandages couldn't blot out the images.

Or justify his returning home when his men hadn't.

He shook off the thoughts and followed her into the bedroom across the hall.

"This is technically the guest room, but it's where I sleep. So I'd like to get some more space in the closet."

"Closet organizers?"

"Yep." She opened the louvered doors. "On this side, I'd like the top shelf raised to make room for double rods. I'll keep a single rod on this side. In the center, I'd like a small set of drawers with a shoe cubby above. Twenty or thirty slots, if possible."

He eyed her with raised brows "You got enough shoes?"

"You don't know the half of it." She grinned up at him.

Warmth filled his chest, and he grew serious. "It's good to see you again, Nicki."

"Yeah, same here. I've missed you."

He held her gaze for several moments. The years melted away, and they were once again connected by that invisible bond that tied his heart to hers. Distance hadn't severed it and neither had time. Did she feel it?

She turned, and he followed her into the hall. When she reached the large room at the end, she made a wide sweep of her arm. "As you can see, this is my work area."

He walked to a table where a partially completed stained glass scene lay. Peaks and valleys rose and fell, outlined in what looked like copper. Some kind of flowering trees occupied the foreground.

"The room has a *his* and a *hers* closet." Her words drew his attention, and she swung open one of the doors. "I'll leave the smaller one as it is, with the rods and all, because if I ever have company, this is where they'll sleep." She motioned toward the daybed against the far wall, then turned back to the closet.

"I want to have several shelves installed on all three sides here. Right now, I'm storing a lot of stuff in bins, and it'll make my life a lot easier to have everything more accessible."

"Let me know what you want, and I'll build it."

"Awesome." She pulled a pushpin from the corner of the bulletin board and handed him a sheet of paper. "Here's my wish list. Do you think you're up to it?"

"And then some." The work she'd laid out would keep him occupied for quite a few evenings. And it would give him somewhere pleasant to focus his mind, far away from the horrors of war.

"Are you out for good now?" She walked from the room and headed down the hall.

He followed her into the living room, shaking his head at her uncanny way of reading his thoughts. "I'm out for good."

"They can't call you back?"

"Nope." They'd retired him. And he was still trying to find his purpose.

She leaned back against the entertainment center.

"I thought your first months or years out, they can always recall you."

"Not always."

His clipped answers weren't what she was looking for, and he knew it. But he didn't want to talk about it.

The progression from enlisted to retired didn't happen overnight. Those things never did. They reassigned him to a warrior transition unit for a year. The cast eventually came off his arm, but the skin graft procedures seemed to go on and on. Finally the doctors decided he was as good as he was going to get, and the medical board made their determination. He could no longer do the job. And that was that.

He shifted his gaze to the window overlooking her front yard. Drapes in earth tone patterns hung on each side, connected by a matching valance. Lacy sheers occupied the space between, partially obscuring whatever lay in the lengthening afternoon shadows. Another task he would add to his to-do list—installing some blinds behind the sheers. The bedrooms had them, but the living, dining and kitchen areas didn't.

"How should I go about getting the materials you need?"

Her words pulled his attention from the window, but movement in his peripheral vision snapped it back. For a brief moment, a vague shape hovered at the left portion of the sheers, then disappeared. He tensed and raised a hand. What had he seen?

"Stay here."

He made a dash for the door, jerked it open and pulled it shut behind him. As he rounded the corner of the house, a figure melted into the woods lining the back of Nicki's property. Tyler pounded through the grass and ran into the tree line a few moments later. Seeing no one, he stopped to listen.

A rain-scented gust whipped the trees around, the steady *shhh* drowning out the rustle of the intruder's movements. He turned slowly, all senses on alert. Some distance to his right, the snap of twigs underlay the steadier sounds of nature. He moved in that direction, his own footsteps little more than a whisper. His pulse picked up as he closed in on his prey.

Soon a voice drifted to him, soft and distinctly feminine. Then another, this one male. Both young. And a flash of clothing. Moments later, two figures came into view, and he shook his head. He'd followed a couple of teenagers on an early evening hike. And the intruder had gotten away.

As he approached, the guy took her hand, pulled her to a stop and drew her into his arms. Fifteen years ago, that had been him and Nicki. The hanging-out, walking-through-the-woods part, anyway. The other had been only in his dreams.

He cleared his throat, and they both started.

"Did you see anyone pass by in the last few minutes?"

They shook their heads. There was no sense continuing his search. Nicki's Peeping Tom was long gone. And she was probably inside wondering if he'd lost his mind. He hadn't taken the time to explain.

When he got back, though, Nicki wasn't in her house. She was standing at the edge of the sidewalk, face angled downward. She looked up as he approached.

"You were supposed to stay inside." His tone was stern.

"I did, for a minute, anyway. What's going on?"

Judging from the furrows in her brow and the concern in her eyes, he could have asked her the same thing. He cast a glance down. A wicked-looking knife lay in the flower bed, partially obscured by the daylilies planted there.

"Where did that come from?"

"It's my chef's knife. It's been missing since my house was broken into. I thought I'd misplaced it."

He frowned. "Someone was at your window. By the time I got around the side of the house, he was disappearing into the woods. I took off after him, but I didn't get a good look at him."

"Find anything?"

"'Fraid not. I ended up following a rabbit trail." At the question in her eyes, he continued. "I heard something, which led me to a couple of teenagers." He glanced back down at the knife. "We need to call the police and have that fingerprinted."

Another gust swept through, the rain even closer, and Nicki moved toward the front door. "The intruder must have taken the knife, then dropped it the night he broke in. I've been in and out this way with Callie, but I wasn't paying any attention to the flower bed at the time. So I didn't notice it."

He nodded. That was one explanation. Except he didn't buy it. His own interpretation was much more sinister. He stepped onto the porch and opened the door for her, then followed her inside. "Maybe you're right and he dropped it the night he broke in, or..."

"Or what?"

He turned her to face him and took her hands. He

would do everything he could to protect her. But she needed to be armed with the facts.

"Maybe he took it with him the night he broke in, then brought it back tonight, fully intending to use it."

THREE

Blood.

So much blood.

It covered the woman's body, seeping outward in an ever-expanding circle. She lay facedown on the floor, hand curled into a fist, as if she was spending the final moments of life in an angry protest against the void creeping over her.

She drew in a final shallow breath. The fist tightened, then released.

Nicki bolted upright with a gasp and pressed a hand over her racing heart. It was only a dream. One nightmare of many. This one was probably triggered by the visit from the two detectives and all the talk of her mother's murder. The knife lying in the mulch might have played a part, too.

She slid from the bed and bent to stroke Callie's head, trying to shake off the final remnants of the dream. She was no stranger to nightmares. Scary movies triggered some of them, the evening news others. Growing up, she'd seen things no child should ever see, watched movies that would terrify the most hardened adult.

But often her dreams held elements of the past—leering grins, sinister glances and whispered threats. Louie had landed a starring role in more than one.

As she removed a T-shirt and shorts from the chest of drawers in the corner, her gaze slid toward the closet. She'd left the doors open last night. Shoes lined the bottom, and her clothes hung in organized sections, although packed in way too tightly. Lavender once again occupied his spot on the shelf.

She hadn't been able to bring herself to throw him away. So she'd bought a needle and some matching thread and set to work. Now, with the exception of dozens of tiny stitches crisscrossing his belly, he was back in the same condition he'd been in before the attack—one eye missing, pale purple fur matted and stuffing so compacted his head listed pitifully to one side.

All these years, she'd held on to him. He was the only thing from her early childhood she'd managed to keep. She'd started out with a bin of personal belongings, but through the series of foster homes, one by one, the items disappeared. Some she accidentally left behind, but more often, other kids took them. Once someone tried to take Lavender. The foster mom had to pull her off the other child. The next day, she was on her way to another home with her beloved stuffed rabbit.

Callie nudged her hand, letting her know she'd dallied long enough. It was time for a walk. And after that, breakfast. Like most dogs, she approached both with equal enthusiasm.

Once showered and dressed, Nicki hooked up the leash. As soon as she stepped outside, uneasiness sifted through her. She scanned the yard, then shifted her gaze to the flower bed. Nothing was there, no threatening objects. She tried to shake off the apprehension. It was broad daylight. And Callie was with her.

But finding her chef's knife lying in the mulch Friday night had shaken her more than she wanted to admit. And although neither she nor Tyler had seen hide nor hair of the intruder in the day and a half since, tension continued to wrap itself around her body.

She glanced toward Andy's, then headed down her drive. Tyler was probably back inside, having long since finished Sasha's walk. Maybe she should try to coordinate Callie's walks with Sasha's. She would feel safer, and the company was nice. Reconnecting with Tyler had been a pleasant surprise.

But he was different from the boy she'd known long ago.

Friday night, when she'd asked him about his military service, she could feel him shutting down. Her questions had been innocent. But he'd clammed up so tight she couldn't have pried the information from him with a crowbar.

He never used to be that way. During those balmy days, sitting in the tree in her backyard, sharing stories as daylight became dusk and finally darkness, there'd been no secrets between them. But those experiences had happened a lifetime ago. That Tyler was gone. Maybe that Nicki was, too.

When she reached the road, she looked in both directions. She hadn't gotten up as early as she did during the week. Maybe if she had, she could have avoided the nightmare. If that was the case, the extra hour of sleep hadn't been worth it.

She took in a deep breath and increased her pace to

a jog, giving Callie the opportunity to work out some of that inexhaustible supply of energy. Yesterday after Tyler had finished his work at the inn, they'd made a run to Crystal River for materials. Today he had the day free and planned to tackle her bathroom vanity installation in the afternoon, as soon as she got home from church. Andy refused to work on Sundays. Tyler didn't have any such compunctions.

Callie skidded to a stop so suddenly, the leash jerked Nicki's arm backward before she could halt her forward movement. She frowned down at the dog, who'd stepped off the pavement and was busy sniffing the ground. "A little bit of warning would be nice."

Nicki let her gaze drift down the street. A short distance away, a car sat parked against a patch of woods. When Nicki started moving again, the engine cranked up. The driver made a U-turn and sped away, heading toward downtown.

Her chest tightened, and she tried to push aside the uneasiness. The driver was probably a lost tourist consulting a map, then discovering he was on the wrong part of the island. That was a logical explanation.

Except for the break-in and the note and the knife left near her living room window.

Unfortunately, she hadn't gotten close enough to make out the tag. Other than the fact that it was small to medium size and white, she couldn't even say what kind of car it was. She wasn't good with car models. She'd always been a truck girl herself.

A few minutes later, she turned around and headed in the direction of home. Callie would keep going if Nicki let her, all the way to town. But long walks alone had lost their appeal. There were too many deserted stretches along Hodges.

Back at the house, she opened the front door and removed Callie's leash. The dog made a beeline for the kitchen, then stood watching her enter, eyes filled with eagerness. After opening a can and dishing up a generous serving of a smelly concoction named Savory Beef Stew, she poured herself some cereal and sat at the kitchen table.

Yesterday's mail was still piled at the edge. She'd been busy cleaning when she saw the mailman stop and hadn't taken the time to go through it. Then she'd set to work on one of her stained glass projects until Tyler arrived to take her to Home Depot.

She picked up the top piece and tore open the envelope. Central Florida Electric Cooperative. The charges were every bit as high as she'd expected. Summers in Florida were hot and it showed on the power bill. Of course, that was all she'd ever known. At least she had air conditioning, which was more than she could say for her early years.

The next envelope contained a credit card offer, which she intended to run through the shredder. Beneath that was something from Chase. One of her credit cards was through them. But the page showing through the windowed envelope looked more like a letter than a statement.

As she scanned the type, dread slid down her throat, lining her stomach with lead. Someone had applied for a credit card in her name, likely before she'd placed the fraud alert. She hadn't gotten home till Sunday night. And she'd called them Monday morning. If her intruder had come in on Friday, he'd had two whole days to wreak havoc with her credit.

She laid the sheet of paper on the table and sat back in her chair. She'd have to call Chase and cancel the request. This was what she'd feared the moment she saw her information spread across the table. One week had passed, and it was already starting.

The doorbell sounded, and her tension ratcheted up several notches. Who would be ringing her bell at eight-thirty on a Sunday morning? She looked through the peephole, and the tension dissipated. When she swung open the door, Tyler stood on her front porch.

He wasn't smiling. In fact, his jaw was tight, and vertical creases of concern marked the space between his eyebrows. When he spoke, the concern in his features came out in his tone. "Are you all right?"

"Yeah, other than the fact that someone just applied for credit in my name."

Of course, Tyler wouldn't have known about her identity theft concerns. Something else must have put those creases of worry on his face. "What's going on?"

He held out a folded sheet of paper, which she hadn't noticed until that moment, and a chill passed through her. "What is it?"

"Whoever has been harassing you has apparently decided to carry it next door. I don't think this is aimed at my brother, even though he's the one who retrieved it from the front door a few minutes ago. It wasn't there when I walked Sasha this morning."

She took what he held and unfolded it. Like the other note, it was written in all caps with bold, angry strokes that could belong to almost anyone.

WATCH THE COMPANY YOU KEEP. IT CAN
GET YOU KILLED.

Her blood turned to ice and her heart almost
stopped.

She looked up at Tyler, her jaw slack. Her heart had
resumed a frantic pace, and moisture coated her palms.
"He was watching us. He saw us leave for Home Depot
together." She took a step back, shaking her head. "You
have to stay away from me."

He moved closer until he was standing at the threshold. "Do you really think I'm intimidated by this creep
who's too much of a coward to show his face?"

"Maybe *you're* not intimidated, but *I* am. I'm not
willing to risk you getting hurt. This is my battle, not
yours." Although she had no idea what she'd done to
get drawn into it.

He took a step closer and put both hands on her
shoulders. Now he was inside her entry area. "It's *our*
battle. Friends stick together. Or have you forgotten
that?"

She dropped her gaze. No, she hadn't forgotten.
When some of the snooty rich girls at school had given
her a hard time about being adopted, he'd gone to bat for
her. And she'd returned the favor when those same girls
and their boyfriends had egged the principal's house
and tried to pin it on Tyler.

He laid a finger against the underside of her chin,
encouraging her to look at him. His eyes held a warmth
that had never been there before. Or maybe it had and
she'd been too young and naive to recognize it.

When he finally spoke, his tone was low, the words

heavy with meaning. "I never run from danger. Especially when it involves someone I care about."

She swallowed hard, unable to look away. His words suggested more than simple friendship. So did his tone.

The thought scared her more than anything had as yet.

Tyler moved through the darkness at a brisk walk, the beam of his flashlight illuminating the road ahead of him. It was 1:00 a.m. on a Monday morning, and Hodges was deserted, all the houses dark except for the soft glow of porch lights shining from a few of them. Gulf Boulevard didn't show any more signs of life than Hodges had. According to Andy, a lot of his neighbors escaped the heat and humidity and spent summers up north. In the wee hours of the morning, that sense of isolation was even more acute. Most sensible people were in bed.

He'd tried. For almost two hours, he'd chased sleep. Finally he'd grown tired of tossing and turning and had slipped out into the quiet night.

He should have been tired. Actually, he was. Physically, anyway. He'd worked hard all afternoon and evening, pushing to get Nicki's new sink and vanity installed and the plumbing hooked back up. He'd even started on the shelves in the master bedroom closet. But when he'd dropped into bed at eleven, his brain had gone into overdrive.

The note Andy had pulled off the front door that morning was in the hands of the police. But they probably wouldn't be any more successful lifting the intruder's prints from it than they had been from the first one. Or from Nicki's house, for that matter. All the viable prints belonged to her. Her intruder had apparently worn gloves.

Tyler slowed his pace to catch his breath and cross to the other side of the road. He'd walked about a mile and a half. Maybe by the time he got back, he would be ready to sleep.

But the tension that had coiled through him as he lay staring into the darkness was still very much there. The second note had disturbed him as much as the first. Not because of what it meant for him. He wasn't afraid for his own life. The note was likely an empty threat. But he understood the purpose behind the words. Whoever wrote them was trying to isolate Nicki from her friends. To weaken her and make her a better target.

It wasn't going to work. It would take more than a written threat to tear him from Nicki's side. It would take mortars, RPGs and a couple of Abrams tanks. And even that wouldn't stop him if he could help it.

As he neared her house, he cast a glance in that direction. Light trickled through the trees that bordered her yard. She would be sound asleep inside, Callie nearby. The dog's presence brought him a measure of relief. Otherwise, he would insist on loaning her Sasha to stand guard. Or move in himself.

He dismissed the thought as soon as it entered his mind. The nightmares were too frequent. Too real. He'd gotten pretty good at waking himself up before the scream building in his throat escaped. But sometimes the terror refused to release its grip until it was too late. Though it hadn't happened yet, it was only a matter of time until he jarred Andy and Joan from a sound sleep. That was going to be embarrassing enough. He wasn't about to show Nicki how messed up he was.

He rolled his shoulders, then ran his hands through his hair. When he reached her property line, he again shifted his gaze toward the house. To the right of the front door, a rattan rocker sat bathed in soft yellow light. A short distance away, an American flag hung from a short pole attached to the corner post. Further to the right, her Ram sat in the carport.

In total darkness.

He drew his brows together. When he'd headed out thirty minutes ago, both the porch light and the carport light were on. Had she gotten up and turned the second one off? Or had someone else extinguished it, not wanting to be seen?

He clicked off the flashlight and squinted into the night, worry coiling in his gut. But beyond the glow of the porch light, everything was black. Clouds obscured most of the stars, and the sliver of moon he'd seen early yesterday morning wouldn't be visible until just before daylight.

He retraced his steps, then slipped into the trees bordering her yard. A twig snapped beneath his foot, the sound amplified in the silence. He hesitated. He had a gun. It just wasn't with him. With his flashbacks and nightmares, he'd figured it was best to leave his weapon with a friend for safekeeping. Only a week and a half had passed, and he was already rethinking that decision.

Staying within the tree line, he continued to move away from the road, eyes on the carport. Once he was even with her truck, he stopped, listening. The skin on his arms prickled. Someone was there, or had just been there.

Dropping to his hands and knees, he clicked on the light and shone it under the truck, then swept the beam side to side in an expanding arc. Seeing no one, he sprinted to the back of the truck, then crept around it.

When he shone the light on the door of her house, he heaved a sigh of relief. It was undisturbed. He shook the tension from his shoulders. Of course it was undisturbed. No one was getting past the lock he'd installed. At least not without an ax or sledgehammer.

So maybe no one had been there. Maybe the light had burned out. He reached into the fixture. The bulb was still hot. It was also loose. He rotated it a quarter turn and light flooded the carport.

His stomach tightened as he stepped back from the door. His first instinct had been right. Someone had been prowling around her house in the dark. He scanned the side of the house. The laundry room window was the only jalousie left. According to Nicki, the prior owner had changed all the others to single-hungs.

Icy fingers traced a path down the back of his neck. Two of the four-inch by three-foot panes of glass stood against the house. The metal tracks that had held them were warped and bent outward. And the intruder had started on a third. Another thirty minutes and someone would have been inside, in spite of the locks he'd installed.

A sense of protectiveness surged through him, and he clenched his fists. Whoever wanted a piece of his longtime friend was going to have to go through him first. He stalked toward the front door, pulling out his phone as he walked.

After calling 911, he lifted his hand to ring the bell, then hesitated. That probably wasn't the best option. He'd startle her out of a sound sleep, and she'd be terrified, not knowing what threat stood at her front door.

He dialed her number, and she answered on the second ring.

"Tyler? What's going on?" Her tone held hesitancy.

"Come to the front door. I'm right outside."

A light went on some distance to his left, filtering through the slats in her miniblinds. A minute later, the front door swung inward.

And his breath caught in his throat.

Nicki stood just inside, auburn hair framing her face in wild disarray. Her eyes were wide, fear swimming in their green depths, and it shot straight to his gut. She stepped back to allow him entrance, then stood motionless, her silk robe fluttering with every jagged breath. She looked so vulnerable.

And so beautiful.

As he stepped inside, he lifted a hand to reach for her, then mentally shook himself. She was his friend, nothing more. It was all she'd been back then, and there was even more reason to keep it that way now. In less than two months, he'd be finished with his business in Cedar Key and once again hit the road. In the meantime, he wouldn't lead her on with promises he couldn't keep.

"What are you doing here?"

He shut and locked the door. "I caught someone trying to get in your laundry room window. He already had two panes of glass out and was working on the third."

Blood leached from her face, leaving it with as little

color as the pale ivory robe. She took a faltering step backward, shaking her head. "I didn't hear anything. Callie apparently didn't, either."

He closed the gap between them and took her hand. "The police are on their way. Let's sit." He led her to the couch, then eased down next to her. When he draped an arm across her shoulders, she leaned into him. A faint floral scent teased his senses. He closed his eyes and forced himself to focus.

"You need to think about moving in with Andy and Joan."

"I don't want to impose." She leaned away to look over at him. "Will you stay for a while, though? Just tonight?"

He pulled her against him again. "I'm not going anywhere. If you want to try to get some sleep after the police leave, I'll be right here on your couch. Come daylight, I'm picking you up a more secure window."

In some areas, changing windows required a permit. If that was the case in Cedar Key, he'd beg forgiveness later.

Because nothing was going to stop him from doing what he needed to do. Come nightfall, the house would be secure. Nicki would be safe.

And that was all that mattered.

Nicki shut off her computer monitor and pulled her purse from the bottom desk drawer. It had been a hectic day. But she wasn't complaining. Busy days went faster. And she was thankful for the job. The week she'd moved to Cedar Key, the receptionist at city hall had moved away, leaving the position open. With Nicki's five years in management, she was overqualified. But the pleasant people and the laid-back environment were just what she needed.

Now that the day was finished, fatigue was creeping over her. She'd barely been asleep two hours when Tyler called. Though she'd been back in bed less than two hours later, sleep had been a long time coming.

She hated to even speculate about what would have happened if Tyler hadn't walked by when he had. She never did ask him what he was doing outside at that time. That should have raised her suspicions, but it didn't. Something told her she wasn't the only one with nightmares—memories kept at bay in the daylight, waiting to invade the subconscious in the wee hours of the morning.

She slipped her purse strap over her shoulder and moved toward the double glass door, but before she could get there, a female voice stopped her.

"Nicki, can you come into my office for a moment?"

She stopped midstride to face her boss, Miranda Jacobs. Nicki's chest tightened, and she tried to shake off the uneasiness. There was no reason to be nervous. She hadn't done anything wrong. Not that she knew of, anyway. But there was something in her boss's tone, a cool professionalism, hinting that there might be a reprimand coming.

"Have a seat." Miranda motioned toward one of two chairs, then settled herself behind her desk. "I've been very happy with your work performance. You're catching on to everything quickly."

Nicki nodded, waiting for Miranda to continue. Why did she sense an imminent *but*?

"I received a complaint this afternoon, though."

Nicki frowned. "What kind of complaint?"

"A woman called, a Jane Wilson. Do you remember helping her this morning?"

"No, I don't. But I'd have to look back through my notes to be sure. Did I do something wrong?"

"She said you were rude to her."

Her jaw dropped. "Rude? I haven't been rude to anybody."

Miranda gave her a sympathetic smile. "Dealing with people all day long can be stressful. But no matter how annoying someone is, we have to bite our tongues and be pleasant, even if it's the last thing we feel like doing."

Nicki shook her head. "I promise you, I wasn't rude to anybody. What did I supposedly say?"

"She claimed that she asked you some questions and you were short with her, that you cut her off and said you didn't have time for her."

Nicki snapped her mouth shut. It had sagged even further during Miranda's explanation. "That's not true. She's making things up."

"Why would someone do that?" Miranda's brows were raised in question. Or maybe it was suspicion.

"I don't know why." She drew in a shaky breath. Someone was out to get her.

"Have you made any enemies?"

"No." Well, maybe one. Peter hadn't taken it very well when she dumped him. He somehow thought it reasonable to expect her to wait for him to do his time, then pick up where they left off.

But it wasn't Peter who'd made the complaint. It was a woman. Of course, he could have put someone up to it.

She drew in a deep breath. "I apparently have an

enemy I don't know about, because I promise you, I haven't been rude to anyone. You've heard me talk to people who come in, and you've listened to my side of phone conversations. Have I ever been at all short with anyone?"

Miranda hesitated before responding. "No, you haven't."

"Please believe me when I tell you I wasn't this time, either."

"All right." She gave her a small smile. "I have to admit, when the woman called, what she was describing didn't sound like you at all, even though she mentioned you by name, first and last."

"When I'm helping people, I always identify myself by my first name only. This Jane Wilson, if that's even her real name, apparently knows me outside of work."

Miranda nodded. Nicki wished her farewell and walked from the office. After climbing into the Ram, she backed from the parking space, mind still spinning. Who would want to get her in trouble and possibly fired from her job? The same person who was leaving threatening notes and had tried to tamper with her credit. Someone had set out to destroy her. But she had no idea who.

She pressed the brake and eased into her turn onto D Street. Over the years, she'd stuck her neck out a few times, provided help to friends who needed a little extra gumption to walk away from good-for-nothing men. Maybe it was coming back to bite her.

Or maybe it was her own good-for-nothing man. Peter had gotten pretty angry the last time she talked to him. He was out on bond, still awaiting trial, and before she left for Miami, he'd called to make one last-ditch effort to talk her into staying with him. His pleas hadn't worked. But was he that vindictive? Something about the scenario didn't ring true.

Maybe it wasn't anger driving him. Maybe the threats and attacks were all part of an elaborate plot to send her running back to him. The notes, the break-in and subsequent attempts, the knife left behind—it was all unsettling. In fact, she was scared. She'd be lying if she said otherwise.

And the attack on her credit and her job were almost as disconcerting. If she ended up unemployed, with her credit destroyed, she'd soon find herself in serious financial trouble, in spite of the little nest egg she'd inherited from her parents.

She squared her shoulders and tightened her grip on the wheel. Peter was underestimating her. She'd been through a lot worse and survived. No matter what happened, she didn't need a man to take care of her.

She made the final turn on her four-minute commute. Hodges wasn't in a subdivision. Most of the houses were spaced far apart, some almost hidden in the trees. The secluded setting was what she'd wanted. A month ago, anyway. Now one of those postage-stamp-size lots in the city had a lot of appeal.

But she had good neighbors. Andy and Joan had extended their friendship the day she moved in, with freshly baked cookies, and had made regular visits since. Now Tyler was there, at least for the time being. He and Andy wouldn't be home yet. But she'd see him tonight. He was determined to have the laundry room window changed out before she went to bed.

And he was equally determined to ignore the threat

against him. She pursed her lips. The note had said, "Watch the company you keep. It can get you killed."

Was Peter capable of murder? She hadn't thought so. But she hadn't thought he was capable of embezzling a hundred grand from his employer, either. Which proved one thing—she really didn't know him at all.

She pressed the brakes and made a right turn into her driveway. She'd unwittingly given Peter a reason to go after Tyler in earnest. Late Saturday afternoon, she'd left with Tyler and not come back for three hours. They'd even had dinner out. It had been totally professional. Their *date* had consisted of roaming the aisles of Home Depot.

But Peter wouldn't know that. He'd think she'd found someone new, which would make his chances of winning her back zilch. Of course, they'd been nonexistent anyway. But Peter wasn't one to give up easily.

She drew in a stabilizing breath. As soon as she got inside, she'd call Amber, or maybe Amber's brother Hunter. He'd been a Cedar Key cop a lot longer. She wasn't ready to file an official report, because she didn't have enough evidence to make an accusation. But Hunter would be able to advise her.

As she moved up the drive, she scanned the house's concrete block face. Everything looked the same as it had when she'd come home at lunchtime to take Callie out. Except…

Dread wrapped around her like a cloak. Something was attached to her front door.

Heart pounding in her chest, she jammed on the brakes, jumped from the truck and hurried to the porch. A sheet of paper was folded in half, its creased edge affixed to the door with a small piece of tape.

She extended her arm. She wouldn't risk destroying prints. Touching only the top edge, she folded it back and scanned the words.

YOUR WORLD UNRAVELING? YOU HAVEN'T SEEN ANYTHING YET.
YOUR HOME, YOUR JOB, YOUR FRIENDS, YOUR LIFE.
I WILL TAKE IT ALL.

Bile rose in her throat, and she stepped back, clutching her stomach. Why would Peter go after her like this? The first note had said, "The party's over." But he, better than anyone, knew her life had been anything but a party. She'd told him a little about her childhood and her years in foster care. Not all of it. There were some things she hadn't told anyone except Tyler.

But Peter knew enough. And he'd been there the night she got the news of her parents' deaths. She'd had plenty of hardships over her twenty-nine years and fought far too many battles to get where she was.

None of that mattered. She knew that now. Peter was a lover spurned. He was selfish and angry, maybe even a little off.

It was a combination that could turn out to be deadly.

FOUR

Nicki turned back the cover on her notebook and passed it across the table to Meagan Kingston. "It's just a rough sketch, but what do you think?"

Meagan studied what she held, then showed it to Hunter next to her. He was dressed in his police uniform, on break during his shift. Besides enjoying dinner with his wife, he'd be dispensing some advice. Nicki had already forewarned him.

Meagan tapped the page with her other hand. "I like it. But I think I want a little more detail on the trees."

Nicki nodded. She'd treated herself on her birthday with a Meagan Kingston painting, and now Meagan was ordering some Nicki Jackson stained glass to hang in her dining room. The three of them sat on the back deck of the Blue Desert Café, two half-eaten medium pizzas in the center of the table. Usually in July, the deck would have been unbearably hot, even at dusk. But a thunderstorm brewed somewhere off the coast, sending refreshing gusts of cooler air over the water.

After wiping her fingers on a paper napkin, Meagan removed a pencil from her purse, then held it poised over the paper. "Do you mind?"

"Not at all. You're the artist."

"Looking at what you have displayed at Darci's and the co-op, I'd say you are, too." She put the pencil to the paper and sketched some lines, then did some shading.

While Meagan worked, Nicki took a bite of pizza, then lifted her gaze to the dock extending out over the shallow water. Near the shore, palmettos partially obstructed the view. Further out, other greenery broke the horizon. Cedar Key was a series of islands, some connected by bridges, others accessible only by boat.

Meagan handed her back the pad. "Is that doable?"

"Definitely. Now for colors." She pulled several pages of swatches from the back of the notebook and, after handing them to Meagan, turned her attention to Hunter.

"You've probably heard about what's been happening around my place."

"The break-in and the notes, yeah. We've been having units drive through and patrol the area."

"I appreciate it." She cut off a piece of pizza but didn't put it in her mouth. "Yesterday I had another note."

"I heard." Hunter frowned. "Those were some pretty serious threats. Any ideas on who could be making them?"

She opened her mouth, but the words stuck in her throat. When she'd made the decision to talk to Hunter, she'd been sure of her course of action. What if she was wrong? Peter was in enough trouble without her adding to it with false accusations.

But what if she was right? What if he refused to accept that it was over and would stop at nothing to get her back? Or worse, what if he had accepted it and decided if he couldn't have her, no one else could, either?

She drew in a deep breath. "Let's just say there's a guy who isn't very happy with me right now."

"An ex-boyfriend who can't seem to walk away?"

"Fiancé. I was supposed to have gotten married last month."

Meagan looked up from the color blocks, concern in her eyes. From what Nicki had heard, her new friend had her own horror story involving an ex-fiancé. "I take it you're the one who broke it off."

"Yes." At least she was trying. She wasn't sure she'd accomplished it yet. "He thinks I should give him a second chance."

Hunter didn't respond, just waited for her to continue, which was turning out to be a lot harder than she'd thought it would be. It was as if Peter's bad choices were somehow a reflection on her.

In a way, they were. They showed what a bad judge of character she was.

She pursed her lips, then continued. "He got caught embezzling from his company and was arrested. He was shocked I wasn't going to stand by him through it. First he tried playing the sympathy card, blaming it on being poor and deprived growing up and needing to feel secure. Then he tried to guilt me into staying with him, telling me that he did it all for me."

She stifled a snort. Material possessions had never ranked high on her list of priorities. The first nine years of her life, she hardly had any. When she finally landed in the Jackson home, there were too many other new things to experience—love, security and life without fear. Baubles didn't mean much. Peter knew that as well as anybody.

She pushed a bite of pizza across her plate with her fork, then again met Hunter's eyes. "When that didn't work, he got angry. That was the last conversation I had with him, about two weeks ago." She'd witnessed a side of him she'd never seen before. Once she'd made it clear it was over, he called her several choice names and disconnected the call. Was he angry enough to attack her in the way someone had in recent days? Angry enough to want to kill her? It was hard to imagine.

"Did he make any threats?"

"No, just said some pretty hateful things. I figured he was hurt and was lashing out." But maybe it was more serious than that. Maybe over the next few days he'd let the anger simmer and had plotted ways to get even.

She sank back in her chair. "I'm not sure what to do. I don't want to accuse him in case he's innocent."

Hunter nodded. "Where does he live?"

"Crystal River." An hour away. Too close for comfort.

"I'll check out his mug shot and be on the lookout for him. I could also go talk to him, see what he's been up to. If he *is* the one behind everything that's been going on, maybe having a cop show up on his doorstep will be enough to convince him to stop."

"That sounds good." She released a small sigh. A little bit of the weight lifted.

Hunter popped the last of his pizza into his mouth and stood. "I'd better get back out there."

She smiled up at him. "Thanks for letting me talk shop during your dinner break."

"Anytime." He pulled a pad from his pocket. "Give me your ex's name."

"Peter Gaines."

"I'll check him out." He bent to give Meagan a kiss, then stepped off the deck and headed up the narrow gravel drive toward the road.

Meagan slid her chair closer and laid the samples on the table between them. "I think I have my colors picked out."

By the time they finished their pizza, several color names surrounded the sketch, with arrows drawn and notes in the margins. "I should have this finished in about a month." Nicki tucked the notebook into her bag and flagged the waitress to bring their checks.

Meagan rested her chin in her hands. "I'm nervous about you staying at your place alone."

"I'm not alone. I've got Callie."

"Callie doesn't carry a .45."

Meagan had a point. "I do have someone keeping an eye on me." And he likely did carry a .45. Or something comparable. "Andy's kid brother." Since they all went to the same church, Meagan knew Andy and Joan.

Her brows shot up. "Oh, yeah?"

"No, not like that." She'd made a vow. No more serious relationships. She was through with men. "We're just friends."

Meagan grinned. "I've heard that before."

Nicki sighed. Meagan was enjoying giving her a hard time. "I'm serious. We were friends as kids, in Crystal River. Then he and his mom moved away, and we lost contact."

"And now he's back. Well, I'm glad he's there."

Yeah, so was she. Their childhood friendship made him a little more than a concerned neighbor. Over the past few days, he'd spent a lot of his spare time at her house. Of course, he'd had a good excuse. He'd gotten through most of the work she'd assigned him.

In fact, he was there tonight, installing a closet organizer in her bedroom. She'd left him with his tools, a pencil tucked over his ear and the room in total chaos. She'd probably be sleeping on the daybed tonight, unless he worked really fast.

She looked out over the water. The trees were now dark silhouettes against a sky stained shades of orange and pink. Soon dusk would fade to darkness. By then, she'd be headed home. Tyler would likely still be there.

He'd changed a lot since those early days. That everpresent chip on his shoulder seemed to have lessened. Maybe with maturity, his anger with the world had evolved into acceptance.

It wasn't an easy acceptance. Tension emanated from him, a brooding silence that hadn't been there before. Beneath the adult confidence was a tortured soul, something he'd never be able to hide from her, because she knew him too well. And she knew herself. Their shared traumas formed the invisible cord that would always tie them together.

When she looked at Meagan again, she was wearing a knowing half smile. Nicki shrugged it off. Let her think what she would. She valued Tyler's friendship too much to throw it away on yet another failed attempt at something more.

After they'd paid their checks, Nicki rose and followed Meagan off the deck.

"I'll keep you posted on my progress. I've got two other projects to finish first, but they're small."

Meagan leaned against the passenger side of her car. All the parking for the Blue Desert Café was along the street. "No rush. We're still dealing with remodeling dust. My goal is another two weeks, but a month is more realistic."

Nicki's gaze drifted past Meagan to the house across the street. "Then it should be perfect ti—" She stopped midsentence, tension spiking through her. A figure stood in the shadow of a tree a few yards from the side of the house.

Meagan turned. "What's wrong?"

"Someone's watching us." Either that, or he'd stepped outside for a smoke and she was letting her imagination run away with her. Between the distance and the shadows, she couldn't say what he was doing or see any kind of identifying characteristics.

Moments later, the person scurried away, moving deeper into the woods. Meagan pulled her cell phone from her purse with one hand and grasped Nicki's arm with the other. "Stay here. I'm calling Hunter."

"Trust me, I'm not going anywhere." She wasn't the type to follow a stranger into the woods unarmed. She'd leave the heroics to the cops.

The cops showed up in the form of Hunter ten minutes later. He'd searched the area and found no one suspicious. She wasn't surprised. Whoever had been watching her from the shadows was the same person who was making all the threats. She had no doubt. If he was smart enough to not leave behind any prints, he wouldn't stand around and wait for the police to arrive.

She climbed into the driver's seat of the Ram and

started the engine, thankful she wasn't going home to an empty house. But Tyler wouldn't be around indefinitely. Eventually he and Andy would finish their work on the inn. And Tyler would be gone.

She pulled from the parking lot, an odd sense of loss stabbing through her. It wasn't just the thought of the protection she'd no longer have. And it wasn't the loss of the companionship she was growing accustomed to.

No matter how she tried to fight it, Tyler was becoming much more than a friend.

Andy turned his truck onto Hodges, and Tyler took off his baseball cap and laid it in his lap. It was covered in drywall dust. His clothes had been, too, but he'd managed to brush off the majority of it before getting into Andy's truck. A cool shower had a lot of appeal. Then he'd see what Nicki was doing.

He'd finished the closet organizer project late Tuesday night, after she'd come in from dinner with her friends. Last night she'd gone to church. Nicki had invited him twice, Andy and Joan more than that. But each time he'd come up with an excuse.

It wasn't like he'd never been. After his father left, his mother hadn't known how to deal with his anger, so she found a small white church two blocks away and started taking him. It didn't help. He hated not getting to sleep in Sunday mornings and resented giving up time hanging with his friends.

When his mom got sick, though, everything changed, and he tried to make a bargain with God. If God would keep his mother alive, he'd be in church every time the doors opened. Hey, he'd even have been willing to become a preacher if that was what it took.

Apparently God didn't listen to angry teenage boys. Because in spite of his mother's good fight and his own pleas and promises, the cancer took her anyway. And he hadn't darkened the door of a church since.

"So what are your long-term plans?" Andy's words cut across his thoughts.

"I don't have any."

"Are you thinking about maybe settling in Cedar Key?"

He shrugged. "Hadn't considered it. Why?"

"I don't know. You've been spending a lot of time with Nicki. I figured you might think about staying here permanently."

Tyler slanted his brother a glance, but Andy's attention was focused forward.

"I've been spending a lot of time with Nicki because I've been working for her."

Now Andy did look at him. "You know, you're going to have to stop running at some point."

Tyler nailed him with a glare. "Twenty years ago, you were bigger than me, so you got away with bossing me around. It's not going to fly now."

Andy lifted his shoulders and let them fall. "Have it your way. But as long as you're here, I'm going to work on you. I want you to be happy, bro."

"I *am* happy." He crossed his arms in front of him, then dropped his hands to his lap. The first pose had looked anything but happy.

When they approached Nicki's house, she was walking down the driveway with Callie. Tyler lowered the passenger window, and Andy eased to a stop. When Tyler called a greeting, Callie picked up the pace, tail wagging, pulling Nicki with her. She stopped at the side of the truck, then stood up, resting her front paws on the door. The dog had taken a liking to him. Or maybe she just associated him with her buddy Sasha.

He reached through the open window to pat her head while he talked to Nicki. "Will you be home tonight? I was going to see if I could stop over."

"Make it after eight. I'm feeding Callie, warming up some leftovers for myself, then heading up to The Market for groceries."

"Let me get cleaned up, and I'll go with you."

She waved away his offer. "I'm sure you have better things to do than follow me around the grocery store."

"It's no trouble. I need to go myself. I'm sure Andy and Joan are out of something. If not, I'll pick up another jar of peanut butter." He grinned. "You can never have too much peanut butter."

She returned his smile. "All right. In that case, I'll let you tag along. Come over in about forty-five minutes."

After Nicki pulled Callie away from the truck, Andy took his foot off the brake and gave him a crooked smile.

Tyler shrugged. "She's in danger, and I'm right next door." A touch of defensiveness had crept into his tone. His brother knew about the break-in and notes and didn't need to be giving him a hard time.

Andy pulled into his driveway and turned off the truck. "She's a nice girl. I'm glad you're taking an interest."

Tyler responded with a grunt.

A short time later, he was on Nicki's front porch, clean and pleasantly full from Joan's cooking. Before ringing the bell, he'd scanned the area, making sure they were alone. It appeared they were. Of course, with woods all around, he couldn't say for sure.

Nicki grabbed her purse and, after giving Callie her usual command to behave herself, closed and locked the door. She pressed a button on her key fob and the locks on the Ram popped up. "How is the work at the inn coming along?"

"Right on schedule." He slid into the passenger seat next to her. "Actually a little ahead of schedule. We've been at it almost two full weeks. If everything goes as planned, another five should do it."

She nodded, her lower lip pulled between her teeth.

He reached across the cab of the truck to rest a hand on her shoulder. "Nicki, I'm not leaving until I know you're safe."

"Thanks." She gave him a half smile. "Under normal circumstances I'd tell you not to change your plans on account of me. But I feel a lot better having you around."

She cranked up the truck but didn't back from the drive. "I might know who's been doing this."

He studied her in the growing afternoon shadows. "Who?"

"Peter, my ex-fiancé. I broke things off with him about three months ago. The first few weeks, he was pretty persistent, trying to get me to go back to him."

His gut tightened. He'd heard too many stories about vindictive exes. And he wouldn't mind getting his hands on this one. "Have you given his name to the police?"

"I told Hunter about him Tuesday night. He's Amber's brother, also works for Cedar Key. Anyhow, he called me this afternoon and said he'd talked to Peter.

Apparently he hasn't been outside Citrus County. Even has the witnesses to prove it."

"So our only lead has been eliminated."

She shifted the truck into Reverse and backed into the street. "Not necessarily. These people aren't with him twenty-four seven. He could drive over here, stay a couple of hours and be back before anybody misses him. Or maybe he's getting someone else to do his dirty work."

Tyler shook his head. Neither scenario sounded good. No, leaving Cedar Key before this was resolved was out of the question.

A few minutes later, Nicki pulled into a parking space. The Market at Cedar Key was the only grocery store on the island. It wasn't big, but it had all the basics and then some. Which was good, since Joan had come up with a fairly lengthy list.

Nicki tilted her head toward the Prius next to them. "Meagan's here. I'll introduce you."

As soon as they were inside, Nicki waved him forward and made a beeline for the cash register. A woman with long blond hair gathered three bags, looping two of them over one arm before picking up the third. Her face lit up when she saw Nicki. She shifted the single bag to her left hand to give her a hug, then extended her hand his direction.

"Meagan Kingston. You must be Tyler. Nicki told me about you." She smiled. "It was all good. I promise."

After the women chatted for a minute or two, Meagan glanced down at her bags. "I'd better get this stuff home."

Nicki nodded. "I'm glad we ran into you. When I

saw that shiny silver Prius out there, I knew you were inside here."

Meagan frowned. "The poor thing had to be towed yesterday."

Nicki's brows went up. "You broke down? You haven't had it that long."

"No, the engine was fine. It was the tires, all four of them. I got up yesterday morning, and someone had taken a knife to them."

Nicki's jaw dropped and the blood leached from her face. "Someone slashed your tires?" She pressed her hands to her cheeks and took several steps back. "This is my fault. You were with me Tuesday for dinner. And he was watching. We saw him. He's watching everything I do." She looked frantically around her. "He retaliates against anyone who dares to be seen with me. You have to stay away."

Meagan rushed toward her, then stopped Nicki's flow of words with a hand on her arm. "You don't know that."

Nicki jerked her arm away and backed up further. "Tyler and I left for the evening to go to Home Depot, and the next morning, there was a note on his door telling him to watch the company he keeps, that it could get him killed. Anyone who dares to be seen with me will pay for it. I should leave."

Tyler draped an arm across her shoulders and pulled her close. "Whoever is doing this will follow you. He's trying to isolate you. If you leave Cedar Key, you'll be playing right into his hands. You need to stay here where you have friends, people looking out for you."

"Tyler's right. I won't abandon you, and I'm sure if we talked to our other friends, they'd say the same thing. And I know for a fact that the Cedar Key police are working on all this." Meagan looped the last bag over her arm so she could take both of Nicki's hands. "Promise me you'll stay." When Nicki didn't respond, Meagan spoke with more force. "Promise me you'll stay. Give Hunter and Amber and the others a chance to solve this. Okay?"

Nicki nodded. Her face was still pale, her eyes wide and filled with fear. "I don't want anyone getting hurt. If anything happened to any of you guys, I'd never forgive myself." She hesitated, eyeing him with raised brows. "You carry a gun, right?"

"No, I don't."

"Do you have one?"

"Not here."

She studied him, brows raised in question at his clipped answer. But he didn't talk about his experiences in Afghanistan with anyone. And he certainly didn't discuss the mental and emotional issues that had followed him home.

He dropped his arm from her shoulder to take her hand. "Come on. Let's get our shopping done."

Whoever was tormenting her meant business. By spending so much time with her, Tyler was putting himself in the line of fire, especially if her tormentor was a jealous ex.

That was a chance he was willing to take.

All through their friendship, he'd been there for her. And she'd been there for him. He wasn't about to let her face this alone.

FIVE

A man knelt in the semidarkness, straddling the figure beneath him. He raised his arm, and a shaft of light caught the blade of a knife. For one tense moment, he held it suspended. Then he plunged it downward. The figure on the floor jerked, and a high-pitched scream pierced the night.

The arm rose and swung down a second time. The head lifted from the floor, and stringy hair fell over the side of the woman's face as another scream was wrenched from her throat. Again and again, the knife plunged into her back. The screams became gurgles, then faded to silence.

Nicki came awake with a start, her own scream dying on her lips. The remnants of the dream held on, chilling her all the way to her core.

This was the second time she'd dreamed of a woman being killed. Twice in less than a week. The other time, she didn't witness it, just saw the aftermath. The woman's final breath. And the blood. Lots of blood.

Callie nudged her hand and released a small whimper. The dog had gotten into bed with her sometime during the night. Nicki pushed herself to a seated position and patted Callie's head. "It's okay, girl. It was only a nightmare."

Where were the dreams coming from? And why now?

She was under a lot of stress. The constant uneasiness, the sense of being watched. The threats against friends. Maybe she hadn't been able to turn it all off when she crawled into bed at night. And the detectives reopening her mother's murder case gave her mind the fodder it needed to congeal all the fear and anxiety into one terrifying scenario.

She glanced at the clock on the nightstand, its red numerals glowing in the darkness: 4:45. She didn't have to get up for another hour. But trying to go back to sleep would be pointless. Her heart pounded in her chest, and tension still threaded through her muscles.

She swung her feet over the edge of the bed, trying to shake off the final tendrils of the dream. Callie jumped to the floor with a thud, then trotted to the open door, tail wagging. For Callie, morning meant two things, both equally exciting—a walk and food. It wasn't time yet for breakfast. And since Nicki didn't know who was lurking in the darkness, taking her for an early run alone was out of the question. Callie would have to wait.

Nicki stood and padded from the room. She'd work on one of her stained glass projects before starting her day. She always found the work therapeutic. Anything creative calmed her. Over the years, she'd spent many hours hunched over her sketch pad.

Sometime later, she sat back in her chair and stretched her arms skyward. She'd gotten a lot accomplished. While she worked, the nightmare had gradually released its grip. It wasn't daylight yet, but it was time to quit.

She rolled the chair back from her work table, and Callie perked up. For the past hour, she'd lain with her head resting on her front paws, eyes closed. Now that she knew a walk was imminent, she pranced from the room and down the hall, casting backward glances as she went.

The doorbell rang, and Nicki smiled. All week long, Tyler had been there at 6:00 a.m., like clockwork. After finding someone at her window, he'd insisted they time their walks together. She hadn't argued. The dogs hadn't objected, either.

She swung open the door and greeted Tyler with a smile and Sasha with a firm scratch behind the ears.

He lifted a brow. "You look perky this morning."

"I probably look perkier than I feel. I've been awake since shortly after four-thirty."

"Trouble sleeping?"

"Nightmare."

He grimaced. "I can relate."

Yeah, he probably could. Though he'd never mentioned it, he'd probably had more than his share of bad dreams.

At the end of her drive, she scanned Hodges in both directions. Tyler was doing the same thing. But the street was deserted. They turned left and headed down the road.

"Any new news?"

"Since ten o'clock last night?" She grinned.

He returned her smile. "Patience has never been one of my virtues."

"I think I remember that." She kicked a piece of gravel along the asphalt. "Since the Peter lead was a dead end, I'm guessing there won't be any opportunity for breaks until whoever is harassing me tries something again."

His smile faded. "You might be right."

When they'd once again reached her drive, he hesitated. "How about letting me take you to work?"

"Thanks, but I think I'll be safe driving in broad daylight. Besides, I don't want to be without my truck. I'd be stranded until you came to get me."

"Let me at least see you from your house to your truck."

She gave a sharp nod. "That I can do. I'll call you when I'm ready to leave."

She stepped onto her porch and bade him farewell, but he still seemed hesitant. She rested a hand on his forearm. "I'll be fine."

When she slipped out the side door forty-five minutes later, he was waiting next to her truck, this time without Sasha.

"I wish I could be here when you get home every night."

"I'll be all right. I'll keep my eyes open and won't get out of the truck until I'm sure I'm alone. Then it's only a few feet to the kitchen door." She pressed the fob and strolled toward the Ram. "And if all goes as planned, when I get home tonight, I'll be armed."

He raised his brows. "You bought a gun?"

"No. I don't know how to use a gun." She didn't like them, either. One of the men her mother brought home had one. Used to get it out regularly, too, wave it around and make threats with it. Several times he aimed it at her mother, explaining that with a twitch of his index finger, her brains would be all over the wall behind her. He'd even pointed it at Jenny once.

"When I got home from the Blue Desert Café Tuesday night, I went online and ordered some mace. I had it shipped to the office and paid for two-day delivery. According to the email confirmation, it went out Wednesday and will arrive today."

Relief flashed across his features. "That makes me feel a little better. Not as good as being here myself, but better than the thought of you walking in unprotected."

She climbed into the truck and fastened her seat belt. "I don't know how to use a gun, but I can handle a tube of mace. And if I ever feel threatened, I won't hesitate." She grinned at him. "So make sure you never sneak up on me."

"Thanks for the warning."

She held up a hand in farewell. "Later."

He closed the door, patted the roof twice, then watched her back from the carport. By the time she reached the end of the drive, he was halfway through his trek back to Andy's. The two men would be leaving shortly and wouldn't return until after seven. At least, that had been their usual schedule.

She backed onto Hodges, then headed toward town. She wasn't in a hurry. She had fifteen minutes to make the four-minute drive. Her to-do list waited on her desk, completed the afternoon before. No matter how crazy things got, she never left work without outlining her tasks for the next day. She wouldn't hold to it— her plans would change a hundred times. But starting with everything laid out in black and white gave her a sense of control.

And control was important. Maybe because the first nine years of her life, she'd had none.

She turned onto D Street and stepped on the gas. Some distance ahead, a group of six or eight people stood beside the road, waiting to cross. Tourists, more than likely.

As she approached, the man standing at the head of the group stepped into the road, and the others followed. None of them looked to be in a hurry, another indication she'd been right in labeling them tourists.

Nicki depressed the brake pedal, then, with a gasp, released it to jam it down again. Both times, it went all the way to the floor. Panic stabbed through her as the distance between her and those ambling across the road decreased. Hand on the horn, she grabbed the lever beside her and jerked it upward, but the emergency brake was as useless as the other.

A half-dozen faces turned in her direction, then registered the same panic spiraling through her. She jerked the wheel to the right and bounced up over the curb and onto the sidewalk. Not twenty feet away, a telephone pole stood framed in her front windshield. Before she could react, a deafening crash mingled with her own scream, and the truck jerked to an abrupt halt.

For several moments, she sat motionless, drawing in calming breaths and trying to still her racing heart. She'd almost hit those people. When she shifted her gaze to the side mirror, one of the men in the group stalked toward her, face red and arms flailing.

She groaned. She'd just had one of the biggest scares of her life and now had to face some stranger's wrath. As soon as she opened the door, the words assaulted her.

"What were you doing, lady? You could have killed us."

She stepped from the truck, and for a brief moment, her legs threatened to collapse under her. Steadying herself against the door, she lifted a hand. "I'm so sorry. It was my brakes." She drew in another shaky breath. "I pressed the pedal and didn't have any."

Her words apparently didn't soothe his anger. "Brakes don't just go out like that." He snapped his fingers on the word *that*.

She squared her shoulders, her own patience growing thin. She didn't need this. "Well, mine did. I had new pads put on six months ago, and the brakes were working fine until just now."

He dropped to his hands and knees in front of her door. After inspecting the underside of the truck for a half minute, he rose, then went to the back. His head and shoulders again disappeared under the truck. When he stood a minute later, he was rubbing his right thumb and fingers together.

"Lady, you got a problem."

His tone was somber, all traces of anger gone. A cold block of fear moved through her, leaving a frozen trail. She preferred the anger. "What do you mean?"

"I've been working on cars since I was sixteen, and it looks to me like somebody punctured your brake lines."

Her chest clenched. "They're cut?"

"Not cut. Judging from the way brake fluid is sprayed all over the undercarriage, someone poked holes in them, front and back. If we went around to the passenger side, we'd probably find the same thing. This way, instead of the fluid all leaking out in your driveway, your brakes wouldn't fail until after you'd depressed them a time or two." He pulled a tissue from his pocket and wiped the oily substance from his fingers. "The mess under there was intentional, because whoever did this also cut the cable to the emergency brake." He shook his head.

"Somebody wants you dead."

Tyler's tennis shoes pounded the pavement, and his breath came in heavy pants. The moon rested low on the horizon, a swollen crescent, waiting to be pushed aside by the morning. But even at that early hour, a solid sheet of moisture hung in the air, promising another hot and humid day.

Andy and Joan were still asleep. At 4:30 a.m., so was Sasha. He had been, too, until about twenty minutes ago, when the whoosh of incoming RPGs had invaded his dreams. After a series of brilliant flashes and earth-rocking explosions, he'd sprung from the bed and slammed into the wall, a scream clawing its way up his throat.

So he'd thrown on some clothes and shoes and headed outside. Exercise helped. Movement of any kind helped. It almost gave him the illusion that he could outrun the memories tormenting him.

He slowed to a stop, then stood bent at the waist, hands on his knees, trying to catch his breath. Two years ago, a run like he'd just done wouldn't even have left him winded. Now, with the slightest exertion, his damaged lungs worked overtime, never quite able to keep up with what his body demanded.

He moved again, this time at a more reasonable pace. No sense sapping all his strength before getting the day started.

Today would be a shorter workday. Saturdays always were. But first, he'd check on Nicki. She'd been pretty shaken yesterday after her accident. Actually, *he'd* been pretty shaken. She'd again resisted his pleas to move into Andy's place, but she was at least going along with his demand that she not go anywhere alone. In another hour, he'd be on her doorstep with Sasha. This afternoon, they'd take another walk, then make a trip to Enterprise in Chiefland to get her a rental car. The Ram was repairable, but it was going to be out of commission for some time.

The hum of an engine sounded in the distance, and he cast a glance over his shoulder. There was no sign of headlights. In fact, the closest street lamp was some distance away. And the dim glow of the porch light on the nearest house wasn't much more help than the sliver of moon barely visible over the treetops.

He shrugged it off and continued walking. Sometime between those morning and afternoon walks, he needed to talk to Bridgett. His sister hadn't called in almost two weeks, which was unheard of. Of course, she probably had some level of comfort knowing he was staying with Andy. At least she knew he wasn't dying under a bridge somewhere.

The hum grew louder and closer, and he cast another glance over his shoulder. Still nothing. What was he hearing? It was too close to be someone's air conditioner kicking on. And if a car were approaching, there would be headlights, especially on such a dark night.

Moments later, the hum raised in pitch and volume,

building to a roar in the span of a second. Now he had no doubt. It was a car. And it was close.

His heart beat out a jagged rhythm, sending blood roaring through his ears. He shot sideways toward the woods a few feet away. Blinding light engulfed him, and he swiveled his head. The car was right on him. In a split-second reaction, he threw himself onto the hood and rolled up the windshield, then landed in the grass with a thud. The car careened back onto the road, and the taillights brightened. The driver was hitting the brakes.

When he tried to sit up, his battered body protested. His right leg and hip were bruised, maybe even broken. Already his back muscles were drawing up, and pain shot through his left shoulder and wrist with the slightest movement.

He pulled his cell phone from his pocket, and his heart fell. A strange pattern of psychedelic colors shone from behind the shattered screen. Twenty yards away, the car made a U-turn. The headlights again went black and the engine roared.

It was coming back.

With a groan, he rolled onto his hands and knees and scrambled into the woods. The car raced past. He plopped onto his side and lay motionless in the underbrush. If the driver got out to finish what he'd started, Tyler would be doomed. He was in no shape to fight.

He pushed himself to a seated position and clenched his fists. He didn't survive three tours in Afghanistan to be taken out by some driver with an ax to grind. Or a jealous ex-fiancé.

The car made one more pass to head toward town and probably off Cedar Key. And for several minutes,

Tyler sat there, testing joints and taking inventory. By the time he crawled from the woods, the promise of dawn touched the eastern sky, now a pale charcoal.

With the help of the nearest tree, he pulled himself to his feet, then took a small step. Everything still worked. Apparently nothing was broken.

He put a shaking hand to his chest, trying to calm his pounding pulse. That was no accident. The extinguished lights, the racing engine, the erratic path off the road—it left no doubt. Someone had tried to kill him.

But this wasn't about him. He didn't have any enemies. Not on this side of the Atlantic, anyway. This was about Nicki. And the note. He'd been warned to stay away from her or else. Tough. No way was he letting her face this creep alone.

He stepped away from the tree that had been supporting him for the past couple of minutes and limped toward the road. He was a good mile from Andy's. Stumbling back with every joint and muscle screaming at him was going to be pure agony.

By the time Nicki's driveway came into view, the eastern sky had faded from black to gray, the first hint of approaching dawn. He'd call the police from Nicki's house. Already he was probably ten or fifteen minutes late for their morning walk, and he didn't want her heading out alone.

He'd made it three quarters of the way up the drive when the door swung open and Nicki called his name. She eyed him with concern. "What happened? Where's Sasha?"

He stepped onto her porch and winced. "I left early

to go for a walk and almost didn't make it back. Someone tried to turn me into a hood ornament."

Her mouth fell open and her brows drew together. "Are you all right?"

"I don't think anything's broken, but I can pretty much guarantee you, come tomorrow, I'll wish I'd stayed in bed."

She took his arm and draped it across her shoulders, then looped hers around his waist. Once she had him inside, she locked the door and led him to the couch. "Have you called the cops?"

"The impact killed my phone."

She pulled hers from her pocket and, without further comment, punched in the three numbers. There would be nothing the police could do. The car was long gone. And he couldn't even describe it. Year, make, model, even the color—it was all a mystery. The only lead he could give them was to look for a car with a body-sized dent in the hood and roof.

While she waited for the dispatcher, her gaze swept him. "You need to go to the hospital."

"I'll be fine. I just need some ice." Several bags. Maybe an ice bath. Because his body was now beyond protesting. It was shouting obscenities.

After reporting everything, Nicki pocketed the phone and headed toward the kitchen. When she returned a minute later, she held two dish towels and zippered bags filled with ice. He wrapped both packs, trying to analyze which body parts hurt the worst. Probably his hip and shoulder.

"What about Callie?"

"I'll take her out in the front yard when the police get here."

"You don't have to work?"

"Not on Saturday."

Oh, yeah. She was off. And unless he did some incredible mending over the next hour or two, he'd be off, too.

She sank onto the couch next to him and put her face in her hands. "This is my fault."

He dropped the ice pack from his shoulder into his lap so he could give her leg an encouraging pat. He'd known this was coming, that once she was no longer occupied with taking care of him, she'd heap the guilt on herself. "That didn't look like you behind the wheel."

"You know what I mean. You were told to stay away from me. You should heed those warnings." She stood and started to pace. "I'm putting everyone in danger. I need to leave."

He once again pressed the ice pack to his shoulder. "We've already had this discussion. I'm sticking with you through this. And so is everyone else. We're going to catch this guy."

She stopped pacing to stare at him, her eyes wide and filled with worry. "And who else will be hurt in the meantime?"

"We'll all be careful. I'm sure the police will be stepping up surveillance, too." And he was going to see to it that they checked out this Peter character. He'd better have a pretty watertight alibi for where he was between the hours of four and six this morning.

He forced a smile. "How about getting us some breakfast?" She needed to occupy herself with activity again and stop all this ridiculous talk of leaving.

For several moments, she stood motionless, eyes

swimming with indecision. Finally she gave a sharp nod and disappeared into the kitchen. Moments later, the clanging of pots and pans announced the beginning of breakfast preparation. Soon the police would arrive and make a report. Meanwhile, he'd rest. Now that his pulse rate had returned to normal and his system had absorbed all the extra adrenaline, exhaustion was creeping over him. He hadn't gotten enough sleep. Or maybe it was having almost been killed.

He let his head fall against the padded back of the couch and closed his eyes. As the pleasant aromas of frying bacon and eggs wafted through the house, an odd sense of contentment slid through him, that cozy warmth synonymous with home. It wrapped around him, holding him in its soothing embrace.

Home. What every soldier dreams of during each seemingly endless stint. The reason to survive against all odds.

He moved the ice pack from his shoulder to his knee and pushed the thought from his mind. He wasn't even going there. Because home didn't last. That was life.

Good things ended way too soon.

And the fewer attachments he formed, the better.

SIX

Nicki slashed through the final envelope, the rip of paper eclipsing the other office sounds. She'd just come back with the morning mail and was determined to get it dispersed before lunchtime. It had been a busy morning. One more day and the week would be over.

She laid the letter opener on her desk and removed the contents of each envelope. There were the usual items—invoices, customer payments, letters and other business, along with a healthy stack of junk mail. She began separating everything into stacks based on recipient. One letter, however, was simply addressed to "Manager." That was typical for form solicitation letters. But this one looked more personal.

She leaned forward and began to read. Below the City's address were the words "Re: Complaint about employee."

Uneasiness chewed at the edges of her mind. Last week, someone else had made a complaint. About *her*. That one had come from a Jane Wilson. This letter was from a man, a Thomas Abbott, according to the bottom of the letter. The return address portion of the envelope was left blank.

As she read, the uneasiness morphed to dread in one swift stroke. The first sentence pointed out the offending employee—Nicki Jackson. The author of the letter claimed to have applied for a permit for which he had to pay one hundred fifty dollars, but that when he arrived home, he found the receipt had been made out for seventy-five dollars.

Nicki's jaw dropped, and a cold lump settled in her stomach. She wasn't being accused of simple rudeness this time. The author of the letter accused her of dishonesty.

The next paragraph began, "Clearly she pocketed the other seventy-five." And he had his own opinions about how to handle it, suggesting that she be terminated and investigated for embezzling.

Nicki dropped the sheet of paper on her desk and flopped back in her chair, her thoughts tumbling over one another. Although she wanted nothing more than to make the letter disappear, she couldn't do it. She had to give it to her boss. Maybe Miranda would see it for what it was—nothing more than a vendetta. Peter had embezzled, and she'd refused to stand by him. So he was accusing her of the same crime.

She rose and headed toward her boss's open door. She'd been able to convince her the first time. But she was a new employee. And this was the second complaint in a week and a half. How many more would she be able to ward off before Miranda gave in and let her go?

As soon as she stopped in the doorway, her boss motioned her in. Maybe she should have given the letter to the police. But what was the point? The envelope had been handled by too many people. She stepped forward and handed Miranda both the letter and the envelope. "This came in the mail today."

Without speaking, Miranda took what she held. When she finished studying them, she looked up, brows raised, a question in her eyes.

Nicki steeled herself, ready to make her defense. "Lies. Every bit of it."

"I'd tend to agree."

The tension drained from her body. "You would?"

"No return address on the letter or the envelope. No contact phone number. He claims he was bringing in the paperwork for his sister, who is the one having the work done, but didn't give us her name, so there's no way to verify any of this. I smell a skunk."

Nicki slumped against the doorjamb and released a sigh. Her job was safe. For the time being.

After thanking Miranda, she headed back to her desk to retrieve her purse. No more trips home at lunchtime to walk Cassie. The dog was now spending her days with Joan and Sasha. And Tyler was watching Nicki come and go from the house each morning and afternoon.

But a short walk downtown in the middle of the day would be safe. Today, especially, she needed the break from the office. She'd do lunch out, maybe text Tyler to see if he had time to talk.

She stepped outside and looked both ways down Second Street. The car she'd rented on Saturday sat parked at the curb. Several people strolled down the sidewalks.

She crossed the street then headed toward Tony's Seafood Restaurant a block away. In an hour, she'd return, refreshed, settled and ready to work. She opened the wooden door and drew in a fragrant breath. Yes, this was what she needed—a bowl of Tony's world-famous clam chowder. And a long talk with her oldest and dearest friend.

Friend. That was all Tyler was. That was what she had to keep reminding herself. Especially with the way he looked at her. The gentle concern he showed. That fierce protectiveness.

She sighed, then moved to one of the small tables. After the server had taken her order, she pulled her phone from her purse. Tyler hadn't been without his for long. The day he was hit, she'd driven him to Chiefland for a replacement. He'd wanted to be easily reachable if she needed him.

When she swiped the screen, ready to place the call, her phone showed one text received. The number belonged to her private investigator, and the message was short and sweet—Call when you get a chance. Her pulse picked up. Tyler would wait.

When Daniel answered, she dispensed with the pleasantries. "You have news?"

"Sort of." He paused. "I caught up to her in Gainesville yesterday, met her face-to-face. She was waitressing in a small mom-and-pop place. I told her who I was and why I was looking for her. This was about four o'clock. She said she'd get off at seven and I should come back then."

"You came back, and she was gone."

"I never left. I took a seat in a corner booth, got the Wednesday special, and settled in to wait her out. Shortly after five, I didn't see her anymore. Checked, and she'd slipped out the back. At first no one would tell me where she went. They all seemed to be covering for her."

"Then?"

"Then one of the women broke down and gave me what I needed. She and her brother had been separated when they were young and recently reunited, so she has a soft spot for siblings trying to find each other. She didn't have the address, but she'd picked Jenny up for work a few times when Jenny's car broke down, so she was able to give me the name of the apartment complex and the location of the apartment."

"I take it by the time you got there, she'd run again."

The waitress returned with a glass of tea, and Nicki swirled the ice with the straw. The investigator had gotten close this time, had actually gotten to meet Jenny. But the rest of the story was going like all the previous times. Jenny still didn't want to be found.

"Yes. Jenny's roommate was there. She said she didn't know Jenny, that she lived alone. Of course, the neighbors said otherwise. I staked out the place all night, until about eleven o'clock this morning, and she never returned. When I went to the diner, I learned she was scheduled for the breakfast and lunch shifts and never showed up."

As Nicki listened, an idea began to form. Jenny's roommate was protecting her. With all the trouble Jenny had been in, who knew what she was running from? She'd view any stranger looking for her as a threat. Even Daniel. After all, he could be a cop, his story about looking for a long-lost sister nothing but a cover to get information.

But if a woman showed up on the roommate's doorstep, someone who bore a strong family resemblance

to Jenny, maybe she'd talk. Even with the five-year age difference, Nicki had looked like her. They'd had the same green eyes, the same small bone structure, the same angled features.

"Give me the roommate's name and address. I'm going to pay her a visit and see if she'll talk to me. I'm sure Jenny's gone, but maybe the roommate has a clue where she went."

Nicki pulled a piece of paper from her purse and jotted down the information, then disconnected the call. Gainesville was a little more than an hour away. She'd leave right after work. She didn't have her truck back yet, but the rental car would get her there just fine. Now to call Tyler.

He answered on the first ring.

"Am I pulling you away from work?" she asked.

"No, we just broke for lunch. What's up?"

"I'm going to Gainesville."

"What's in Gainesville?"

She smiled. "Jenny's roommate. I got a call from the PI. Jenny has disappeared again, but I now have her roommate's name and address. I'm going to pay her a visit."

"When?"

"I'm leaving right after work."

"I'll get off early." His tone was emphatic. "I'm going with you."

"Won't that put Andy in a bind?"

"Andy will survive. I'm not letting you drive over there alone."

The determination and protectiveness behind his words sent an odd warmth coursing through her. She

tamped it down. He'd always been protective of her. It didn't mean any more now than it had then.

"It *will* be nice to have some company."

The waitress returned with a steaming bowl of clam chowder and placed it in front of her.

"My lunch just arrived."

"What are you having?"

"Tony's clam chowder."

"I haven't tried it."

"You need to." She spooned some into her mouth and savored it. "Spicy. The best."

"Better than my cold bologna sandwich?"

"Living with Joan, you're not eating bologna."

"You're right. Today is beef stroganoff. I was trying to drum up some sympathy."

She grinned. His quirky sense of humor was usually buried under a pensive soberness, but occasionally it slipped through, giving her a glimpse of the old Tyler. "It didn't work."

When she'd finished her soup and paid for her meal, she took a final swig of iced tea. "I've got to get back to work."

"Me, too. I'll meet you at city hall at five."

"Sounds good." She crumpled her napkin and stood. "Later."

"You always say that. I've never heard you say *bye*."

"*Goodbye* is too final." That was what she'd told her parents the night before they were killed—*bye*. She hadn't meant it. What she'd meant was *see you later* or *talk to you tomorrow* or any number of other ways to sign off. Instead, she'd told them *bye*, and that was what it had ended up being, their final goodbye.

What she'd said hadn't made a difference. She knew

that, at least logically. But she hadn't been able to bring herself to mouth the word since.

She walked out the door and headed toward the office, pushing the thought from her mind. She had more important things to think about. After over six months of searching for her sister, with countless ups and downs, a reunion might be in the near future. The thought brought eagerness mixed with trepidation.

Nicki wasn't kidding herself. Jenny was messed up. Even with love and a stable environment, she wouldn't be right for a long time. Maybe ever. Reaching out to Jenny might saddle her with Jenny's problems for years to come. But she wasn't about to quit now.

Finding Jenny had become even more important with the visit from the detectives. Given that Jenny was five years older, she probably remembered more. She was possibly home at the time of the murder. Maybe even witnessed it.

Whatever faults their mother had possessed, she hadn't deserved to die in the way she had. For twenty-two long years, someone had gotten away with murder. But now, justice might soon be served.

When it finally happened, Nicki would be able to close the door on the past.

Then maybe the nightmares would stop.

Andy pulled into a parking space in front of City Hall, and Tyler stepped from the truck. His F-150 was still sitting in the driveway at his brother's place. He wouldn't need it. This trip was Nicki's deal, so she'd insisted on driving.

He moved up the front walk, stiff after his short ride there from the inn. Although six days had passed since the car had struck him, he still had some sore joints and ugly bruises. He reached up to rub his shoulder, then glanced in through the glass door. The room was the obvious site for town meetings. A table stood at the front, several microphones positioned along its length. Wooden pews arranged in neat rows provided seating for attendees.

To the left, a window opened into Nicki's work area. She stood there talking with someone, papers spread out on the counter between them. Nicki looked in his direction and gave him a quick smile before returning her attention to the customer.

He turned to his right, where three glass-encased bulletin boards lined that side of the walk. He was a couple of minutes early. And if the paperwork on the counter was any indication, Nicki was going to be more than a few minutes late.

The first case held meeting agendas—city commissioners, historic preservation board and local planning agency. The second held a variety of announcements, from Scrabble at the library to vacation Bible school next month. The sleepy town of Cedar Key was more active than he'd realized.

He'd just moved to the third board when the door opened and the man Nicki had been helping walked out. A few minutes later, Nicki was ready to leave, too. He smiled at her as she came out the door. "You got through your work quicker than I thought you were going to."

"I planned it that way." She grinned. "I figure if we get there before dark, this Gina Truman will be more likely to open the door."

"You're probably right." He followed her to the rental car. "So, what do you know about her?"

"Her name and address."

"That's it?" He raised his brows. "I'm glad I'm going with you."

"I don't think I have a whole lot to worry about. She's more likely to avoid me than mug me."

She started the car, then dropped it into Reverse. "I had another attack today."

His stomach clenched. "You didn't tell me."

"I was going to. Then I talked to the PI, and that has consumed my thoughts ever since."

"What happened?" He scanned the length of her body. She didn't look injured in any way, so it must not have been a physical attack.

"Another complaint at work. This time it was a letter, someone claiming I'd charged him a hundred fifty dollars for a seventy-five-dollar permit. The letter said I should be fired and investigated for embezzling. Fortunately, my boss didn't take it seriously. There was no return address on the letter or the envelope."

His tension uncoiled. The threat was serious. Someone had made some grave allegations. But this time it was her job instead of her life. He suppressed a relieved sigh. With Nicki facing the possibility of losing her means of supporting herself, she probably wouldn't appreciate the gesture.

An hour later found them in a less-than-desirable part of downtown Gainesville. The businesses had bars on the windows, and trash littered the edges of the road.

Tyler frowned over at her. "Are you sure you're in the right place?"

"Positive. I pulled up the directions on MapQuest and also plugged it into my GPS. They agree, so that's a good sign."

He nodded, his uneasiness over her quest increasing with every passing minute.

Nicki succeeded in driving them directly to Jenny's apartment complex. It was two stories, made of concrete block covered in peeling paint. A metal stairway zigzagged up the side of the building, its railing continuing all the way across the front.

Nicki pulled into a parking space and turned off the car. "Stay here, at least for the time being. She'll be more likely to open the door if it's just me standing there."

He crossed his arms. "I don't like you going in there alone."

"You don't have a choice. Now that I've gotten this close, I'm not going to risk you scaring her off."

He frowned. With that determination in her eyes, arguing with her would be pointless. But if she went inside and didn't come out within ten minutes, he was going to break the door down.

She looped her purse strap over her shoulder, and as she stepped out of the car, he opened his own door. They were parked a couple of spaces over but from his vantage point in the car, he could see Gina Truman's apartment door and hear any conversation that took place. Until Nicki disappeared inside. His stomach clenched. It was going to be a long ten minutes.

But before Nicki had even reached the front bumper, the door to apartment 112 swung open and a young woman stepped out. If there was any family resemblance at all between Nicki and her sister, the woman he was looking at wasn't Jenny. The woman on the front stoop was short, not much over five feet, but solid, a little on the chunky side. Chances were good they were looking at Gina Truman. If so, Nicki wouldn't even have to go inside.

Nicki moved in her direction, and their words drifted back to him.

"Gina?"

"Yeah?" The single word held a lot of hesitation. Her gaze flitted over the parking area.

"I'm looking for Jenny. I'm her sister."

Gina's eyes snapped back to Nicki's face, and she visibly relaxed. They stood facing one another, both in profile to him.

Gina nodded. "Y'all look enough alike. I can see you're sisters. So the guy yesterday was telling the truth." She shook her head. "I couldn't take any chances. A while back, Jenny crossed some bad people down in Miami. If they found her, it wouldn't be good."

Tyler's gut tightened. So Jenny wasn't just running from the police. Her problems were more serious. Worry circled through him, settling in his chest. With a crazy ex after her, Nicki had enough to handle without exposing herself to her sister's mess of a life.

Nicki shifted her weight to the other foot. She was still dressed for work. Her black dress pants and modest heels were a sharp contrast to Gina's short shorts and flip-flops. "I don't know how much Jenny told you about her childhood."

"Not much. She's a pretty private person. Tough, but private."

"When she was twelve, our mom was murdered. We got put into different foster homes and haven't seen

each other since. About six months ago, I started looking for her." Nicki paused, studying the other woman.
"I'd like to help her if I can."

Gina sighed. "I wish I could tell you where she
went, but I don't know."

"What did she say when she was leaving?"

"Nothing much. She came tearing through the front
door and ran straight to our room. Then she started
throwing her stuff in bags. She said they were closing
in, so it was time to run again."

"Did she give you any hint about where she was
headed?"

"Not at all. She just said she had to disappear. But
first she was going to see a wrong made right."

"Any idea what she was talking about?"

Gina shook her head. "I asked her, but she was
being real mysterious-like. I got the idea it was something before all the Miami stuff. Something from a
long time in her past."

"If you hear from her, will you let me know?"

"Sure. Give me your number."

While Nicki fished in her purse for a pen and
paper, a door opened upstairs. A woman stepped out
and moved down the walkway, five-inch heels click-
ing against the cement floor. Her leather miniskirt
stretched taut across her hips, and the thin tank she
wore left little to the imagination. She made her way
down the stairs, weaving between three young men
who sat at varying heights, sharing a smoke. Based on
the sweet smell that wafted to him, it wasn't tobacco.
When she reached the bottom of the stairs, she moved
toward the parking lot.

Tyler shifted his gaze back to Nicki, but not before taking in the sunken cheeks beneath the woman's heavy makeup and the creases around her eyes and mouth. She probably wasn't more than thirty, but she'd lived a hard life.

Nicki climbed into the driver's seat and cranked the engine. "She doesn't know where Jenny went, but she's going to call me if she gets word from her."

"Yeah, I heard." He studied her for several moments. She wasn't going to like what he was about to say, but he couldn't keep quiet. "Gina said Jenny has some bad guys after her. Doesn't that worry you?"

"A little." She backed from the space, then headed out the same way they'd come in.

"Whoever is after her, you don't want her to lead them to you. Maybe you should stop your search. Sometimes it's better to leave well enough alone."

Her hands tightened on the wheel, and her eyes filled with that determination he knew so well. "I won't turn my back on her."

"You've got enough of your own problems. Do you really want to take on Jenny's?"

"I want to find her, whatever it involves. You have a brother and a sister. I have no one."

You have me. The thought shot through his mind, but he immediately dismissed it. She *didn't* have him. She had his friendship, at least for the time being. Then, once this was over, once Nicki was safe and the work on the inn was complete, he'd be gone.

A block away, she braked to ease around an old man pushing a heaped-up shopping cart down the edge of the road. "These people have it rough."

"A lot of them choose the lifestyle they have."

"No, they don't. It chooses them." She stopped at

a traffic light, then turned to look at him. "Do you think they want to live that way? Like the woman who walked past you a few minutes ago. She'll spend the night turning tricks. Maybe she'll still be alive in the morning."

The light changed, and she stepped on the gas. "Even Gina. On the surface she seems okay. But you didn't look in her eyes and see the hopelessness there."

He smiled over at her, but her expression didn't soften. "You've always stuck up for the underdog."

"That's because I've been the underdog, more times than I can count."

Yes, she had. So she would always have a heart for those less fortunate. It was innate, an intrinsic part of her.

And that was one of the things he loved about her.

SEVEN

It was dark, except for a narrow shaft of light spilling into the room from somewhere down the hall. But it wasn't silent. There was a tussle, panting, then curses.

A woman ran into the room, a man right behind her. He pushed her to the floor and pinned her there.

Light glinted off the blade of a knife. He raised it and plunged it into her back, again and again. Screams echoed through the room, then fell silent.

The woman lifted her head and turned it to the side to mouth a single word—"Run."

Nicki jumped from the bed and stumbled backward until the dresser stopped her. Bile pushed its way up her throat, and she clamped a hand over her mouth. The scene was the same as the other two times she'd had the nightmare. Just as real, just as bloody.

But what had chilled her the most was the woman's face—the pain and fear and desperation.

And her own recognition.

The face had belonged to her mother.

Cassie nudged her hand, then pressed her body against Nicki's legs. Nicki dropped to her knees to wrap both arms around the dog's neck and bury her face in the soft fur. For several moments, she clung to her, the lifeline linking her to sanity. Gradually her racing pulse slowed and her spinning thoughts stilled.

What had just happened?

She'd dreamed of her mother's murder, as real as if she'd been there. And her mother had warned her—or somebody—to run.

Was it more than a dream? Was it a memory?

No, that was impossible. She hadn't been there. She'd been next door, with Lizzie and her family. While Lizzie had waited in the doorway to her room, Nicki had gotten her things together—pajamas, clothes to put on in the morning, her toothbrush and toothpaste, a brush and ribbons and barrettes for Lizzie and her to play beauty parlor. She'd never forget that night, because it had been the end of an era. After that, everything had changed. Her whole life had been turned upside down.

The next morning was just as clear in her mind. She'd woken up to Mrs. McDonald shaking her gently, the woman's face streaked with tears, telling her that something awful had happened, that her mother was gone and people would be coming to get her, people who'd love her and take care of her.

So why was she dreaming about her mother's murder as if she'd been there and witnessed it?

She pulled a T-shirt and pair of shorts from the dresser. It was four thirty on a Saturday morning. She should go back to sleep. But that was the last thing she felt like doing. What she wanted to do was walk.

She moved to the nightstand and picked up her phone. At this time of night, most normal people were asleep. But there was a good chance Tyler wouldn't be. She keyed two words into the phone.

You up?

The return text came moments later, a frowny face. Her thumbs slid over the screen again.

Walk?

Be right there.

By the time she finished dressing, brushed her hair into a high ponytail and clipped on Callie's leash, Tyler was at the door with Sasha. She stepped onto the porch, and he looked at her with raised brows.

"Another nightmare?"

"Yeah. You?"

"Yeah."

"What about?"

He shrugged. "Just stuff."

She released a sigh. He was as tight-lipped as ever. But she didn't expect otherwise. She stepped off the porch and headed down the drive. "I've had nightmares most of my life. But the ones I'm having lately are different." She was going to sound crazy, but she needed to talk to someone. And if there was anybody she could be herself with, it was Tyler.

If only he could be himself with her.

"I keep dreaming I'm seeing my mother's murder."

"Since when?"

"The last couple of weeks."

He nodded, his expression thoughtful in the light

of the half moon. "After all these years, the event was probably pushed to the back of your mind. The visit from the detectives a couple of weeks ago put it front and center. And all the stress you've been under hasn't helped."

What he said made sense. But it was more than that. "I don't know. Aside from the fact that I'm just an observer, it doesn't feel like my other nightmares. It seems so real. It's almost like I'm…remembering."

He looked over at her, brow creased. "You said you weren't there."

"I know."

"Is it possible you were?"

"No. I distinctly recall going to Lizzie's house. My memory isn't the slightest bit foggy on that. She came home with me to get my stuff together. Then we went to her house. We took turns fixing each other's hair, and her mom made chocolate chip cookies, brought them to us hot out of the oven."

She smiled at the memory. The time spent with Lizzie and her mother had been the one bright spot in an otherwise dreary and terrifying childhood.

"A little while later, we went to bed. The next thing I remember is waking up and Mrs. McDonald breaking the news to me."

In the distance, headlights angled toward them, someone coming from the direction of town. Tyler grabbed her arm and pulled her into a neighbor's yard. The dogs followed without hesitation. All while she had spoken, he'd listened with tense alertness, his eyes taking in their surroundings. They ducked behind a tree, and the vehicle moved past at a normal rate of speed. It was an SUV. As it neared her house, it didn't slow or make any other suspicious moves.

Tyler let out a breath. "False alarm." He led her back toward the road. "Cars in the dark make me a little more nervous now than they used to."

She cast him a sympathetic smile. "With good reason."

By the time they returned to the house, the first hint of dawn had touched the eastern sky. He stepped onto her porch and watched her unlock the door.

"What are your plans for today?"

She shrugged. "Some cleaning, laundry. Work on a stained glass project or two." The problem was, none of what she mentioned appealed to her in her current state of mind. "Maybe I'll go into town, bum around some of the shops. Or hang out at the park." Anywhere that would take her thoughts away from threats and nightmares for a while.

"If you go this morning, I'll go with you."

"You have to work."

"Andy's doing a half day today, not going in until this afternoon. Joan's got him tied up this morning."

"In that case, how about a trip to the park?" Sitting on a bench overlooking the water, with the happy voices of children drifting to her from the playground, would go a long way toward soothing her frayed nerves. Especially with Tyler sitting next to her. As long as he was there, he wouldn't let any threats near her. "Nine o'clock?"

"Nine o'clock." He lifted a hand in farewell.

"Later."

After breakfast, she dove into her housework. In spite of her lack of enthusiasm, she managed to get quite a bit accomplished over the next three hours. When the doorbell rang, she'd just finished putting away the laundry and had all the cleaning except the vacuuming done. She was apparently looking forward to this outing with Tyler more than she'd realized.

After checking the peephole, she swung open the door. He stood on her porch, this time without Sasha. His black F-150 sat in her driveway.

He motioned in that direction. "I brought my truck over. You seemed a little cramped in the Fiat." He grinned. "Not to mention me with my long legs."

"I'm supposed to get my Ram back Monday or Tuesday." She walked with him to his truck. "I've always had trucks, never owned a car. My first vehicle was a blue Silverado pickup with chipped paint and several dents. But I was so proud of that thing."

He walked her to the passenger's side, and when she had climbed in, he closed the door. As he backed from the drive, she continued.

"At sixteen, I got a part-time job at the ice cream parlor in town. For over a year, I saved every penny I made, until I had enough to buy myself a vehicle."

The Silverado hadn't looked great, but she'd paid for it herself, and that had made all the difference. Some of her friends had gotten new cars for their sixteenth birthdays. Six months later, half of them had wrecked those same new cars. But the Silverado got her all the way through college and was still chugging when she'd traded it in four months after graduation.

Tyler shifted into Drive and headed down Hodges toward town. "I didn't have to buy a vehicle until I got out of the Army. When I was a teenager, we didn't have the money, with Mom being sick and everything.

By the time I hit seventeen, she wasn't driving anymore, and I was helping my aunt get her to and from her chemo and doctor's appointments. So her Camry sort of became mine."

Nicki watched him as he spoke. His tone was casual, but she wasn't fooled. His mother's illness and death had devastated him. She could see it in his eyes, in the hard lines of his jaw.

Tyler eased around the curve from Dock Street onto A, then pulled into a parking space. On the grassy area in front of them, a father worked with his boy to get a kite airborne. Beyond them, children scurried over a variety of playground equipment painted cheery shades of yellow and blue. Beyond that was the beach. The water was like glass, the line between sea and sky blurred, except for the green mass that was Atsena Otie Key.

Nicki stepped from the truck, then walked with Tyler toward the beach. Mornings and evenings were popular times at the park, when the July heat and humidity were much more bearable.

After a leisurely walk on the beach, she sank onto a wooden bench overlooking the water, and Tyler sat next to her. A barely there breeze whispered past them, and Nicki closed her eyes. But instead of drawing peace from the sights and sounds of nature, she had the opposite reaction. Tension wove through her body, drawing her nerves taut. Out in the open, she was too exposed, too vulnerable.

She glanced nervously around her. A short distance down the beach, a man and woman held fishing poles, two buckets between them. In the other direction, a young couple stood, hand in hand. At the playground, parents conversed with one another while keeping one eye on their charges. A man stood alone near the pavilion, leaning against a tree. Was he watching them?

When Tyler's arm came across her shoulders, she jumped.

"Are you okay?"

"Yeah, just a little tense." She rolled her shoulders, then gave him a shaky smile. "I guess I need to chill, huh?"

She settled in against his side, reveling in the safety she felt there. She shouldn't. If Peter was watching...

But he wasn't. She'd looked. Aside from the one guy standing near the pavilion, all the park's visitors seemed to be involved in their own activities, oblivious to Tyler's and her presence.

His arm tightened around her. "That's better."

She tilted her head to the side to smile up at him. "I guess I can always relax when you're around, huh? You stay alert enough for both of us."

"I try." He paused. "How about hanging out with Joan this afternoon?"

"I've got work to do at home. I promise I'll stay locked inside all weekend. Except for church." She cocked a brow at him. "You could go with me."

"Or you could ride with Andy and Joan."

"You act like I'm trying to drag you back into battle or something. Something must have turned you off."

He shrugged. "I don't see any purpose in it."

If that were the case, he'd be apathetic. She straightened on the bench so she could turn to face him. The set of his jaw and the stubbornness in his eyes said the opposite.

"I think you're angry with God. What happened?"

When he didn't respond, she continued. "You feel He let you down."

He crossed his arms over his chest. "Will you stop trying to psychoanalyze me?"

The angry response told her she was uncomfortably close to the truth. "He's not Santa Claus, you know."

"What is that supposed to mean?"

"You can't give Him a list and expect Him to give you everything you ask for."

"So what you're saying is God *doesn't* answer prayer."

"That's not what I'm saying. God always answers prayer. But sometimes the answer is *no* or *maybe*."

The sound he emitted was halfway between a sigh and a snort. "You're letting God totally off the hook."

"Look, I don't have all the answers. I'm new at this stuff myself. But there are a few things I've figured out. One is that bad things sometimes happen to good people. It doesn't mean God has turned a deaf ear to their prayers. We don't always understand why things happen the way they do. We don't see the big picture."

She studied him for a moment. If she was getting through to him, he wasn't letting it show.

"The second thing is that whatever happens, God walks with us through it. We don't have to face anything alone. He gives us strength and comfort, and when we come out on the other side, we're better people. But that part's up to each of us. We can let the bad stuff make us better or we can let it make us bitter."

For a long minute, a heavy silence hung in the air between them. Finally he stood and held out his hand. "I need to get home or Andy's going to be upset with me."

She put her hand in his and forced a smile. "Thanks for coming here with me. I needed this."

"Anytime."

When they arrived home, he walked with her onto her porch. She unlocked the front door and swung it open. Callie was waiting just inside, tail wagging furiously.

"I'm going to take her out."

"Then I'll hang around a few minutes longer."

Nicki stepped inside and hooked up the leash. When she walked back out, her gaze shifted to the side. At the edge of the woods was a flash of movement, with a simultaneous *phsst*. Callie let out a squeal, and Nicki dropped to her knees. Blood seeped from a wound behind the dog's left shoulder.

"Callie's been shot!" She jerked in a jagged breath, heart beating double-time.

Tyler grasped her arms and pulled her to her feet. "Inside, quick." He half dragged her over the threshold, tugging on the dog's leash. Callie yelped again when she put weight on the injured leg, then lay on the tile floor. Nicki ran to get a towel and dropped down next to her dog. Tyler was already on the phone, reporting the incident.

When he finished the call, Nicki looked up at him. "We need to find a vet." She should have established herself with one long before now. But Callie's shots weren't due for another eight months, and there'd been no reason to take her.

Now Callie was in trouble, and she had no idea who to call. She pressed the towel to the wound. The dog whined but didn't resist.

Tyler still held his phone, touching the screen several times. "I'm not pulling up any vets on Cedar Key, but there are some mobile vets who service the area."

"She might need surgery to remove the bullet."

"Our best option is to get her to a vet in Chiefland who's open on Saturday." He fiddled with his phone for another couple of minutes. "Family Pet Vet. They're open till noon. I'll let them know we're on our way."

While he waited for the call to connect, he knelt and inspected the wound. "Pellet gun."

"Are you sure?"

"If it was a regular bullet, Callie would be dead. They'll remove the pellet and she'll be fine."

Relief swept through her, mixed with anger. She'd been attacked in almost every way possible—her job, her finances, her friends. What kind of person would take out anger on a defenseless dog?

Peter wasn't an animal person, something he'd admitted right from the start. But he'd never been cruel. At least, she didn't think he had.

But maybe the shot wasn't intended for Callie. Maybe she or Tyler was the target. If that was the case, the shooter meant to harm, not kill. Otherwise he'd have chosen a different weapon. The realization didn't bring the comfort she longed for.

Tyler pocketed his phone and handed her his keys. "They're expecting us." He bent to scoop up Callie. "You drive and I'll hold her."

As she opened the front door, a Cedar Key police cruiser pulled into the driveway. Relief rushed through her. If their attacker had had any thoughts of hanging around for another shot, he was likely gone now.

Nicki locked the front door, and when she turned back around, Amber was stepping out of the car.

"We've got to get Callie to the vet. She's been shot." Of course, Amber probably already knew that.

"Where did the shot come from?"

Nicki pointed, then climbed into Tyler's truck. She'd get Callie the help she needed and leave Amber to do her investigation.

At the park this morning, she'd been tense, worried about what threats lurked in the shadows.

She'd been wrong. No one had been watching them at the park. While she and Tyler were there, someone was right here, waiting for them to return. Looking for the right moment to exact vengeance.

Poised and ready to strike when the moment came.

And Callie was the victim.

It was bound to happen eventually.

Tyler stalked down the street, his tread heavy. He didn't have Sasha with him, but the dog was awake. Andy and Joan were, too, thanks to him. He'd known it was just a matter of time. But that didn't make his shame any less.

Once again, his mind had taken him back to the place of darkness and smoke and the stench of burning flesh. His own screams had mingled with the screams of his men. And Andy's had, too. Apparently Andy had stood there for some time, hollering his name, smart enough to stay out of harm's way, but determined to release his mind from the prison holding it.

Several blocks down, he turned around and headed back toward his brother's house. He was going to have to face them. Might as well get it over with.

When he stepped inside, Joan was in the kitchen making a pot of coffee. Andy sat in his recliner, a magazine open in his lap. He looked up from what he was reading.

"Feeling better?"

Tyler shrugged and sank into a chair. "Better than I was thirty minutes ago. Sorry I woke you guys up."

"No need to apologize. From everything I've read and seen, it's to be expected."

Yeah, it was, but that didn't make it any easier.

"How about going to church with us this morning?"

He stifled a snort. "You think that's going to fix me?"

"It sure can't hurt."

Andy had invited him every week since he got there. Joan had chimed in a couple of times, too. Even Nicki had asked him to come.

But religious platitudes weren't going to fix what was wrong with him. Neither had counseling or anything else he'd tried. In fact, his therapists had been pretty up-front about the battles he was going to face. They'd warned him the flashbacks and nightmares could go on for years, maybe even a lifetime.

He pushed himself to his feet. "No thanks. I'll hang out here."

"Why are you so dead set against going with us?"

"Let's just say I'm keeping a promise."

He ignored Andy's raised brows and strode to the kitchen. After pouring himself a cup of coffee, he moved down the hall. He'd been in such a hurry to get away from the house, he'd stayed in the gym shorts he'd slept in and thrown on the first shirt he could find. But he wanted to make himself more presentable before meeting up with Nicki.

When he returned to the living room, Sasha lay next

to the recliner, waiting for the scratches Andy regularly delivered over the side of the chair. Tyler removed the leash from the coat rack by the front door, then clapped his hands. "Come on, girl, it's time to meet Callie. You'll just have to be easy with her."

He walked out the door and looked toward Nicki's. The sun sat low on the horizon, blocked by the trees separating the two properties. They'd agreed to a later meet-up time since it was Sunday. After yesterday's scare, starting the walk in daylight had a lot of appeal.

When he rang Nicki's bell, a half minute passed before the door opened.

"How's Callie?"

"Sore. She's limping, and she hates the cone."

He smiled. "They always do. But without it, she'd have those stitches pulled out in no time."

He'd been right about it being a pellet gun. The object had lodged in the soft tissue right behind the shoulder joint. The vet had removed it, put in three small stitches and sent them home with an antibiotic, some pain medication and the plastic cone around her neck.

"Last night we didn't go much past the front door. This time we'll see if she can make it all the way to the end of the driveway."

Letting Callie set the pace, they moved toward the road. The limp wasn't as pronounced as he'd expected. Another week or so and she'd probably be back to normal.

He frowned over at Nicki. "I'd feel a whole lot better if you'd move in with Andy and Joan and me." They'd had the conversation yesterday, and he hadn't gotten anywhere with her. Moving in with any of her Cedar Key friends was out of the question. She wouldn't put them in danger. And she wouldn't consider staying with someone off Cedar Key because she wasn't willing to give up her job. Moving in to one of the area hotels wasn't doable, either, because of cost.

"I'm not going to impose on them like that."

"It's not imposing. I already talked to them, and they agreed." Maybe he needed to have Andy and Joan walk over and appeal to Nicki themselves.

"There are only two bedrooms."

"You and Callie can have mine. I'll sleep on the couch."

She shook her head. "I'm not putting you out of your room." She sighed and continued. "I'll be all right. I'm being careful. And you're next door."

"Nicki, someone shot your dog." His exasperation came through in his tone. Sometimes she was too stubborn and independent for her own good.

"With a pellet gun. If he'd intended to kill Callie or me, he'd have used something a lot more lethal."

"Maybe next time he will."

When they reached the end of the drive, Callie stepped off into the grass and squatted. This was likely as far as she'd go. Once she finished her business, she'd be ready to head back to the house.

"What time are you leaving for church?" He might as well drop the other topic of conversation. Convincing Nicki to move in with Andy and Joan wasn't going to happen. Her mind was made up.

"Around ten." She raised her brows, hope in her eyes. "You thinking of coming with me?"

"No, I just want to make sure no one bothers you on the way to your car."

"What about from the car into the church and from the church back to the car?"

She had a point. "That's why I suggested riding with Andy and Joan."

"They go a lot earlier than I do."

He frowned. This conversation wasn't going much better than the other one had. But she was right. Andy played guitar for worship and practiced before the service, and Joan taught Sunday school.

"Okay, I'll go."

"Awesome!" A victorious smile spread across her face.

Yeah, her victory, his defeat. But not really. He wasn't reneging on his long-ago vow never to set foot inside a church. He was going to see to her safety. He had no intention of paying God any kind of homage.

As promised, he was back at her house at ten o'clock sharp. She swung open the door, and his breath caught in his throat. She was elegant, sophisticated, beautiful. And utterly feminine.

Growing up, he'd never seen her in anything but jeans and shorts. Except for the dress pants and blouses she wore to work, that was still her usual attire.

Not today. Apparently she wore dresses to church. This one was made of some soft, silky fabric with bold splashes of color. It was sleeveless, V-necked and cinched at the waist with a wide blue belt. The flared skirt fell just below her knees, swirling as she moved. High-heeled sandals the same shade of blue as the belt put her eye level with him.

"You look great."

She stepped out the door and pulled it closed behind her. "Thanks."

As he climbed into his truck, he glanced at his watch. This wasn't how he wanted to spend his Sunday morning. But in another two hours, it would all be over.

They arrived fifteen minutes before the service would begin. As soon as they stepped from his truck, a short, perky woman, whom Nicki introduced as Darci Stevenson, ran over to greet her with a warm hug. Her husband Conner was with her, along with their two sons.

Inside, Nicki introduced him to several other friends. He'd met Meagan previously, along with her husband Hunter and his sister Amber. The rest of them, he didn't know. He eased himself into a seat between Nicki and Meagan and looked around. Several people conversed softly, faces animated, as if they wanted to be there.

After an opening prayer, the musicians led the worshippers in several songs. The music wasn't what he'd expected. He'd intended to shut it out. But it wove its way past his defenses, catchy tunes that made him want to sing along in spite of the worshipful lyrics.

And when the pastor finally took his place, there was nothing irrelevant about his message. The theme was "Cast your cares on Him, because He cares for you." There was something appealing about the whole idea. Tyler couldn't say he believed any of it, but he wasn't able to ignore it, either.

Church was different from what he remembered. Or maybe *he* was different. He was no longer an angry teen being forced to do something he thought was pointless. Instead, he was a floundering adult, here by his own free will. Sort of.

When the service was over, everyone filed out of the rows, and several people gathered in groups to chat. Nicki led him out of the building behind Hunter and Meagan. Once outside, Meagan faced them.

"Game night's at Blake and Allison's this month." She winked at him. "You're welcome as Nicki's date."

Nicki smiled at him. "The last Friday night of the month, there's a group of us who get together for games. It'd be nice to not be the odd man out for a change."

He glanced at those around them. They all seemed to be couples. He nodded. "Sounds like fun."

After farewells, they all headed toward their vehicles. Darci and Conner were parked two spaces over. They stopped at their car, but instead of getting in, removed something from the windshield.

Tyler frowned, lead settling in his gut. All the notes he'd seen lately hadn't been good. He watched Darci as she skimmed the page, the color leaching from her face. Hunter apparently saw it, too, because within moments, he was next to her.

"Don't handle it." He took it from her, touching only the corner. "We'll try to get prints."

"What does it say?" Nicki's voice was paper-thin.

Darci's hands shook as she read. "'Stay away from Nicki Jackson, or harm will come to those little boys of yours.'"

Nicki stepped back, her face now as pale as Darci's. She held up her hands, her eyes darting from face to face. "You have to stay away from me. I can't be near any of you. I won't come here anymore. I won't put all of you in danger."

"No."

Tyler turned toward the female voice at his back. Sometime after Darci had pulled the note from her windshield, Allison and Blake had stepped up behind them. So had Sydney and Wade, two other friends.

Allison continued. "You can't stay away. It's times like this when you need your church family more than ever. I can't speak for everyone else, but Blake and I are standing with you."

Wade stepped forward, holding his wife's hand. According to Nicki, he was a Cedar Key firefighter. "Sydney and I are with you, too."

Hunter spoke next. "We need to leave Darci and Connor out of this. They have the boys to think of. But Meagan and I are with you, too."

Tyler put his arm around her and pulled her close. "And you already know where I stand."

The three couples formed a circle around Nicki and Tyler and joined hands. When Tyler looked at Darci, standing to the side with her small family, her eyes were moist.

A tear slipped down her cheek. "Nicki, when I was in trouble, you were there for me. I don't know what I'd have done without you. Now you're the one who needs help, and I'm turning my back on you."

"No," Nicki argued. "Don't worry about me. Take care of your boys. They come first."

Darci nodded and got into her car. Tyler pulled Nicki even closer. She'd refused to give up her search for her sister, because Jenny was the only family she had left.

She was wrong.

Maybe Nicki didn't share any blood with these eight people.

But they were family, in the truest sense of the word.

EIGHT

Nicki sat in Tyler's truck, staring out the front windshield, conflicting emotions tumbling through her. She was a danger to everyone. She should leave and start over somewhere else.

But it wasn't that simple. A good bit of her inheritance was tied up in her house. She had her job and two great outlets to sell her artwork. If she walked away with nothing but her reduced savings account, she'd starve before she got on her feet. And who was to say the person tormenting her wouldn't find her again as soon as she got settled somewhere else?

Tyler pulled out of the parking lot, then reached across the truck to squeeze her shoulder. "You okay?"

She swallowed hard. "I don't know what to do. I'm putting everyone in danger by staying here. But I don't know where to go."

"You need to stay right here in Cedar Key. Hunter and the others are going to catch whoever is doing this. It's been only three weeks. We need to give them time."

How much time, and who'd be hurt in the interim? It wasn't just her own life. There were too many others who could be caught in the crossfire. All of her wonderful new friends. Darci's autistic little boy. Conner's nephew Kyle who'd already experienced far too much heartache before Darci and Conner adopted him.

Tyler squeezed her shoulder again. "Okay?"

She nodded slowly. What else could she do? Leaving was out of the question. And she couldn't isolate herself. Her friends wouldn't let her.

She laid her head back against the seat and closed her eyes. Her friends. They were more than friends. Allison had referred to them as family, her church family.

All through foster care, *family* had seemed like some glittering concept that would remain forever out of reach. Then, against all odds, she'd landed in the home of Doris and Chuck Jackson. And the impossible dream had become a reality.

The moment she learned her adoptive parents had been killed, her whole world had collapsed into the giant black hole left by their absence. And soon, the desire to reconnect with the last living person who could fill the role of family had been overwhelming.

But Tyler was right. Bringing Jenny into her life would also bring all of Jenny's problems down on her. Was that what she wanted? Her own problems would be over once the police caught whoever was harassing her. But Jenny's problems would go on indefinitely.

Tyler's gasp cut across her thoughts, and the engine revved. She opened her eyes. Ahead and to the right, smoke billowed into the sky. Her back stiffened, and she leaned forward in the seat, straining to see where the billowy charcoal-colored column was coming from.

Someone's house was on fire.

Her heart pounded out an erratic rhythm, picking up speed the closer they got. It was either her house or the one on either side of hers. Within moments, she had no doubt. Her house was engulfed in flames.

Callie!

She hooked her purse strap over her shoulder, gripping it until her fingers cramped. Without waiting for Tyler to bring the truck to a complete stop, she swung open the door and stumbled out. Her sandal contacted the edge of the pavement, and her ankle twisted, throwing her sideways into the grass. Without pausing to survey the damage, she pushed herself to her feet and ran up the drive. Pain shot through her right ankle with every step, but she didn't slow down. Callie was inside. She had to get to her.

As she neared the house, high-pitched barking punctuated the ominous crackle of flames. She pulled her keys from her purse and, with shaking fingers, inserted one into the lock. The next moment, a deafening explosion rent the air as the living room window exploded outward in a burst of flames just ten feet away.

Strong arms wrapped around her, pulling her backward, and she fought for all she was worth. She couldn't let Callie die in the flames.

"Let me go!" Her voice was loud and shrill. She twisted and brought her right elbow backward. It connected with Tyler's ribcage with a solid thud. She followed it with several more blows.

They didn't even faze him. With his arms still wrapped around her waist, he picked her up and carried her away from the house. She continued to scream at him and kick her feet. Several times her heels connected with his shins, and he swore under his breath.

"Stop fighting me." He forced her to the ground and pinned her there. "You can't go in there or you'll die."

She stopped resisting and let the tears flow. "Callie's in there. You can't let her burn to death."

"I'll see what I can do. But you have to promise me you won't try to go in."

She drew in a sobbing breath and nodded her head.

"I'm going to release you, but you've got to promise me."

She nodded again. "I promise." Her eyes widened. "We need to call 911."

He glanced to the side, and she lifted her head to follow his gaze. Andy rushed toward them from the road, where he had left his truck, his phone pressed to his ear.

Tyler released her and stood. "I think my brother already has."

She pushed herself to her feet and followed Tyler to the house, staying back several feet. The barking had become even more frantic and seemed to be coming from the master bedroom.

When Tyler reached the house, he pressed his hands to the bathroom window. "She's in here, and the glass is cool."

He peeled off his shirt, and her eyes locked on his bare back. He'd never talked about that final mission and the injuries he'd sustained. But now she knew at least part of what had sent him home. Pale skin stretched across his upper back, down toward the curve of his waist and up over his right shoulder. Some places were mottled, others unnaturally smooth. All of the mended area was different from the surrounding olive-hued skin. He'd been badly burned and likely undergone months of painful skin grafts. And now he was going in to save her dog.

He wrapped the shirt around his fist and thrust it through the window. One blow shattered the glass. After ripping the miniblinds from their brackets and tossing them aside, he knocked the remaining shards of glass free from the frame. Then he ducked his head and shoulders inside. Moments later, he backed out, and a blond head and front paws followed him.

Nicki rushed forward in an exclamation of laughter mixed with tears. Sliding her hands under Callie's stomach, she helped Tyler lift her through the opening. Then they moved away from the house, Tyler carrying Callie.

After putting her down on the lawn, he shook out any shards of glass clinging to his shirt and put it back on. "It's a good thing you had Callie closed up. That helped keep the majority of the smoke away from her."

She looked at him sharply. "I didn't. I always let her have the run of the house. At least, I do now that she's well past her destructive phase."

He drew his brows together. "That's odd. She was in the bathroom with the door closed."

She nodded. "She closed doors a couple of times at the other house. When I first got her, she'd start playing, chasing her tail and whatnot, and bump into all kinds of things. I'd say she went back there today, trying to get away from the fire. Then, as she got more and more frantic, she hit the door and slammed it shut."

Sirens sounded in the distance, and Nicki glanced up the road. Over the next couple of minutes, they grew closer, then stopped as a fire truck came to a halt in front of her house. The next moment, the crash of shattering glass split the silence. On the carport side of the house, the roof collapsed, and a swirl of sparks rose into the sky.

Two firemen ran toward the house, pulling the hose as it unreeled behind them. One was Wade Tanner, his firefighting gear probably thrown quickly over the clothes he'd worn to church.

Moments later, a thick stream of water shot from the end of the hose, traveling in a gentle arc. A sharp sizzle rose above the other sounds, and smoke billowed into the air as the water extinguished the flames.

Nicki stood frozen, watching it all. Pain shot through her, so intense it brought her to her knees. She wrapped her arms around Callie's neck and buried her face in her fur. Everything was going to be a total loss—all her stained glass supplies, the incomplete projects, her clothes and dishes and furniture. The figurines and jewelry and everything else that had belonged to her parents. And the pictures—years of photo albums holding precious memories.

A sob welled up in her throat, and she tried to tamp it down. Callie was still alive, unhurt. Her possessions would be replaced by insurance. The memories of her parents, she'd forever hold in her heart. No one could take those from her.

She raised her head to look at Tyler, and her blood ran cold.

Although he was standing right next to her, he was somewhere else. His fists were clenched. His jaw was tight, and his eyes were squeezed shut. Sweat ran down his face, far more than what could be blamed on the heat and humidity.

She rose to her feet. "Tyler?"

"No." He shook his head, but he wasn't communicating with her. He was reacting to whatever was going on in his mind. "No, no, no." Each word was louder than the last. He lifted his arms to press his palms against his ears.

"Tyler." She gasped, her thoughts spinning. What was he seeing? She moved to stand in front of him, her back to her smoldering house. "Tyler, it's Nicki. Look at me."

She put her hand on his arm, her touch featherlight, and he started. He opened his eyes and looked at her. But not really *at* her. More like *through* her, to something only he could see.

She slid her fingers beneath his. "Tyler, you're here with me. And Callie." She pulled his hand away from his ear and lowered it to Callie's head. "See? Callie's here."

His gaze gradually cleared. "I'm all right."

She continued to study him. His posture was stiff, his focus straight ahead. He *wasn't* all right. Her jaw went lax. Her fire, his burns… "Watching my house burn, you were reliving that last mission, weren't you?"

He swallowed hard, his Adam's apple bobbing with the action, but he didn't respond.

"It might help to talk about it."

He answered without meeting her eyes. "No war stories, okay?"

She wrapped her arms around his neck and pulled him to her. Her heart broke for him, for the agony he'd lived through that refused to release him. And it broke for herself, for all that lay destroyed in the smoldering ruins behind her.

"Hold me," she whispered. The words slipped out of their own accord.

She pressed her cheek to his, feeling his breath in her hair, and his arms came up to circle her back. He tightened his hold, and she reveled in the security she felt in his embrace.

Maybe she'd one day escape the clutches of the past, and he would, too.

Maybe together they'd find healing.

Tyler sat on the couch, feet propped up on the coffee table, Nicki next to him. She was sitting close, tucked under his arm, which was draped across the back of the couch. Callie and Sasha lay at their feet. An older romantic comedy played on the TV, something light and fun and a little bit senseless. Just what he needed after the day they'd had. A period of zoning out would probably do Nicki a world of good, too.

It had been a crazy afternoon. Amber had shown up shortly after the fire was out and called Hunter, who'd had the day off. He then told Meagan, who got in touch with Allison and Blake. Soon half the people he'd met at church that morning were in Nicki's front yard, offering their support.

Allison was tall like Nicki and the closest to her size. So after Nicki had answered the investigator's questions and called her insurance company, Allison had loaded her in her car and taken her home. Forty minutes later, they returned with several bags of clothes. Allison even had shoes Nicki could wear. Then Tyler had taken her to the Chiefland Walmart to stock up on anything else she needed, mostly toiletries and underclothes.

Nicki still hadn't been inside the house. That wouldn't happen for some time yet. Since everyone suspected arson, Chief Robinson had called in the state fire marshal. The scene wouldn't be released until the investigation was complete. The first time into the house would be heart-wrenching for Nicki, but Tyler planned to be right by her side.

He glanced over at her. Her head was tilted back, resting against his arm, and her eyes were almost closed. She was exhausted. He could relate.

He'd had his own ordeal that afternoon. As he'd watched the flames consume her house, he'd suddenly been back in Afghanistan. Explosions rocked the landscape, brilliant flashes of fire lighting up his surroundings. Smoke enveloped him, pungent and suffocating. Then came the screams of the trapped and dying—gut wrenching howls of agony that went on and on.

Nicki had brought him back.

She'd stood in front of him, understanding shining from her eyes, the gentle breeze lifting her hair and swishing it about her shoulders. When she wrapped him in her arms and drew him to her, he'd wanted to melt into her and stay there forever.

The shame he'd expected to feel over his display of weakness hadn't been there. They were two of a kind—lost souls trying to find their way through the quagmire of life's circumstances.

When the credits began to roll, he looked again at Nicki. Her chest rose and fell in the steady rhythm of sleep. Her eyes were closed, her lashes fanned out against her cheeks. Some pale blue shadow covered her lids. The peach lipstick she'd applied that morning for church was long gone, but a hint of color still touched her cheeks.

Her eyes fluttered open and she turned her head to look at him. "I missed the last part of the movie."

He smiled. "I like watching you sleep."

"I hope I didn't do anything embarrassing."

"No, you didn't snore. There weren't any snorts or other strange noises."

She swiped her hand across her chin. "And I didn't drool, so I guess I'm okay." She pushed herself to a more upright position. "I guess I should let you go to bed."

"No rush." He liked having her sitting there with him. After almost two weeks of trying, he'd finally convinced her to move into Andy and Joan's house.

"I feel bad running you out of your room."

"You didn't run me out. I left willingly." He patted the cushion beside him. "The couch is quite comfortable."

"I still feel like I should be the one sleeping out here, not you."

"Absolutely not." He stood and held out his hand to help her up. "Ladies need their privacy. Us guys, we can crash anywhere."

She let him pull her to her feet. "I have to admit, a nice, soft bed sounds really good about now."

He watched her disappear down the hall, then fluffed the bed pillow lying on the end of the couch. He'd changed into a pair of shorts and a T-shirt as soon as he'd gotten home. He'd sleep in them just fine.

After turning off the lamp, he swung his legs up

onto the couch and lay on his back. Moonlight washed in through the front door's oval glass inset, casting the room in its soft glow.

A welcome sense of contentment washed through him, the result of having Nicki so close.

Partly because he could now keep her safe.

And partly because that was where he'd always wanted her to be.

He slipped silently into the kalat *and stopped, M4 at the ready. Tension spiked through him as he scanned the shadows. Five others filed in with him, each with a preassigned sector. He moved toward a doorway and stepped inside the adjoining room, weapon swinging around in a controlled arc.*

The telltale whistle of a mortar round rent the silence, the explosion following a fraction of a second later. Pure adrenaline spiked through him. He spun back through the open doorway and strained to see into the cloud of dust and smoke that enveloped the area. The rugs had ignited, and flames licked at the pillows and cushions lining the room. A gaping hole in the front wall gave a clear view of the outside.

Small arms fire erupted, and he snatched his radio from his vest, struggling to make out his men in the haze. Three were crouched, having moved to positions away from the front wall. Two were down. Marty lay faceup on the cushions at the back of the room, bloodstained hands clutching his stomach. Steve sat against the wall nearby, empty space where the lower part of his leg should have been.

Tyler raised the radio to his face. "This is Wildcat

two-one. We're caught in an ambush and receiving fire. Over."

The cushion beneath Marty erupted in flames. Tyler stepped in that direction as another mortar round whizzed into the room. The explosion threw him backward, slamming him into the side wall. A bone snapped, and pain shot through his left arm. The staccato rhythm of AK-47 fire continued, and another man went down. Where was that other squad?

An agonized scream rose over the sounds of the small arms fire. Marty was engulfed in flames. Steve would be next. With his left arm hanging, Tyler moved toward them on his knees, firing off several shots through the damaged wall. Another mortar round slammed into the building. Mud bricks and debris crashed over him, knocking him flat.

The next moment, a series of creaks sounded above him. That section of the roof was giving way. He threw his good arm over his head just before the full weight of it crashed down on him. Steve's screams joined Marty's, forming a hideous chorus.

He tried to rise, but he was pinned. Flames spread to the newly fallen support beams, and his own screams mingled with those of his dying men. He had to get out. His men needed him.

Suddenly his arms were free. He threw his hands back, fighting his way through the debris holding him. His fist connected with...something.

The screams faded and disappeared, replaced by barking. Dim light crept into the room from somewhere else. He blinked several times. He was in Andy's living room. A figure lay on the floor on the other side of the coffee table, barely visible in the glow of the light seeping in through the front door. A dog flanked each side, still barking.

"Nicki?"

He flew to his feet and clicked on the lamp, a vise clamping down on his chest. If he'd hurt her...

"Are you all right? Tell me I didn't hurt you."

The dogs settled down but still eyed him warily. Nicki pushed herself onto her hands and knees and sat back. Her left cheekbone was turning an angry shade of red. Callie gave her several sloppy kisses on the side of her face. Nicki grimaced, then ran a shaking hand down the dog's back.

He dropped to his knees and gathered her into his arms. "Oh, sweetheart, I'm so sorry."

"It's not your fault."

"Yes, it is. I hit you."

His brother appeared at the end of the hall, followed by Joan. "Everything okay? We heard a scream."

Nicki spoke. "Tyler had a nightmare. Everything's fine."

"No, it's not. I hit her." And he hated himself. He was a danger to those around him. He'd thought if he just kept his weapon locked away, he couldn't hurt anyone. He'd been wrong.

"I shouldn't have approached you." Her eyes held concern mixed with understanding. "I was awake and heard you thrashing around. By the time I got out here, you were talking in your sleep. Something was apparently going horribly wrong." She cast a glance at his brother. "Andy and Joan would probably appreciate me not repeating your exact words."

He cringed. "Sorry about that."

"Your talking got louder and more agitated, and

I tried to wake you up by calling your name. When that didn't work, I put my hand on your shoulder and shook you. Then you screamed and started swinging. I tried to twist away, but I didn't escape fast enough."

He shifted his gaze to the coffee table, and his stomach filled with lead. "I hit you hard enough to knock you over the table."

"Not totally. I was already off balance, my weight shifting that direction. You just helped." She started to smile, then winced.

Apparently having decided the danger was over, Andy and Joan disappeared back down the hall. The dogs must have sensed it, too, as they lay back down. He tightened his hold on her and buried his face in her hair. "I'm so sorry."

"Don't apologize." Her words were the softest whisper.

She turned so she could wrap her arms around him, and for several minutes they sat, locked in a comforting embrace. He breathed in the faint floral scent of her shampoo, letting her soothing presence drain away the last of his tension.

He'd cherish it while it lasted. Because like every other good thing, his time with Nicki would be all too fleeting. Soon he and Andy would finish their work on the inn. Eventually whoever was tormenting Nicki would be caught. Then Tyler would leave.

He'd entertained thoughts of staying, of trying to make Nicki feel something more than friendship. That had been nothing but a pipe dream. Tonight had proved it.

Because if he stayed, if they became more than

friends, he'd never know when he might hurt her. He'd always be a threat.

Maybe as much of a threat as whoever was after her.

NINE

Nicki couldn't help shaking her head as she hung up the phone. Tyler was still sitting at the kitchen table, and she plopped into the chair next to him. After he and Andy had worked a short day at the inn, the four of them had had a late lunch, and Andy and Joan had run into town. Tyler was probably thankful for the afternoon off, since they'd stayed out way too late last night. At least he'd enjoyed his first game night with her friends.

She turned to him now. Almost a week had passed since the fire, and she'd just gotten her first piece of news. "That was Chief Robinson. The preliminary report shows the right rear burner under the pan I'd fried eggs in was left on medium high."

Tyler raised his brows. "You forgot to turn off the stove?"

"No, I didn't." She was too much of a double-checker to walk away with her stove on.

"Maybe you were distracted."

"I'm positive I turned it off. Besides, I fry eggs on medium, not medium high."

She rose from the table and began to pace, a knot

forming in her stomach. She'd hoped it was faulty wiring or some other accidental cause. This proved otherwise.

Tyler nodded, mouth set in a firm line. "If that's the case, someone turned it on, maybe trying to make it look like a grease fire to hide the fact that it was intentionally set." He drew his brows together. "Would Callie let a stranger into the house when you're gone?"

"I doubt it. But if someone broke the kitchen window, he could stretch across the counter and reach the knobs without even coming inside, since they're on the back of the stove."

It was a distinct possibility. The kitchen window had been broken. So were several others. The day before yesterday, she'd gone in with Tyler and taken a look around. The tour had been heartbreaking. Ashes littered everything, charred remains of most of her earthly possessions.

The room she used as her workshop had been the least damaged, leaving her stained glass tools and supplies salvageable. There was a lot of smoke damage, but fortunately, the insurance company had arranged for cleanup.

The rest of the house hadn't fared so well. The kitchen and living room were a total loss. The curios holding all her collectibles were reduced to a few warped and charred pieces of wood and blackened panes of glass. The figurines lay in pieces amid the destruction.

Her bedroom was almost as bad. The flames had swept through the room, turning everything fabric to ash. It was all gone—curtains, blankets, bedding, clothes. And Lavender.

Nicki sighed. After the first attack, she'd carefully stitched the rabbit's belly back together and returned her to her place on the shelf. This time there would be no repairing her. Lavender was gone.

She sank back into the chair and laid her phone on the table. "The investigator said the glass is still being tested to determine whether it was shattered from the outside first or burst from the inside due to the heat. Since the doors were still locked, I'm guessing they'll find that at least one window was shattered from the outside." She was pretty sure it was the one in the kitchen.

Before Tyler could respond, her phone lit up and the ringtone sounded.

"You're popular today."

She frowned at the phone. She didn't recognize the number. She swiped the screen and said a tentative hello.

"Nicki?"

Her pulse began to race. There was something familiar about the voice, a certain lilt that, even after twenty-two years, she'd never forgotten.

"Jenny?"

"Yes, it's me."

She closed her eyes and clutched the phone more tightly. After seven long months of searching, and a couple thousand dollars, her dream was about to become a reality. She was going to be reunited with her sister. "Where are you?"

"On my way to Cedar Key. I just need your address."

The front door opened and closed, and several moments later, Andy and Joan stepped into the kitchen.

Nicki sprang from her chair and pointed at the phone, mouthing her sister's name. Now that she'd gotten over the initial shock, she could hardly contain her excitement. She gave Jenny directions, then moved into the living room at a half skip.

"How soon will you be here?"

"About thirty minutes."

"I can't wait."

After disconnecting the call, she bounded back into the kitchen. "Jenny's on her way here."

Joan squealed and hugged her. Andy patted her shoulder. "That's wonderful news."

Only Tyler didn't share in her joy. He sat with his arms crossed and his jaw tight. Annoyance slid through her, and she tried to tamp it down. He was just concerned. Once he saw that everything was going to be okay, he'd be happy for her, too.

At least, she hoped everything was going to be okay. Because the doubt chewing at the edges of her mind was hard to ignore.

For the next thirty minutes, she alternated between pacing and parting the blinds to stare out the window. When she thought she could stand it no longer, a small white car pulled into the driveway. She opened the door and stepped onto the porch.

The driver's door swung outward, and a woman climbed out. Platinum-blond hair brushed her shoulders, and long legs emerged from cut-off denim shorts. A baggy T-shirt ended a couple of inches above the frayed hem. Sunglasses hid her eyes. She stopped just before reaching the porch.

Nicki closed the remaining distance between them and wrapped her in a tight hug. Tears sprang to her eyes, and she had to choke back an unexpected sob. Jenny returned the hug, but not as enthusiastically as Nicki had initiated it.

Nicki released her. Jenny was holding back. Nicki understood that. They had so much catching up to do. After twenty-two years, they were virtual strangers.

"Come on in. I want you to meet my friend Tyler and his brother and sister-in-law."

Once inside, Jenny moved her sunglasses to the top of her head. Her eyes were the same green Nicki remembered. But there was a hardness to them, and creases fanned out from the outer edges. Jenny had other wrinkles, too, vertical troughs between her eyebrows and frown lines around her mouth, signs of the hard life she'd led.

Nicki made introductions, and Joan extended a warm handshake. "Can I get you something to drink?"

"No, thanks. I had something on the way over." She gave everyone an apologetic smile. "I was hoping Nicki would show me around Cedar Key. I feel like the two of us have so much to talk about, I don't know where to begin."

Tyler stepped up. "How about if I chauffeur you? Then you guys can relax and enjoy the ride and not have to worry about a thing."

Jenny patted Tyler's arm. "I'd like some alone time with my sis. I appreciate the offer, though."

A hardness settled in his eyes, and Nicki flashed him a warning glare. He was entitled to his opinions about her sister, but he needed to keep them to himself. She'd been waiting months for this reunion and she wouldn't let him spoil it.

She put her phone back into her purse, then followed her sister out the door. When she removed her keys, Jenny stopped her.

"I'll drive. Just tell me where to go."

"All right." Nicki slid into Jenny's passenger seat. "So, what would you like to see?"

"You pick. Show me whatever you think is noteworthy."

"How about if we start at the co-op?"

Jenny's brows went up. "Co-op?"

"The Cedar Keyhole Artist Co-op. It's where local artists sell their work—pottery, jewelry, leather, metal, paintings, you name it. I have some stained glass there. I'd love for you to see it."

Jenny shrugged. "Sure."

Nicki directed her through a few turns until they reached Second Street. Two blocks down, Jenny pulled into a parking space, and Nicki led her into the colorful building.

Over the next several minutes, she introduced her to several people, pride swelling inside. *My sister.* She shook her head. It still seemed surreal, probably would for a long time.

After stopping to study some blown glass, she grinned over at Jenny. "I could live in here. Every time I come in, there's something different." She pointed ahead. "There's my stained glass."

Jenny followed her but seemed distracted, almost agitated. Or maybe she had no interest in art and was bored.

"Is there something else you'd rather do?"

"I was thinking it would be nice to go for a walk somewhere, just the two of us. We've got a lot of catching up to do. I want to hear all about what you've done over the past twenty years."

"Sure." She swung the door open and held it for Jenny to walk out ahead of her. "The Railroad Trestle Nature Trail would be perfect. It's quiet and peaceful and private. It's one of my favorite places to go."

When they arrived at the trailhead, the single parking spot was empty. Jenny stepped from the car and looked around her. "You're right. This is perfect."

Nicki slipped her phone into her pocket and headed into the woods, Jenny next to her. "You wanted to hear everything that's happened since we got separated." She grinned. "I'll give you the abridged version." She picked up a piece of a broken limb and tossed it away from the trail. "Foster care was the pits. By the time I got out of there, I was ready to fight anybody and everybody, no matter how big."

"Yeah, if you don't learn how to stick up for yourself, you can get eaten alive."

Nicki continued her story without slowing down to admire the scenery. Along the sides of the trail, a couple dozen signs identified many of the plant species there. She'd read them before. But not this time. If looking at the endless variety of art had bored Jenny, she wouldn't care to read botanical signs.

By the time they reached the end of the trail, Nicki had just finished telling her about losing her parents and inheriting the house. She looked out at the old trestle posts poking up through the shallow bay, remnants of the bridge that had carried the trains across the water. Now she would hear Jenny's story. And maybe through the process of telling it, Jenny would find healing.

Nicki headed back down the trail the way they'd come. "So did my PI catch up with you, or did you talk to Gina?"

"Both. Gina gave me your number yesterday. But your investigator found me a few times before. Though we didn't personally talk, his messages got to me. At the time, I wasn't ready to see you." She hesitated, and an odd coldness entered her eyes. "Now I am."

Unease darkened Nicki's thoughts, a shadow passing through her mind. She shook it off. Jenny had no reason to want to hurt her. They hadn't even seen each other in over twenty years. Before that, they weren't close, but that was because of the five-year age difference. They'd gone to separate schools, had their own friends and varied interests.

Besides, even if Jenny did feel some kind of animosity toward her, she wouldn't be stupid enough to try anything. Too many people had seen them together.

Nicki cast her an uneasy glance. Jenny stared straight ahead, her whole body radiating tension. Finally she spoke.

"We both got shipped off to foster homes the day after Mom was killed. That's where I spent the next six years. Messed-up twelve-year-olds aren't nearly as adoptable as cute little seven-year-olds."

Nicki's uneasiness ratcheted up several notches at the bitterness in Jenny's tone. She put her hand over her back pocket, which held her cell phone. If things got too bad, maybe she could shoot off a quick text to Tyler.

Jenny continued, the bitterness increasing. "I never had the opportunity to go to college. And I never had a cushy job."

"I did go to college, but I've always had to work my tail off at my jobs." She forced a laugh. "If you find out where the cushy ones are, let me know."

Jenny moved ahead as if she hadn't spoken. "I never owned my own home, either. Of course, I never had anyone to leave me everything when they bit the dust."

Nicki's jaw dropped, and anger surged through her. "I'd give it all back for another day with my parents."

Jenny ignored her again. "Always surrounded by friends and family. You have no idea what it's like to have no one." She shook her head and continued. "Two sisters. One given all the advantages. The other nothing. Do you think that's fair?"

Nicki gasped, realization slamming into her with the force of a freight train. No, it wasn't fair, so Jenny was here to level the playing field.

It wasn't fair she had the "cushy" job, so Jenny tried to make her boss doubt her, even fire her.

It wasn't fair she had good friends, so Jenny threatened them, hoping to isolate her from them.

And it wasn't fair she had her home and all of her possessions, so Jenny set fire to it and destroyed it.

Jenny had told Gina she was going to see a wrong made right. And that was why she'd come to Cedar Key.

To make sure the sister who had it all would end up with nothing.

Including her life.

Nicki glanced around, heart pounding in her throat. They were at about the halfway point on the trail, with mangroves and water on one side, marshes and more mangroves on the other. And not another human being in sight.

She drew in a stabilizing breath. If she could keep Jenny talking, maybe they'd be back to civilization before things got ugly.

"The problems I've been having, it's been you all along, hasn't it?"

Jenny snorted. "Finally figured it out? You're not the brightest bulb in the pack, are you?"

It had taken her that long to unravel the mystery because she'd focused her attention in the wrong direction. Peter was angry. But he wasn't vindictive. And he wasn't crazy.

Jenny apparently was.

In one smooth motion, Jenny pulled a folding knife from her pocket and extended the blade with a sharp flick of her wrist. Then she took a predatory stance, knees slightly bent, as if ready to pounce. "Now it's my turn."

Nicki raised both hands and stumbled backward, a cold knot of fear in her stomach. She curled her toes against her sandals, every instinct shouting at her to run. But she didn't stand a chance with Jenny in tennis shoes. And if she screamed, Jenny would kill her instantly.

Jenny's eyes narrowed. "Try to run and I'll slice you up and leave you for the vultures."

Nicki swallowed hard. "Jenny, you don't need to do this. Come back with me. You can move in with me, and we can be real sisters again. It'll be like old times."

"Old times?" Jenny released a disdainful snort. "Old times was Mom protecting you because you were the baby, while her men slapped me around. Or worse."

Nicki's heart fell. No wonder Jenny resented her so much. The anger began long before their mother's murder. She'd blamed their lack of closeness on the age difference and normal sibling rivalry.

Now she knew. They weren't close because Jenny hated her.

Her phone buzzed in her back pocket, and she started. "Someone sent me a text. Everyone's watching me. If I don't answer, they'll know something's wrong, and half of Cedar Key will come looking for me."

Jenny tightened her grip on the knife. "Read it to me."

She pulled her phone from her back pocket and swiped the screen. "It's from Tyler. 'Everything OK? Worried about U.'"

Jenny nodded, lips pursed. "This is perfect. Tell him this: 'Fine. Jenny left, but I'm hanging out. Will catch a ride home. Thanks for checking.' Let me see it before you send it. Try anything, and I'll kill you right here."

Nicki entered the words exactly as Jenny had dictated them, with one small exception.

What she'd done was so minimal, so innocuous, Jenny would never catch it.

She held up the phone. Jenny read the message and gave a sharp nod. As Nicki hit Send, a sliver of the tension slipped away, pushed aside by a desperate hope. Jenny had approved the message, just as she'd keyed it in.

Jenny didn't see the clue.

Unfortunately, there was a distinct possibility Tyler wouldn't, either.

Tyler stared at the phone in his hand, doubt circling through him. She'd said she was fine. So why the nagging feeling that something was wrong?

He read the text again.

Fine. Jenny left, but I'm hanging out. Will catch ride home. Tx for ckg. Bye.

He tried to shake the tension from his shoulders. She was fine. Even thanked him for checking. He laid the phone on the coffee table and began to pace. She wasn't with Jenny anymore. But with everything that had gone on in recent weeks, he hated to let her out of his sight.

He moved to the front window and parted the blinds, willing a familiar car to pull into the drive— Allison's Camaro or Meagan's Prius. Or any other mode of transportation, as long as Nicki was in it. But the driveway was empty except for Nicki's newly repaired Ram and his, Andy's and Joan's vehicles.

"Are you all right? You're like a caged tiger."

He started at the female voice behind him, then spun to see Joan watching him with raised brows.

"Yeah." Except for the ever-present tension coiled in his belly. He was too used to watching for danger, always on the alert, ever cognizant of the fact that every second could be his last. It had been almost two years since he'd seen combat, but sometimes it seemed like yesterday.

The only way he was going to shake the uneasiness was to see Nicki for himself. He snatched up his keys. He'd probably find her downtown hanging out with her friends. Or strolling through the artist's co-op, feeding her creative side. Perfectly safe activities in broad daylight.

When he picked up his phone, he scanned her words once more. A solid block of ice hit his core.

She'd ended the text with *bye*.

"Nicki's in trouble. I'm going to find her."

"What do you mean?"

Ignoring Joan's question, he ran out the door, dialing 911 as he went. As he made the short trip into town, his heart pounded out an erratic rhythm, and he gripped the wheel so tightly his knuckles turned white. The dispatcher probably thought he was crazy. He heard her hesitation when he explained how he knew Nicki was in trouble.

But he had no doubt. That single word was a code, a way to let him know she was in danger without raising Jenny's suspicions. Unfortunately, he had nothing to go on. He had no idea where they'd gone. Over an hour had passed since they'd left. They could be a good distance from Cedar Key by now.

And he didn't have Jenny's tag number. He'd watched them leave and hadn't even thought to look at it. If they were still in Cedar Key, the car would be easy to spot. It was a white two-door Sunbird that had seen better days. The driver's side had long scrape marks running its entire length. A twelve-inch section of the front bumper was caved in, bearing a permanent imprint of a pole or tree trunk, and the hood was warped as if something had been dropped on it.

Something heavy…like a body. *His body.*

Jenny was the one who'd hit him. The one who'd broken into Nicki's house and tried to get her fired from her job. The one who'd been threatening her and had tried to isolate her from her friends.

And now Nicki was alone with her.

He turned onto Whidden, then pulled into a parking space. He sat for several moments, staring at the Cedar Key water tower, trying to get control of the panic circling through him. He had to rein in his scattered thoughts. Focus.

He pulled out his cell phone and went to his contacts. A half minute later, Hunter answered. Nicki had given Tyler both Hunter's and Amber's personal cell numbers.

"You on duty?"

"Not till this afternoon. What's up?"

"I've figured it out. Nicki's sister is the one who's been threatening her. Nicki's with her now."

"Where?"

"I don't know. The two of them went off alone together. I sent Nicki a text. She said she was fine, then ended with *bye*. Nicki never says *bye*. She always says *later*."

"You're right." Hunter's voice was thick with concern. "Something's wrong."

"I know." He filled Hunter in on everything he'd given the dispatcher. "I'm sure they've set up a road block on 24, so they'll catch her if she tries to leave Cedar Key."

If she hadn't already left. Enough time had passed, so it was a distinct possibility.

He continued. "I'm going to drive around the island looking for the car. Beyond that, I don't know what else to do."

"You can pray. And rest assured, I will be, too. God's in control, and he can lead us right to her."

"Thanks." He disconnected the call and pulled back

onto the road. He'd talk to people in town and see if anyone had seen them, starting at the artist's co-op.

And he'd leave the praying to Hunter.

Maybe Hunter's prayers would do some good. From everything Nicki had told him about the man, he had that kind of faith.

Tyler eased to a stop in front of the artist's co-op. Hunter had said God could lead them to Nicki. Actually, Tyler couldn't argue the point. He'd always believed God *could* answer prayers.

The problem was, when it had mattered more to him than anything in the world, God *didn't*.

TEN

Nicki looked frantically around her, willing someone to come down the trail. Jenny had become more agitated with every word out of her mouth. She waved the knife as she spoke, several slashes coming much too close.

Nicki took another step back. "Why are you doing this?"

"Don't go acting all innocent here. You brought this on yourself."

"How?"

"You had to go and find me. You couldn't leave me well enough alone. I was minding my own business, had completely written you off. I figured I'd never see you again. But you pushed your way back into my life and forced me to check you out. When I saw your perfect existence with your nice house and comfortable job and disgustingly sweet friends, I had to do something. You think you're someone, don't you?" She gave an irreverent snort. "It's easy when you've had all the breaks."

Nicki shook her head. "I haven't had all the breaks.

I've had to work hard for everything. But I'll share it with you. You're the only family I've got."

"Share?" Jenny spat the word. "I don't need to share. When you're gone, everything will go to me anyway as the only surviving relative." She grinned, but the gesture was grotesque instead of reassuring. "I think I'll even see if I can get your boyfriend."

Jenny took a step forward, eyes blazing hatred. Nicki moved back further. Perspiration coated her body, and a watery weakness had settled in her legs. Nothing she'd said was working. She swept her gaze to one side, then the other, not taking her attention off Jenny for more than a second.

Her heart pounded harder. A limb hung three feet to her right, barely connected to the tree. If she could break it loose and swing, maybe she could disable Jenny long enough to get away. It was a desperate move. But she was out of options. *Lord, please let this work.*

Jenny's eyes narrowed. "After all these years, it's time for you to die and me to live."

She raised the knife and swung downward in an arc, aiming at Nicki's chest. With a scream, Nicki stepped to the side and spun in a full circle, grasping the tree branch on her way around. It held on for a fraction of a second, then broke loose with a crack of splintering wood. A half second later, it connected with the side of Jenny's head and shattered into several pieces.

Nicki didn't wait to see the result. She sprinted down the trail, terror pounding at her heels. The blow wouldn't slow Jenny down for long. The branch had been too rotten.

A searing pain shot through her back, and she stumbled and fell to her knees. Jenny had thrown the knife. The next moment, Jenny was standing over her.

Understanding hit Nicki like a bolt of lightning.

The dreams. They weren't memories. They were warnings. She was going to be murdered the same way her mother had been. *Please, no.* She'd made her peace with God, but she was too young to die.

Another pain shot through her as Jenny pulled the blade free. Before she had time to react, Jenny threw her onto her back, dropped to her knees and raised the knife again. As she plunged it downward, Nicki screamed and rolled away.

"Nicki!"

The voice belonged to Tyler. He'd come for her. And there were sirens, too, in the distance. Relief rushed through her. Help was coming. She was going to survive.

But only if she could hang on until they got there. *Lord, please help me.*

She rolled over and pushed herself to her knees. But before she could get to her feet, Jenny slammed into her, knocking her to the ground.

She released another scream as weight pressed down on her lower back and fingers entwined in her hair. She was pinned.

Jenny was straddling her. Just like the man in her dreams.

No. She wasn't going out like this. Especially with Tyler moments away. She screamed again, twisted to the side and swung. The back of her fist connected with Jenny's jaw. Several expletives rolled from her sister's mouth, and her eyes blazed with fire. The hold on Nicki's hair tightened, and the knife came up again.

Footsteps pounded against the ground, and a moment later, a body slammed into Jenny.

Suddenly Nicki was free. She pushed herself to a seated position, her breaths coming in short pants. A few feet away, Tyler lay on top of Jenny, wrestling the knife from her hand. The sirens had stopped.

More footsteps sounded and two uniformed officers came around the bend on the trail, Hunter right behind them. The officers cuffed Jenny and one of them tried to read her her rights. But Jenny wasn't listening. A steady stream of hate-filled words flowed from her mouth. Nicki dipped her head. All of the anger was directed at her.

Tyler dropped to his knees beside her and grasped her shoulders, his gaze sweeping her from head to toe. Then he wrapped her in his arms and rocked her back and forth. His cheek was against hers, his mouth so close she could feel his breath against her ear. "When I got your text, I was frantic. I'm so glad I found you when I did. God answered Hunter's prayer."

Hunter's prayer? She'd have to ask Tyler about it later.

Tyler started to release her, then froze. "There's blood. You're hurt."

She shifted her position and winced. "She got me in the back."

Tyler pulled out his phone, but Hunter stopped him. "They're already here. The fire truck with the paramedics pulled up just as I headed down the trail. An ambulance will arrive shortly."

As if on cue, Wade Tanner and another man jogged up next to her, carrying a gurney and a medical kit.

After checking her wound, they loaded her on the stretcher and stood.

She reached for Tyler's hand. "How did everyone know where to find me?"

"I know how you love the artist's co-op. So I figured that's where I'd start and see if you'd been there. You had, and on your way out the door, someone overheard you mention coming here."

She closed her eyes, emotion sweeping through her. God had answered *someone's* prayer. Whether hers or Hunter's, she'd take it. If she and Jenny had waited until they were outside to have that conversation, there was a good chance she'd be dead. Thankfulness swelled inside her. Her back was on fire. But she was alive.

Commotion nearby drew her attention to her sister. The officers had her on her feet, trying to lead her up the trail, but she wasn't having it. She kicked at one of them. He sidestepped and managed to avoid the blow.

Jenny twisted to throw a malicious glance over one shoulder, her eyes locking with Nicki's. "Someday you'll get yours. He's coming after you, you know."

Nicki pushed herself partially upright, unease chewing at the edges of her mind. "Who?"

"Mom's killer. He knows where you are. I told him."

"Wait." She held out a hand, and the officers dragging Jenny up the trail stopped. "You know who killed her?"

Jenny tossed her head and lifted her chin. Her eyes held an odd sense of pride, mixed with disdain. "I was there, but he didn't see *me*."

"Who killed her?"

"What do you mean *who killed her*?" Jenny looked

at her for several long moments. Then her jaw dropped. "You're serious. You don't remember."

"Of course I don't remember. I wasn't there." She'd said the words with as much conviction as she could muster, but doubt wove its way through her mind, shattering the reality she'd held on to for so long.

She hadn't been there, right? Otherwise she'd remember. There would be some sliver of recall, some disjointed image.

Like in her dreams.

Coldness settled in her core, and she closed her eyes. No, the nightmares were just that—dreams. Nothing more. They weren't real.

When she opened her eyes again, Jenny was smiling.

"Oh, you were there." The smile broadened.

"What's even better is that he knows it. And he knows how to find you."

Nicki leaned over the railing of the observation deck and stared into water tinted a bright aquamarine. Shouts rose from the swimming area, visitors enjoying the relief the cool spring water provided from the steamy August day.

As she leaned over farther, pain stretched across her back. But she wasn't complaining. She had a lot to be thankful for. Jenny had intended to kill her. Instead, she'd barely nicked her lung. Over the past few days, the pain had retreated to a dull ache, and other than three days in the hospital, a hefty insurance deductible and some residual soreness, she was fine.

Except for the nightmares.

Tyler had shaken her awake from two, and last night

he'd insisted on taking her someplace where she could relax and put the events of the past five weeks behind her. After an internet search, he'd settled on Fanning Springs State Park in northern Levy County. Right after church, they'd traded dress clothes for shorts, T-shirts and tennis shoes and headed out with a picnic lunch. Andy and Joan were dog-sitting.

It was over. She was safe. Jenny's final words were nothing but a lie, a last-ditch attempt to steal her peace. It wasn't going to work.

She straightened and smiled up at Tyler. They'd made a pact to avoid discussing anything related to Jenny. It was a welcome break.

"How is the work on the inn coming?"

"We're ready for appliances. Next week we'll start rebuilding some decks."

"Sounds like you're winding it down."

He leaned against the railing, resting on one elbow. "Yeah. Another two weeks and that should pretty well do it."

Heaviness filled her chest. Was he still planning to leave? She couldn't bring herself to ask. Just the thought left a big hole in her heart.

He turned away from the railing and extended his arm, palm up. After placing her hand in his, she let him lead her down the wooden stairs. At the bottom, concrete steps led up away from the pool area. When they reached the top, he turned right and headed toward the picnic area.

He squeezed her hand. "Tell me what else you did after I left."

She smiled. She'd already told him several stories

from her later teenage years. "I can't think of anything else."

"Tell me about your first real boyfriend."

She looked at him askance. "I thought you didn't
like war stories."

"I like hearing other people's war stories."

"I have quite a few." More than she wanted to admit.
"I seem to attract the users and the losers." When Peter
came along, she thought she'd broken the pattern. He
was attentive, romantic, good-looking and successful. But two other adjectives had been lacking—*honest* and *law-abiding*.

"My first real boyfriend was Junior. His idea of a
romantic date was taking me to his friend's house so
I could watch them play video games. Fortunately, his
friend also had a girlfriend who was as bored as I was.
One night, we both got tired of competing with Halo
and gave up. She called her brother to come and get
us. That was the end of Junior and me."

"Sounds like he needed to grow up."

"Yeah. I'm afraid that describes too many of the
guys I've dated."

Tyler took a seat at one of the picnic tables, and she
sat next to him. A small playground lay a few yards in
front of them. Both swings were occupied, and four
other children slid down green plastic slides. Midway
between the playground and a pavilion, two adolescent boys stood talking, kicking pine needles and stray
pieces of mulch.

Nicki angled her face toward Tyler and rested her
chin in her hand. "Okay, now it's your turn. Tell me
about your first crush."

"That's easy. My first crush was a scrappy eighth

grader who always had a chip on her shoulder and would never back down from a fight, especially if her best friend was the one being threatened." He grinned and gave her a gentle nudge in the ribs with his elbow.

She elbowed him back. "Hey, I'm being serious. Tell me about your first girlfriend."

He shrugged. "I didn't have much time for dating. As soon as I turned sixteen, I got a job after school working at a local fast-food place. When school let out, I went to work with a friend. His dad owned a small construction company."

Nicki studied him as he spoke. But he wasn't looking at her. Instead, he faced straight ahead, his eyes taking in the activity on the playground and scanning the woods beyond. An underlying tension flowed through his body, a ready alertness.

She was used to it. The only time he seemed truly relaxed was inside Andy and Joan's home, with the doors locked and the blinds drawn.

He continued, his gaze shifting to the right, where the two boys she'd observed earlier appeared to be trying out some pseudo karate moves on each other.

"My friend's dad didn't let me run the power tools. Maybe he wasn't allowed to, since I was underage. But he taught me a lot. I worked with him two summers."

"Then you joined the Army."

He nodded, his attention still focused on the boys. "But not till October. I was supposed to start college in the fall, but Mom's cancer had spread, so I stayed with her."

Some distance away, the shorter boy kicked at his taller friend, who grasped his foot and flipped him onto his back. Tyler stiffened and sat up straighter.

"I'm glad you got the time with her."

"We were able to keep her at home until…" His voice trailed off.

"Tyler?" She followed his gaze to where the boys were tussling. The larger one pressed his friend's shoulders to the ground, then straddled him.

Tyler shot to his feet, stepped over the bench and stalked that direction.

"Tyler!"

She stood and followed him, shouting his name again. But he marched straight ahead, picking up his pace. He took the final few yards at a jog.

Before she could stop him, he grasped the taller boy by the shoulders and threw him aside, then stood over him glaring, fists clenched. Both boys sat up and scooted backward, eyes filled with fear. He took another step, closing the gap between them.

"Tyler, stop! They're just playing." Her voice was loud and shrill. If she didn't stop him, he was going to hurt one of them.

He took another step. Both boys scrambled to their feet and took off in a spray of sand. Tyler stared after them as if unsure what to do. She ran in front of him, grasped his arms and shook him.

Finally the wildness left his eyes. He twisted free of her grasp, spun and walked back the way they'd come at such a brisk pace, she had to run to keep up with him. He jogged down the steps toward the spring, taking them two at a time, but instead of continuing to the water's edge, he made a sharp right and headed down the boardwalk. His pace slowed to a brisk walk, and she moved up beside him.

"What happened back there?"

He kept walking, eyes straight ahead, jaw tight.

She grasped his arm. "Tell me what's going on."

Again he shook himself loose from her grasp. For another minute, they walked in silence. Cypress trees rose all around them, shading them from the afternoon sun. Hundreds of cypress knees protruded from the ground beneath, ranging in size from a few inches to five or six feet. The setting was almost magical. But she knew Tyler wasn't seeing any of it.

She heaved a sigh. Keeping everything buried inside couldn't be good for him. But getting him to open up seemed almost impossible. He refused to discuss any of his experiences in Afghanistan.

She glanced over at him. "Tyler, stop. Tell me what's going on."

He didn't slow down, and he didn't look at her. His features were set in stubbornness, his fists clenched.

She bit her lower lip. Soon he'd have to stop. He wouldn't have a choice. Up ahead, the boardwalk ended in a square, covered area overlooking the river. Two couples stood there taking pictures with their phones. As she and Tyler grew closer, the women glanced their way, and the four of them began to move back down the boardwalk.

Tyler stepped under the structure and stopped at the end, hands clutching the wooden railing. Several more moments passed in silence.

She put a hand on his upper arm. "Tyler, please talk to me."

His muscle twitched under her palm, but he didn't jerk away from her. His eyes held a steely hardness. "I'm all right."

"No, you're not. If I hadn't stopped you, you might have hurt one of those boys."

"I was breaking it up. I thought the bigger boy was attacking the smaller one."

"They were playing."

His gaze dropped to the water below. "I know that now."

"And everyone else knew it then. There was never any doubt in anyone's mind except yours."

He allowed her to turn him away from the rail, and she took his hands in hers.

"Anywhere we go, you look as if you expect to be attacked at any moment. You're always assessing your surroundings, looking for threats. I thought it had to do with me and all the things that have been going on in my life. But that's not right, is it? It started long before you came to Cedar Key."

His hands tightened around hers, but he didn't respond.

"Talk to me, Tyler."

He shook his head. "You don't want to hear this."

"If I didn't want to hear it, I wouldn't be asking. Come on, Tyler. Talk to me. We used to tell each other everything. If anyone can understand what you're feeling, it's me."

She released his hands and raised her arms to rest both palms against the sides of his face. "What happened over there?" She was no longer talking about the playground. Instead, her thoughts were focused halfway across the world. Judging from the distant look in his eyes, his likely were, too. "Tell me what happened that sent you home."

For some time, a silent battle ensued. Then all the tension flowed out of him, and he released a heavy sigh.

"It was our last mission. We were all shipping home the following week. That day, there was a meeting planned with community leaders in a nearby village. I was tasked with route clearance. We go ahead of the command representatives and secure the route, looking for IEDs and ambush sites. These meetings are usually held in the home of one of the leaders, and we go in and make sure there are no booby traps, look for security vantage points and so on."

He released her hands and turned back to the rail, resting his palms on its surface. "There were six of us. We loaded into two MRAPs. I was with Marty and Steve. We were all talking about what we were going to do when we got stateside, who'd be running onto the field to greet us."

He smiled down at her, but there was sadness behind the expression. "The deployment homecoming ceremony is a big deal. The whole unit goes home together, so there are around eight hundred of us. The families are all in the bleachers, holding signs and banners welcoming us home. We'd been downrange for just shy of twelve months, so there was going to be a lot of excitement and emotion. Marty had a wife and a four-month-old baby. Steve was making plans to propose to his high school sweetheart."

He fell silent, and she didn't prod him to continue. He'd finish his story when he was ready. She laid her hand over his and curled her fingers into his palm. Finally he continued.

"Everything was fine. There were no problems en route. Nothing seemed out of the ordinary going in.

Then Taliban forces fired the first mortar round into the building, and the rugs and furnishings caught fire. More rounds followed, and this whole time, the enemy kept a steady barrage of AK-47 fire coming at us. That pretty well kept us pinned. I radioed the perimeter squad, but it seemed to take them forever to subdue the enemy."

He closed his eyes. "Marty and Steve were down after the first mortar round. Pretty soon, both of them were engulfed in flames." His hand tightened around her fingers, his other one clenching into a fist. "I listened to their screams as they burned to death, but I couldn't get to them. I tried. The explosion of another mortar round knocked me backward. Then the roof caved in on me."

"What about your other men?"

"Gone, every one of them. One took a mortar round and was killed instantly. Two others were taken out by small arms fire." He pushed away from the rail to sink onto the nearby bench, then put his head in his hands. "Every one of them had so much to live for—girlfriends, wives, children. All they had to do was make it through one final mission. They didn't and I did." He lifted his head to look at her. "How is that fair? I had no one, just Andy and Joan and my sister, Bridgett. So why did I come home when none of the others did?"

She sat next to him. "It wasn't your time yet."

"And it was theirs? Marty with a four-month-old baby who is never going to know her father? Steve at twenty-one, who hardly even got to taste adulthood? You're telling me it was their time? How?"

"Some things we just have to accept, because trying to find an explanation will make us crazy."

He pulled his hand from hers and rose to his feet. "I can't accept it. And I never will. I keep imagining Marty lying there with a hole in his belly, Steve with his leg blown off. Flames swallowing both of them." He shook his head. "When I was watching your house burn, I was back there in that *kalat*, listening to their screams."

She closed her eyes, her heart twisting in her chest. He'd experienced unimaginable horrors, and now, when it should be over, he was reliving them again and again. As a teenager, he'd been tormented. And she'd known what to do. Often just her presence and a listening ear would soothe his troubled heart.

That was nothing compared to this. He'd seen things no one should have to witness. And they'd scarred him. Maybe permanently.

She wrapped her arms around him, offering comfort in the only way she knew. "I want to help you. I just need you to tell me how."

His arms circled her waist, then tightened around her, and he buried his face in her hair.

"You were always there for me." His words were muffled against the side of her neck, his breath warm.

"We were there for each other." And more than once over the years, she'd missed it desperately.

He stepped back to meet her gaze. "We were crazy to let that go."

She nodded, ready to agree with his statement. But the words stuck in her throat. His eyes were warm, raw emotion swimming in their depths. Her stomach rolled over, and all the oxygen seemed to exit her lungs, leaving her breathless.

She'd hugged him numerous times in the past. And other times, he'd watched her without saying a word.

This was different.

The way he was looking at her wasn't how a friend looks at a friend. The intensity in his eyes said a whole lot more.

Before she had a chance to ponder it further, he leaned closer. A bolt of panic shot through her, followed by calm. Because whatever he was feeling, she felt it, too.

The next moment, his mouth slanted across hers. Sensation burst across her consciousness, bright and hot, searing a path to her heart. This wasn't the boy she'd known fifteen years earlier. This was Tyler now—one hundred percent man. Capable of setting her pulse racing with a single kiss.

But in many ways, he was the same. The same caring person who felt deeply and bore scars as a result. The one who could read her moods and instinctively know what she needed most.

Her best friend in all the world.

She stiffened and backed away. If they allowed their friendship to become anything more, there would be no turning back. Eventually their relationship would end. Her track record had proved that. His wasn't much better. He was as damaged as she was. When everything fell apart, there would no longer be any friendship to fall back on.

"What's wrong?" Concern filled his eyes.

She stepped out of his arms, letting her hands fall

from his neck. "You're my best friend. I'm not willing to throw that away for a brief fling."

Hurt pushed aside the concern. "Why would it have to be just a brief fling?"

"Because good things don't last. You know it as well as I do. This is one season of your life. It'll pass and you'll be off on your next adventure."

For several moments, he stood silent and still. Then he gave her a sharp nod and started back down the boardwalk.

She fell in behind him, disappointment swirling inside her. She'd halfway hoped he'd argue with her, tell her that they could make it work, that they'd overcome all the obstacles together.

But he hadn't, because he knew she was right.

ELEVEN

Tyler held the two-by-eight joist in place and swung the hammer, the sharp thuds piercing the tranquility of the summer day. A bead of sweat ran down the side of his face. The bandanna did a pretty good job of keeping it out of his eyes, but within an hour of starting work in the summer heat and humidity, his shirt was usually soaked and plastered to his chest.

Especially when he was working like this.

He removed another twelve-penny nail from his pouch. After three good whacks, it was flush.

"You know, we have air tools for that."

Tyler cast a glance at Andy over his shoulder. He was sitting on a camp chair in the shade of a tree, a glass of iced tea in one hand and two of Joan's oatmeal cookies in the other. The open thermos still sat on the ground in front of him. Thirty minutes ago, it had held homemade vegetable beef stew. Now it was empty, every last savory drop scraped from the wide mouth. Tyler's own thermos was in the same condition. When it finally came time to leave Cedar Key, he was going to miss Joan's cooking.

That wasn't all he was going to miss. Reconnecting

with Nicki had been a bonus he hadn't anticipated. Or yet another means of torture.

Especially now that he'd kissed her.

During most of their two-year friendship, he'd longed for more, had wondered what it would be like to hold her with more than the comforting hug of a friend, had dreamed of kisses in the moonlight.

The actual experience was so much sweeter than all those childhood fantasies. And he was having a hard time getting it out of his mind.

He pounded in several more nails, then stood back to survey his work.

"You think the deck is going to last longer if you build it by the sweat of your brow?"

Tyler ignored his brother's taunt. The deck wouldn't last longer, but swinging a hammer was a great way to work out some of his pent-up frustration.

Andy screwed the lid on the thermos and, after dropping everything into the lunch tote, ambled toward the unfinished deck.

"Now that you've spent the last ten minutes beating the deck half to death, you want to talk about what's ailing you?"

"Nothing's bothering me. I'm fine." He wasn't about to discuss his woman woes with his brother. Or anyone else, for that matter.

Andy planted both hands on his hips. "I think my pretty neighbor has been getting under your skin the past few weeks."

Yeah, he had that right. He was just wrong about when. Nicki had gotten under his skin fifteen years ago. Now she was there again.

Or maybe that was where she'd been all along.

He'd always had all kinds of excuses for avoiding serious relationships—too little time to date because he was working and caring for his mom, the transient military lifestyle with its lengthy deployments, the nightmares and flashbacks that regularly plagued him.

Maybe the real reason was Nicki, the knowledge that having a relationship with anyone else would be settling, that he'd never be truly happy.

The fact remained, he was too messed up for an intimate relationship. He'd proved it a few nights ago, when he'd accidentally punched Nicki and knocked her over the coffee table.

And yesterday at the park. He'd watched the activity on the playground—the children swinging, climbing on the equipment, going down the slides. And the boys making up karate moves.

He'd seen a threat that wasn't even there. And eliminating the threat had consumed all his thoughts, trumping common sense. If Nicki hadn't stopped him, he might have ended up in jail for battery. Or worse.

No, he wasn't fit for anything more than causal friendship, no matter what he felt for Nicki.

Andy put a hand on his shoulder, drawing him back to the present.

"I don't know her whole story, but I think she's good for you." He gave Tyler a couple of rough pats and continued, his tone serious.

"Think about it. Maybe it's time to stop running."

Tyler pulled into a space at The Market and put the truck in Park. The gentle lecture his brother had given him that afternoon still circled through his mind. He tried to shut out the words. Andy didn't know what he was talking about. If running was what it took to avoid hurting Nicki, that was exactly what he would do.

"I owe you an apology."

Nicki's words cut into his thoughts, and he turned to look at her. "You do?"

"I didn't appreciate you being so distrustful of Jenny. I got a little annoyed at you."

He grinned. "I thought I was imagining it."

"I'm listening to you now."

Yeah, she was. And that was why she was with him. It was a quick trip to The Market for orange juice, something she'd forgotten to pick up the last time she went. But he still wasn't willing to let her out of his sight except when she was at work. He didn't want to let her out of his sight there, either, but he couldn't very well make himself a permanent fixture in the meeting area at city hall.

He stepped out and headed toward the passenger side. Nicki met him at the front of the truck. Fortunately she'd agreed when he insisted on taking her to the store, which was good, because he wouldn't have backed down.

Jenny had said their mother's killer was coming after Nicki. Was it the one the cops were investigating, this Louie character? Or was it someone else?

Or was it anybody? Nicki didn't think so. She was sure Jenny was just blowing smoke, trying to torment her by keeping her looking over her shoulder. Chances were she was right. But he wasn't confident enough to gamble with her life. Until the investigation was over and Louie was either exonerated or taken off the street, he wouldn't relax.

He swung the door open and motioned Nicki inside. Halfway down the aisle, a young woman stopped her.

"A friend of yours is looking for you. He came into Kona Joe's for brunch today. I waited his table."

Nicki's brows shot up. "Oh?" Tension underlay the word, a strong dose of caution.

"He asked if I knew a Nicki Jackson. I told him I did. He wanted to know where he could find you. He said he'd been by your house, but there'd obviously been a fire, and it was vacant." She gave Nicki a sympathetic smile. "I heard about the fire. I hope you didn't have too much damage."

Nicki tried to return the smile but wasn't quite successful. "Thanks. I'm afraid it was pretty bad." She paused, then continued. "So, did you tell him where he could find me?"

The young woman shook her head. "I didn't know. I figured you weren't in your house anymore, but I didn't know where you'd gone."

Nicki released a soft sigh, but her body was still rigid with tension. "Did he give you a name?"

"No. When I told him I didn't know where you were staying, I asked for his name and said I'd have you get in touch with him when I saw you again. But he told me not to worry about it, that he'd catch up with you eventually."

Nicki's face lost a shade of color, and he draped a protective arm across her shoulders. He didn't like the sound of that, either. If the whole situation was legit, the guy wouldn't have a problem with leaving his name.

He pulled Nicki closer. "Can you describe him?"

"Probably late forties, early fifties, dark hair with some gray."

"A big guy?" Nicki's voice held a slight quiver.

"Not heavy, just really muscular. He was sitting at the table, so I don't know how tall he was. But he'd definitely spent some time at the gym."

Nicki thanked her and headed toward the orange juice.

Tyler followed Nicki to the refrigerated case and stopped next to her. "Did that description sound like Louie?"

"I don't know. Louie was big. Muscular *and* heavy."

He frowned. Based on what she'd learned from the detectives, he'd spent two thirds of the past twenty two years in jail. Maybe he'd lost a lot of his girth on the prison diet. Or maybe whoever was looking for her wasn't Louie at all.

She paid for her orange juice and followed him out the door. "It can't be Louie."

"Why do you say that?"

"Even if he *did* kill Mom, he has no reason to come after me. I didn't see anything. I wasn't there."

He walked her around to the passenger side of his truck and opened the door. "What if you were? What if you saw the whole thing but suppressed the memory?" It was possible. The mind was a complicated and unpredictable thing.

She climbed into the seat. "I wasn't. If I had been there, I'd have some sliver of memory, something."

"What about the dreams?"

She swallowed hard. Based on the set of her jaw, the thought hadn't been far from her mind. He circled around to the driver's side and got in next to her. "Try to remember everything you can about that night."

"I have. Again and again."

"Try one more time." He started the truck and backed from the space. He needed to get her home if Louie was the one looking for her. Sitting in the truck at dusk, they were too vulnerable.

She took a deep breath and expelled it, letting her head fall back against the seat. "It was a Friday. I'd gone over to Lizzie's right after school. We were playing with her dolls. Her mom invited me to stay for dinner, and Lizzie asked if I could spend the night."

She stopped speaking, and he glanced over at her. Her eyes were closed, her hands folded in her lap. When she started speaking again, her tone was wistful.

"The McDonalds were dirt-poor, as poor as we were, but I loved it over there. Those were the only times I truly felt safe."

She drew in another breath and opened her eyes. "As soon as we'd eaten, Lizzie and I ran over to my house to get my stuff together. No one was there but Mom and Jenny. I was glad. I hurried through what I needed to do, because I never knew when Louie or one of my mom's other men was going to show up."

He shook his head, his sympathy for the terrified little girl warring with his anger at the irresponsible parent.

"We packed up my stuff—pajamas, a change of clothes for the next day, my toothbrush and hair brush. And we got out of there as fast as we could. When we left, there was still no one there but Mom and Jenny. Lizzie and I took turns fixing each other's hair. Then we watched a Disney movie and went to bed. That's the last thing I remember before waking up the next morning to Mrs. McDonald telling me my mom had been killed."

She turned to look at him. "If Louie did it and thinks I know something, why didn't he come after me sooner? Why wait till now?"

"You said he was in jail the first fifteen years after your mother's murder. By the time he got out, he probably figured he'd gotten away with it. It would have been riskier for him to hunt you down and kill you than to let it go." He pulled into the driveway and turned off the truck. "Besides, he wouldn't have had any idea how to find you. You didn't even have the same last name."

Nicki put her hand on the door handle, then sat motionless, staring straight ahead. "The risk wasn't there before, but it is now, with my mom's murder case being reopened and the detectives talking to me. After twenty-two years, that loose end would need to be tied up. And if Jenny was telling the truth, finding me won't be a problem."

Her eyes filled with fear. "I'm sure she's given him everything he needs to know."

Nicki watched Joan lay out cake ingredients, her attention split between the woman's cheerful chatter and Tyler's one-sided phone conversation. As soon as they'd stepped into the house, he'd called Hunter, insisting that neither of them make any decisions until getting advice from their law enforcement buddy. Until then, the one thing he'd been adamant about was that she wasn't leaving Cedar Key without him.

Now that she'd gotten inside and calmed her thoughts, her circumstances didn't seem nearly as dire. In fact, maybe there was no danger at all. The person looking for her could have been anyone. Someone she'd known in college, a former coworker, a past neighbor. Maybe he didn't give Libby his name because he wanted his visit to be a surprise.

Tyler's voice drifted to her from the living room, louder now that he was once again facing the kitchen. Since beginning his phone call, he'd paced back and forth, his voice fading in and out. He'd finished telling Hunter about Louie and was currently relaying the conversation they'd had with Libby in The Market.

Nicki leaned against the counter as Joan pulled two mixing bowls from the cupboard, then proceeded to measure dry ingredients into the larger one. When finished, this creation was going to be a red velvet cake decorated with cream cheese frosting and pecan halves. Knowing Joan's skill in the kitchen, it would be as pretty as the one pictured in the cookbook.

Tyler's voice once again faded, and Nicki sighed. Jenny had done everything to destroy her happiness. And when all her attempts failed, she'd made one last desperate parting jab. Leaving her looking over her shoulder, terrified to step out of the house, was exactly what Jenny had wanted.

Joan cracked two eggs into the smaller bowl, then added the oil, milk and vanilla. The final ingredient was a one-ounce bottle of red food coloring. It split the oil, some penetrating to the bottom of the bowl, the rest spreading along the surface of the other ingredients.

Like blood.

Nicki closed her eyes against the image intruding into her thoughts. The woman being stabbed. Her mother. Blood everywhere. Pouring from her body, seeping into the carpet.

No. There was no reason for her to be haunted by those images. She hadn't been there. She'd gone to spend the night with Lizzie next door.

And she'd forgotten Lavender.

The realization was a physical blow, knocking the air from her lungs. She'd forgotten Lavender and couldn't sleep without him. So while Lizzie and Mrs. McDonald slept, she'd slipped out, across the yard and to her own house.

All she'd done was grab Lavender and run back to Lizzie's, right? Surely she didn't see her mother's murder. She'd have remembered it if she had.

Without any effort on her part, the events of the night unfolded, playing through her mind like an old film reel. She followed the path of her younger self into the house, through the living room, down the hall and to her room, where she snatched Lavender from her bed. Jenny was asleep in the other one. In the bedroom at the end of the hall, loud voices erupted. Her mother and a man. An angry man.

She squeezed her eyes shut more tightly, and suddenly, it was all there, every gory detail dredged from the dark recesses of her mind. She leaned over the counter, hands splayed on the cool surface.

"Nicki?"

She straightened and spun in the direction of Tyler's voice. He'd apparently finished his conversation with Hunter and stood in the doorway to the kitchen. Her legs buckled, and she slid down the front of the cabinet to the floor.

Joan stood staring at her, mouth agape, a wire whisk

in her hand. Nicki struggled in a constricted breath. With three large strides, Tyler crossed the kitchen, then dropped to his knees in front of her. "What is it, sweetheart? Tell me what happened."

"I was there." Her tone was flat. The shock and fear had drained away, leaving her cold and numb.

Joan knelt on the other side of her and rested a hand on her shoulder. "What do you mean?"

"My mother's murder. I was there."

Tyler's brows drew together. "How? You'd gone to your friend's house."

"I ran back home to get Lavender." And she'd seen everything. Jenny was right.

Tyler sat next to her and pulled her into his arms. Joan straightened and stood, one hand clutching the other fist, the whisk still trapped inside. For several seconds, her lips moved, but no sound came out. Knowing Joan, she was probably praying.

Nicki pressed the side of her face to Tyler's chest. His warmth surrounded her, helping to thaw the frozen places inside her.

"Before I could leave, there was a fight, my mom and a man. My mom screamed, and I ran from my room at the same time she ran from hers. A man was right behind her." Her voice dropped to a whisper. "I recognized him."

And she'd been terrified. All these years later, she could still taste the fear, knowing that if he saw her, he'd kill her.

"I couldn't make it to the door, so I slipped behind the recliner in the living room, planning to hide until he was gone. It was dark, except for some dim light coming from the end of the hall. I stood there and waited."

She drew in a shaky breath. "My mom ran past, but before she could get out of the room, he caught her, spun her around and threw her to the floor. He had a knife, and he stabbed her eight or ten… I don't know how many times. It went on and on."

A shudder shook her body, and Tyler's arms tightened around her. For several moments, she sat in silence, drawing from his strength.

"I saw the whole thing. I stood there frozen, staring over the back of the recliner, holding on to Lavender. Then Jenny was there, almost beside me. She looked at Mom and Louie, then at me. Then she disappeared down the hall. Eventually Louie stopped. My mom raised her head one final time, looked at me and mouthed the word *run*. That's when he saw me."

"Who?"

"Louie. He looked right at me. The light shining down the hall illuminated his face, and what I saw there was pure evil."

She shuddered again. Now that she'd remembered, she'd never forget. That menacing glare would haunt her for the rest of her life.

"I panicked. I had no doubt he was going to kill me just like he did my mother. So I ran back to my room, slammed the door and locked it. Jenny had been there when I'd gotten Lavender, but she was gone then. Or maybe she was hiding under the bed. A few seconds later, the doorknob rattled. Louie was trying to coax me to open the door, telling me he wouldn't hurt me. I didn't believe him." By the tender age of seven, life had taught her a lot of lessons, one of which was never to trust the men who wandered in and out of her home.

"I opened the window, pulled my desk chair over and climbed out. Then I heard a crash. Louie had kicked in the door. But I didn't look back. I ran as fast as I could to Lizzie's, jumped into bed and pulled the covers up over my head. For the longest time, I lay there waiting for Louie to step into the room with that bloody knife. Even though I'd locked the back door, I was sure he was going to come after me. But he never did, and I finally fell asleep."

And somehow over the course of the next few hours, the memory of what she'd seen had retreated to a remote corner of her mind, where it remained buried, undisturbed for twenty-two years.

Louie knew she was a witness. And he was coming after her. He was already in Cedar Key. It would just be a matter of time till he learned where she was staying.

And showed up on Andy and Joan's doorstep.

Her mouth went dry. Whatever happened, she wasn't going to bring Andy and Joan into it. Or Tyler, either, for that matter. Her mind raced. If she called the police, they'd likely put together twenty-four-hour surveillance.

But she was a sitting duck. All it would take was one well-aimed shot fired from inside the woods.

Or one shot that wasn't so well-aimed and took out the wrong person.

No, there was only one way to ensure her friends' safety.

Leave Cedar Key.

TWELVE

Nicki stiffened and pushed herself from Tyler's arms. When she twisted to look at him, her eyes were wide and lit with fear.

"He's coming after me. I have to go." She rose to her feet. "I can't stay. If I do, I'll lead him here."

Tyler stood, too, and grasped her hand. "You can't leave. If you're alone, you won't stand a chance."

"I won't put you guys in danger." She pulled her hand from his and spun away from him, then stalked toward her room.

He followed, leaving Joan standing in the kitchen. Andy had gone to the church for a men's meeting and wouldn't be home for some time yet, which was unfortunate. Tyler could have used the reinforcement.

He stopped in the doorway of the bedroom. "What do you think you're doing?"

"Packing." She snatched the duffel bag she'd gotten from Allison the afternoon of the fire and stuffed clothes into it.

His chest tightened. When Nicki had her mind made up, it took an act of Congress to change it. "Nicki, stop. Let's calm down and think this through."

"There's nothing to think through." She picked up the bag and pushed past him. "He'd kill you to get to me."

He waited in the hall while she pulled her toiletries from the bathroom medicine cabinet. "I'll take that chance before I let you walk out of here alone."

"I'm not giving you that option." She stuffed each of the items into the side pouch and jerked the zipper closed. "I'm not giving Andy and Joan that option, either. I need you guys to take care of Callie for me."

He followed her into the living room and put a hand on her arm. "Hang loose until I call Hunter. You need to tell the police what you know. Once Louie is behind bars, you'll be safe. In the meantime, the authorities will protect you."

She picked up her purse but didn't head for the door. Maybe he was starting to get through to her.

Joan stepped up beside him. "Tyler's right."

Several more seconds passed. Finally Nicki released a long sigh. "All right. Call Hunter."

A ringtone sounded, but it wasn't his. Joan waved a hand. "That would be my weekly call from my sister. I'll call her back later."

Nicki gave her a weak smile. "Go ahead. I'm all right now. I promise I won't run."

Joan paused, then dashed to the kitchen for her phone. When she headed down the hall toward the master bedroom, Sasha trotted along behind her, with Callie in the rear. Nicki sank onto the couch, and Tyler redialed Hunter.

He answered on the first ring. "I was getting ready to call you back. I have some disturbing news. I did some checking, and Louie has disappeared from Jacksonville. So there's a distinct possibility he's the one who was asking about Nicki."

The knot of worry in Tyler's gut grew to boulder size. "That's what I was afraid of. But there's more than what I told you before. Nicki was there the night her mother was murdered, and Louie is the killer. She remembered everything."

Hunter let out a low whistle. "We'll get a couple of units out right away. We need to get a report and make contact with the detectives who are investigating the other murder. Until Louie is picked up, Nicki is going to need around-the-clock protection. We'll call Levy County in."

Tyler breathed a sigh of relief. Between the two agencies, someone would be watching her every moment of the day or night. He didn't intend to let her out of his sight, either.

When he finished the call, he laid the phone back on the coffee table and filled Nicki in on what Hunter had said. Finally she nodded and rose from the couch.

"All right. I'll stay here." She gave him a small smile. "I guess I need to unpack."

Instead of heading down the hall, she veered into the kitchen and poured herself a glass of water, then sat down at the table. "I'll stay for now, but if I even think you guys might be in any danger, I'm out of here."

"Just trust the professionals. They know what they're doing."

He circled around to the other side of her. As he pulled the chair away from the table, he looked past her to the living room. A shadow passed in front of the oval inset of the front door.

He tensed, all senses going on high alert. It was too

soon for the police to have arrived, and Andy's meeting would still be going strong.

The doorknob moved a fraction of a turn and back again. Then the other direction. Someone was trying the door.

"Nicki."

Though he'd whispered her name, she'd apparently picked up on the urgency in his voice. She sprang to her feet, eyes wide. He grabbed her hand and pulled her further into the kitchen, putting a wall between them and the front door. A boom split the silence— the thud of a foot hitting the door, accompanied by the sound of splintering wood. A fraction of a second later, the door crashed into the hall tree next to it.

Nicki gasped but didn't scream. As quietly as possible, Tyler turned the lock and swung open the back door. If they could make it out before Louie discovered where they were, they might have a chance at escape. He hoped Joan would have the presence of mind to stay hidden in the back.

With Nicki's hand still in his, he darted across the backyard toward the woods. As they reached the tree line, a series of shots sounded, and bark splintered, spraying him in the face.

Explosions sounded around him, a volley of mortar rounds. Then small arms fire. He spun and dropped to one knee, reaching for his weapon. It wasn't there. Why didn't he have his weapon?

Hands clamped down on his shoulders, then shook him hard. Someone said his name in a harsh whisper.

Nicki.

He pressed his palms to the sides of his head. He wasn't in Afghanistan. He was in Cedar Key. And if he and Nicki had any hope of making it through the night alive, he had to hold it together.

Heavy footsteps pounded in the distance, moving closer. He sprang to his feet.

"Run," he hissed. "I'm right behind you."

Louie was much too close. It was only a few seconds, but Tyler had lost them precious time. Thankfully, Nicki had brought him back. Again.

No matter what happened, Nicki would always bring him back.

Renewed determination surged through him. He'd sworn to protect his men. And he'd failed every last one of them. Now he had another vow to keep. The night he'd seen Nicki standing in her drive, shaken over her break-in, he'd sworn to protect her. She meant too much to him to do otherwise.

She was the best friend he'd ever had. But what he felt for her went much deeper than that. He'd loved her then, and he loved her now. Through all their years apart, he'd never stopped.

Whatever it took, tonight he would save Nicki's life. Even if he had to sacrifice his own.

Nicki ran like she'd never run before, one hand stretched forward in the darkness, the other shielding her eyes against the branches slapping her in the face. Her breath came in heavy gasps, as much from fear as exertion. She didn't dare slow down. Heavy footsteps pounded behind her. She hoped they belonged to Tyler rather than Louie.

She cast a quick glance over her shoulder but couldn't see who was there. Beneath the trees, the darkness was complete. Her sense of direction wasn't the greatest, but if she wasn't too far off, she was probably paralleling 166th Court. Eventually she'd reach the water and have nowhere else to go.

Hopelessness washed through her. Tyler's phone had been lying on the coffee table when they'd run from the house, and hers was in her purse. And Tyler didn't carry a gun. *Lord, please protect us.*

The woods disappeared, and a distant streetlight cast a soft glow over the area. Tyler bounded up beside her. He was stumbling forward, slightly bent at the waist, struggling to take in quick gasps of air. She slowed her pace and cast a frantic glance around, trying to get her bearings. She knew this place. It was the Cedar Key Museum State Park. And it was much too open.

Pulling Tyler with her, she dove under one of the trees separating the parking lot from the museum grounds. If they could make it across to the area north of the buildings, they'd once again have cover.

Tyler put a hand on her shoulder. "Listen."

Other than the gentle rustle of the branches overhead, the dark night was quiet. She shook her head. "I don't hear anything. Maybe we lost him." Now they might have the opportunity to call for help. If they could find someone home. A lot of people headed north for the summer. And for the year-round residents, August was a popular vacation month.

After gesturing for Tyler to follow, she darted through the parking lot toward 121st Lane. The street came off at a sharp backward angle and, though well-shaded, was more densely populated than 166th. But the first several houses were dark.

Staying under cover as much as possible, she jogged through the front yards, Tyler next to her.

In the distance, a motor roared to life. She cast him a sharp glance. Based on the alertness in his eyes, his thoughts were following the same path as hers. If they could reach the boat before its captain headed out, maybe they could get some help.

He held out a hand. "Come on."

She let him lead her between two houses at a full run. Away from the streetlights, the darkness was thicker but not complete. Though the crescent moon she'd seen early that morning wouldn't appear for another several hours, the night sky was awash with stars, their minimal light trickling over the landscape. In front of them, the ground sloped downward to where the yard grasses gave way to marsh. A dock stretched out over the water, a boat tied to it. This one was empty and quiet.

Tyler made a left and ran toward the roar of the motor, pulling her with him. A few houses down, they located it. As they approached, the driver of the boat looked up. Her breath escaped in a rush. It was Wade Tanner.

He froze midway through untying the rear dock line and scanned the landscape behind them. "You guys look like you're running from something."

"We need to call for help." She'd explain later. "Do you have your phone?"

He stood and pulled it from his pocket. Tyler stepped onto the dock to reach for it at the same time a shot rang out. Ten feet away, the ground erupted in a brief fan-shaped spray.

Her heart leaped into her throat. Louie had found

them. He was too far away to aim accurately, but he'd have that remedied in moments.

Wade tossed his fishing pole and tackle box onto the dock. "Get in, quick."

Tyler jumped in as Wade shifted into forward. The boat was already starting to move when she stepped in. Tyler grabbed her around the waist to keep her from toppling over the side, and she landed in his lap.

He pushed her to the floor. "Stay down."

She twisted in time to see Wade give the throttle a sharp turn. Instead of rising in volume and pitch, the motor sputtered and fell silent.

Another shot rang out, this one hitting the dock. Wood splinters sprayed into the boat, wrenching a startled scream from her throat. Wade gave the rope two sharp yanks. His efforts were met with the turning of gears, then silence. Louie fired a third shot.

"In the water, quick." Tyler stood, pulling her to her feet and throwing her overboard in one smooth motion. Her knees and feet met the sandy bottom at the same time her head plunged beneath the surface. The water was warm, only about three feet deep even though it was high tide.

The surface wasn't more than six inches below the deck boards of the dock. The frame came down even further. She slipped beneath, and moments later, Tyler, then Wade surfaced beside her.

For what seemed like forever, she crouched in the water, hardly daring to breathe. A tense silence permeated the air, broken only by the gentle sloshing of the waves against the dock posts.

Then there was a heavy footstep, boot against board. Louie had stepped onto the dock. A second footstep followed, and a third. Her blood turned to ice in her veins.

Sirens sounded in the distance, moving closer. Joan had probably called them. Relief washed through Nicki, but hopelessness doused it immediately. The authorities would never reach them in time.

A shot rang out, accompanied by a splash near the shore. Three more sounded, each splash growing closer. Louie was shooting through the deck boards.

She looked frantically around her, heart pounding out an erratic rhythm. Tyler pressed the side of his face to hers and spoke in the softest whisper. "Duck under and swim. Don't come up until you absolutely have to."

She sucked in a huge gulp of air, dropped as close to the sandy bottom as she could and propelled herself through the water with short kicks and wide sweeps of her arms. Would Louie be able to see her movement in the dim starlight? Or would the relative darkness conceal her?

She continued to swim, each stroke taking her farther from danger. The urge to breathe became almost overwhelming. She needed air. Fear pumped through her with every beat of her heart, using up the oxygen even faster. Her lungs burned, and she willed herself to not breathe. Just a little farther.

Finally she turned and surfaced as quietly as she could, resisting the urge to burst from the water. She drew in huge gulps of air, her gasps sounding amplified in the quiet night air.

Louie stood in the center of the dock some distance away, little more than a menacing shadow in the semi-darkness. With pistol raised, he spun in her direction. As she dipped back beneath the surface, he fired off three more rounds, their muffled sounds reaching her through the water.

She changed the angle of her path. Louie couldn't see her. Otherwise he'd have hit her by now.

But what about Tyler and Wade? Worry tightened her gut. In the brief moments after she'd surfaced, she hadn't seen them. If anything happened to either of them, she'd never forgive herself.

No, they had to be swimming, the same as she was. If Louie had shot them, they'd be lying on the beach or floating on the surface of the water. *God, please keep them safe. And please let the police get here in time.*

She knew they were nearby. She'd heard the sirens. But they'd have gone to Andy and Joan's. Unless someone else had called to report gunshots.

She surfaced again, and almost immediately, a shot sounded. The resulting splash a foot away sent a surge of adrenaline through her. She ducked back beneath and lunged sideways. Louie fired two more shots, and she swam, praying the panicked half breath she'd taken would somehow last.

When she surfaced the third time, her heart almost stopped. Tyler had stepped onto the dock and crept toward Louie. Wade was in the yard a little further back, moving in their direction. Louie obviously hadn't seen either of them.

His attention was on her.

He leveled the weapon, and she gasped. But before she could duck beneath the surface, Tyler called out and broke into a full run. Louie spun, pulling the trigger as he turned, and Wade fell to his knees on the grass.

Dear God, no, not Wade. They should never have involved him.

The next second, Tyler plowed into Louie, knocking him to the dock. The gun hit the boards and tumbled to a stop a few feet from the end.

Louie roared, then threw Tyler off him. Tyler hit the boards with a thud and an audible grunt. When Louie rose and lunged for his weapon, Tyler grabbed his ankles and jerked his legs from under him. Louie landed facedown and released a string of curses.

For a brief moment, Tyler looked past Louie. His eyes locked with hers, and she knew what she had to do. She stumbled through the waist-deep water, making her way toward the dock. Tyler would fight with everything in him to protect her. But Louie was a formidable foe. And if Tyler couldn't keep him from getting his hands on that weapon, he'd gun her down in the water without a moment's hesitation.

Louie pushed himself to his feet and faced his opponent. He wore the same attire she remembered, cutoff jean shorts and a wifebeater shirt. He stood with clenched fists, muscles rippling beneath the tattoos covering his arms and chest. Although he'd lost some of his girth, everything left was solid steel.

He let out a bellow of rage and swung one meaty fist at Tyler's face. Tyler twisted to avoid it, then countered with his own punch. It connected with Louie's nose. Tyler wasn't as big as Louie, but all those years of military physical training showed. Louie released another bellow, then shook his head. Blood and sweat sprayed from his face in an arc.

Nicki crept closer, moving silently through the water. She approached at an angle, with Tyler facing her more fully than Louie. Unless Louie turned, she might be able to approach the dock undetected.

And get the gun.

Once she got it, she wasn't sure what she'd do with it. Other than one target practice session with a long-ago ex-boyfriend, she'd never held a gun.

On the dock, Tyler aimed a volley of punches at Louie's face. Louie managed to block half of them. The other half didn't have nearly the effect they should have had. A lesser man would have been facedown on the deck boards.

When Louie's next punch connected with Tyler's jaw, she had to clamp a hand over her mouth to keep from crying out. The two men exchanged several more punches, until both of their faces were battered and bleeding.

Suddenly Louie slammed into Tyler, knocking him to the dock and landing on top of him. Several moments passed.

Come on, Tyler. Get up.

Instead, he rolled his head side to side as if trying to clear it. With no chance to break his fall, he'd hit it hard.

Fight, Tyler, just a little longer. She reached the end of the dock, then moved along its side. Louie rose to his knees, made a fist and slammed it into Tyler's temple.

What hitting his head on the dock hadn't done, that final punch had. Tyler's eyes closed and his body went limp.

Nicki released a strangled cry. Louie turned, his gaze settling on her, then shifting to the gun. He rose and lunged for it at the same time she grabbed it.

It was heavier than it looked—cold and hard and

lethal. And it felt foreign in her hands. She clutched the handle in her right hand, then wrapped her left around it, palm up. If she could at least *look* like she knew what she was doing, Louie would be less likely to attack her.

She backed away, putting some distance between them. Louie stepped to the edge of the dock.

"You won't shoot me."

Confidence oozed from him, the same cockiness she'd observed as a child. He lowered himself to the dock, letting his legs dangle in the water. "You're not a killer. You don't have it in you."

She continued to back up. Louie was right. She wasn't a killer.

But what if the only choices were to kill or be killed? Could she do it then? Tyler had killed. Numerous times.

Louie slid into the water and moved toward her. Her pulse jumped to double-time, her heart threatening to beat out of her chest. Her hands shook, betraying her fear.

Louie's eyes dipped to the barrel of the gun, which seemed to have developed a mind of its own. It waved up and down and side to side.

The edges of his mouth curled up in a wicked grin. "See? You can't do it. Give me the gun, Nicki, and everything will be all right. I won't hurt you."

It was the same promise he'd made that night after killing her mother. Unlock the door and everything would be all right. She didn't believe it then, and she didn't believe it now.

She gripped the gun more tightly.

"One more step, and I'll shoot." The strength in her tone surprised her.

Louie's brows shot up, and for several moments he stood motionless. Then he laughed, an evil, menacing sound. "No, you won't."

She rested her finger on the trigger, poised and waiting. Louie had said she wasn't a killer. She wasn't. But she wasn't a victim, either. Not anymore.

Louie took a step. A deafening *pow* reverberated through the air, and the gun kicked, throwing her arms upward. A scream shot up her throat, and her hands opened. The weapon fell into the water with a splash.

Louie stood about ten feet in front of her, mouth agape, hands clutching his stomach. Blood seeped between his fingers. He dropped to his knees, then fell forward, face in the water.

Nicki gasped and took a step toward him. If she didn't do something, he was going to drown.

And the world would be a better place.

No, she couldn't do it. Pulling the trigger in self-defense was one thing. Letting him drown when she was standing ten feet away was another. She closed the distance between them.

Movement in her peripheral vision drew her attention. Four figures were running toward the shoreline—two officers in uniform and Hunter and Amber in plain clothes.

Another siren split the silence, increased in volume, then stopped. When she reached Louie, she grasped his shoulders and lifted his face out of the water. The next moment, his hand came up and clamped around her throat. Panic shot through her, and she struggled to take in a breath through her constricted windpipe. When she tried to pry his fingers from her neck, he squeezed harder. Her head pounded and her ears began to ring. Blackness encroached from all sides.

Suddenly Louie's hand relaxed, and he fell forward. Her knees buckled as Hunter reached her.

He looped an arm around her waist. "Whoa, steady. Are you all right?"

"I'm fine." Her voice was little more than a croak. "Wade needs help. He's been shot."

"They're already attending to him."

She looked toward the shore, where two paramedics knelt on either side of him. She breathed a sigh of relief. *Lord, please let him be all right.*

"And Tyler's hurt."

As if in response, a moan came from the dock. She waded over and climbed onto the wooden structure. Tyler still lay on his back with his eyes closed. His lower lip was swollen and split open, and caked blood had dried in several places on his face.

She put a hand on his chest. "Tyler?"

He moaned again, and one eye fluttered open. The other was too badly swollen.

"It's over. Louie is—" What, injured? Dead? Someone had dragged him from the water and laid him on the beach. Two more paramedics had arrived and were working on him.

Conflicting emotions tumbled through her. If Louie survived, she'd live with the knowledge that someone out there wanted her dead. If he died, it would be at her hand. Neither was a good option.

Tyler's good eye closed. "Louie is what?"

On the shore, one of the paramedics shook his head

and they both rose. In that moment, all she felt was relief.

She took Tyler's hand and squeezed it. "He'll never be a threat to anyone again."

THIRTEEN

Tyler clawed his way to consciousness, the sounds of explosions still ringing in his ears. It was only a nightmare. He was no longer in Afghanistan. But where was he?

Near his head, something emitted rhythmic beeps. Like medical equipment in a hospital. That was it. He'd been injured and they'd flown him to Landstuhl, Germany.

There was more, but remembering required too much effort. He tried to open his eyes. They refused to cooperate. He was drifting, floating.

The telltale whistle of a mortar round blazed a path through his mind, jarring him back to semiconsciousness.

Burns. He'd been burned. His right shoulder and the upper part of his back. He remembered now. There would be weeks of skin grafts. The doctor had already warned him.

The doctor at Brooke Army Medical Center. He wasn't in Germany. He was back stateside, Fort Sam Houston, Texas.

The grafts were going to be painful. Burns were always painful. He'd deal with it.

But the pain he'd prepared himself for wasn't there. At least, it wasn't in his shoulder and back. Instead, he had the granddaddy of all headaches. And he felt as if he'd tried to dive face-first through a slab of concrete. What was going on?

He tried again to open his eyes. This time he was successful. With one eye, anyway. The other was glued shut. His mouth didn't feel right, either. His jaw was stiff, his lips dry. When he ran his tongue over them, the lower one seemed huge.

He rolled his head to the side. Someone sat in the corner, curled up in the chair, sleeping. A woman. Her head rested on the arm of the chair, and her knees were drawn up to her chest. Bright auburn hair had fallen over her face, hiding most of it from view.

Nicki.

The fogginess cleared in an instant, and memories of the past days' events flooded his mind. He reached for the control to raise the top part of his bed. The gentle hum joined the other sounds of the room.

Nicki sat up, sweeping her hair out of her face and tucking it behind her ear. Her eyes widened. They held relief tinged with concern. A slow smile climbed up her cheeks.

"You're awake." She swung both feet to the floor and stood to approach him. "How do you feel?"

"Like I've been used as a punching bag."

"I think you have." The smile faded and she took his hand. "You saved my life. If you hadn't tackled Louie when you did, he'd have shot me."

"When I saw him take aim, I almost had a heart attack. All I could think about was that I was going to lose you." And for the first time in twelve years, he'd prayed. No bargains or promises this time. Just heart-felt pleas for protection for Nicki and strength and success for himself. And God had answered.

He pressed his free hand to the side of his head and winced. "How's Wade?"

"The bullet lodged in his right lung. He was in surgery a couple of hours, but he's going to be all right."

She lowered her head. "I feel terrible. We should never have involved him. All I wanted to do was borrow his phone. Instead, I ended up getting him shot."

"It wasn't your fault. All the blame is with Louie." He shifted position and winced again. His head and face weren't the only places that hurt. He was probably going to be finding muscles he didn't know he had for the next three weeks.

"Speaking of Louie, what happened to him?"

"Dead."

He raised his brows. "How did that happen? The last thing I remember is having my head slammed into the dock and everything going black. I think there might have been another punch in there, too."

"There was." She gave him a sympathetic smile. "After you were knocked out, I grabbed the gun. I warned him, but he came after me anyway."

Pride swelled inside him, but he didn't congratulate her. Too often, victory didn't feel so good. "Are you all right?"

She nodded a little too quickly.

"Having killed someone isn't an easy thing to live with. Trust me, I know." It was likely to haunt her for years to come. "If you ever need to talk about it, you know where to find me."

"Thanks."

He closed his eyes. "My head feels like it's stuffed full of cotton. I think my brain is firing on only two cylinders."

"You have a concussion and lots of bruises, but fortunately, nothing's broken."

"You couldn't prove it by me." He shifted to get more comfortable, then gave up. "It looks like Andy might be finishing the renovations on his own. We were only a few days from having it complete."

She nodded. Sadness seemed to emanate from her. "What are your plans once you've mended?"

He searched her face. Did she want him to stay? He couldn't tell. Her eyes were shielded, fixed on their joined hands.

No, she'd already answered all his silent questions at the park. Whatever she felt for him, and he was sure it had deepened over the past few weeks, she wasn't willing to sacrifice their friendship to explore it.

And if that was all she wanted, that was what he'd take. But it would have to be long-distance. Being with her every day, hearing her sparkling laughter as she played with Callie, seeing her crooked half smile when she teased him, all her little quirks—it would be pure torture. And he'd had enough of that in his life.

"I guess I'll be heading out again." He pivoted his head to stare at the darkened TV screen on the opposite wall. *Please say you want me to stay.*

But she was silent, except for the small sigh that escaped her mouth. Was it disappointment?

No, it was likely relief. She probably didn't want

to deal with his problems. And he couldn't blame her. The nightmares and flashbacks, never knowing when he might get violent or lose it in public—no one deserved to be saddled with all that.

She gave him a slow nod, the movement drawing his gaze back to her face.

"Where will you go?"

"I'm thinking about Montana this time." At least, as of two seconds ago. Until that moment, he'd avoided all thoughts of leaving her. He gave her a half-hearted smile. "Big Sky Country."

"Montana is awfully cold."

He shrugged. "Maybe I'll leave again before the snow sets in."

Before answering, she swallowed hard. "This time we need to do a better job of staying in touch."

"I agree. I'm not sure what happened last time."

One side of her mouth lifted. "I think you dropped the ball."

"I think it was you."

"Maybe it wasn't either of us. That final letter might be trapped in some crevice in the back corner of the Atlanta post office, covered in dust."

He smiled, then let it fade. "No excuses this time."

She nodded. "Not with texting."

"And Facebook. We need to be friends." He squeezed her hand. "I don't want to lose you again, Nicki."

She nodded again, but this time the motion was jerky. "I'm going to let you get some rest." She pulled her hand from his grasp. "I promised I'd try to come in to work this afternoon."

He watched her walk from the room, then lay his head back against the pillow and closed his eyes.

Leaving was the right·thing to do. It just wasn't easy. But often the right thing wasn't.

Footsteps sounded outside his door, and he opened his eyes in time to see Andy walk into the room.

"It's good to see you awake. How do you feel?"

Tyler stifled a moan. "Ask me in a few days."

"Pretty bad, huh? You don't look so hot, either."

He started to lift a brow, then stopped. Even that small motion hurt.

Andy moved the chair closer to the hospital bed and sank into it. "I met Nicki getting off the elevator. What did you say to her?"

"Nothing."

"Don't give me that. She was crying. What did you do?"

Annoyance surged through him. He didn't need his big brother meddling in his affairs.

"I told her we were almost done with the renovations, and once I got out of here I'd be leaving." He glared at Andy. "Nothing that's any concern of yours."

Andy shook his head. "When are you going to stop running? You've found a good woman who's crazy about you, and you're ready to throw it all away. For what?"

"I'm not throwing anything away. We're friends. That's all. And wherever I go, we'll still be friends."

"You're an idiot."

"Thanks, bro. I love you, too."

Andy heaved a sigh. "Maybe you and Nicki *are* just friends. But you're not satisfied with that. I recognized it almost from your first day here."

"It doesn't matter what I want."

"What about what Nicki wants? Aren't her wishes important enough for you to get your act together and settle down?"

Tyler crossed his arms over his chest. "Look, if you came here to beat me up, you can go back home."

"Okay, I'll drop it for now. But this isn't over."

Yeah, it was over, whether Andy wanted it to be or not. Before Tyler could say as much, a nurse entered the room.

"I see you decided to join the land of the living. How do you feel?"

"Like I've been run over by a truck."

She checked his vitals, made a few notes on the clipboard she carried, then added something to his IV.

"There. That should have you feeling better soon."

He closed his eyes and let the medicine do its work. Already the edge of his pain seemed a little duller.

He drew in a deep breath and let it out slowly. Nicki had so much to overcome—the memories of her mother's murder, the fact that her own sister tried to kill her, the terror of being pursued by Louie, his death at her hands. Whatever she needed, he'd always be there for her. As a friend. Asking to be anything more wouldn't be fair to Nicki.

She'd had her share of users and losers. But someday, someone would come along who would value her uniqueness. Who would be awed by her beauty, both inside and out. Who would appreciate her toughness but be sensitive to her vulnerability.

Who would love her the way he did.

The pain that pierced his heart almost took his

breath away. He clenched one fist and put it over his chest.

The monitor beeped and the IV dripped fluids into his veins, but the pain refused to abate.

Unfortunately, this was the type for which the doctors had no cure.

Nicki jammed the spade into the dirt and grasped a weed with her left hand. After a couple of gentle tugs, the roots slid free of the ground holding them, and she tossed the plant onto the growing pile next to her.

They were Joan and Andy's weeds, not hers. Her own flower beds were in pretty bad shape, between neglect and too much foot traffic over recent weeks.

She cast a glance in that direction. The carport side of her house was still a burned-out shell, but renovations would be starting soon. She'd settled on a contractor, and the insurance company had approved his quote. Once all the work was done, she'd tackle beautifying the yard.

But today, she was focused on repaying Joan and Andy for some of their kindness. And avoiding Tyler.

He was inside packing, getting ready to head for parts unknown. She had no choice in letting him go, but she didn't have to watch him make the preparations.

She focused her attention on the task in front of her and attacked the weeds with renewed vigor. The doctor had discharged Tyler yesterday. She'd visited him several times over the past few days. There'd been no talk of future plans for either of them. He'd kept his conversation casual and so had she. But an undercurrent of tension had run between them.

What happened to the easy camaraderie they'd shared all those years ago? It almost felt as if they were strangers. Or former friends with too many hurts between them to move past.

At some point over the prior weeks, their friendship had morphed into something else. And now she was kicking herself. She'd done it again. Four months out of one failed relationship and she was running head-long toward another dead end. But unlike several of her exes, Tyler wasn't a user *or* a loser. He was just afraid to commit. Of course, she'd had more than her fair share of those, too.

She moved over a couple of feet, then sat back on her heels, ready to tackle the next section. Letting herself feel anything deeper for Tyler than friendship had been stupid. But what she felt wasn't one-sided. The kiss at Fanning Springs had proved it.

And she'd stopped it. She'd been too afraid to explore this new spark between them, scared that if it didn't work out, their relationship would be ruined.

But the damage was already done. They'd crossed that line from friend to something else, then tried to step back over it again. What they were left with was neither.

Now Tyler was leaving.

The front door opened, then shut, and she stopped her work long enough to watch him load his bags into the passenger side of his pickup. He circled back around to the driver's side, then stopped to face her.

"I guess that's it. We'll stay in touch, right?" His tone was hesitant.

"Sure." She pushed herself to her feet, spade still

in her hand. Should she go hug him? Not unless he initiated it. After all, he was the one leaving, not her.

He shifted his weight to the other foot but made no move to open the door. He seemed troubled. Lost. And her heart broke.

She wasn't the only one with fears. Tyler, who'd faced down the enemy, boldly served his country and survived three tours of duty, never knowing whether each minute would be his last, had fears, too. And when everything got to be too much, he pulled up roots and ran.

The first time he'd left her, he hadn't had a choice. Now he did. When faced with the thought of settling down and letting someone close enough to share his traumas, he was choosing the easy way out.

Well, not without a fight.

She dropped the spade and stalked toward him, then stopped with her back against his closed driver's side door. She crossed her arms and glared up at him.

He raised his brows. "What are you doing?"

"When are you going to stop running?"

His jaw tightened. "What, have you been talking to my brother?"

"I haven't needed to. Do you think I don't know what you're doing? Just when you get settled in somewhere and start getting close to the people around you, you take off again. You're so afraid someone's going to see past that tough exterior of yours. Well, too late. I already have."

He matched her stance, arms crossed, legs shoulder-width apart. "I'd planned to stay only until the work on the inn was finished. You knew that from the start. Nothing's changed."

No, nothing had changed, yet everything had. They'd spent almost every spare moment together since he arrived. They'd shared their fears and fought for their lives. Now she was in love with him.

But she wasn't going to beg him to stay. She uncrossed her arms and let them fall to her sides. "All right, then. Go." She stepped away from the truck and opened the door. "Keep on running. What you're hiding from is always going to find you."

He made no move to get into truck, just stood there watching her. Indecision flashed in his eyes, and a muscle twitched in the side of his jaw.

"Well?" she prodded him.

"You're asking me to stay."

"I want to be there for you, Tyler, as a friend and more, if you'll let me."

He closed his eyes and clenched his fists. His jaw was still tight, further evidence of the struggle going on inside him.

He sighed and once again met her gaze. "I have nightmares."

"So do I."

"Mine are dangerous. You've experienced that first-hand."

"I think I can handle it."

"You've been through so much—your mother's murder, foster care, the death of your adoptive parents. Your sister, then Louie." He shook his head. "You need someone stable."

Her heart fell. "So I'm good enough for friendship, but not anything more."

"That's not what I mean." He slipped his keys into

his jeans pocket, then took both of her hands. "I care for you too much to saddle you with my issues."

His touch was reassuring, his hands calloused, strong but gentle. Like the man. "Sometimes the best way to take your mind off your own problems is to help someone else with theirs."

Without releasing her hands, he stepped closer, until she had to tilt her head backward to look at him. His face was inches from hers.

"Do you know what you're getting yourself into?" His voice was the softest whisper, his breath warm against her lips.

"I think I have a pretty good idea." Her tone matched his, low and smooth, belying the turmoil inside her. If they hadn't passed the point of no return before, they were getting ready to now.

He leaned closer, and her eyes drifted closed. His lips met hers, gentle at first, tentative, testing. She didn't pull away. He deepened the kiss, and she still didn't pull away.

All her fears and past mistakes faded into the background, and a whole world of new possibilities opened before her. There was no cause for concern, no reason to hold back.

Because this was Tyler. Her best friend. The one who was there through those troubled early teenage years and would be there for whatever lay ahead.

The one who knew her better than anyone in the world.

And he loved her anyway.

EPILOGUE

Nicki walked along the raised dirt trail, Tyler's hand in hers. A gentle breeze rustled the trees around them, but otherwise, the late August morning was silent.

She drew in a clean breath. The air was hot and humid. Maybe it would help warm some of the chill that had settled inside her the moment she stepped out of Tyler's truck.

Though she loved the old Railroad Trestle Nature Trail, she hadn't walked it since that day with Jenny. She'd tried. Several times she'd parked her truck at the trailhead, then turned around and gone home without even stepping out. Once she'd gotten as far as the large sign at the entrance. She'd stood there and read every word. She'd learned the history of the Cedar Key Railroad but hadn't been able to bring herself to step through the open gate.

Today she was going to walk it. The whole thing. She couldn't preach to Tyler the importance of facing his fears if she wasn't willing to do it herself. But she didn't have to do it alone.

She smiled up at Tyler. Behind the mangroves to her right, sunlight glistened on the surface of the water.

On her other side, marsh grasses filled a small clearing. Callie and Sasha trotted ahead of them.

Almost three weeks had passed since Louie had pursued them through the woods. She was still living with Joan and Andy, but the work on her house was progressing nicely.

And the inn was completed, furnished and scheduled to open next weekend. They were going to open with a bang—every room was booked. Of course, it was Labor Day weekend. But according to Andy, the coming weeks didn't look too shabby, either.

Tyler smiled down at her. "I'm enjoying my last weekend off for a while."

"Me, too." Saturdays together were going to come to a screeching halt.

Although the renovation work was done, Paradise Inn was going to be a true family venture. Andy was the owner and manager, Joan would handle housekeeping, and Tyler would be in charge of maintenance and whatever else needed to be done to keep things running smoothly.

Up ahead, the branches of a red cedar arched over the trail. Nicki recognized the spot immediately. Strength drained from her limbs, leaving behind a watery weakness. Tyler, always sensitive to her moods, squeezed her hand.

"Right there under that tree is where Jenny attacked me."

She shuddered, and Tyler released her hand to wrap his arm around her. Her life had almost ended that day. As she'd lain bleeding on the sandy trail, her knife-wielding sister on top of her, she'd been sure she was going to die the same way her mother had.

"I'm ready to go home now." She'd revisited this place too often in her dreams over the past few weeks. Why go there now, when she was fully awake and had a choice? "Callie, come." The dog walked toward her, enthusiasm dampened.

Tyler turned her to face him, resting both hands on her shoulders. "You love this place. Are you going to let Jenny take that away from you?"

She drew in a shaky breath. Tyler was right. Several times she had walked the trail with her sketch pad and a fold-up camp chair, then sat at its end, overlooking the water and mangroves. There was no reason to not go back to those peaceful outings. Jenny was in jail, where she'd maybe get the help she needed. And Louie was dead.

"All right." She put her hand in his. She could do this with Tyler next to her.

He flashed her an encouraging smile. "That's my girl." He began walking, leading her down the trail. "You're a fighter. Always have been."

As they passed under the cedar, she scanned the ground. There was no sign of what had happened there four weeks earlier. Not that she'd expected there to be. Any scuff marks in the dirt would have long since been washed away by the summertime rains. So would any bloodstains.

When they reached the end of the trail, the breeze that had rustled the trees around them blew wisps of hair into her face. She tucked them behind her ear and looked out over the water to the mangrove-lined shore beyond. Sasha and Callie occupied themselves with sniffing their surroundings, and Tyler stepped up beside her. There wasn't another soul in any direction.

A blanket of tranquility lay over the landscape, wrapping her in a soothing embrace.

She smiled up at him. "Thank you."

"For what?"

"For making me come out here. Sometimes the best way to banish bad memories is to make new ones. Happy ones."

He took both of her hands in his. "I'm planning to make lots of happy memories with you."

She cocked a brow at him. "That sounds kind of permanent." Though he hadn't talked of leaving since that day in Andy's driveway, he hadn't talked long-term, either. They'd spent every spare moment together. He'd gone to church with her, listened to her stories and shared his own. But she still sensed he was taking life one day at a time.

"It does sound permanent. But that's my intention." He drew her into his arms. "When I was a scrawny fifteen-year-old, angry at the world, you reached out to me. You listened to all my ranting and were always there for me. I loved you back then, and I love you now more than ever."

Nicki swallowed hard. This wasn't the first time he'd said he loved her. Over the past two weeks, he'd told her several times. And she'd told him. But something was different this time. There was a solemnness in his gaze as if he was preparing for an important announcement.

Her stomach turned several flips, and her heart started to pound. She waited for him to continue.

"A life with me won't be easy, but I'm pretty sure you know what you're in for. Do you think you can put up with me?" He gave her a crooked smile.

Her heart pounded harder. "If you can put up with me."

"I don't think that will be a problem." He squeezed her hands. "I know you've had a lot of bad experiences with men, and they've made you apprehensive. I'm not perfect. I've got a lot of faults. But I love you with all my heart, and I'd never intentionally do anything to hurt you." He squeezed her hands. "Nicki, will you marry me?"

Her mouth went dry and her heart skipped a beat. It was her second marriage proposal in a year. She'd accepted the first one, and look where it had gotten her.

When Tyler showed up, she hadn't been looking for a relationship. In fact, she'd sworn off men unless God plopped one in her lap.

Tyler didn't exactly land in her lap, but his appearance was just as sudden and unexpected.

"Nicki?"

Concern had crept into his eyes. She'd waited too long.

She pulled her hands from his grasp to wrap her arms around his neck. Committing to marrying Tyler wouldn't be repeating past mistakes. There were no secrets between them. And there would be no surprises.

"Yes, I'll marry you."

Relief flooded his face, then pure joy. His arms went around her waist, and he pulled her to him. Then he kissed her long and deep, proving anew his love and devotion.

And all her hesitation, each concern, every doubt floated away on the salt-scented breeze.

* * * * *

SPECIAL EXCERPT FROM

*When a guide dog trainer becomes a target
of a dangerous crime ring, a K-9 cop and his loyal
partner will work together to keep her safe.*

Read on for a sneak preview of Trail of Danger
*by Valerie Hansen, the next exciting installment
to the* True Blue K-9 Unit *miniseries,
available September 2019 from Love Inspired Suspense.*

Abigail Jones stared at the blackening eastern sky and
shivered. She was more afraid of the strangers lingering
in the shadows along the Coney Island boardwalk than
she was of the summer storm brewing over the Atlantic.

Early September humidity made the salty oceanic
atmosphere feel sticky while the wind whipped loose
tendrils of Abigail's long red hair. If sixteen-year-old
Kiera Underhill hadn't insisted where and when their
secret meeting must take place, Abigail would have
stopped to speak with some of the other teens she was
passing. Instead, she made a beeline for the spot where
their favorite little hot dog wagon spent its days.

Besides the groups of partying youth, she skirted
dog walkers, couples strolling hand in hand and an old
woman leaning on a cane. Then there was a tall man and

enormous dog ambling toward her. As they passed beneath an overhead vapor light, she recognized his police uniform and breathed a sigh of relief. Most K-9 patrols in her nearby neighborhood used German shepherds, so seeing the long floppy ears and droopy jowls of a bloodhound brought a smile despite her uneasiness.

Pausing, Abigail rested her back against the fence surrounding a currently closed amusement park, faced into the wind and waited for the K-9 cop to go by. His unexpected presence could be what was delaying Kiera.

"Come on, Kiera. I came alone, just like you wanted," Abigail muttered.

Kiera had sounded panicky when she'd phoned.

"Here. Over here" drifted on the wind. Abigail strained to listen.

The summons seemed to be coming from inside the Luna Park perimeter fence. That was not good since the amusement facility was currently closed. Nevertheless, she cupped her hands around her eyes and peered through the chain-link fence. It was several seconds before she realized the gate was ajar. *Uh-oh. Bad sign.* "Kiera? Is that you?"

A disembodied voice answered faintly. "Help me! Hurry."

Don't miss
Trail of Danger *by Valerie Hansen,*
available September 2019 wherever
Love Inspired® Suspense books and ebooks are sold.

www.LoveInspired.com

WE HOPE YOU ENJOYED THIS BOOK!

Love Inspired SUSPENSE

Uncover the truth in these thrilling stories of faith in the face of crime from Love Inspired Suspense. Discover six new books available every month, wherever books are sold!

LoveInspired.com

SPECIAL EXCERPT FROM

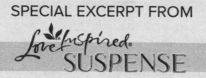

*When a rookie K-9 cop becomes the target of a
dangerous stalker, can she stay one step ahead of this
killer with the help of her boss and his K-9 partner?*

Read on for a sneak preview of
Courage Under Fire *by Sharon Dunn,*
the next exciting installment to the
True Blue K-9 Unit *miniseries, available in*
October 2019 from Love Inspired Suspense.

Rookie K-9 officer Lani Branson took in a deep breath as
she pedaled her bike along the trail in the Jamaica Bay
Wildlife Refuge. Water rushed and receded from the shore
just over the dunes. The high-rises of New York City,
made hazy from the dusky twilight, were visible across
the expanse of water.

She sped up even more.

Tonight was important. This training exercise was an
opportunity to prove herself to the other K-9 officers who
waited back at the visitors' center with the tracking dogs
for her to give the go-ahead. Playing the part of a child lost
in the refuge so the dogs could practice tracking her was
probably a less-than-desirable duty for the senior officers.

Reaching up to her shoulder, Lani got off her bike and
pressed the button on the radio. "I'm in place."

The smooth tenor voice of her supervisor, Chief Noah Jameson, came over the line. "Good—you made it out there in record time."

Up ahead she spotted an object shining in the setting sun. She jogged toward it. A bicycle, not hers, was propped against a tree.

A knot of tension formed at the back of her neck as she turned in a half circle, taking in the area around her. It was possible someone had left the bike behind. Vagrants could have wandered into the area.

She studied the bike a little closer. State-of-the-art and in good condition. Not the kind of bike someone just dumped.

A branch cracked. Her breath caught in her throat. Fear caused her heartbeat to drum in her ears.

"NYPD." She hadn't worn her gun for this exercise. Her eyes scanned all around her, searching for movement and color. "You need to show yourself."

Seconds ticked by. Her heart pounded.

Someone else was out here.

Don't miss
Courage Under Fire *by Sharon Dunn,*
available October 2019 wherever
Love Inspired® *Suspense books and ebooks are sold.*

www.LoveInspired.com

LISEXP0919